Moderation

Moderation

ELAINE CASTILLO

VIKING

VIKING
An imprint of Penguin Random House LLC
1745 Broadway, New York, NY 10019
penguinrandomhouse.com

Designed by Nerylsa Dijol

LIBRARY OF CONGRESS CATALOGING-IN-PUBLICATION DATA
Names: Castillo, Elaine, author.
Title: Moderation / Elaine Castillo.
Description: New York : Viking, 2025.
Identifiers: LCCN 2024056767 (print) | LCCN 2024056768 (ebook) |
ISBN 9780593489666 (hardcover) | ISBN 9780593489673 (ebook)
Subjects: LCGFT: Novels.
Classification: LCC PS3603.A8754 M63 2025 (print) |
LCC PS3603.A8754 (ebook) | DDC 813/.6—dc23/eng/20241230
LC record available at https://lccn.loc.gov/2024056767
LC ebook record available at https://lccn.loc.gov/2024056768

First published in hardcover in Great Britain by Atlantic Books, London, in 2025.
First United States edition published by Viking, 2025.

Printed in the United States of America
1st Printing

The authorized representative in the EU for product safety and compliance is
Penguin Random House Ireland, Morrison Chambers, 32 Nassau Street,
Dublin D02 YH68, Ireland, https://eu-contact.penguin.ie.

Come with me if you want to live.

T-800 to Sarah Connor, *Terminator 2: Judgment Day* (1991),
written by James Cameron and William Wisher,
directed by James Cameron

Still New Bedford is a queer place. Had it not been for us whalemen, that tract of land would this day perhaps have been in as howling condition as the coast of Labrador. As it is, parts of her back country are enough to frighten one, they look so bony. The town itself is perhaps the dearest place to live in, in all New England. It is a land of oil, true enough: but not like Canaan; a land, also, of corn and wine. The streets do not run with milk; nor in the spring-time do they pave them with fresh eggs. Yet, in spite of this, nowhere in all America will you find more patrician-like houses; parks and gardens more opulent, than in New Bedford. Whence came they? how planted upon this once scraggy scoria of a country?

Go and gaze upon the iron emblematical harpoons round yonder lofty mansion, and your questions will be answered. Yes; all these brave houses and flowery gardens came from the Atlantic, Pacific, and Indian oceans. One and all, they were harpooned and dragged up hither from the bottom of the sea.

Moby-Dick, Herman Melville

Little Brown Fucking Machine

Girlie was, by every conceivable metric, one of the very best. All the chaff, long ago burned up by unquenchable fire: the ones who had hourly panic attacks, the ones who took up drinking; the ones who fucked in the stairwells during break time, the ones who started bringing handguns to the office, the ones who started believing the Holocaust had never happened, or that 9/11 was an inside job, or that no one had ever been to the moon at all, or that every presidential candidate was picked by a cosmic society of devils who communicated across interplanetary channels; the ones who took the work home, the ones who never came back the same, or never came back at all. The floor was now averaging only three or four suicide attempts a year, down from one or two a month. The ones who remained, like her, were the wheat: the exemplars, tested paladins, the ones who didn't throw up in the hallway and leave the vomit there. They'd been, to continue speaking of it biblically, separated.

None of the white people survived. Not that there were that many of them to begin with. Young middle-class hopefuls bulging with student debt, they'd shown up around the time the position was still being called *process executive*, back when the site was still in the Bay Area. Back when she still lived in the Bay Area; back when any of them still could. Most of the white candidates didn't make it past the initial three-week training course; the ones who did left within a year. The majority of the workers had been Filipinas, with a smaller minority of Cambodian, Indonesian, Laotian, Vietnamese workers: people who knew about the job through that reliable network still unmatched by LinkedIn, otherwise known as family— people who'd grown up knowing their mothers and aunts had been moderators, and so too would they follow. Sometimes a particular year—she'd started to think of her surviving cohort as a kind of graduating class, although what they were graduating from or toward, she did not know—would have one or two working-class Korean Americans, one or two Black Americans, usually people who were married to Filipina or Viet employees and had heard about the job through them. Of the two hundred or so who worked at the Vegas site, nearly all were women. Nearly all the women were Pinay.

To pass her final assessment, Girlie'd had to stand in a conference room of no great nor small size, indistinguishable from the nine other conference rooms in the building, and, in front of her peers and potential future colleagues, moderate a video of a tied-up and blindfolded young girl of about six or seven who was being made to fellate an unseen man. The girl had bruises along her shoulders. The man, who was recording and audibly enjoying the act, had gray in his pubic hair. The trainees had already been reminded that they wouldn't be allowed to pause the video or remove the audio during their presentation.

Earlier that morning, a young Cambodian American trainee who wore three soft friendship bracelets around his left wrist—two fraying, one new—had moderated a video of a young man, about the same age as himself, being stabbed multiple times, gurgling bright blood into a Champion sweatshirt as he abortively begged for something; not quite yet his life. In the middle of his presentation, the young trainee, without pausing the video, discreetly crouched behind his podium to throw up into a wastepaper bin he'd presumably positioned there for this very reason. By the time it was Girlie's turn, the room still smelled of pepperoni and bile.

Girlie stood in front of her prospective coworkers and managers, presenting a carefully supported case for why the video of the tied-up girl should be banned from the social media site in question, on the grounds of child pornography. On the one-to-five scale they'd all been taught, the video was a solid five.

One of her potential supervisors challenged her, face stony: How did she know the girl was a child, and not a consenting adult?

It was true, they could barely make out the girl's face, behind the blindfold, on the blurry blown-up image beamed on the matte-white projector screen, in front of the forty faces waiting, as in a court of law, for a verdict. It was true, there were plenty of small-breasted, small-boned women in the world, Girlie among them; it was true, there were plenty of people who cried during sex, or liked rough play of all descriptions. This was the real test of the moderator, in the end: being able to sift through, again and again, each workday's thousand and one true things. This was the real work, beyond the stabbings, the rapes, the paranoia, the conspiracy theories, the hate speech, the carved-out crater in the living world where belief had collapsed in on itself like an exploding star. Reaching into the wound with two clean fingers, pulling out the still-steaming metal slug. "The socks," she said.

Girlie asked for permission to rewind the video. Permission was granted. Then she aimed her laser pointer toward a corner of the frame, where one of the girl's feet was barely visible.

By this point four women had left the room, one crying. The red light pinned to the girl's ankle and did not shake.

"The socks feature an illustration of a main character from the animated Disney film *Frozen*," Girlie continued. "Judging from the scale of the TV remote control next to her leg, I would estimate a girl's size three or four."

Girlie got the job. So did the young man who threw up before her; he'd thrown up, but he hadn't paused the video. That was good enough. She was proud of herself, but knew she had no real reason to be; the hiring managers weren't all that picky, in the beginning.

· ·

Think of yourself as someone who makes our social media family a safe and fun place for everybody, that early job description read. *The best candidates will not only be able to apply content policy and execute handling procedures with consistency and efficiency but will also be able to identify subtle differences in the meaning of digital communication and accurately enforce the client's terms of use. Here at Reeden we believe that a community that learns together, grows together—you will actively benefit from and participate in employee assistance programs, program reporting initiatives, and appropriate training to foster your well-being and the well-being of our entire employee family. You may find that we love a good party, and you can usually expect one to be happening on campus somewhere! Now come on, we need your full concentration—it's time to imagine what it's like being a Content Moderator!*

At the beginning there were user-experience researchers floating around—UXRs, they were called—forever doing some study or another, there to observe the lives of the moderators, the better to improve said lives. There was the Day in the Life method, in which a UXR would shadow one moderator throughout the workday, sitting po-faced at her side while she rewound a video of someone's partial decapitation, scribbling in a notepad. There was card sorting, a method meant to "uncover the user's mental models, to improve informational architecture," in which the UX researchers would hand the moderators a deck of index cards labeled with categories—sometimes examples of content to be moderated, like DISEMBOWELED HORSE, sometimes pictures of famous Hollywood actors, to be categorized according to the character they most embodied: ACTION HERO for Schwarzenegger, ROMANTIC LEAD for Clooney, et cetera. Girlie looked at the film still of Schwarzenegger as the T-800, put him in the MATERNAL ROLE MODEL category. She didn't receive any feedback about what this said about her informational architecture.

Every single one of the UX researchers was a middle-class woman. Oh, they were diverse—white women both Bostonian and Scandinavian, Black women both Southern American and West African, Asian women both Korean Californian and Indian immigrant—but in that Tolstoyan way of all happy families being alike, all middle-class women looked the same to Girlie.

The solutions they found were the same too: the studies, ultimately, all found that the moderators could benefit from a variety of wellness tools, as well as regular team-building events to encourage decompression and foster camaraderie. Girlie hadn't asked for weekly cake parties. Girlie had replied "a raise" when a researcher asked how her job could best be improved. She didn't get a raise; the funds, it seemed, had been allocated into the social activities budget. They got a karaoke machine.

By the time the initial flurry of these researchers and tech reporters had dissipated, employees were merely encouraged to attend two wellness coaching sessions a year, and at least one wellness group session a month. Every few months or so the company still held a Mental Health Symposium, full of indispensable tips and crucial training about how to protect her internal space, set up boundaries, and not hesitate to make use of the resources at hand, nearly all of which were helplines that went straight to an answering machine, or infrequently monitored email addresses programmed to auto-send a PDF about anger coping skills, mostly recommending different forms of deep breathing.

After the first year was over, Girlie skipped both her one-on-one visits and the group sessions, all the cake parties and symposiums. She had a job to do, and she was doing it. If she hadn't been as productive, perhaps the mandatory wellness sessions would have been more stringently enforced—but the company policy, in general, was that if you looked like you were doing okay, they left well enough alone. Even if you didn't look like you were doing okay— someone at another site, it was rumored, had a heart attack at their desk and died there; there was a new moderator at that desk within the week—they left well enough alone. There was just so much to do.

At first, there were no official specializations in the moderation department—"our aim is to upskill all of our moderators," the Bay Area manager had said in those early days, "so they can action all potential abuse types." But there was an unspoken understanding that certain employees were particularly gifted in specific genres of abuse, and so in training they would be partnered with—or would become, themselves—unofficial subject matter experts.

MODERATION

No one wanted the title *Hate Speech Expert* or *Head of Child Sexual Abuse* on their LinkedIn, but it was known amongst the moderators that if you were struggling with a racist abuse issue, you went to Maria (one of the four moderators named after the Virgin; this one was ex–grad student Maria—to be distinguished from the other three, who were all older Pinay women, none of them particularly good at identifying tendencies toward racial abuse, in particular their own).

If you had trouble judging whether or not a video contained scenes of animal torture, you went to Robin, the uptight young Pinoy nerd everyone said was the youngest employee Reeden (well, not Reeden, exactly) had ever hired, recent UC Davis grad, never talked to anyone, didn't flinch or cry like that one white guy—last one left on the floor—who quit after seeing the video of someone beating a bag of puppies to death with a baseball bat.

If murder and gore were your bugbears, you went to Rhea—former ER nurse, McCain Republican, self-proclaimed gun enthusiast, sometimes found cooing on the phone to her geriatric Italian husband, and who'd started moderating after her retirement, just to bring some extra cash in. Rhea, alternately known as Ray, not quite a deadname since Rhea switched back to it whenever she felt the privileges or protections of being Ray were superior, usually when they had to accommodate a senior manager visit. Rhea was a consummate capitalist ex-provinces girl in the school of Girlie's own mother, which was to say: nothing was dead if value could still be extracted from its ghost.

The young Cambodian American trainee who'd thrown up, Vuthy, was Rhea's apprentice now, following her around like a puppy, showing her pictures of shotgun wounds and asking for her advice, so they'd often be found chatting pleasantly in the hallway about the difference between birdshot, buckshot, and slug, how to look for the scalloped edge around a wound, what powder tattooing looked like at close range.

And if child sexual abuse was your issue—whether someone being fucked within an inch of their life was a four-foot-eleven adult Asian woman or a child speaking choppy French to appeal to his expat clientele, how many photos of naked children wearing angel wings constituted a cache of pornography, which ever-changing code words to flag on which ever-disappearing Passport Bros message boards, which cities were the hot spots for meeting places for affiliates and the newly initiated, how to differentiate between a right-wing nutcase endlessly SWAT-ing a laundromat from an actual potential trafficking bust—you went to Girlie. Girlie didn't have any apprentices.

Later, perhaps in recognition of the need for aspirational examples of workplace advancement, the specialists were officially called SMS. Subject Matter Specialists; the word *Experts* being a touch too self-actualizing. They even received a raise: one dollar more per hour.

The Vegas site was the highest-performing location in the national network; they hovered around a 97 percent accuracy rate, just a percentage point short of the company's set target, which was never achieved by any site, and was in effect a built-in justification for all future budget cuts and layoffs—they were perpetually ever so slightly underperforming, always as a direct result of the previous year's budget cuts and layoffs. Accuracy rate meant that when the people in Vegas thought something was child trafficking, it was child trafficking. When the people in Boston or Dallas thought something was child trafficking, it was usually just a brown mom and her mixed-race kid in Target. The managers had talked a lot about learning algorithms. Clearly the concept—that is to say, learning—hadn't quite reached critical mass in human beings yet, but one could be hopeful about machines.

Girlie's own accuracy rate was around 99.5 percent. The old judicial joke about pornography was, in Girlie's case, both the earliest of life lessons and the ultimate performance review. When it came to child sexual abuse, Girlie knew it when she saw it.

As for why so many of them were Filipino—well, what was there to say that hadn't been said in 1765; in 1899; in 1946; in 1965? The bootstraps way of putting it was to say they excelled, frankly, in the manner of people who had been formed to excel in these very specific theaters: because they spoke and read good English, because they respected chains of command, because they kept a positive attitude, because they would take a fifth of an American worker's pay, and most of all: because they were familiar. They knew Americans; what they liked, what they didn't, the ditties they sang, the food they ate, what they looked like when they were horny, what they looked like when they were dying, the psalms that struck their hearts, the way their women set their curls, the shift of air around a man before his fist hit flesh, the hours of night when God was least visible. There was no other country in the world, no other people in the world, better suited to the content moderation of America. And from America, to the world. Ad astra, et cetera.

Well, why not? Her mother was a nurse, her aunts and distant cousins all nurses and maids and cleaners scattered everywhere from Jeddah to Singapore to Rome. There was a glowing line that trailed through them, all the way back to that first early Pinay, a twentieth-century almost-girl, being taught by a white woman how to administer quinine to a malaria patient.

A glowing line through them, like a lava-bright rift in the earth, which traveled all the way to Girlie: there in the office park, cleaning the feeds of their stubborn stains of rape and bludgeoning; there in the Vegas desert, far from home; there in that soul-shaped place called heredity.

••

There was, of course, an attrition rate. The turnover in the content moderation racket was—high, to say the least. Management liked to give the impression they were concerned when employees showed signs of needing a break, or wanting to leave.

In terms of "signs-that-a-worker-was-going-to-leave," there was the story of Maring.

Not quite one of the fake Marias, too young to be an aunt to anyone, Maring never said hello, never met Girlie's gaze, wore a beige peacoat buttoned all the way to the top, collar popped to cover her neck, never took it off even when she sat at her desk on the moderator floor, not in springtime, not even in summer.

Girlie had just assumed that Maring was one of those newish Pinay immigrants who didn't like to be seen associating with other Pinays, thought of Pangasinan as the province good only for producing slaves for the Middle East, referred to Pangasinense as "Panggalatok," that type. Maring wasn't light-skinned, but Girlie was now evolved enough in her socioeconomics to know being an uptight mestiza wasn't necessarily a class giveaway. Though Maring did have about her person the rigid primness of someone who knew she didn't belong there, but who through the stormy winds of fate and martial law had somehow ended up a contract laborer in Vegas, rather than being driven through EDSA in an air-conditioned Lexus by an Ilocano chauffeur. This, Girlie believed, without having spoken to her once. Girlie, not for the first time, understood she was perhaps prone to judgmental thinking.

Ultimately, Girlie didn't spend that much time thinking about Maring; she certainly wasn't the only moderator who seemed to be on edge all the time. It was a silently understood thing that you couldn't sneak up on a moderator from behind, couldn't tap anyone's shoulder without clearing your throat unless you wanted a reflexive elbow in said throat. Everyone had moderated a hundred, thousand videos of someone coming in from behind to end somebody's world.

Like Girlie, Maring was another SMS, and her specialty was teenage internet usage, in particular campus violence threats. No one knew the whole story, but the rumor was that she'd kept reporting one kid in particular for hate speech.

He'd been on specific forums, standard stuff, making threats, saying men should enslave women for sex and food, kill the ones that didn't listen. He was also on a number of gun fandom forums: asking how to get an assault rifle without a license, how to skirt the holding periods, was it better to grind, file, or drill off a serial number, various locked posts repeating the same question about Dremels.

Maring kept reporting him. It wasn't just her; other moderators had flagged that user as well, but Maring had seen his posts for the longest period of time, had followed his user behavior over nearly two years, likely knew more about him than his own parents. He'd been banned from some forums, but came back under a different username, masked IP. Reeden HR kept insisting his constructive vision for the future of womankind—which was to say, raping them in all their factory-issue holes and then in all the holes you modded for them aftermarket, preferably with the dullest knife possible—was a free speech issue.

The teenager later shot thirteen students and two teachers at a high school in Ohio. Rhea said Maring recognized the boy's face on the news. That was the last conversation Maring had with anyone at Reeden. She turned in her resignation the day after the shooting, then drove her car into a tree—0.4 percent blood-alcohol level.

There were no signs, was the conclusion, after the investigation into her death. Unless one considered the work itself a sign. Management upped the free meditation workshops.

As for her own wellness: Girlie lifted weights regularly, drank a protein shake every morning and one again before her macro-balanced lunch, ate her five a day. She continued to please her primary-care physician at every routine visit: her metabolic panels, her lipid panels, her hormones, her blood glucose, her high good cholesterol, her low bad cholesterol, every measured metric came back sterling; solidly, stolidly above average (except, occasionally, the BUN/creatinine levels, which were a little elevated; typical meathead lifter results, too much protein, too little water).

The closest thing she had to a physical ailment was something that had started in her midthirties: she'd started smelling cigarette smoke, on and off, but with increasing frequency, so that for months she thought someone in the family had secretly taken up smoking. Girlie started looking around the house for everyday items being used as secret ashtrays, caches of stubbed-out butts in beer bottles or bathroom wastebaskets. On most days, she ignored the smell, went noseblind to it, the way she'd gotten used to the broken smoke detector that had beeped for decades in the old Milpitas home. It was still beeping the day they left the Bay. She figured it was probably just a symptom of an undiagnosed stroke, so that was something to look forward to.

Dr. Shamsie, her bright young new Vegas GP, whose online bio said she "focused on healthy eating and preventative care" and "loved hiking with her husband and two dogs in her free time," said no, it wasn't likely to be a stroke, that it was probably either just dehydration or, at worst, olfactory hallucinations, which could be a symptom of early menopause—rarer, but not unheard of for women in their mid- to late thirties. Do you have hot flashes? Premenstrual cramps? Mood swings? Increased irritability before your period?

"Oh, you mean like hating everyone and everything around you and wanting to lie down in traffic instead of have a conversation?" Girlie asked, trying to make it sound like a joke.

Dr. Shamsie frowned at her. "Yes," she'd replied evenly. "Like that."

In the end, Dr. Shamsie prescribed calcium supplementation, deep breathing. There was a worksheet.

All in all: Girlie didn't have a relationship to fuck up, a partner to cheat on with a coworker or three, a kid to come home to and distractedly parent while killing a bottle of red. She was a college-educated woman with no dependents, and after over a decade on the job— unheard of, for a content moderator—she showed minimal signs of acute mental distress, had accepted a first offer of twenty-eight thousand dollars a year, after tax, and after five years had accepted a raise to thirty-two thousand a year. It got a bit better after that. Moderators couldn't get full benefits, being not full-fledged employees but "contractors," under ever-changing contract company names. The one currently on her pay slips was calling itself Paragon; that name would change in a year. That was textbook traceability training for any Fortune 500 company. You didn't directly employ the wet work.

She never took longer than a thirty-minute lunch break, rarely took her daily nine-minute wellness break, and used her two fifteen-minute breaks to walk around the small campus and get her steps in, despite being otherwise physiologically and morally opposed to cardiovascular exercise (deadlifts counted as cardio). She recognized the chain of command, avoided the fights, never stole the toilet paper, never collapsed weeping at her desk. She hit her targets and kept to herself. She was, in short, the ideal employee. There was no better proof of her wellness, indeed her resiliency, than the fact that she was still there.

2

Anagolay, Goddess of Lost Things, Drops the Ball

*T*he regular SDX bus was late, so Girlie ended up on a Deuce; there was no avoiding tourists if you took a bus to the Strip on any night of the week, but tonight a group of white Australians on a budget stag night was holding court, singing what sounded like an endless chain of football or rugby cheers about anal sex. When they started going around the bus trying to get people to join in, Girlie muscled past them, got off at the Mirage stop—she could walk the rest of the way to the Bellagio, where Maribel should've been nearly at the end of her shift at Dram. If she tried to take public transportation all the way home, it'd add another two hours to her commute. Using the Bellagio as her subway stop, and her younger cousin's car as the solution to her last-mile problem, seemed a particularly Vegas state of affairs.

She stepped once more into the surround-sound din of the Strip, its eternal chirp of human need as high and sharp as lark-song: here, the Venetian, where gondoliers rowed tourists beneath the painted sky, singing "Nessun dorma" so it echoed all the way from the Rialto Bridge to the new McDonald's; there, all the strangers she'd never see again—the lovers kissing in front of the Roman soldiers, Romeo's hand extended to take a selfie; the laughing friends vomiting in the foliage in front of the Mirage, one holding back another's hair; the millions of palm-size fliers of women in bikinis, advertising unforgettable nights at unbeatable prices. She'd never lived in such a big city before, and now she lived in at least ten. Hadn't she, too, eaten crepes in Paris and won two hundred dollars at a *Game of Thrones* slot machine in the Luxor? And her, a kid from Milpitas.

Tomas, the security guard kuya at the entry to the main floor of the Bellagio casinos, recognized her and tipped his hat. He had insisted she call him kuya, even though she was pretty sure she was older than him, protracted youthfulness being a perk of her mother's genes. There had to be at least one perk.

"Sup, fam," he said as she passed. "Have a good night."

"You, too, kuya," she said. Thus were civilizations maintained.

Dram was at the other end of the hotel, past the steakhouses, past Hermès, past the Conservatory and Botanical Gardens where the seasonal display was still up, twenty-foot Christmas trees, crystal-encrusted sleighs, shining green and red and gold baubles the size of a Kia Soul. There were three main bars in the hotel: one big caviar and vodka bar where rich Russian, Chinese, and Middle Eastern gamblers tended to congregate; an elevated tiki bar that was uniformly attended by the white over-fifty-five crowd, too poor for a Maui vacation. And then there was Dram, which was supposed to be the cool young person's bar, industrial-Sinatra-mob vibes, the Bellagio's concession to what might be expected of old-school Vegas, but for a Gen Z clientele. Because of this anxious and cluttered stab at

brand identity, Dram attracted an unexpectedly catholic crowd—
you could, it turned out, romanticize Sinatra at any age or class
bracket.

The people who stumbled into Dram could be wealthy Singaporean
tourists, or young self-appointed food reviewers from the East Coast
sipping at black sesame cocktails, or drunk white women tourist
groups out on last-chance benders, flashing their legacy-admissions
damage at everyone like ID cards. The nightclub scene, on the other
hand, was a completely different ecosystem, one which most Vegas
locals Girlie knew either avoided or aged out of, whichever came
first. Girlie had no patience for bottle service, VIP tables, thirty-strong
groups of SoCal Asians taking ten to twenty Patrón shots apiece until some poor girl had to be stretchered out to the tune of David
Guetta. She didn't need a nightclub; if she wanted to see her community being a mess, all she had to do was track everyone's credit score.

On her way to Dram, Girlie passed by the big Tiffany & Co. store,
caught Sam's eye through the window display, avoided the look on
instinct, and kept walking—until she remembered.

She cursed under her breath, stopped in the middle of the walk-
way; thought about it. She could keep going, send a text to confirm
the reservation, or just wait for the email, even though she'd been
waiting for the email for a month (that was a Pinoy business owner
for you). Resigned, she walked backward a little, rewinding herself
through time and space, then turned around.

Sam was still looking at her, had seen the rewind move, a nice little *really, bitch* look in her eye, curtained by demi-wispies. Girlie
steeled herself.

"How'd your mom like the earrings," Sam was saying over her
shoulder, walking Girlie toward her station near the Elsa Peretti
displays, diamonds by the yard. "I saw them all over Facebook."

"Says she loves them."

"Does she actually wear these ones?"

Girlie shot her a heavy look. Sam laughed, because Sam had a mother who didn't just preserve all of her daughter's gifts in the amber of the Facebook wall; drank her Maxwell House instant coffee from Tiffany Blue bone-china coffee cups, well stained. "At least you know she drives the Tesla. Maybe you have to get her a car every year. Ha!"

Girlie had only dated Sam for two months, almost six years ago, so Sam's tendency to be overfamiliar was something she knew she had to muscle through, to get to her ultimate goal. She couldn't lead her on—though Sam wasn't actually a person who could be led on, which Girlie respected—but if she was *too* mean during the encounter, even that could have an unwelcome erotic charge. Sam was still commenting on Girlie's mom's Facebook posts, **wow auntie ang ganda!! Beautiful Goyard bag. What a good daughter you have. Happy Birthday and God bless.**

That was how Girlie and Sam met, all those years ago; Girlie, there to buy some starter Tiffany for her mother, doing what every eldest daughter did with her paycheck: tithing. She'd been planning on a nice little Elsa Peretti heart necklace in sterling silver, but couldn't help lingering by the more sculptural pieces, so that was how Sam had first laid eyes on her: out of character; looking for herself, for a second.

"You get enough money from me." Girlie turned her back to the display. "Did you talk to your brother about the reservation?"

"I *told* you it's confirmed for thirty people."

"I didn't get an email."

Sam threw Girlie a look of her own. "It's not my fault you won't just DM him! You know what he's like with email. You guys are the ones who keep changing the date."

"Maribel's got people from everywhere flying in, the Bay, East Coast, she wants to accommodate everybody, I just want to make sure it's locked in—"

"Y'all can't lock down the whole month of March. Tell your cousin to talk to my brother."

"She said the date is final—"

"She said that two dates ago—"

"The date is final," Girlie repeated, hard. "I'm vouching for it."

"Fine then, confirmed, you already got it," Sam said. "But if you guys change it again—"

"It's on my head. Thirty people."

"I *said* thirty people," Sam huffed, appearing to remember why she and Girlie weren't friends.

Girlie nodded. Objective secure. "Okay. Thanks, mare."

Sam rolled her eyes. "Is that all, because I got actual clients waiting. Buy that cuff from me sometime, I need the commission. Support your community."

"Two percent commission on an eighteen-hundred-dollar cuff makes a difference to your finances, that's on you," Girlie muttered, already walking back toward the door. There were no clients waiting.

Resuming the walk back to Dram, Girlie again put her collar up, arms crossed, chin down, face hard once more against the tide of the wondering world. For a time, she'd worn a fake wedding ring, but that had made a negligible difference to her would-be trappers, which in Vegas could be singletons with moxie, drunken bachelors and their reckless grooms, retirees flush with chips, or comp sci majors on spring break.

Girlie had no false modesty about her own beauty, found it stupid to be humble about it, pretend about it, to make it smaller so others—ugly men and fear-compliant women, particularly that racially diverse coalition of women with an ex-boyfriend who'd started dating an Asian woman, ever a reliable solidarity—could feel bigger. She was not a shy person—silently ever-judging, yes, but not shy—and would not pretend at shyness to make her beauty seem accessible, would not diminish herself to appear oblivious to it and therefore escape condemnation for it. A mere babe in the woods, a diamond in the rough, a cerebral virgin ignorant of lash curlers and mascara: this was the ideal posture of the beautiful, according to the traditional owner class of Filipina women's beauty (suffice to say, the workers did not own the means of production).

But to simper and shrink and be coy about her birthright was contrary to Girlie's fundamental nature (kingdom: asshole / phylum: know-it-all / genus: first-generation eldest daughter). She refused to be a tenant of her face, rather than its owner. The heirloom of this beauty had been her mother's prize possession—sole possession, really—in her impoverished youth back in the Philippines; it was the only form of intergenerational wealth Girlie knew.

For a while she tried to share the beauty around a bit; she'd been pan, then bi, then queer—that was when she was still in college, where people said stuff like *queer* and quoted Judith Butler. At heart Girlie was nominally bi, but it was like a driver's license she'd gotten as a teenager and had let expire; she could probably still drive the car but that didn't mean she'd be safe on the road. A more relevant sexual identity: she'd been called a ho since she was eight or nine, the word aimed at the shape of her hips, the resting expression on her face, her indio mouth, too full of opinions.

When she was very young, she'd leaned into it—wore low-cut

tops, short skirts, smiled with adolescent pride whenever she was catcalled by adult men on the street. Later she learned hypersexuality was a common symptom of sexual abuse. She hadn't investigated further; she figured googling "hypersexuality as a ten-year-old" would probably put her on a list; probably one she'd have to moderate.

She stopped being so generous. That Girlie was the most beautiful cousin in their family, that she'd been beautiful even as a child—she would be more beautiful, her mom and aunts and grandma mourned like clockwork, if only she were light-skinned like her mother instead of morena like her father—was fact. But in the end, although perhaps it would have saved her family, she didn't have the natural charm or interpersonal fortitude for a career as an IG model; go to Dubai and get shit on by oil sheiks for six figures and a Birkin 25 (leather: Togo / color: gris étain / hardware: palladium).

So ultimately, this beauty, this ancestral inheritance, this halfway holy thing, was just a natural commodity; a mine that had been tapped, here and there, and which she'd since chosen to close. The only way to survive hotness was to have clarity about it: both its reach and its limitations. She had it; it would one day dry up on its own; until then, she just had to live with it. And Girlie was honest enough to know that the day-to-day experience of living as a 24-karat hottie was, on the whole, pretty bearable.

..

Maribel's shift was almost over. Here she was now, sliding the rum cocktail to the East Coast–looking Asian girl—Midwest or East Coast presumably, because she was there with three white girls—then holding up a hand at Girlie, five minutes, and disappearing into the back room. When she came back out, still in her tuxedo trousers and shirt but without the bow tie and vest, old Aritzia puffer thrown over it, saying "Hi, ate!" in that sunny, culturally deferential way that Girlie pretended not to draw internal strength from, Girlie slid off the bar stool and began walking in step with her cousin, out of the bar. "You look so pretty!" said Maribel, who began most conversations with a compliment, appeasement being her preferred form of survival. "I need to find one of those jackets too."

"I sent you all the eBay links."

"Yeah, but I never find the same stuff! It doesn't look the same." Then Maribel made a theatrical crying motion, fist rubbing at the side of her eye. "Avery's still a little sick! But she's getting better. I brought her some pho before work. At least it's not COVID."

"I told y'all to get your flu shots early this year."

"Night, Maribel," said Joshua, the Pinoy security guard at Dram who'd been making eyes at Maribel for years, even after she'd finally broken up with the terrible DJ and, instead of falling straight into Joshua's arms, ended up dating a white girl from Chicago.

"Night, kuya," Maribel said brightly; Maribel, who was incapable of ever letting an iota of love, however pained or fledgling, go unthanked. Girlie watched the hit register on Joshua's face. Innocent people were capable of anything, Girlie thought, looking at Maribel, almost impressed.

Once they were in Maribel's car, a newish leased blue BMW Series 1 from a dealer in Henderson, Girlie watched Maribel check her phone, then frown at it. "What," Girlie asked.

Maribel held up her phone screen to Girlie; it was a text from Auntie Stella, Maribel's mother, on the family group chat: **here late! Come by!** was all Girlie could read before Maribel pulled the phone back, slumping back into her seat. "They're at the Orleans if we want to join them," she explained glumly.

Maribel's parents Stella and Dodo had cottoned on to the local wisdom that the jackpot chances at the Strip were next to nothing, geared as they were to tourists—there were better odds at the smaller, more rundown casinos off the main Strip, the nicest of which was the Orleans on Tropicana. First it was just a sliver off Stella and Dodo's mortgage contributions, going to the blackjack table (Dodo) or the penny slots (Stella). When it started to be nearly half, Girlie and Maribel had to intervene. Stella and Dodo had finally gotten the habit down to only a couple days before payday; abundance mindset.

"I'm good," she said, dry as a bone.

Maribel squeaked out a distressed laugh, still reading the text thread, her mouth turned down.

Now Girlie really looked at her. At the end of the day, Maribel was your classic youngest daughter with two brothers in the military and an absentee mother: all she wanted was an older girl to solve her problems, fight the bullies, take her to Sephora. Sometimes it was hard to look at Maribel and not see the infant whose diapers Girlie had changed when she herself was still in grade school; the ocher-yellow color of her newborn shit.

Girlie began to prepare herself for the night's possibility, the old routine of swinging by the Orleans under the pretense of being in the mood to play slots, just to peel away Maribel's parents with as little friction as possible from the dulling opiate haze of some Buffalo Instant Hit Machine that Auntie Stella kept insisting was about to burst. She took a deep breath. "You want to go pick them up?"

But Maribel shook her head, put her phone away. "Nah. Let's just get some food and go home."

As they drove down the strip in silence, Girlie could see Maribel drawing up her courage to ask a question; opening her mouth, then closing it again; taking in a breath, then saying nothing. Girlie grimaced—so that's why they weren't going to the Orleans; something else on the docket.

"I actually wanted to talk to you—about my birthday party," Maribel began.

"I just got the confirmation from Sam, we're on for Rocky's at the date you said, it's all taken care of," Girlie said, before Maribel could do something typical, like change the date again. The party wasn't going to be for a couple of months, but—Girlie shrugged internally—Pisces culture. Maribel had been obsessed with this birthday since she turned twenty-nine, having decided to use the occasion of her thirtieth birthday to do something no one in the family had done since they'd all escaped to Vegas: throw a big Filipino party. Girlie hadn't been particularly excited by the idea from the beginning, but early on Maribel had asked her for ideas for cool places in Vegas that they could maybe rent for a party, "not necessarily a fancy place, but like, nice, and cool, something you'd like."

"What do I know about cool places," Girlie had retorted at the time. "You ever see me go out?"

"Yeah, but you *know* about these things. Like which places are overrated. You read reviews."

"Just go on the Vegas subreddit once in a while, you'll know things too."

"But I don't have your taste in things. Nice things."

"I don't have a taste for nice things," Girlie had argued, despite the fact that she was wearing a vintage Rolex Prince Elegant on her wrist, a Canadian eBay score for less than six hundred dollars, someone who was selling off their dead grandpa's belongings and didn't know what they were selling, i.e., a relatively rare 1930s Art Deco doctor's watch, rhodium-plated, now so battered and worn you could see the cloudy stainless steel starting to peek through. The manual-wind movement, when she finally set and wound the watch, was fucking loud as hell, sounded like a tractor, its harsh post-Depression tick-tick-tick slicing time into portions like a butcher.

Girlie was in denial, but Maribel was right: it was known that Girlie had taste, that she had an instinct for things that were—a word Girlie hated from her marrow—*classy*, but not just classy; cool, sensual, vibey, things that smelled of a soul: the actually decent modern restaurants owned by progressive, second-gen Asians reclaiming their once-reviled grandmother's recipes; which dealers were basically giving away anything that wasn't a Pepsi GMT, like a skinny 14k gold Jaeger-LeCoultre manual-wind watch with a ribbed integrated mesh bracelet, the case so tiny it might have the historic Calibre 101 inside, if Girlie ever worked up the nerve to go into the Jaeger-LeCoultre store and get it serviced. She knew the right places to score vintage Helmut Lang denim jackets from the '90s, or old Belgian army quilted jackets for ten dollars that looked like the ones being sold by Scandinavian contemporary brands for five hundred, if you could just get over the fact that the person who wore it probably murdered a bunch of Congolese people on the job. The special thing about vintage clothing was that it came with history. Lots of *Vogue* articles said so.

"And you still think Rocky's is cool," Maribel said tentatively, a question in her voice, but not forward enough to commit to the punctuation of it.

"Yes," Girlie said, making her authority-figure approval very clear so Maribel could extract the requisite validation from it. Sam's brother, Rocky, had worked at some Michelin-starred establishments before opening his wildly successful ode to Pacific barbecue; they used the word *decolonial* on the website but had a sense of humor about it; the prices were bourgeois aspirational, not flat-out oligarchic. "Yes," Girlie said again, more gently. Maribel closed her eyes and nodded, nearly consoled.

Maribel, almost a decade younger than Girlie, had forever been overawed by her eldest cousin, but as they all got older—and particularly after the family's move to Vegas—Maribel's worship began to run deeper, sing keener, bruise-tender. Girlie knew Maribel was proud of her, proud to be warmed beneath her great sturdy wing, proud of Girlie's beauty like it was a shared family asset, proud of the way Girlie had paid off twenty thousand dollars of her mother's IRS debts within the first two years on the job, then bought her mother a Tesla Y after her first raise, financed, while Girlie herself still took the bus.

"Okay, so—okay. There's another—bigger part—that I wanted to run by you," Maribel was saying now. Girlie felt her body go into fight or flight.

"It's—okay, you're the first person I'm telling this to, but: I want to propose to Avery at the party."

Girlie's brain briefly went offline. "Okay," she began, rebooting, and Maribel, as expected, started freaking out, glancing over at her with a fraught sort of beseeching energy.

"Wait, okay, I know, ate, I know what you're going to say—"

"This is not a good idea."

"I know, I know, and that's why I haven't told anyone, and I'm not—I'm not completely decided on it"—that meant not only that Maribel was indeed decided on it, but it was the thing she wanted to do most in the world—"and if you think it's a bad idea obviously I—obviously I'm not gonna do something stupid—"

"Public proposals are always stupid, and a form of coercion—"

"Okay, yes, but! But!" Maribel was still taking her eyes off the road with a frequency Girlie did not enjoy. She'd had nearly ten more years of life than Maribel; if only she'd enjoyed them before they both died here. But on the bright side, at least Girlie wouldn't have to help plan a proposal dinner. "I knew you were going to say that, and totally, you're right, but—but—Avery and I had this exact conversation, about public proposals, and I brought up that some people think they're coercive, and I can see that—like don't ask your girl to marry you at the Olympics, fam—but! But then Avery said she actually thinks public proposals are really romantic. ESPECIALLY"— Girlie considered telling Maribel she was becoming hysterical, but Maribel had recently been educated in the white feminist history of witch persecution via Avery and some Marxist Italian texts, and Girlie, already trapped in one argument, didn't need to borrow credit for another—"for queer women, because a public showing of queer love is radical, especially now. Okay? So it's not my idea, it's because Avery said, herself, that she thinks public proposals are romantic. And then she showed me a bunch of TikToks of guys getting engaged and crying."

"Okay," Girlie said.

Maribel waited. Then: "Okay?"

"Far be it for me to hold the movement back. What does that have to do with the restaurant reservation?"

"What—I—okay. That's it? I thought you were gonna fight me for longer."

"I'm old, I don't have the cardio for long fights," Girlie said. "You want the setting to be proposal-worthy, that's it?"

Maribel finally started smiling. "I was thinking the outdoor terrace. Too much?"

Girlie sighed. The restaurant had a very nice terrace full of tropical plants, Kentia palms, birds of paradise. She started calculating how much more it would cost per hour to reserve the whole thing; she was already imagining the conversation she was going to have with Rocky, let alone Sam. She sighed again.

"Budget'll go up."

"I could work days."

Girlie waved her hand, silently indicating that she'd take care of it, but Maribel shook her head, "No, no. You've done enough"—*Oh have I, okay then*, Girlie thought blankly—"I'm gonna work days. I already decided."

Girlie put that skirmish aside for now. "Guest list still twenty?"

"Well—if I tell Avery she should invite some of her Berkeley friends—I'd want them to be there for a proposal—"

And this was why Girlie had reserved for thirty. Clown car. "How many?"

Maribel winced. "Could we do thirty? Would they do thirty? Would they do specific Filipino dishes if we special order, you think? I know we already got them to do the pancit for long-life thing but Avery loves ube brazo, we had that on one of our first dates, and I thought it'd be nice if—on the proposal evening, she has some—but I know it's not on their menu—"

You, bitch, are also in possession of Google and an email address is what Girlie should have said, but then what would her use value as an ate in this community be? She sighed again, heavy, recruiting everyone from dead ancestors to circumstantial acquaintances to sworn enemies into the sigh, Igorot headhunters, Hokkien grandmothers, the Spanish and the English and the Americans, hell, even Dutch pretenders from the Battle of Manila Bay in 1646, get everybody in there, build bridges for once, look at this dumb bitch. "I'll ask Rocky. If not, we can just bring it from Goldilocks."

Maribel beamed. "We should bring at least two!"

Maybe it was because Maribel's ilk were the post–search bar generation; they didn't have to search for things anymore, algorithmic benevolence having already figured out what they were looking for just by the scent trail of their fingertips, the crumbs they left around the world for someone else to vacuum up, a million undying lights in the gloaming. Or maybe it was just because they weren't eldest children; learned helplessness being one of the more malignant comorbidities of being a family's last born. It did seem like a skill, maybe even a valuable one: Knowing what you wanted. Knowing how to look for it. Knowing how to recognize it, when it appeared.

• •

They stopped to pick up dinner on the way home, two bobas and the All-In Bundle at Wingstop, which Girlie paid for, as usual, after Maribel put up an impassioned protest, also as usual ("I just got paid" was tonight's futile campaign), with Girlie, deadfaced, muscling past her to the register, gently elbowing Maribel's battered old Coach Outlet wallet out of the way, saying "Her money's no good here" to the girl behind the register, who knew the whole routine by heart, clearly found the entire family annoying as hell. There was not yet a universe in which Girlie was going to allow any of her food to be paid for by a younger cousin. Civilizations, etc.

From there, they drove quietly toward the gated community on the west side of Enterprise, the part that hadn't been incorporated into Henderson, squeezed at the foot of Desert Hills and Buffalo Rock, bordered to the east by Paradise, to the north by Spring Valley. All of it Paiute land; long before the railroad workers, the gypsum miners, the twenty-first-century California refugees fleeing financial illiteracy. Which Maribel and Avery both made sure to honor, with bumper stickers on their cars that said YOU ARE ON NATIVE LAND, bought from Puha, the Native-owned weed lounge downtown they regularly frequented, more often toward payday— further away from payday, beer was cheaper than Orange Sherbet pre-rolls.

It was time to say hello to the last Filipino security guard of the night. Tito saluted them, military perfect, uniform too big for his frail body. He worked in the entrance booth next to Dominic, younger Guatemalteco cat, heavyset and a little browbeaten by daily life under Tito's martial confidence, who pressed the button while barely checking them over. The gate lifted.

Here they were again: the rolling green lawns, the palm trees, the eighteen-hole golf course not one person in the family ever used, the two-mile walking path promising relaxing vistas of the community. Girlie had never hiked in her life. There was the basketball court, the tennis court, the playground, the outdoor pool with water park "for summer fun," including cabanas, a lagoon, at least three spas, a lap pool, a rope bridge, sixteen water slides, and most important of all, several squirt-gun stations. There was the recreation center, where Maribel said she and Avery sometimes played pickleball, a concept outside of Girlie's realm of comprehension. The water park had been closed for "renovations" for over a year; someone had drowned in the lagoon.

They drove up the long black streets of the "oasis of the Southwest," or so the old early 2000s brochure had called it, passed Pine Shores, and Misty Springs, until they reached Living Edens Court, a name Girlie couldn't have come up with for their new address in her meanest hours.

Once more into the breach. She looked up at the house that wasn't yet theirs: the great hulking curse of it, the great hulking raft of it, the copy-paste Spanish-tiled dreamer's monstrosity that had ruined them all, and was all they had left: their colossal victory, shameful and triumphant; a successful hunt, crammed with buckshot. They were home. It was a word Girlie thought of now with an asterisk next to it. Home*.

· ·

The early 2000s. It was the age of rhinestones, the age of velour, the age of shock and awe, the age of that most rhinestoned, most veloured, most shocking and awesome of things: the adjustable rate mortgage.

Everyone was buying houses. Girlie's mother and three of her aunts all bought—*bought*, term used with extreme prejudice—houses all the way from California to Nevada, everywhere new housing was being thrown up against the scrubland like a rash: houses in Livermore, houses in Dublin, houses in Pleasanton, houses in Visalia, houses in Las Vegas. The houses were all puffy McMansions, neo-eclectic Goliaths, cloistered away in planned gated communities penned in by fields of blistering foxtail grass, each one with five to seven bedrooms, curved double staircases, oiled MDF balustrades, oak veneer.

Girlie's mom took equity from the house in Milpitas—their comparatively modest but paid-off family home, the one for which her parents had slept all night in a car on an empty lot back in the early '80s just to be first in line for the housing lottery—to buy a huge Mission Revival house in Livermore and an even bigger neo-Mediterranean house in Las Vegas.

"The rich never pay off their houses," one Pinoy financial adviser said. "You have to think of them as assets. Buy and sell. A house will never depreciate in value," he said. Day-Date 40 on his wrist, after-market diamonds. Then 2008 came.

For a while, it felt like everywhere Girlie looked was an inferno; everyone sequestered in their own private circle of hell, aflame. Everyone she knew lost something. Most of the people she knew lost everything. The aunt who'd bought—*bought*—some giant house in Milpitas Hills lost the house, along with everything (and, given her husband left her and took the kids to be raised by his mistress, had lost, at least by most accounts metaphorical, spiritual, and judicial: everyone) in it. Another aunt went fully bankrupt and had to move back in with the brother who'd abused her throughout their childhood, taking his kids to school, shopping at Costco with his third wife. The classmate whose family had owned a popular Pinoy bakery in Milpitas lost their main home, the three homes they'd bought with the equity, and the bakery itself. The classmate had to drop out of school to help chip in. That bakery quickly became a Domino's, more popular than the bakery had ever been.

Girlie's mother lost—everything. Which meant that in 2008, ten years away from her supposed retirement age, her mother was a million dollars in debt.

The Livermore house—underwater. The Las Vegas home—underwater. With the Livermore house, they managed to avoid foreclosure with a short sale; which, no idea why it was called a short sale, because the entire process of selling a home for less than it was worth—transferring a property from a "distressed seller" to a "qualified buyer"—took three times longer, involved long, shameful months of long, shameful conversations between Girlie's mother and the long, shameful carousel of lenders and real estate agents, her mother putting so much effort into speaking English clearly, enunciating every syllable, trying to sound slow, even, and assured. But in her speech were bursts of scratchy, uncontrolled terror, like an amateur putting too much tension on the strings of a violin.

With the Las Vegas house, they again avoided foreclosure by a hair's breadth with a stroke of genius. In order to keep Stella—the youngest of Flo's six sisters, nineteen years younger than Girlie's mother, barely even walking yet when Girlie's mother had left Mangaldan for Tennessee on a nursing visa—and, by extension, Stella's large family, from becoming homeless, Girlie's mother magnanimously offered the Las Vegas home to them, saying she'd cover half the mortgage if they'd cover the other half; Stella, her husband, Dodo, and their three kids all chipped in. Stella and Dodo got jobs at Walmart; Martin and Melvin enlisted; Maribel got the job at the Bellagio. Which just left the Milpitas house to deal with.

If someone had told Girlie when she was a kid that Milpitas would one day be gentrified; if someone had told her that the town that famously smelled of shit and had the best Southeast Asian food in the Bay and whose contours would remain as known and loved to her as the body of any lover, would one day demand over a million dollars for a newly built townhouse out in the weedy backlots south of the mall, she would have—laughed, probably. Died, maybe. Asked what alternative universe they'd come from. But she didn't know yet that there were thousands upon thousands of universes crumpled up like a bad draft in God's back pocket; that it was easy to tumble out of one and into another.

Girlie's mother sold the Milpitas house in 2009 for a fraction of what they would have gotten if they'd only been able to wait a decade—but they couldn't wait a decade. They couldn't cover both the Milpitas mortgage and the Las Vegas mortgage; they couldn't keep up the middle-class drag of being a family with multiple houses, a portfolio, a Catholic school–educated daughter now at Berkeley, a bright future for the clan. The Milpitas home was so much smaller than the Vegas home; there wasn't enough space on the raft there for everyone to be saved. And so Girlie's family completed the exodus out of the Bay, avoiding the lookback so they wouldn't be turned to salt. Everyone moved to Vegas.

Girlie's mother got a job at a Henderson hospice care center—most of her friends and fellow nurse coworkers had already long since retired, way past the age for it, left the game before the pandemic hit then watched in horror as the younger frontline daughters and nephews came home from their shifts with bruised faces, dead eyes, spirits charry as the interior of a burned-out car. But Girlie's mother had famously said she'd retire at the age of one hundred and two; said it as a testament to her work ethic rather than her debt load, which meant Flo sometimes joined in on the COVID-era TikTok dancing health-worker videos meant to stave off total breakdown, always the oldest one in the lineup; shared posts on Facebook saying **PLEASE WEAR YOUR MASK IT PROTECTS BOTH YOU AND ME.** As it was, three of Flo's cousins went down, in America, Canada, and the Philippines; no public funerals. Flo said she'd pay for the burials, gave the families some money so they could get back on their feet. Girlie covered her mother's share of the mortgage those two years.

Nowadays Flo worked the one p.m. to twelve a.m. shift, which meant she and Girlie rarely, if ever, crossed paths, unless it was a birthday or major holiday and Girlie had a Goyard bag or bonus mortgage contribution to sacrifice on the altar of filial piety. They communicated mostly by texting—Girlie's mother, at Costco, asking Girlie if she needed anything; Girlie saying either *no, thank you,* or *Maribel says we're out of peanut butter.*

The Vegas house wasn't paid off yet, not even with what they'd made from the sale of the Milpitas house—but the finish line wasn't that far, comparatively speaking. Three, four hundred thousand dollars far. Girlie couldn't remember when she'd started measuring in debt.

Girlie had once read, to her amusement, an article wondering at how families in the Philippine diaspora had some of the highest household incomes despite largely being employed in working-class jobs. Indeed: hers was a seven-income family, in a gated community, all on the same Costco club card.

Girlie knew of some Bay Area transplant kids who'd kept the 408 in their email addresses and IG handles, who still made the ten-hour drive back to San Jose every couple of weeks just to feel the sting of it, who led every conversation in Vegas with *But really I'm from the Bay*—

Girlie, from the beginning, refused such rituals. When people asked where she was from, she said she lived in Vegas. In the end, she knew, they'd never been meant to thrive: not here, maybe not anywhere. They'd long ago been mutated, that was the capital-F Fact: remade lifetimes and lifetimes ago to be forever-tourists, just passing through, lifted by the dominion of the centuries to live always just an inch off the ground, so no root ever stuck and no foundation went unshaken. Maybe it was because of this that she was more inured to such losses and indignities; maybe it was because of this that she bore such daily disasters with the self-preserving impassivity that made her, in the end, so good at her job.

At least, that was the front she'd chosen: the defrag she'd made of her person, all bulky files and partial folders duly consolidated, secreted away to save time and space. The other option was actually confronting the fact that her mother had sold the only thing any of them had to their name right out from under them. That her mother had been born in the kind of poverty in the Philippines that had made her, as a girl, dig crabs out of the ground and eat them, shell and all, just to have something in her stomach; that she had spent her entire life in a breakneck run from that poverty, had deformed every single decision in her life around the soul-curdling vow of never, ever, ever feeling poor again—and in the winter of her life, here her mother was: poor again. In the early 2000s, someone told Girlie's mother she could feel rich, and she signed on the dotted line.

. .

"Home sweet home," Maribel murmured, as she did every night, as she drove the car into the garage, turned the engine off. Girlie scoffed a little; as she, too, did every night.

But now was the time when a hush came over them, when neither knew quite what to say to the other. Girlie waved off Maribel's help carrying the food into the house, and they made their way past the triple-height ceiling entrance, leaving their shoes at the door, moving silently in socked feet across the fake marble floor toward the kitchen, where Maribel turned on the lights. Someone, probably a pre-casino Auntie Stella, had left a Styrofoam package of store-bought assorted turon on the kitchen island, a single fly already picking over a shiv of caramelized sugar.

In silent concert, they divided up the portions, pulling out mismatched cutlery from the drawers, replacing the paper towel roll when it ran out, rummaging in the garage for the giant torn-open plastic package of twelve rolls, stuffed in between stacks of laundry detergent, old canned food and toilet paper, dozens of pairs of tsinelas, some used, some still in their crackly plastic packaging from a trip to Baguio in 1993, little burgundy velour wedges with plastic beads on the toe box, fitting anyone size 5 to 11, enough for a family of twenty, unused.

"You don't wanna—watch a movie, or something—" Maribel tried, too casually.

Not for the first time, Girlie wished Maribel would just figure out she was an asshole already, and finally find somewhere else to park her gargantuan need for love and acceptance, and let Girlie off the fucking hook.

Tonight, Girlie looked down at her hands, left one holding her boba—oolong tea, crystal boba, oat milk—and right one just about to lift her plate, heavy with wings, tenders, fries, and the Hickory Smoked BBQ and Mango Habanero sauces.

"I—was just gonna do some emails then crash," she said, which was a lie, she never had emails to do for work; not that any of them knew that, NDAs being good for something, at least. She wanted to eat in front of her laptop and let her brain simmer on low for the rest of the night, maybe watch some gamer's old YouTube playthrough of *Red Dead II*, or a four-hour video of a Christie's auction: one million pounds for a small Greek bronze head of Eros, twelve thousand pounds for a three-piece Dietrich-inspired Harris Tweed suit from the Vivienne Westwood estate, forty-five million Hong Kong dollars for the only surviving pair of Frères Rochat gold and enamel singing bird pistols.

She saw out of the corner of her eye Maribel already nodding, waving her hand. Forgiving her for yet again refusing, forgiving herself for yet again trying.

"No, no, of course, no doubt—I should check on Avery anyway—"

"Next time," Girlie said, already on her way out the door toward the stairs to her room.

"For sure, for sure, for sure," Maribel said, still at the kitchen island, putting all the tenders on her plate with great care, not looking up.

..

When they moved to Vegas, all the pictures they'd brought with them remained in boxes. They'd never unpacked them, never put them on display; with two families living in the same house, they had somehow silently agreed not to put any personal photos up, as if in keeping the home neutral, it would draw less attention to the fundamental unsustainability of the project—the project being family. Which meant there was only one place to look at pictures of the old Milpitas house.

So late at night, just before going to bed, no more than once or twice a month: Girlie allowed herself to open up Zillow in an incognito tab.

Girlie began by flicking through the old familiar image gallery, rememorizing the details of each photograph like she was playing an extended game of Where's Waldo with her own life. Each time she visited the SOLD listing, she was half afraid that they'd take it down, or worse, that there'd be a new listing up—that the house would be on sale again, for twice the price than she privately dreamt to herself that she might be able to afford one day. That it would be entirely redone, renovated from the guts up—*put your own stamp on it!*—and that someone else, some other cash-rich millionaire from the New Bay Area via Boston or Guangdong or Punjab would snap it up again, and she'd have to start the dream over from scratch.

But tonight, the house wasn't for sale. There was just a note in the corner of the listing, which said, *Make Me Move!* It meant that the current owners weren't actively selling the house, but were open to potential offers, if the offers were competitive enough. They weren't attached to the home for the home's sake, it meant. They could be bought out.

Girlie looked at a picture of her childhood kitchen, the ghosts of grease stains above the stove that not even the industrial cleaning, forcefully recommended by their estate agent, could've erased. Looked at it until her eyes burned, until her throat burned, until every part of her hurt.

It had taken her a little while to come up with the name Girlie Delmundo. In the early days, they were encouraged at Reeden to use pseudonyms, which wasn't exactly a hard-line requirement, except for when the odd reporter came sniffing around. Then, a fake name was forcefully suggested for the employee's protection—which meant, of course, for the company's protection. They'd all had to sign NDAs about the job, couldn't tell their family members that they worked for the same company that let them share Christmas photos and Bible verses and donation links across the entire diaspora. Most people stopped using their fake names after the first couple years or so—but Girlie held on to hers. It made no difference, really; no one in her life ever called her anything but *ate* or *anak*. The last time she'd heard her own name called was at her college graduation.

Landing on Girlie was easy; it rhymed, in a way, with her actual name, and moreover it seemed like the most obvious confirmed-bachelor Pinay auntie name she could think of (other options: Baby, Nene, Pinky, Lala)—and she was, as ever, trying to be the change she wanted to see in the world.

The last name took longer. At first she wanted some defiant little precolonial name, like Dimasalang, Dimaapi, Dimacuha, Dimaisip, Dimalanta, Dimapasoc, Dimasupil, but by the time she'd finished scrolling through the Ds on the "Find Your Filipino Surname and Its Meanings!" website on her phone in the middle of the night, the idea of calling herself *untouchable, unoppressable, unobtainable, unfath-*

omable, untiring, unbreachable, and *unvanquishable* felt—just slightly—like overkill.

She went with Delmundo because that was the last name she'd glimpsed before finally falling asleep crushed-face-first on top of her phone, right before Dimasalang. Girlie Delmundo. She had no fucking clue who that person was. It felt right, then, to become her.

Some of her coworkers had chosen the names of iconic political figures—Reeden, surprisingly, didn't prohibit this—and so on the moderator floor there had been Gandhis and Malcolms and Baldwins and Tandang Soras and Mulans.

She knew she didn't want a historical name. Oh, all names were historical, she knew that. She didn't want an important name, she meant. She was tired of Jose Rizal, tired of Aguinaldo and Bonifacio, tired of history and heritage. She didn't want a boulevard name, a monument name, a national hero name.

The most popular names, by far, were the names of the dead. Private dead, communal dead, dead of public dignity or secret infamy or some arranged marriage of the two. She couldn't think of anything she was more tired of than the dead: tired of the dead, and death, and all its shrouds and songs. Tired of dining at its table, tired of its ceaseless stalker's attention, tired of always having to leave it on read. The coworkers bearing like heraldic flags the revolutionary names of the dead always said things like: *remember to be proud of us, remember to know your history, remember to let them know we're out here.*

She was tired of pride, tired of us, tired of knowing her history, tired of being out and here. Tired of having to be so emphatically who she was in order to redeem whoever the hell they had been, tired of having to hold up the heaving ceiling of the ramshackle home they'd left her, still mortgaged. Most of all she was tired of forgetting that the world was over; that it was over before any of them even got there. That the disaster had already happened, and from its indifferent trembling had formed this ill-starred shade of a world, and now they were just—here, day two, clocking in for the shift. She was tired of carrying it all; she was going to put it down. The first thing she was going to put down was her name.

The next morning, as always, she woke up in bed drooling, laptop dead at her side, neck bent halfway to broken. The screen was black; the Zillow listing was gone.

By the time she was on the bus to work, any residue of the dream would be gone; she was Girlie Delmundo again. She couldn't even remember who the hell had ever lived in that house; what her name had ever even been.

3

The Sin-Eaters Orientation

hen, one day, opportunity came in a well-cut suit. Girlie knew something was up, not just because of the ammonia and lemon in the air, the freshly wiped floors—all the regular signs pointing to an impending senior management visit—but because of the way the man in the doorway dressed.

People didn't dress up like that; not in Las Vegas, certainly not on the first floor of the Reeden Content Moderation department—not even the overly polite on-the-border-of-condescending European tourists looking for sex workers on the Strip dressed like this.

The man was in a sharply cut dove-gray suit, not a wrinkle on his narrow shoulders, starched white dress shirt with only the top button open at the collar, no tie—a concession to the unspoken rule of the new Western corporate fashion, she thought, where an excess of elegance would be deemed effete and tryhard. The collar looked a little disturbed; maybe he'd left the tie back in the cupholder of his car, probably a Mercedes S-Class, silver or black; his dad's generation would've had one in champagne. By Western, she meant the American West, not the global; the man was Asian, sure, but her first thought when she saw him was that he was probably from the East Coast. Only when the man opened his mouth, and the careful, not quite posh, faintly Hong Kong–inflected British English of the well-traveled meritocratic business elite came tumbling out, did she startle.

"Good afternoon," he said to the room at large, smiling a little wryly, as if he and the entire content moderation floor were in on the same running joke.

Standing next to him was Joseph, their on-site manager, and Aditya, Director of Content Moderation, who only appeared during company socials and team-development exercises, usually to give a long, grinny speech about disruptor culture.

From his time in the Bay Area, Aditya had picked up the habit of calling them *the talent*, of sidling up next to the Filipina mothers and joking about lumpia (it was the only Filipino food item he knew), shamelessly deploying the material fact of his brownness to obscure the equally material fact of his bossness. He talked a lot about "radical candor" in his meetings. What that meant, no one really knew, and the meaning could not be derived from context.

Among the aunties who still had connections from the closed-down Bay Area site, it was widely rumored that Aditya had been removed from his previous position in the Bay Area for discriminating against lower-caste Indian employees, namely by refusing to promote or even speak to employees with Dalit last names, and then going to stalk the LinkedIn profiles of said employees, reaching out to their bosses, and asking creepy "good faith" questions about their performance. But like your average Catholic priest, instead of being fired once his behavior was reported, he was merely transferred to a different department.

Much to the relief of everyone involved, Aditya flourished in his new position. He loved playing benevolent ruler over the mostly Filipina employees in his care; loved the clarity of the hierarchy, so crystalline it allowed him to pretend, when he was feeling sentimental, that it didn't exist at all.

"The difference of working in a company like Reeden," Aditya said, "is that at heart, we're really a family. One Team." "One Team" was an internal slogan they were trying to make happen at Reeden, always capitalized so you knew it Meant Something.

Joseph, a sheepish white man in his early thirties, was much less chummy than Aditya, and lived in seeming mortal terror of offending the older Filipina moderators, so quick was he to acquiesce when they blandly refused to do some task he'd been sent down by management to deliver. He let them smoke in the stairwells, turned a blind eye to the employees who fucked in the wellness studios, and never said anything when he caught them binging Netflix on their secondary computer monitor, provided they met their targets on the first. With his stretched earlobes, he seemed like he should have been serving specialized coffee flights at a café in Portland, so how he'd stumbled into content moderation was a bit of a mystery to everyone. Joseph had mentioned that he'd worked at a doomed start-up, some type of augmented reality app, but the only real thing he said about his experience was one single solemn proclamation, after some of the moderators complained about the off-brand candy bars in the breakroom: "The first sign a start-up is going to fail is if the snacks are expensive."

"But we're not a start-up," Rhea pressed. Joseph deflated. Some of the branded candy bars came back. Girlie liked Joseph just fine.

Joseph, who already looked like he was sweating. "Hey, everyone, hey—hey. So Aditya and I are here to show around—"

Senior management visit. At this, most of the moderators on the floor visibly started tuning out, though they remained facing Joseph, appearing, at least to an untrained eye, to be listening intently. No one was better than a content moderator at dissociation.

Joseph was saying, "We'll just be moving around the floor, so don't mind us—"

Girlie caught Rhea's eyes, rolling upward. Rhea was making a dick-sucking gesture with her tongue in her cheek. Girlie let no expression pass over her face, which she knew would transmit her unequivocal and culturally specific agreement. She put her earpods in and went back to work.

On Girlie's desk there were two computer monitors; one screen showed an image of a large two-sided dildo made of neon green silicone, moving athletically between a vagina and an anus. The other screen showed a gamer's Animal Crossing livestream—tips on how to build a cozy cottagecore island. She didn't think the vagina was a kid's. Normal explicit content flag and ban.

"Ah—hey—hey," Joseph said from behind her—when the fuck was he going to learn not to come up on the moderators from behind? "Sorry to, sorry to bother you there, can we—"

Girlie took longer than she needed to take out her left earpod—labor resistance took all shapes—then finally turned around in her swivel chair.

Joseph, Aditya, and the man were all standing behind her desk. Aditya was grinning widely, as usual; he didn't seem to have a lower-frequency grin. The man was still looking wry, still in a suit, still looking like he'd last-minute decided to leave a silk tie in the cupholder of his car. Shining black shoes, long toe box, large feet, maybe a thirteen. Up close there were slight lines around his mouth, and one deep line between his brows, but no lines around his eyes, like his smiles never quite reached there. Impossible to tell how old he was. Her age, maybe. Impossible to tell how old she was either.

One of Joseph's hands was clenching and unclenching; he so hated confrontation, Girlie thought with an affectionate kind of cruelty; hereditary trait. She shouldn't bully him. But still she left the dildo picture on the screen.

"Is something wrong," she asked, eyes round with oppressed peasant worry, laying it on thick, Oliver Twist please sir can I have some more vibes. The new man's mouth twitched.

"No—! No," Joseph said, looking around furtively. Rhea had already started glaring at him from behind her monitors. "Not at all, just—hey, can we borrow you for a second?"

"Right now?" Girlie was not, normally, one of the employees they trotted out for senior gladhanding. Her strengths were legion, but corporate analingus did not number among them. She could've been floor manager herself by this point, Rhea kept telling her, if she'd just dole out some positive reinforcement every now and then.

"If you don't mind—"

Girlie took her time turning around, took her time closing the dildo window, the Animal Crossing window. Took her time removing the other earpod, putting them back in their case, pushing her chair back. Probably something to do with all the skipped wellness sessions this year, she thought with an internal sigh. The man didn't look like HR, but who knew. They might have a new Global Leader of Resiliency. They might be making an example of her. Now she'd probably have to do yoga on the roof by the company pool.

As they walked, Aditya and Joseph immediately launched into some competitively hollow conversation about bouldering, which had been the last mandatory team-building activity Girlie'd had to suffer through: waiting stiffly while the climbing gym owner helped fasten her carabiner, some poor guy who needed to pay the rent, couldn't turn down bread-and-butter corporate events. "Good times, good times," Aditya was saying to a nodding Joseph.

In passing, Girlie caught the new man's eye. He nodded politely at her. Come to think of it, he hadn't introduced himself yet. That was odd. All of these Heads of Whatever always introduced themselves before you even managed to get a breath out, hands out for a firm handshake, Submariner or GMT-Master II on display.

They reached the managerial floor, light flooding in from the floor-to-ceiling windows, the brightly lit vending machines serving coffee, candy, smoothies—the largest machine was even a mini supermarket, which had become mythic to the moderator floor, where you could buy laundry detergent, lightning cords, chargers, condoms, organic protein bars, all for at least twice the price they'd usually go for at any grocery store or cash-and-carry.

"Nice watch," Girlie found herself saying at the man's Reverso as they walked.

Stainless steel, unless he was going stealth and it was actually white gold or platinum, but she knew the shine of precious metal, and this wasn't it. Colonial polo player drag, she thought, starting to relax into a sneer, happy to dismiss him, happy to feel sorry for him, seeing his whole life unfurl before her, little Asian British boy, maybe a scholarship kid, trying to fit in with the aristocrats, bought himself a Jaeger-LeCoultre Reverso Grande GMT so he could pretend to check the close of the stock market in both America and England. The other watches in his collection, she'd place a moneyline bet on it at the Bellagio: an entry-level hobnail Calatrava, probably inherited, some kind of Seamaster (English and European men got the Seamaster, American men got the Speedmaster; it was the James Bond/

Buzz Aldrin dichotomy), hell, maybe even a fucking Nautilus 5711 if he was a real incel. Drove a Mercedes S-Class or maybe a hybrid Lexus SUV if he was trying to be a man of the people. I got you, she thought mirthlessly, almost regretting being correct. I got you.

He was looking at her, smiling very faintly when she finally brought her gaze up to meet his. She smiled back at him, with all the patronizing benevolence of the sure. He had very dark brown eyes. The pockets of fat just under his bottom lashes were thick, giving him a somewhat incongruously boyish look, which belied the very deep eyebags just below them, almost bruise-brown, the two lines under the bags sprayed over with faint brown freckles.

Then the man said coolly: "Likewise," without looking down at her watch, or looking away from her face at all. The very dark brown eyes didn't blink. "Thirties?"

Girlie's smile went tight; she could feel it, but she couldn't stop it in time. "About there."

"Very nice patina," he said, still not looking down at her wrist. "Quite rare."

"Thank you," she said thinly. Somehow they'd started walking next to each other, locked in step. The new man was tall, just around six feet, even though he stooped toward her slightly, likely a habit from when he was younger; she didn't like that even in lug-sole boots she only came up to his chin, that the height of him cast a shadow on her when they walked. It struck her as—gendered, in a way that felt politically irritating. He also smelled like cigarette smoke, but that could have been the undiagnosed stroke talking.

Finally, Joseph showed them all into a small conference room, holding the door open so Aditya could sweep into it first, then hold out his own arm like he was the one welcoming the remaining two into his kingdom. "Here, have a seat anywhere, guys!"

Joseph was still hovering on the threshold. "Do you guys need anything to drink, can I get you a water, a—"

"A coconut water would be great," she said. When on the managerial floor, she thought.

"Sure, sure—Aditya? William?"

Girlie met the man's gaze. They were standing in front of their respective chairs. He'd started smiling again, that inside-joke smile. He extended his hand out to her. She took it; good temperature, colder than warm, good pressure, firmer than soft, over before she could make any further judgments.

"Hello. William Cheung. I didn't get the chance to say."

Joseph's entire face flushed. "Oh—I'm so sorry! I thought we'd introduced—sorry, sorry. William, this is—this is Girlie, this. Girlie, this is William. He's—well, I'll let him introduce himself."

Girlie smiled at Joseph's back as he rushed out of the room. Rhea and the rest of the aunties had really fucked him up good. "Coconut water for me too!" Aditya yelled after him. Joseph nodded then frantically looked over at William, who shook his head, holding his hand up in benediction like the pope.

"Great guy, great guy," Aditya said.

"Yes," William said, looking like he could not have meant it less.

Then: "Girlie," William said again, more to himself than to her. He turned his head in her direction, his thin shadow still heavy on her. She crossed her arms. "Real name?"

Now his voice was pitched slightly lower, but not low enough, as if he purposely wanted Aditya to hear that the question was not for him.

Girlie met his eye and smiled acidly. "William, was it?"

William laughed. "Touché. Though it is actually my birth name."

Girlie stopped smiling, sensing that the smile might soon turn genuine. William seemed to catch that, and stopped smiling himself. But this joint not-smiling felt like an inside joke, too. She sat down, pulling her chair out with a jerkier hand than she meant to; she realized, a beat later, that she hadn't wanted him to pull her chair out for her.

Joseph came back hugging three coconut waters and three bottled waters tight to his chest. "Here we go, here we go, and that's for you—"

"So. Girlie!" Aditya said, after gulping down half of his coconut water. Aditya, bless him, was wearing his Hulk Submariner instead of the customary Apple Watch; he only took the former out on special occasions, it was clearly his bossing-up amulet. "Let me just begin—first of all, you're not in trouble, just in case you were worried."

"I wasn't."

Aditya clapped his hands. "Good! Confidence. We love that here! Well, I hope everyone at Reeden has made you feel just how valuable you are to our entire community, as one of our longest-serving employees. One of our MVPs!" Girlie opened her mouth to respond, but then quickly discerned that no response had been required or indeed desired on her part, Aditya's conversation being a self-regarding and thus self-renewing resource. "And it's because of that, that track record of performance, of achievement above and beyond the standard"—Girlie started tuning out; this praise wasn't about her, but reflexive praise about Aditya's management skills, a theater of one with an audience of one, Aditya performing Aditya to someone above him in the hierarchy—"but I think William can do an even better job of explaining than I can. And you know I don't give up the floor to just anyone! Ha. Ha."

"Thank you, Aditya," William said evenly, with the particularly

British talent of making a *thank you* sound like a death wish. Girlie was glad she'd watched the first season of *The Crown* so she could recognize it.

William leaned forward in his chair, clasping his hands neatly on the shining white surface of the desk. "Ms. Delmundo, can I just ask—how familiar are you with Playground?"

Girlie blinked. She hadn't expected that question. "Playground? The VR thing?"

"Yes."

"I mean—yeah, sure. I've been to the one in the Bellagio. And a couple of the early ones, over at Westfield Mall."

"Oh, excellent—which ones?"

"At the Bellagio, it was the *Star Trek* one and the, uh"—she was annoyed at herself for this *uh*—"the Marvel one, the *Avengers* one."

"And how did you enjoy them?"

"I—they were great," Girlie replied, then cursed that other initial stutter again. She wasn't even lying; they were—great, those Playground things, box sites, on-site VR, whatever they called it. Fun. They'd started popping up around 2016, like the twenty-first-century version of laser tag. It was a type of immersive virtual reality gaming experience, as far as she could remember. At the beginning, they started off as small pop-ups in malls, minimalist green spaces no bigger than a public school classroom, and the simulations were fairly basic, usually first-person shooters or ultimate fighting games, sometimes branded content like the *Star Trek* or *Avengers* simulations.

It was their cousin Melvin's idea to check out the new Playground site in the Bellagio. Melvin and Martin had both been back in Vegas on leave at the same time, and it was the first time Maribel and Girlie had seen Martin, in particular, in a minute. Melvin, stationed out at Travis Air Force Base, was happy-go-lucky as ever—he was the only one in the family still living close to the Bay, out there in Fairfield, biding his time until he EAS'd. But Martin, the eldest, was stationed out in Doha.

He said it was a cushy base, but Maribel still put money on his Eagle Cash card so he could pay for a round of drinks at the Zink or the Kasbah, make friends easy. Melvin was in the habit of saying things like, "My big brother's out there fighting the *real* fight, fighting the bad guys in the Middle East," sounding alternately proud and jealous, but from what Girlie heard from Maribel, Martin was mostly cheating on his girlfriend, getting into little squabbles with the SECFOR guys who never put dumbbells back on the rack, and trying to avoid getting hep B, C, or HIV, because rumor was the base clinic wasn't properly sterilizing the scopes for gastro procedures—no surprise, since munitions storage was a shit show too.

On this trip, it became obvious that Martin was dealing with some issues none of them were quite calling depression or CPTSD; he'd broken up with the girlfriend; started taking longer to reply to their messages; started keeping to himself, drinking more, complaining about his CO, then shutting up for the rest of the night, glooming into his beer. It was around the same time all the videos of Asian women and Asian elders being sucker-punched on the street in the Bay started circulating, so he'd start ranting, somewhat incoherently, but with a real, vibrating anger—which had an inevitable vibe-killing effect of about a twenty-foot radius—about Filipino slaves in the Middle East, about the "women who looked like mom" who'd had their passports stolen and were left with trumped-up debts they'd never be able to pay back. That he hadn't fully contributed for the last two mortgage payments to help ease the debts of the actual woman who looked like his mom—that is to say: his mom—did not strike him as being in contravention of his position.

When Martin, Melvin, Maribel, and Girlie first entered the box and the Playground employees started outfitting them with all the gear—the heavy motion-sensor vest, the heavier Playground backpack with the computer tucked inside, the unwieldy helmet and glasses, the headphones—Girlie had a sudden jolt of claustrophobia, and turned to Martin, thinking that this was all a mistake, that he'd have a berserker fit the minute they put the helmet on him, why did they think being trapped in a virtual reality PvE game would be a good idea for a person who was like walking unexploded ordnance, one bad day away from going active shooter? But Martin was grinning at everybody in his tactical vest, looking more relaxed than he'd been since he'd gotten back.

The Playground scenario they'd chosen was standard: alien planet, away mission, retrieve data, unexpected monster-snake things, protect the important data while disarming the enemy. Girlie's shooting accuracy rate had been a predictably terrible 46 percent—no surprise, she was a console loyalist who'd spent most of her time in *Red Dead Redemption II* hunting legendary animals and looking for dinosaur bones, not robbing trains and testing her Lancaster Repeater on civilians. Martin and Melvin, Xbox and PC gamers raised since infancy on *Halo* and *Call of Duty*: 86 and 82 percent, respectively. But there was a moment in the game when she'd turned and seen an alien with a huge saber rushing intently toward Maribel's unassuming back, and Girlie had moved forward out of cover before she knew what she was doing, emptied her clip—a weapon not very *Star Trek*, but perhaps the VR game designers thought phasers too peaceable a dispatcher—into its center mass until the alien exploded in a burst of purpling blood.

Afterward, Melvin, sweet summer middle child, laughed about it, her reckless waste of ammo ("It's about single-kill headshots if you want the points, atc!"), but Martin had looked—not impressed, exactly, but: sharp, discerning.

Maribel, for her part, only tucked her shoulders in shyly and said, "Aw, ate. You saved me."

"Are you a gamer, yourself?" William asked now, still in that patient, even, evaluating tone. "I noticed you were gaming on your monitor—Animal Crossing, was it—"

The fucker. "That—I wasn't the one gaming. It was a stream. I'm—I wouldn't call myself a gamer, no." William kept looking at her, his face performing its own openness; he was waiting. That wouldn't be answer enough, then. Girlie carefully managed her breath so as not to be seen sighing. Maybe those deep-breathing worksheets were good for something after all.

"I mean, I game. Like anyone. I don't really do first-person shooter games. I do some open-world gaming, immersive, adventure—that kind of thing—*Red Dead, Ghost of Tsushima, Assassin's Creed*, cowboys and samurais, just the mainstream ones, nothing special. Most of the Playground games were shooters, which aren't really my thing, so. That's why I've only been once or twice," she volunteered; there was one tooth, pulled. "My cousins, the younger ones who play *Call of Duty*, that kind of thing—they liked it more."

Girlie shrugged. "I guess the at-home devices everyone's using now are supposed to be fun though. Playground Home?"

William visibly perked up. "Yes—do you own one?"

"No—not myself. Sort of seemed—clunky. Didn't think I'd really use it. One of my cousins wanted one though. But he's stationed in Qatar, so."

"Yes," William said, like they had agreed on something previously that Girlie had missed.

Girlie leaned back in her chair and crossed her arms, then uncrossed them, aware that he was reading her body language. "So you work for Playground then?"

Aditya clasped William's shoulder, grinning. "Don't be so humble, give her a little history, man! He was one of Playground's first employees, was there pretty much from the very beginning—you're looking at Playground's first Global Head of Content Moderation!"

William's smile looked to Girlie like a wince, which finally put her somewhat at ease.

"Yes," he said. "I've been with Playground almost since its inception—our founder and former CEO, Edison Lau, started the company in London, where we met at university. He'd already been at the forefront of developing some of the more innovative uses of virtual reality with the VR research department at Imperial before I came onto the project. We worked on a wide range of projects, in the research and development phase; most notably on virtual reality's uses in the clinical landscape. But Playground the company, the Playground most people are familiar with today, really started to take shape as we began working more closely with L'Olifant, a French company that runs historical theme parks—they've got sites all over France, incredibly popular—you might have heard of them?"

"No."

"I suppose not by that name. They've also expanded in Spain and China and even here, where the parks are called Hero's Horn? You might have heard of that?"

That did ring a bell. "Like the show at the Excalibur? Used to be Tournament of Kings?"

Aditya shot finger guns at her. "This guy!" he said, referring to Girlie, which admittedly she sort of enjoyed.

"Yes, exactly," William said. "The L'Olifant theme parks were originally looking to expand their physical presence further into the United States, beyond just their Excalibur partnership, but the plans for a series of on-site locations were obviously affected by some of the serious travel restrictions brought about by the pandemic and Brexit, not to mention the rise in shipping and construction costs— I'm sure you can imagine. They halted the plans for physical expansion and began exploring something a little more . . . future-facing."

William nodded at Aditya. "That was the point at which Playground was acquired by—our shared parent company," he said.

"Really?" Girlie asked. She looked at Aditya too. "I didn't know we owned Playground too."

Aditya looked pleased at that unthinking use of *we*. "It was all over *Wired!*"

William, for his part, didn't appear to enjoy being described as someone owned. "Yes," he said evenly. "Playground was acquired by Reeden, and as such our resources—obviously—vastly expanded. Along with our corporate remit, shall we say."

"A mountain of money will do that," Girlie said, in her affable little killer's voice.

William smiled again, directly at her. It was a smile she'd seen in faith healers' homes, on altars and on the scapulas hanging from the rear windows of certain cars in the '90s: the doomed smile of protective saints and death-facing minor gods. An angel of history smile; succorless.

"Yes. It will," he agreed. "Ms. Delmundo, I'll cut to the chase. I'm here today to offer you a promotion." Girlie went very still.

"Playground and L'Olifant, under the umbrella of Reeden, have created what promises to be a world-changing development in the fields of both entertainment and virtual reality, as proven industry leaders in both." He sounded, suddenly, like he was reading from a script and knew it.

Then he turned his gaze at her again, and she felt the urge to lift up her arm, shield her face from the tractor beam pull of it. Only by looking down at the heavy machinery of early twentieth-century watchmaking strapped to her wrist, still on the table, could she assure herself that she hadn't moved.

"Ms. Delmundo, I've heard all about your exemplary work here as a content moderator, directly from Aditya and Joseph. I'd like to take you out for a meal today, to talk more about the future of Playground, and your future here with us. I hope at the end of the day you'll find the offer worth considering."

She looked at him. A few months after she graduated from college, not even a year after her father had died, Girlie had taken her first meeting at Reeden. She thought of that day very rarely. On the way home, she nearly threw herself in front of a BART train at MacArthur Station, and then: didn't.

Life was like that, really; a series of executive functions. Of all the iron rings offered to her, she kept picking the brass one. Survival came naturally, if not easily. But what was easy about one's nature.

Then, a couple weeks into the job, she got her first and only set of tattoos; two sets of thin stripes on either forearm, just below the crook of the elbow. It was the gulot; the rite-of-passage tattoo of the young headhunter, marking first kill. The headhunter tattoos of Ilocos were traditionally, of course, for men; the tattoos of the women meant to protect, ornament, beautify. Girlie had been against the trend of cultural reclamation tattoos all her life, never found out what her name looked like in baybayin, didn't give a single fuck. Sure, there were apocryphal half stories, old jewelry, that might have meant people in her blood had been Bontoc, Igorot, Kalinga, but those were just the scattered bullet casings of diaspora, nothing to be sure about.

She'd resisted getting tattooed for years, knew it was cultural appropriation, was wary of the Indigenous revival scene, all the nouveau manongs and their apprentices wearing the chaklag who'd studied Kalinga tattoo traditions, were forever trying and failing to put together a definitive documentary on Whang Od. Culturally, politically, it was a mess: same old revive our ancestral roots while fucking over the girls we're dating bullshit, same old undercooked decolonial zeal, eternal rehearsal for a revolution always deferred. Researching where to get her ink, Girlie had to decipher the beefs between the different schools in the West: which native-pride school was run by people whose family were condo landlords in Quezon City, and which catalyst-for-change studio was protecting the guy rumored to have sexually assaulted that one female tattoo artist who left the game and became, last anyone heard, an influencer with a small calligraphy account on IG.

In the end she picked a sweet-seeming young guy on IG who posted long captions about being influenced by the work of OG Pinoy American flash and the other Asian and Hawaiian tattoo artists of that era, the ones who'd been doing the actual work under Ed Hardy and Sailor Jerry—the Rosie Camangas of the world, inking pirates and gangsters in Honolulu's Chinatown while white tattoo artists took the credit and the fame. She told him haltingly the reason behind her tattoo; said there was no tradition of headhunter tattooing for women, so how could they mark the heads they took: in this era, in this life? *Hundreds of years from now, I'll be the ancestor,* she'd said back then—cringing to remember it now, Girlie could not believe she had ever been young enough, or sure enough of the world lasting hundreds of years, to say such a thing—*so what are those kids going to be able to read off my body, about the kills it took to get here?*

Promotion meant a raise, surely. It was almost four p.m., too late for lunch; that meant she'd get to choose from a full dinner menu.

They might even take her to Nobu. She realized she was still looking at him; that he was still looking back. She gave him her headhunter's gaze, her firing-line gaze; he lifted his chin slightly, didn't blink.

She thought once more of that day in front of the BART. Survival came natural; not easy. But free omakase sushi could be worth living for; today. "Sure," she said.

· ·

Joseph didn't accompany them on the lunch—he didn't even look disappointed when Aditya clapped him on the shoulder and said, "Thanks for your help, man, I'll see you about that thing," as he, William, and Girlie made their way back down the stairwell, which was still fragrant with weed. Through the small hallway window that gazed onto the moderator floor, Girlie could see Rhea's head pop up from behind her monitors, watching them pass. They were already talking about her on the floor, Girlie knew. She hated being an object of gossip. Girlie blinked twice, so at least Rhea would know she wasn't a hostage.

"Your car or mine," Aditya said over her head to William. "I'm fine either way," William replied, which sounded like a lie.

They ended up taking Aditya's driverless Tesla, with him sitting in the primary passenger seat, swiveling it around so he could face Girlie and William, seated next to each other on the side bench. Girlie didn't appreciate the showing off; she hadn't been in that many autonomous vehicles, but most people still sat in them like regular drivers, just in case. Was Aditya also auditioning for a position in whatever William's new Playground venture was? How long had he been Director of Content Moderation at Reeden? Long enough for a move up in the world: Senior Director, maybe even VP.

"Seat belts, please," William said, nodding at Girlie's. Girlie blinked at him, then fastened it.

They didn't take her to sushi. Instead, it was New American, one of the expensive places just opened, outside the revitalized downtown area, full of coastal-lite bars where all the Asians were blond and all the boyfriends were white. Girlie wasn't about to turn down a rib eye, but demurred when they asked what she wanted to drink. Then she felt herself—tried to stop it, couldn't—looking at William; William, who was studying the menu, a deep line between his brows, looking distrustful. She knew, with the certainty of someone who'd quit drinking years ago but refused to call themselves an alcoholic, that she did not want to let herself get drunk around him.

"Tap water's fine," she said to the server.

"So you grew up in California, is that correct?" William asked. She mimed surprise to him. He gestured modestly into the ether. "I do my research. Of course, I talked to Joseph and Aditya. I understand you grew up very close to the site where you first joined Reeden, in San Jose."

"Milpitas," she said, and saw that his face did not register the correction; she couldn't tell if he knew, and had been waiting to see if she would volunteer the information herself.

"Milpitas," he repeated, overdoing the Spanish pronunciation, sounding like a real dickhead. Or, you know. Just an English person. Girlie had to chill. "Yes. You were born in California?"

"Born and raised."

"And your parents come from the Philippines—"

"Both of them, yes."

She was sure, for some reason, that he knew her father was dead.

She'd had to share that information in one of her early interviews, when they'd asked employees about past experiences that might affect their moderation of certain scenes. It was true that, given the choice, suicide was not her favorite content to moderate. "They'd lived in Milpitas since the early eighties."

"And you came to Las Vegas—"

"In 2009."

Their food arrived; they gave the requisite meaningless praise to the server. William speared a piece of bream, but didn't put it in his mouth.

"That's a long time," William said. Girlie shrugged.

"A long time is relative," she said, mostly just to put a pin in this part of the conversation. "May I ask you some questions?"

"Of course."

"How long have you been in the States?"

"About six weeks."

"Were you born in London?"

"Born, no." William looked amused at this obvious attempt to gauge where he was from, a certain *et tu fellow Asian* passing over his face like a squall. But she liked that he didn't rush to explain or defend himself, the way some in her generation did, all indignation, *I'm from Detroit.*

"I was born in Hong Kong but my parents moved to London quite soon after my birth, so I have no memories of Hong Kong. We lived mainly in Bromley. You won't have heard of it. Though David Bowie grew up there."

"You don't sound like him."

"No," William agreed, then furrowed his brow, deepening that line she'd seen. "Americans can't usually tell between English accents."

"I've seen both *The Crown* and *Peaky Blinders.*"

"That's British culture done then," William said.

"And do you ever go back to Hong Kong with your family?"

"No," William said stiffly, after a brief pause. "I've never been back."

Girlie still didn't know why she'd asked the question, hated when people asked her the equivalent question about the Philippines, and now she didn't know what to do with the answer. She stormed past it, sticking with the featureless bravado she'd started with. "And what brought you to Playground?"

"Edison," William said. He did not put down his utensils, but held them incrementally tighter. He still hadn't eaten a bite. "He and I were in the same student residence while at Imperial. More House. Edison was born in Hong Kong as well, but his family moved around a lot, lived in Missouri for a while, then eventually came to London when he was fourteen. We met and became friends at uni. He was still very—American," William said, again in that delicately British way of making a compliment sound like an insult, and vice versa.

William turned to Aditya. "And where did you grow up? I don't think we ever spoke about it."

Aditya lit up. "Well, I moved around a lot when I was very young, too, born in India, lived in Dubai for a few years, and then we came to the Bay Area. Then Vegas, with Reeden—"

Girlie realized that William had made the turn to Aditya to change the subject from himself, from Edison. When he met her gaze, he nodded minutely, as if acknowledging that he'd evaded her, and would return to the discussion in due time. He ate his bream; she couldn't read his face. Her steak was perfect. She ate the fries with fork and knife, which blunted their taste, but it felt unprofessional to eat them with her fingers.

After Aditya had finished describing the business fraternity he'd joined in college and whose pledges he still mentored, William put his cutlery down.

"How lucky they are to have you," he said without a trace of sincerity. "And now, if you don't mind me being so crude—perhaps on to business."

"You talked about a promotion," Girlie said, happy to be crude as hell.

Then: "Thank you," to the server taking her plate, a young Pinay with silver hair and tattoos, who met her gaze and tilted her head in a half nod, half are-you-also-queer-ate ID verification gesture. "Thank you," William echoed to the woman, making eye contact, which Girlie noted with neutral approval.

When the woman left, William turned his gaze back onto Girlie, as if he'd guessed she would be clocking his level of courtesy with service workers.

"I did," he said. "And I was serious about that. But I wonder if you'd allow me tell you a little more about Playground, to sort of—set the scene. This must all seem rather abrupt, I think it'd be only fair to give you some context."

"You mentioned your friend Edison."

"Yes," William said, and there was that look again. "Playground was his passion project, had been, even from the beginning. As you may know, Playground has for some time been at the forefront of virtual reality gaming. The box site you visited at the Bellagio, the Playground Home devices. We weren't always just focused on gaming, though of course that was the most obvious path to commercial viability; all of our architecture was right there, it made sense to focus on creating virtual reality game engines. It was really only when

L'Olifant came calling that Edison was—invited to fulfill some of his most ambitious dreams for the virtual reality space.

"How to expand the limits of experience, make history come alive in an exciting way, do away with some of our preconceptions around—what was past, what was present. But we would've partnered with anyone who had funding, at the beginning."

William laughed, eyes crinkling now, like he'd learned somewhere that to make a smile look authentic, it had to reach the eyes. But his face still seemed unused to the gesture.

"The gaming and medical industries were the real bread and butter of our research, initially. But there was crossover between the two. There'd already been studies that showed that people with traumatic brain injuries who played video games as part of their treatment experienced neurogenesis—the growth of new neurons," William explained, which Girlie didn't appreciate; she knew what it fucking meant.

"Yeah, I've read about it," Girlie said, not realizing she was proving herself until she was doing it. "They say video games help with PTSD—there've been studies talking about how if you game after a stressful event, it stops your brain from—shrinking. Going down traumatic pathways. Embedding the event too deep."

She thought about her own weeknights, playing *Zelda*, hunting in *Red Dead*; she thought of her mother in the '80s and '90s, coming home after a sixteen-hour shift, falling asleep playing *Tetris* on the Game Boy. She thought about how much easier her life would be if she wasn't so easily baited at the slightest hint of underestimation from someone in an economic class above hers.

"It encourages volumetric brain increase," she tried and failed not to say, scowling.

William looked at her; his face seemed like it was smiling, even though neither his mouth nor eyes had creased—it was just some internal light that had turned on, behind the skin.

"Yes," he said. "Exactly. At first we worked with the NHS, developed virtual reality ORs with consulting surgeons; even created VR therapeutic landscapes for a psychosis study funded by the National Institute for Health Research. We still work regularly with consulting physicians, even here in Las Vegas. You may even meet our consulting physician, he'll be working on site. That's still an incredibly important part of our business. Something we're all very proud of."

"Very noble," Girlie said.

William studied her. "But," he prompted.

Girlie lifted a hand. "But—aside from the prestige medical angle— we cure people of their PTSD, et cetera—it's just—it's all a bit of a joke, isn't it?"

Aditya coughed, turning it into a laugh. "Oh ho!" Then he waved an incoming server away imperiously, gesturing that he was still working on his fries.

"Virtual reality, metaverse, polyverse, whatever. I mean, we all watched that VR launch with Zuck and it's—I mean, at best, it's— what is it the kids say, it gives the ick?"

Aditya's laugh took on a violently cheerful edge, like maybe Girlie was actually going to fuck this up and push William too far, and it'd reflect badly on him, like he couldn't get his underlings in line, not even the one supposedly reported to be the best on the floor, which was the only reason she was here in the first place eating a sixty-dollar rib eye. Girlie didn't know why she was punching so hard, showing off, poking holes. But found she couldn't really stop.

"The 'VR revolution,' or whatever you want to call it," she continued, "came and went. It's fun for an alternative gaming option, and I—look, I love Gibson as much as anyone, but—when it comes to virtual reality—it just. It's old news. Clunky tech. People have moved on."

William, to her surprise, was nodding. "Yes, no, of course. I completely agree. Though I'd argue the relative failure, thus far, of virtual reality, as a platform, to really create a watershed moment—something that would cause as much of a revolution as the internet did—or social media for that matter—has meant there's still so much room to grow."

He paused. "With an actually viable product, that is. A truly new proposition."

The deathless dream of the tech entrepreneur, Girlie thought to herself bleakly. Let loose into horizonless fields like a foxhound.

William smiled, now a little acidly himself. Maybe she'd actually annoyed him, at last. "Something that gives less—ick," he added.

Girlie let one corner of her mouth quirk, raising her hands in a peacemaker's gesture. "That was rude. I apologize."

"Accepted, pending review," William said primly.

Then: "Content moderation is going to be an integral feature of the world we're trying to build—it's no exaggeration to say that the entire foundation of Playground's future will depend on it. Active moderation, in particular."

Active moderation meant screening posts and uploads in real time, not just content that had been flagged as objectionable by social media users. Girlie had done a little bit of active moderation early in her start at Reeden—it was tough, pitiless work. Active moderation took more out of an employee than reactive moderation, moderation hours or even days after the fact. Active moderation was a bouncer's world, like playing whack-a-mole with a dozen bloody murders, every hour on the hour, every minute on the minute. There, then. The first catch.

"Perhaps most importantly, if you accept this position, you'll no longer be a Reeden contractor—you'd be a full-time Reeden–Playground employee." William leveled his gaze at her. "With full Playground benefits, sick leave, retirement, and stock options. And, of course, compensation."

"Pay."

"But I'm getting ahead of myself. We can discuss all of that in our official interview, if you're interested—"

Girlie looked around at the restaurant, the lacquered reclaimed wood of the table, its rich shiny whorls, every scar a year, every trace a lost age. "If you ambush a girl in Vegas and take her to a place like this, she'll expect you to write a number on a napkin and pass it to her face down, like in the movies, I'm just saying."

Aditya laughed, banging his open palm on the table. William looked at her.

Then he took a pen out of the inner pocket of his blazer, motioned to Girlie to hand him her mostly clean napkin. She slid it across the table to him, lifting her fingers the moment his touched down. Covering the napkin with his left hand, like a child avoiding being copied by his neighbor, he wrote down something, turned the napkin face down, then slid it back over to her.

She rolled her eyes, smiled indulgently at him, playing along. He didn't smile back, but his dark eyes were soft, in what looked like apology.

Girlie flipped the napkin and felt her throat close up, the blood rushing her temples, churning at the membranes of the veins.

It wasn't real. The number wasn't real. She was dreaming. She was going to wake up, and she would be home, in her bed, and the laptop would be hot on her stomach, fan churning, drool on her face, and—and. The number would be gone, she would be the self that was not herself, and the world would be real again.

Aditya, still laughing, laughed even harder. "Man, did you actually—"

"That's baseline," William said, not looking at Aditya. "You're of course free to begin your own negotiations."

Aditya, now realizing William was serious, shook his head. "We're supposed to have an HR person here! That is *strictly* unofficial, okay, that is *not* on the record," he said to Girlie. Then he laughed again; he was the kind of person who laughed when he was out of his depth, which was starting to be sort of touching. He raised a hand, flagging down their server. "*On* the record, I'm gonna order a dessert—"

William's gaze was fixed on Girlie, which she could not know, because she was finding it physically impossible to tear her eyes from the number on the napkin.

"Full medical and dental," she heard him saying to her ghost. "Three weeks paid holiday. Unlimited sick leave. I did mention the stock options."

Girlie finally ripped her eyes off the napkin. Looked at her maker. "I still don't know what the actual job is."

William relaxed slightly, put the pen back in his pocket. "I do realize this is highly unconventional," he said, speaking now to both Girlie and Aditya, trying to bring the temperature of the room back to normal. "Ultimately, the best way to explain to you what I mean is to show you. The new Playground offices—including my office—have been set up a few floors above your current station. Would you be willing to accompany us for a tour, perhaps tomorrow morning? We can run a more direct demonstration there."

Girlie looked at Aditya. "What about my targets?"

"You've already been signed off for today and tomorrow." Aditya was staring at a picture of a lava cake. "You're a valued employee."

"You're not going to murder me and scatter my pieces across the Mojave when I get back into your car?"

William leaned back slightly. "You asked about your targets before you asked if we were going to murder you?"

"If I don't meet my targets, I might as well be dead."

"That's company policy," Aditya agreed, still not looking up. If only she didn't hate him, Girlie thought, she might actually like him.

William laughed, the stiffness melting from his shoulders, relaxing into his victory. He opened his palm out to her on the table, the way one holds a hand out to a wild and wary stray dog.

"It's just the future, Ms. Delmundo," he said. "Want to take a peek?"

She was still clasping the napkin he'd given her, the carefully written figure still shining up at her in its plainness, its world-swallowing inevitability. She balled it up in her fist, afraid if she looked at the number much longer she'd do something mortifying, like burst into tears, or say yes without having to hear another word. "Okay," she said, like accepting a proposal of marriage. "Yes."

. .

"What happened, where did you go," Rhea demanded when Girlie returned to the content moderation floor so she could collect her things and go home, hoping to slip out and avoid the karaoke as usual. But Rhea was already approaching with a slice of someone's birthday cake—how quickly had she plated that up, Girlie thought, almost admiring the cyborgian efficiency of the move, particularly when Rhea used Girlie's waving hands of protest as a table-setting to put the food on. "Were you fired? Was Vuthy with you?"

So they already recruited Vuthy, Girlie thought to herself. She looked around; Robin wasn't there either, so maybe he'd been recruited too.

"No, I wasn't fired. I haven't seen Vuthy."

Rhea was vibrating with the intractable resolve of someone who'd recently downed a nitro brew pilfered from the managerial floor vending machines and was now speedballing that with chocolate cake. Girlie groaned internally; she had to leave in the next fifteen minutes if she wanted to catch the next bus home. She offered, placating: "They might be moving me to a different department."

That was what Aditya had advised her to say to people who asked; she was surprising herself by actually obeying.

"You'll get a raise?"

A Filipina auntie could detect incipient money, smell it off you like bad B.O. "Maybe. Hope so."

Rhea didn't relax, but nodded sternly. "That's good, then. Okay. Update mo ako when you know more. You're going home now?"

"Yeah, I'm done for the day."

"Okay, say hi to your mom for me." Rhea's sister had once been a patient of Girlie's mother; terminal kidney disease, slow decline, septic shutdown, quick morphine death. As far as Girlie knew, Rhea and Flo had never spoken since. But civilizations, etc. "See you tomorrow then."

If Playground knew what they were doing, they'd hire Rhea too. Who knows, maybe they were going to, or already had, and this was just her sniffing out competition. Couldn't trust anybody; American anthem under late capitalism. "I might be late, I have a doctor's appointment tomorrow."

In the parking lot, she saw William and Aditya again, still chatting in front of the latter's Tesla. They saw her passing and waved. She gave Aditya a lazy subordinate officer's salute, palm of the hand facing correctly down, to the shoulder. His face lit up; he loved that military chain-of-command shit.

William watched her, leaning against the trunk of Aditya's car—she was surprised that he wasn't smoking, so smokerly was his posture, the way he held his arms in front of him, the way his right hand was held carefully away from his body. "Did you park far?" William asked. "I can walk you to your car."

Girlie blinked at him, taken aback by the offer, but then remembered it wasn't a courtly gesture, it was just a post-Asian-hate thing; for female moderators who left late, sometimes a security guard would accompany them to the car. But more and more of the security team had been cut, as the political fervor died down. Now all they had on-site was one receptionist and one frail sixty-year-old guard with a baton, both nine-to-fivers. Built-in security system, on-call police unit, average response time: forty-five minutes. The moderators accompanied each other. Girlie always said she was fine, walked alone, carried pepper gel.

Girlie pointed at a park bench, just outside of the campus. "I take the bus."

"The original self-driving car," Aditya said—he was smoking, she saw, a small black vape half concealed by his left hand. He laughed too loud again, seemingly realizing that he sounded like a dick. "He's an old-school gentleman," he interrupted himself, deflecting at William. "We need more of those nowadays!" William blinked at this unwelcome compliment; Aditya had the grace to look embarrassed by himself.

A flash of headlights; the bus was coming into view, just on schedule. The driver usually waited there for ten minutes, so she had no reason to rush, but it was as good excuse as any—she nodded backward at William and Aditya, then began jogging toward the stop. When she got on the bus, she saw it was Ben, who usually drove her morning route: "Overtime," he explained wearily, to her slightly lifted eyebrows.

Once in her customary seat, Girlie looked out the window to see William's and Aditya's figures, small and faceless. William's body was still turned to the bus, but she couldn't tell if he was watching or not; she had to go with her gut. She lifted a hand in a sardonic royal wave, like the queen she'd seen on television. She saw William's tiny figure bend backward in a sudden jerk that she recognized now as laughter. A tinier hand lifted, waving queenly back.

· ·

Girlie had a subroutine for every day of the week. Monday, Tuesday, Friday, and Saturday were her lifting days, when she was running an upper-lower program. She'd tried a three-day push-pull-legs split before, then tried the six-day bodybuilding bro-split, but found the former didn't give her enough volume on her compound lifts, and the latter didn't give her enough recovery time.

At some point around 2007 or 2008, nearly everyone in her family had become a meathead; all her cousins lifted, mostly the boys at first, but eventually the girls got into it too. There'd been a bodybuilding streak in the community, even back in the '90s-era Bay, but things really took off in the decade between 2007 and 2017. There were suddenly a multitude of perfectly acceptable aesthetic, economic, political, catastrophe-induced, depression-related reasons for self-medicating via barbell.

Girlie was weaker the week before her period, so she usually took the week as a deload. She knew she would never hit truly impressive raw numbers taking a deload every month, but she'd stopped trying to max out, had long ago accepted lifting for maintenance, preserving a certain level of functional strength. Her hip thrust was her strongest lift; typical cis girl lifter, stronger lower body, bench press straight trash. She'd fucked her shoulder up ego-lifting during military press, couldn't even push decent weight over her head anymore.

That was fine; her favorite lift of all time was the deadlift, anyway. She'd started out conventional, then went sumo, then plateaued and went back to conventional for a new challenge. Romanian deadlift, American deadlift, deficit deadlift, single leg deadlift, deadlift with dumbbells, deadlift with the trap bar, rack pull deadlift for when her back was acting up: hallowed, every single one. There was something about the movement that felt as plain and as redeeming as a Eucharist: here was something heavy on the ground she wasn't sure she could lift—and then she did. Again and again. Three sets of ten if she was working volume, five sets of two if she was working power. She'd deadlift every day if she could—and did, at the beginning; stopped only after she was admonished by an older lifter at Barkada, one of those wiry old-man-strength Ilocano lifters who'd knock out a hundred pull-ups easy, looked like he could tear a coconut tree out of the ground. He'd told her she'd overload her CNS if she kept deadlifting every day. "The deadlift is the hardest lift to recover from," he scolded her in a faint Hawaiian accent, brandishing a shaker bottle. "You can lift like that when you're young, but you'll fry your nervous system. Rest."

Of course, like everyone in the community who had the standard old duffel go-bag of trauma in the trunk of the Honda, she'd spent years going through the whole rigamarole of building her body up: all that hard-ass lady vengeance shit, fortress-woman, you shall not pass, but in the end it was just too much work—trying to be the strongest girl in her weight class, the strongest girl in any given room. Turned out that sublimating one's "adverse childhood experiences" into being shredded AF did not, in the end, a personality make. She was just someone who lifted; she didn't have to make the practice an autobiography. Improve your form, eat your protein, keep it moving. That was good enough.

··

"So wait, let me get this straight," Avery was saying, squatting by the platform where Girlie was setting up. Girlie's bench wasn't going to get any stronger doing 3x3s at 65 pounds, but it was a deload, she reminded herself, as she'd already reminded herself to keep 75 pounds on the deadlift bar and not do five sets of ten instead of the rehabilitative three. Still distracted from the meeting, she didn't need to add another shoulder injury to her plate. She'd planned to do deadlift, bench, maybe some accessories for her lats—upper body was really what was holding her deadlift back, she needed to do some barbell rows—and be happy with that. If only Avery, who seemed completely recovered from whatever flu she'd had, would shut the fuck up.

"You're finally gonna let them promote you—who took you out for lunch? Joseph?"

"It was Aditya, and then the new guy. He was some bigwig at Playground."

"Playground?" Avery leaned forward, almost knocking over her shaker bottle, which Maribel swiftly righted. "What, *Playground* Playground? *That* Playground, as in—" She pointed at Maribel, which Girlie understood to mean, *Playground like the Playground box site that's in the Bellagio where Maribel works.* Why have language at all, when you had family and their annoying-ass girlfriends, Girlie thought sourly. And she actually liked Avery; not that she'd ever tell her that to her face. Avery, who'd met Maribel on Tinder, and whose profile had said **Straight women with husbands need not apply. Been there done that.**

"I'm not even sure how much I can talk about it yet, I'm finding out more tomorrow. But they're starting a new kind of—immersive virtual reality thing—they said they need elite content moderators—"

Maribel looked like she was going to have a cardiac event. "*Elite!*"

"And then they took me out to lunch—"

"Where?"

"Some bougie new place, just before you hit downtown, in that new complex they built with the Robuchon restaurant—"

Avery leaned forward. "Wait, wait, wait, is this the new thing for Playground Home they've been advertising? The Hero's Horn thing? L'Olifant?"

Girlie blinked at her. "How did you know about that?"

"They've been advertising it for months! Over in the Playground box and on all the at-home games. You haven't seen the ads? They're even all over YouTube and everything, they've been teasing the rollout ever since the summer Halo thing got released. If you're already a Playground Home user you get a monthlong trial subscription when they roll out."

"Wait, wait, so you're going to work for Playground?" Maribel rocked back on the short stool she was sitting upon, so that the two front legs lifted up off the ground perilously. A young man was hovering behind her, obviously hoping to use the stool for a barbell box squat.

"Did they show you the new mask and gloves? There was a teaser trailer like a month ago, I was thinking of getting on the wait list," Avery said.

Even fucking Maribel was nodding, saying, "Oh yeah! They said you can use Playground with the mask you've already got, but the new one has loads of new features, all the haptics are supposed to be crazy—"

"Can I get a spot," Girlie said, trying to get over the fact that Maribel knew the word *haptics*, which didn't correspond to her internal understanding that Maribel was still seven years old.

She got into position at the bench press station, sliding easily into her arch, then settling her feet flat on the ground. Girlie benched two reps, making a show of difficulty for the third; Maribel touched the bar, featherlight, just to give confidence.

"Up, up, get it up," she coaxed, and Girlie pushed the bar, the whole weight of the world, off her chest; reset it.

Avery, from her position, said, "Oh, spot?" with the expression of someone who saw perfectly well that Girlie hadn't needed any damn spot.

Avery was Maribel's first white partner, and also Maribel's first ever foray into queer relationships, which meant Girlie, as the local battle-hardened bisexual in the family, now had to treat her historically calamitous love life with kid gloves, even more than everyone in the family already treated Maribel with kid gloves, with her being the youngest girl cousin and all. Maribel had spent a lot of her youth dating terrible men, mostly Pinoy, Vietnamese, and Taiwanese first gens; still had a bit of an eating disorder from the years of insecurity and self-loathing, not to mention the mean-ass Asian would-be mothers-in-law fully enmeshed with their sons, so happy to have children and thus be on the right side of oppression at last. Girlie had told her time and time again that being unnaturally skinny attracted bad men—it was a rule—but Maribel never listened, probably because Girlie herself didn't exactly speak with the lived authority of a Rubens Venus, had long worn the chased, eroded frame of a hardgainer. It took enormous effort, at least a hundred grams of protein a day, just to keep enough muscle on for Girlie's basic lifts. Whereas Maribel, when she wasn't dating assholes, could deadlift two times bodyweight in her sleep. Girlie would kill for her bench numbers.

It was thus very politically inconvenient for everyone who loved Maribel, and whose sense of humor depended largely upon lowest-common-denominator white supremacy jokes, that Maribel was now so radiantly happy with Avery, had even in the four years they'd been together gained back some weight, didn't throw up in secret or push rice around her plate anymore, had even quit drinking and started keeping a dream journal, impressed the bar manager at Dram with her adaptogen-laced mocktail recipes—politically inconvenient especially for Maribel, who, having not quite shed the sensitive, worried, pleasing nature of the youngest daughter in a disastered family, was always the first to apologize for having a white girlfriend, the first to comment on how handsome some new Asian American actor was, how charismatic, how talented. No one was more effusive about the beauty of men of color than women of color with white partners.

And though they all bullied Avery when she first showed up— how earnest she'd been about the food, the superstitions; her allyship, her diligent attempts at Tagalog, her overachieving Virgo softbutch determination (having spent some time as an overachieving

Virgo soft-butch herself, Girlie was expected to do most of the on-boarding)—the routine was getting tired. Girlie was too old and it was too far into the century to keep manufacturing beef with some-one's white baby. Let the miracle of love in all its mysterious forms find who it will, come what may, and godspeed. Et cetera, et cetera. Avery's parents were Democrat-voting labor-rights lawyers, unlike some of the anti-abortion Trumper aunties and uncles on Maribel's side who disapproved of the match. It was an advantageous union by any measure.

"You think interracial dating is hard? Try dating within your race," Girlie finally said one night when Melvin was home on leave, making another stale pumpkin spice latte joke. "At least Maribel's with someone who doesn't need a Triple-A guide to find her clit. Or do y'all's generation go down on girls now?" Melvin and the rest of them shut up, after that.

It was a testament to the fact that Avery was gaining confidence in her relations with the family that she actually tried to tease Girlie back every now and then; Maribel still too cowed by the codes of se-niority, the diffuse adoration that saturated, which was to say poi-soned, her relationship with Girlie. Girlie was of two minds about this development. On the one hand, she respected that Avery tried it, because attempting to clown the hardest, most respected member of the clan showed backbone. On the other hand, it was a ticking time bomb when a white partner got comfortable, and if this pre-sumptuous little Berkeley dyke smirked at her one more time, Girlie was going to rumble her in the parking lot. Welcome to the family.

Girlie rolled her eyes at Avery. "Are you just spectating?"

"I'm supporting your growth as you overcome limiting beliefs," Avery said. "Sometimes we turn away from the support of those who love us because we feel we don't deserve it."

"Ed, I'm being racially abused," Girlie called.

From behind rows of protein powder adorning the front desk, Edwin, Barkada's manager, lifted his phone, mishearing them. "You want me to change the music?

"We're good," Maribel interjected hastily.

Girlie gestured for the other young man who'd been hovering behind Maribel this whole time to just take the stool already.

He smiled at her gratefully. "Congrats on the promotion," he said, having overheard them.

"Thanks, fam," she said, with the fatigue of someone who had survived the Bataan Death March. He lingered for a little while, then left with the stool.

"Playground," Avery mused to herself. "She didn't even want to be manager three years ago. Now look at her. Titan of industry."

"But—elite moderation," Maribel fretted. "Is it going to be harder? I mean, harder than—harder than the job now. Psychologically, I mean."

"There is *no reason why you should suspect my job is hard at all, ading,* as my *very strict and very thorough nondisclosure agreement would corroborate,*" Girlie said, emphasizing each word with a glare.

Maribel waved her hand. "Fine, fine, fine. You know what I mean."

"It'll probably be just the same-ass job," Girlie said, trying not to think *active moderation.* "Better pay, at least."

Maribel stopped in the middle of her goblet squats. Incipient money; smell it off you like bad B.O.

"How much better?"

"Pay off the mortgage in full better."

Now Maribel sat up, put her dumbbell down on the bench in front of her. "That's not on you, ate."

"Oh, okay then," Girlie said, turning away from the two of them and peering to see if any of the squat racks were free for her rows. One was; she made her way toward it, set a barbell at the correct height, put 15-pound plates on either side. "You need to warm up first," Avery called. Girlie glowered, took the plates off.

Avery, she remembered, was also an eldest sister, in her own large Chicago family. Girlie didn't enjoy meeting other eldest children, generally. Too much like meeting veterans of the same war. You could swap battlefield stories for a little bit, but then you started to set each other off.

"No, ate, I'm serious," Maribel said, trailing her to the rack. She never put away her own weights, pure youngest child shit. But if you called her out on it, the hurt answer would be, *I was just about to do it.*

"Paying off the house—that's not your responsibility. That's on them, that's on—we can help out, okay, but your job is still to worry about your own life."

Now Girlie laughed, having been holding in a laugh since *that's not on you.* How could she not laugh at it: the word *life*, like any of them had a thing like that; had just the one, had even their own.

Maribel was still talking. "Ate, it's not on us to fix all of it."

"Lol," Girlie said, the whole word, and started rowing the bar.

"Is that the only reason you're taking the job?" Avery had followed them too. She was taking her seat at the lat pulldown machine. Avery had great lats, well engaged in her deadlifts, ideal genetic body mechanics for conventional. Asshat. "More money?"

Girlie started laughing again, now at the word *only* from someone whose parents had sent their kid to UC Berkeley because Boalt Hall was her dream school, paid out-of-state fees. No debt.

Maribel amended: "Will you be happier?"

Finally, Girlie reracked the bar. She turned and gazed at both of them: the babies of them, the soft milk-sweet look of them, the wet little bubble of their good intentions. They were too beautiful to look at; she loved them more than her own life; they were the most annoying people she'd ever met and she couldn't fucking get rid of them.

Girlie slid the 15-pound plates back onto either side of her barbell for the next set, even locked the clamps on. Then she pulled the napkin that she'd crumpled up like a fortune out of the pocket of her hoodie. Handed it to Maribel.

Maribel looked down at the paper, then over at Avery, who gestured her over. Maribel joined her girlfriend. Then, their heads ducked down toward each other, they opened the paper together.

Girlie scanned their faces for the shifts and twitches that would let her know just how differently they would think of her now: for the shock, or the joy, or the helpless giddy greed that might deform their features, the fulsome beaming smile that her mother had started to give her after receiving the Tesla, the bags, a smile that shifted so quickly from delighted to expectant; one hunger sated, another newly starving. But neither of their faces twitched at all. Maribel's face shut down—the light in it going out, fading, fading, until the last spark of it ambered, then ashed.

She looked up at Girlie, helpless. Just a baby cousin. Someone who, in the end, would be taken care of.

They already knew then: there was no way Girlie was going to turn down this job. No matter what it entailed; no matter what it meant.

"When do you start?" Maribel asked softly. Girlie opened her mouth to tell her that she had a second interview, that it wasn't a done deal yet. But though it was true, saying it would have been as good as a lie; she knew when she would start. Whenever they said she could.

．．

The following morning, Girlie approached the normal entrance to the content moderation building, but William was already waiting for her, in a suit whose fit she had no opinion about.

"Good morning," he said. "We'll be using a different entrance today. Please follow me. Aditya's already there."

She followed him, matching his speed, which was slow; until she realized it was he who was matching her speed, restraining his long legs from outpacing her shorter ones. She made an effort to speed up, even though she didn't quite know where they were going; he seemed bemused, then seemed to relax, then seemed to settle into his normal speed, which was—too fast for her, but in for a penny.

When they arrived at the other entrance, a back entrance she'd never used and had assumed was a service entrance for cleaners, Girlie was out of breath, heart racing, a stitch starting under her ribs, but she refused to open her mouth and pant, instead inhaling through her nose, muting her body's strain.

William looked like he wanted to say something, but instead just opened the door, gesturing into it. "After you."

It was when she walked through the doors that it dawned upon Girlie that her own entrance had been the cleaner's entrance all along: that this, in fact, was the main entrance, through which so many senior management visits had been carefully choreographed and coordinated, starting here, and only then leading the VIPs down into the section where she and the other moderators lived, in the bowels of the building—the place she had hitherto (and naively, she now realized) thought of as the heart.

She hadn't even heard the construction going on above them—of course, every floor in the building, particularly the moderator areas, was all meticulously soundproofed. You couldn't force everyone to wear headphones, and no one in Bestiality wanted to hear the Gore soundtrack all day. She'd thought this morning she might have to pass the other moderators on the floor again and have to give them an excuse for where she was going, but the part of the building he was leading her through—even though William took care never to let Girlie walk behind him, perhaps sensitive to the optics of a Filipina laborer trailing a middle-class male boss—was neatly bifurcated from the regular moderator floors.

The lobby was one of the most light-filled rooms she'd ever been in, with a palatial sweep she hadn't thought the building capable of housing, wrought out of cast iron and sheet glass, reminding her of a greenhouse, the upper floors stepped in like mezzanines, with a central transept topped with an arched inner roof, also made of glass, and a glass-door elevator with mirrored sides, the Playground logo printed, or perhaps even hand-painted, onto its panes.

In the waiting area was a cream sofa set—three-seater, two armchairs, glass-and-wood coffee table, minimal Scandinavian chic, a little dated and corporate, not quite brave enough for '70s Italian sensuality, the current interiors trend. Behind the sofa set, there was, upon a slender wooden console table, a sized-down mechanical replica of a working Ferris wheel: the little yellow passenger cars moving, slowly and smoothly with barely a sway, the spokes of the wheel as intricate as a cobweb.

Aditya was already ensconced in the sofa, looking down at his phone. Upon noticing them, he jumped up and waved—he moved so youthfully for someone in his forties—coming over to join them: "Hi!"

Beyond the grand transept were two wide steel staircases, each going in opposite directions then meeting at the top, also balustraded in glass, past which the building became, somewhat disappointingly, more conventional again, with beige hallways in the distance that looked like any in a regular modern office block. Party in the front, business in the back. Or perhaps the funding had run out.

Still, Girlie could feel that she was gawking, craning her neck up in something she wasn't quite ready to admit was wonder. There was a feeling of openness, of limitless space, of endless potential, of there being no place untouched by sunlight, dawn-fingered. It was a lobby tailor-made for press releases and journalist tours.

William lead Girlie and Aditya through the glass-ceiling nave, deeper into the building, into the beige hallways, past a series of closed wooden doors, solid warm Californian oak, midcentury detailing.

"Just to the right here," William murmured, and he pushed a large door open to Aditya and Girlie, holding it open, tilting his head. "After you. And please excuse the mess, I'm still moving in."

There was demonstrably no mess to be observed or excused. A gleaming dark leather sofa, an equally gleaming dark wood desk, with no papers upon it, an office chair that was left pulled out, which was the only sign someone had ever been in the room before them at all and it wasn't just a staged set, rented out to photographers to take stock pictures of "offices" on Getty.

No pictures anywhere, though she looked for them before realizing she was looking for them—something like a framed picture of a wife, a husband, a child or three. Aditya immediately took a seat on the leather couch, crossing an ankle over one of his thighs, responding to an email on his phone. She'd only ever been in Aditya's office a couple of times, but it was smaller than this one; she remembered only that he had two katanas and a samurai helmet displayed behind his desk, because: Aditya.

William opened a sleek mini fridge behind his desk, filled with glass-bottled waters, still and sparkling, and an assortment of LaCroix flavors. "Something to drink?"

"Water's fine, thank you."

He handed her an ice-cold glass bottle of water, his fingerprints leaving smudges of clarity in the condensation. He gestured toward the seating area. "Please."

Warily, she looked between the leather couch Aditya was sitting on, the empty leather couch across from it, and the leather armchair positioned between them, choosing the armchair because its back was to a wall, and it gave a clear view of both the exit and William's desk. When she sat down in the armchair, William's face flickered enough for her to guess this was his usual spot.

She didn't move. She put the water bottle down on the long coffee table in front of her, using one of the hand-carved wooden coasters piled artfully on a long leather tray.

William pulled something out of his inner blazer pocket, with a gesture so unassuming she nearly thought it was a pair of glasses that he was going to clean. But now he was holding a mask, almost like a sketch of a fencing helmet, covered in something soft and fleshlike, not quite silicone or rubber—looked almost like biocellulose, but velvety, so the shape of it fluttered and melted alively in the palm of his hand. Even the lips, or the hollow where the user's lips were supposed to go, seemed to open in a sigh.

"The cover is theoretically disposable," William said. "For hygiene reasons; if people in the same household want to share a mask, for example."

Then he started slipping on a pair of black gloves from within the same pocket, all of which should have ruined the line of his suit jacket, yet the gloves were sleek; she couldn't place the textile, and she couldn't see any of the bulky sensors usually attached to haptic gloves, at least the ones she'd worn in the Playground box. These were shapely, elegant, worthy of Pitti Uomo.

"There's also a bodysuit," William said. He put his hand to his clavicle, opening his collar slightly, a gesture which struck her as decidedly—incongruous to the setting, the sudden sensuality of it making her tense up. Beneath his white shirt she could see just the outline of what looked like a sleek black long-sleeved undershirt, made of material so dark it was nearly Vantablack, so that his chest looked blacked out rather than just black, a void where his sternum had been.

She turned to Aditya, who pulled aside the neck of his polo shirt, showed her that he was wearing one underneath his clothes too.

"It further enhances the immersion," William explained. "But I think for now, for you, just the mask and gloves will suffice."

Like I'm going to change into a catsuit without an HR officer present, Girlie thought darkly.

Now he was playing absently—deliberately absently—with the mask in his hands. The casualness of it was practiced, certainly, but effective enough. He was leaning against the front of his desk, hip cocked, one knee bent softly enough to judder rhythmically, making a good impression of someone riding in a commuter train, listening to a song in headphones, there but not there, projected but rooted.

So the presentation had already begun. He tossed the mask at her, then a pair of gloves he'd removed from his front jacket pocket, encased in a soft sleeve; by the grace of God and luck, she caught both, which she could not believe—she'd never had the best hand-eye coordination. He was trying to show her how discreet the equipment was; she never would've guessed he was carrying all of that in this suit.

"You've seen something like this?"

"I don't live under a rock."

"Have you used any VR headset devices yourself?"

"A clunkier version at those VR box sites, but like I said—"

"You're not a gamer, and you're not impressed with VR."

"Those things haven't reached critical mass because they make you look like a dumbass. Respectfully," she added hastily. "It was good for a viral moment when these things first came out, but how many people actually kept the headsets? Really traded in their consoles for them? Yeah, I could've bought a Playground Home; I bought a PS7. Never went back to the box sites after the first couple of times. Neither did anyone else I know. But for the gamers who want a little something different at home, or maybe even professional gamers, streamers, I'm sure they're a fun option. If you don't mind crashing into your coffee table. You need the space for things like that."

She looked down at the mask, rubbed her thumb across its smooth surface, its nose; not too obviously Western, neutral nose bridge—they were avoiding being canceled on the internet.

"This one feels nicer than some of the ones on the market. I'll give you that. Do well with the Apple bros, I guess. Assuming you comped a few sets to the right YouTubers."

She looked at Aditya. "Haven't we tried to make hardware before? The glasses thing? Augmented reality?"

Aditya put his phone down for a moment. Every time she said *we* it seemed to activate him. "So you do read *Wired* occasionally," he hooted. "Tried and failed! But that's the only real way to get things done. Make mistakes and do better next time." He was possibly the most American person she'd ever met, Girlie thought dourly.

"It's funny you say hardware," William said. "Edison used to say, as a company specialized in virtual reality, that everything, in the end, is hardware."

Girlie snorted. "Failed engineer, is he?"

"—. Not exactly," William replied, after a short pause. He turned away, pulling another mask out of his desk. He slipped it over his head, stretching the soft wide silklike strap around his neck, letting the mask hang there for a moment; letting the room at large enjoy the alien elegance of the figure he cut, spare face hanging below the real one.

How old was he? She still couldn't tell; probably not more than a few years older than her. Same generation, different planet. Different income bracket, which was the same thing. Rich fifty was working-class thirty-five. Maybe forty-two, forty-three, she guessed. Reaching back across his desk, he picked up a remote control and pointed it into the air; upon clicking a button, a white screen began lowering from a slit in the ceiling she hadn't noticed and now couldn't unsee.

"The screen is for your benefit," William said, nodding toward the white sheet. "In case you don't want to use the Playground mask yourself. Aditya and I are more than happy to be the guinea pigs, and you don't have to do anything at all except watch the screen, which will project what we'll be seeing behind our own masks. Without the screen, at least, there'll be no other way for you to see what we're seeing, which would make the entire demonstration somewhat pointless.

"If you do choose to come with us, as you haven't created an avatar yet, don't be alarmed to look down at yourself in-game and see your features blacked out—a shadow avatar is the default setting if you haven't created your own model yet."

He pulled at the mask around his neck, then let it snap back lightly against his chest. "The motion controls are in the gloves themselves, fine movements in your middle fingers will move you throughout the landscape. I'd prefer not to coach you on the mechanics, if you don't mind—they're designed to be so intuitive any newcomer would quickly be able to make their way through the world. You'll be able to find out for yourself."

Finally, he smiled. "But you won't have to worry about breaking the coffee table."

Girlie fingered the mask. She thought of the number. Then she put on the gloves, looking down at her hands; clenching and unclenching her fist, testing the stretch of it. The fit was very good. He'd have had to guess her hand size; he must have clocked her during the meal.

She looked up to see William watching her. "How do they feel?"

"Like gloves."

"Good start," William said. "Will you be joining us, then?"

She slipped the mask over her head, too, letting it hang over her collarbones, just like his. "After you."

Aditya, seeing this, laughed and pushed the neck of the bodysuit up so it became a turtleneck, touching his chin. Then he slipped on his mask and gloves, demonstrating without words how to roll the strap up so it covered his ears, going all the way up the back of his head, the strap meeting the hard side of the mask at the crown of the head, just at the old fontanelles; the spot where as babies they'd all been soft, once upon a time.

William smiled at her. He also rolled his turtleneck up, so his throat was blacked out too. "See you later," he said, and that sounded too American, those weren't his words either—then he put the mask on.

• •

She didn't understand what she was seeing at first. The screen showed first the room itself, William's office, with her and Aditya in it. A front-facing camera, then. Standard Playground stuff. A sign-in page, that looked much like the thousand sign-in pages Girlie knew from her entire twenty-first-century life—and thanks to touch ID and facial recognition, largely ignored—the same sign-in screen for Whats-App, for Instagram, for her online banking app, for her weight-lifting tracking app, for every social media account she'd ever opened and let gather dust, having nothing social in her life to mediate; most of the moderators she knew, for reasons too self-evident to enumerate, kept their online presences minimal.

"Allow me," William's voice said smoothly, and the username WilliamCheungPlayground appeared on the screen, then a micropause, as whatever invisible password the site had asked for was accepted, in the currency of his face, or some other transmission as yet undetectable to Girlie. She realized he'd let her in on that bit of admin to give her the impression of being invited behind the scenes—of being in complicity, as a potential employee. Not sold to, as a potential customer.

The sign-in page disappeared, revealing—a park.

Girlie was a sentient American grunt in the tech underclass; the miracles of CGI and virtual reality were not entirely unknown to her. Maribel had sent her all the Meta memes, Twitter jokes. That photorealism had been reached was par for the course: the overworked graphic artists, the VFX technicians, the independent filmmakers who'd been recruited to give engineered worlds a touch of poetry; the ability to recreate Yosemite, or the Battle of Tannenburg, or the wildest of the Wild Wests, every flower in the Mojave, every pockmark in the moon, every alien landscape imaginable.

Over the years she'd seen the grass in games grow, from blurry green stalks of Nintendo pixels, to the kind of Northern Californian crabgrass she'd stepped on in her childhood home's forever-untended backyard, never a lawn, always fruit trees in a sea of weeds. The military simulations, the surgeons learning to do laparoscopic procedures in VR, the tentpole movies with actors half emoting across computer-generated worlds, the fact that hair and water were still difficult to simulate, but they were working on it: she'd read it all. They'd landed on this century's Moon, only the Moon was just: Earth, scannable. One small step, one giant leap, et cetera. Armed with knowledge, numbed with it even, Girlie was certain that none of this would be new to her.

And yet it was the noise that grabbed her first. The deafening chorus that seemed now to carry her up into its thicket of sound, sacral and crude, a sound of hawking ice cream, a sound in English and then distinctly not in English, a sound mineral as much as animal, a sound of cattle shifting in pens, and a tonnage of water churning and banked—at once a mammoth, mountainous sound, which carried indifferently the daily news of its own vast, ancient, inorganic life, and a glottal, guttural, near-near sound, of corn being chewed to the naked cob and thrown just behind her so it bounced off the ground up almost to brush the back of her knees. And pierc-

ing through the thicket, the sound of a man shouting *Open ye gates,
swing wide ye portals, enter herein ye sons of men and behold the achieve-
ments of your race!*

Girlie looked around her—no, it wasn't a park, or it wasn't just
a park; they were on the outskirts of something, noise bustling in
from just outside the frame; world. In the near distance, Girlie saw a
series of enormous palaces come into view: a marble-white city, gas-
lit and glinting.

Underfoot, there was the whispering slosh of just-melting snow.
Girlie, to her own surprise, like a real noob: shivered.

"Welcome to Playground's first lobby," William said, from next
to her.

Even here, she noted, he'd never once come up on her from behind. Global Head of Content Moderation; he knew the drill. She
turned to face him.

His avatar was just—William, his own face and body, now in a
different suit; navy this time, though if she looked closely, there was
a slight gray checked pattern in the weave. He must've had to sit for
3D avatar modeling; the likeness was very good. If she critiqued the
model at all, she would say only that the face seemed—younger,
than the real William. Though this one did, she noticed, have lines
around his eyes.

"Though at the time we were calling it Fairground," he was saying.

She looked down at her blacked-out arm, the void where her
body was supposed to be. Strangely, she felt her mouth wanting to
smile.

The whole place was familiar, but like a person she'd only ever
seen on television as a kid, she couldn't put a name to a face, just an
eerie sense of intimacy, like a childhood ghost. The shadow of a

Ferris wheel, like the last of a race of monsters, fell over the entire fairgrounds, growing larger the closer they approached and saw the long line of fairgoers waiting their turn to ride. In the distance there were giant lagoons, plazas, pavilions garlanded with naked cherubim and goddesses of vague Greco-Roman extraction, fake Corinthian columns and real ivy snaking up them, giant watchful angels towering on platforms, their bare feet floating above a thousand human bodies.

William guided them forward, turning past the fountains spitting water from fishmouths and the boatmen rowing visitors down a grand lagoon. At the lip of the water, she saw a family, one child reaching down toward the ducks militantly avoiding him. She realized she had been moving, walking through the space, without having consciously made her body walk; her fingers were twitching, like proof of life in a comatose body. He'd been right about her intuition.

Just behind the family, there was a lean dog, a sable German shepherd, seemingly standing guard over the family, although far enough away that Girlie wasn't sure if the dog was even with the family at all. One of the dog's ears twitched. The grand noble head seemed to turn, minutely, toward her gaze, but did not meet it. Girlie felt the force of her own body, stepping forward, without knowing why.

"If you'll follow me to the amphitheater, please, the show's about to start," William interrupted, nonsensically.

Now they made their way through this initial lobby—Girlie guessed they were at the beginning of the twentieth century, and she knew she'd seen that Ferris wheel somewhere before, but whatever it was, wherever it was, she just had to chalk it up to a vaguely Western setting, probably America or England, circa the 1900s—and toward a wide sloping path, up a neat incline, where in the distance a medieval castle loomed, just next to an enormous Roman-style amphitheater: each of the structures were from completely different time periods, completely different regions, yet here they were now all side by side, as in any other theme park, with castles next to haunted houses next to roller coasters next to spaceships.

Even tech noobs knew that the most effective virtual reality scenarios were the fantasy ones—fiction, in the end, was the most potent vehicle for immersion into this particular reality. Better to create a "Western city," not quite exactly San Francisco or Los Angeles, but a palimpsest of a hundred streets, a hundred native plants, a hundred species of trees in a hundred stages of growth, with a hundred diners serving a hundred familiar dishes. That was the crucial detour from Uncanny Valley. If it was fictional, it would be believable. And the believable was more important than the real, in the church of the immersive. The real was an outdoors issue; the believable, an indoors. Girlie checked with her own indoors; this did, indeed, feel believable.

When she turned to look at Aditya, she was startled to see that he was dressed in full knight's armor, smiling at her behind a metal helmet. "Custom skin," he explained brightly. "Not my first rodeo!"

"Not a rodeo at all," William said. "At least not yet. The cowboy locations are still in beta."

He led them through the aditus maximus to the amphitheater, into a kind of VIP section from which to observe the show. Girlie could not help but notice that they'd situated the ima cavea accurately, historically speaking: important members of society not seated above, far away from the action, as in skirts-and-sandals movies—but courtside, front row, kissing-close to the bloodspray and gore. There, the ancient seat of emperors and oligarchs. Someone on the design team had consulted a classicist.

The show had already started; there were two men on horses, charging at each other with large colorful lances. "We're still in the jousts," William said. "After this, the Gauls versus Romans battle begins. They share the same location."

He waved down a popcorn vendor making his way down from the media cavea, and accepted a bucket of caramel popcorn, offering it to Aditya and Girlie.

Girlie watched as Aditya heartily shoved his hand into the bucket; the kernels even moved around his hand like real kernels. She watched him pop some kernels in his mouth, behind the metal helmet.

"Do you taste anything?" she asked, genuinely curious.

"Yeah! They've got caramel popcorn as one of the taste presets," Aditya said. "Your mask doesn't have any customized receptors, so you won't taste anything yet. But at least you can feel the kernels with the gloves, even nonpersonalized ones."

Girlie stuck her hand into the bucket, felt the sticky kernels move around her erased hand. She took one of kernels, examined it with her virtual eye. Then let it drop back into the bucket; heard the sticky dull sound of its fall.

She nodded down at the popcorn for William to take some. He demurred.

"I don't care for caramel popcorn," he said. Girlie stared at his face, which was, like the popcorn, almost a face; she almost tasted something in it.

It was easier to stare at him here, in this space; permissible, even, because his face was part of the landscape they were selling. Permissible, too, because she knew her own body was blacked out, that he couldn't turn and see whatever unbidden expression came to her face when she was watching him—now, free to be a voyeur, hidden like a sniper in the alcoves of her own body.

He kept his eyes on the show, though she could feel the force of his attention still turned to her; as if the side of his cheek, where stubble was just growing in, was staring back at her. Had they individually painted on each of those points of stubble; had he forgotten to shave the morning they'd created the 3D avatar? There was a beauty mark about an inch from his lip that she hadn't noticed in real life; another one under his eye, next to a small white dot of milia. William looked—cared for, in the details. Like he'd been created lovingly.

"I appreciate the lack of hand-holding," Girlie said evenly. "Thank you for thinking so highly of my deductive powers."

William didn't say anything for a moment, then, inexplicably said, almost more to himself than to her: "You're the type of person who researches everything about a city before they visit, am I right"—his voice not lifting in the end, so not really a question.

Girlie thought of the reams of research she'd done on Paris before her six months studying abroad there, the bookstores and patisseries she'd planned to go to until her budget ran out and she'd ended up eating Leader Price biscuits for ten euro cents a packet, getting stalked and told "wo ai ni" and "konnichiwa" by French men of all ages and races. Flaneuse, indeed. Aware of the hypocrisy, she nevertheless, as ever, did not relish being clocked.

"What other cities," she retorted. "Don't you know Americans think the world revolves around them?"

"My being here is proof they're right," William countered, still not looking at her. "It wasn't an insult. Researchers are very important. None of this would be possible without such minds."

She was about to tell him to go to hell, fuck the money, she'd had enough of the sparring and the runaround—knowing there was no universe in which she would ever say something like *fuck the money* to anyone—but now in the center of the sandy arena, there was a giant lion roaring at a group of gladiators, their short swords lifted in defiance, roaring back. "Eyyyyyy," Aditya joined in, cheering with the rest of the crowd around them.

"Have you ever learned about history from a movie?" William asked, staring down at the battle.

"What, like"—she gestured at the amphitheater—"like *Gladiator?*"

"For example."

"I'm a human person in the twenty-first century," Girlie said impatiently, "so yes, sure—*Gladiator* isn't a good example for me because I"—suddenly she felt embarrassed—"I did study classics in college, for a little while. I thought I was going to be a classicist, or something in medieval languages. Medieval French for a while."

"Right," William said; did he ever sound surprised? She was starting to think he had a file on her, not just the one from Reeden, maybe from the FBI. Maybe he already knew she'd written about *Le chevalier de la charrette* for her graduating thesis, on the naming function of Lancelot in the epic. Or maybe that was just his way of being in the world, inured to surprise. Which meant he'd had a bad surprise, probably in childhood. She could recognize a coping mechanism when she saw one.

Or: maybe she was completely wrong about all of it, and that was just how he sounded. She couldn't tell. She liked that she couldn't tell. So many people she'd grown up with put on a posture of faux gregariousness, cursing, bawdy jokes, heavy American accents, making themselves excessively legible just to circumvent the whole inscrutable mandarin thing. But what if you actually *were* inscrutable, Girlie thought. What if you didn't want to be read? What if you weren't, actually, from Detroit? She preferred not deforming her entire life to make her existence a counterargument; she liked seeing someone who made the same refusal.

"Ever watched a film and wanted to be the hero? Batman? Aragorn? Elizabeth Bennet?" William continued, eyes still trained on the spectacle. "Or an old Western, and dreamed of being John Wayne?"

"Cowboy isn't usually the thing I get typecast for."

"I wasn't referring to what other people might imagine you as," William said. "I was referring to one's personal dreams."

"That species died out in 2009."

"Certainly," William said peaceably. "Cowboys and samurais, you said."

Girlie's jaw twitched. "I must have missed the new open-world game about content moderators. Did that launch last year?"

William laughed. "I'm not trying to be antagonistic. Merely trying to assess your relationship to—"

"Escapism."

"Heroic identification."

"Same thing."

"Is it?"

"Don't you know everyone gets the chance to be John Wayne now," Girlie muttered. "Representation matters, or haven't you heard?"

William looked at her a beat too long. "I've heard," he said simply.

She was aware she'd been bantering with him as a way to keep looking at him, because she—because it was no hardship, to keep looking at him. But equally, because it was easier to keep her gaze fixed sideward, rather than turn and finally surrender, head-on, to the awe that was just waiting around the corner for her. Thus far she'd walled off that brewing awe, run up to gain high ground, still glimpsing this world only from the safety of the keep.

But now William was nodding toward the show, and she had no choice—no, she had a choice, it wasn't an order; but it was easier to think she had no choice—and faced the spectacle.

The lion was dead, bleeding out on the ground, several swords stuck into his side. One gladiator was left standing, covered in gore, waving triumphantly at the screaming amphitheater at large. Even the timing of his wave was carefully choreographed, it seemed; victory secured. The music had already started to fade, the gladiator exiting the arena; the platform beneath the lion sank into the ground, the bloody body disappearing. Now it was time for a scene change.

A great roar began rumbling forth from the edges of the theater, where, from an invisible basin, dark-blue water began to pour, ton by metric ton, into the center of the scene. A small island began rising up from the center of the theater, lifting above the water; in it was a gilded rectangular booth, windows on every side, like a kind of shark-watching cage—Girlie could see human faces peering out from within it. "The VVIP section," she distantly heard William explain. The music changed; a low, deep drumbeat. An enormous Roman galley began to row its way into the theater.

Girlie didn't realize she was leaning forward until William, next to her, murmured, "We can get closer if you like."

She followed him to the very front row, down the sandy pale steps that kicked up dust when she hurried, made her hands feel gritty and sunbaked. They leaned up against the short stone barrier of the prima cavea, not more than waist high, to watch.

The red-painted oars were moving in perfect synchronicity, oarsmen in fine military regalia. It was the size of the ship that struck her, the grand inevitable threat of it—this was what it must have felt like to see the Roman fleet coming upon one's home shore; great and grand slavemaker, widowfucker, in all her not yet old glory.

From the other side of the amphitheater, another ship was approaching: the oaken ship of the Gauls, even larger than the Roman ship, leather-sailed and caulked with seaweed; decorated with carved animal heads, all of flying beasts, griffins, and eagles. The ship's high prow dwarfed the Romans, moving ponderously—a beast of burden made to ferry cargo, not make war. The Gauls were screaming; the music sided with them. They were going to lose.

Girlie heard a sharp breath come from somewhere: her own chest. At first she thought she was having a panic attack and was mortified, then, at the idea that she was about to have one, not only for the first time in perhaps a decade, but in front of two professional colleagues, one of whom was offering her a job. Then she realized she wasn't having a panic attack at all, that it had only been one sharp breath— that at the sight of the ships facing each other, she had gasped, unbidden. In terror, and in wonder.

She turned to William, who seemed to have predicted the effect this would have on her. She couldn't tell if he was disappointed that she hadn't maintained her cool, that she had shown herself to just be another easily awed spectator; someone who could be amazed, and therefore sold to. He didn't look disappointed—but how would she know. "The first time is always special," he said only.

..

"The Gauls versus Romans show was the signature spectacle at L'Olifant's early theme parks," William said when the battle was over, as the water drained out of the theater and the two of them began walking back up to where Aditya was still seated in the cavea, eating popcorn. "Although, the physical sites at the time used actual man-made lakes; of course, the ships they built then were much smaller, not one-to-one recreations. To recreate the Battle of Morbihan was no small feat, and I think in some early iterations, they even changed the history around a bit, had the Gauls defeat Julius Caesar, experimented with counterfactual outcomes. But they discovered that, in fact, the local audience was most engaged seeing France—well, the Gauls—lose. Be the underdogs. Perceived defeat can be—galvanizing."

"Heroic identification," Girlie said.

William smiled; the wrinkles didn't show up this time. "Yes. They'd hit upon something, in any case, similar to the comparatively global phenomenon of, say, the Marvel Cinematic Universe: that there was a real audience for epic storytelling on this scale; a hunger and longing for a return to a kind of grandeur, something that merged narrative entertainment, epic imaginative settings, and a sense of real, visceral excitement—battles, romance, valor. But even more than that, something homegrown, distinctly European; not American, not Marvel, not *Bridgerton*, not *Pride and Prejudice and Zombies*. Not contemporary and ironic, with winking anachronisms. Something not afraid to be first degree, as I think the founder of L'Olifant once said. *Premier degré*. Something not so tongue-in-cheek."

"So 'woke,'" Girlie supplied.

William smiled again; now there were wrinkles. "Yes, that word has crossed the Atlantic." He waved a hand at the theater. "But they were limited by the physical component; the theme parks were a huge success wherever they went, but location scouting was expensive, building the sets was expensive, creating man-made lakes, expensive."

"Enter virtual reality."

"Enter virtual reality. Enter Playground, né Fairground," William said. "Fewer and fewer people are going to the movie theater, as evidenced by seemingly every other article in the trade papers about the decline of the film industry. But what if that audience could be served at home, and more immersively than ever? What if the epic setting, unlike a film, could feel so alive, so immediate, that it could even change and evolve, every time you logged on, like many other open world games?"

"It's smart," Girlie said. "You're not trying to be *Second Life* or *The Sims*, virtual reality version. Those things have failed. Or, not failed but: the possibilities have been wrung out. You're not just doing alternate reality. You're doing larger than life. Realer reality. Sensory overload." She paused. "Emotion."

"If you compete with life on life's terms, you'll lose," William said, sounding like he was quoting someone. "But—something *larger* than life, as you put it? Something that feels like discovering a more monumental, and yes, more heroic, dimension of our own lives—our own history—there's a draw in that. L'Olifant had proof of concept in France. They just needed Playground to make them global."

"What did Playground need L'Olifant for?"

William turned to her, so for the first time she saw his entire non-face, each tiny handcrafted cell of it. "Money," he said.

Girlie felt herself smile, and though she knew her face was a blank void, when now he smiled, she felt that it was a smiling back; that he'd expected her to smile, and was imagining it, and betting that he was right.

"Consider me impressed with your CGI budget," she said, turning away, just to get them out of the moment.

She let her eyes survey the arena again. A maiden was now at the top of a tower, waving her silk kerchief at a young knight at the foot of it. "And if I were an active moderator for this scene," she asked, "what would I be doing?"

William nodded toward the popcorn vendor again, still roaming up and down the aisles offering popcorn.

She balked. "That's a moderator?"

"Among others," William said. "There are moderators in the audience; there are even some among the actors in the scene. It's generally undercover work, in these landscapes—you would have a period-appropriate skin customized to the particular area of moderation, and you would go largely unnoticed among the other festivalgoers. Easier to flag and ban users, or note who's behaving badly, who needs to be kicked out of a lobby, if you don't have a giant SECURITY sign on yourself. So we've found, at least. In the tourism landscapes, for example, you'd be dressed as any other tourist; just another American at the Amalfi Coast, taking photos. In the imperial shogunate reneactments, a kimono, or perhaps a ninja costume. And so on, and so forth."

"I've never been to the Amalfi Coast," Girlie said.

"Now's your chance," William said wryly.

"Is it overrated?"

William paused. "I've never been either," he said at last. "But— no. I don't think so."

Girlie looked at the popcorn vendor, selling two buckets of popcorn to a family of four, the kids bouncing in their seats, the mother looking harried. "So all of this, it's—*Cleopatra*, it's *Gladiator*, but it's also a theme park, but it's also—travel. Tourism."

"Essentially," William said. "All of those things, and more. A playground, one might say." Then he laughed at himself. "I apologize."

"Accepted, pending review."

"Yes. Well." William—or William's skin—now looked a little sheepish. "The word you're looking for might be *experience*."

The knight was climbing the tower, to the urgent, high-octave shimmer of a piano. She hadn't even noticed, but all around them night had begun to fall, a curtain coming down on the day; the whole world now lit up by one thin sliver of moon, just a taste of it, glowing and lonely. The knight had reached his lady; they were kissing. Then came the high scream of fireworks, shooting off into the sky: huge fiery blooms of saltpeter raining down on them, blue and white and red, with soaring minor strings now swelling from sources so hidden it may as well have come from her own heart. It had to be a kind of lizard-brain evolutionary thing—she hadn't even watched the buildup of the courtship. And yet the combination, the alchemy of it all, was working on her now, drawing out of her a feeling, like a magician plucking a coin from behind her ear and pretending it'd always been there. The music, the gunpowder in the sky, the remote Moon, the remoter Earth. The knight and lady had reunited—but the minor key augured separation. It was night, she was cold, the amphitheater was vast, the whole aching world was dense with lovers; she was alone. The fireworks glimmered and died; now before her unrolled the blackened-blue sky, full of stars. She lived in Vegas—it was the first time she'd seen the stars above her in years.

"You might," William said, his face in shadow, reaching forward to hand her the popcorn bucket in the dark, "also find it fun."

The exchange was careful, professional, with his hand supporting the bucket and nowhere near where she took it, by the lip, fingers closing around the oily paper, and yet the tips of her fingers felt singed, stinging, alive with the sensation of it, the carnival smell of caramel and corn, and the indentation in the bucket where William's fingers had been, where she now placed her thumb, feeling her own pulse beating in it, down to the tips of her fingernails.

William disappeared first from the body in front of her, the mask frozen in place. Even in the virtual reality world, she could tell when an avatar was—*ensouled*, was the only way she could think of putting it. That someone was alive in there. He'd signed out.

She turned around to see Aditya had done the same, his knight's body stuck in a joyous wave, before his body blinked away. The rest of the scene was continuing around them, as the show came to an end; like in any other theme park, the guests were starting to mill out, except the way they exited the theater, much like William, was to log off, so she saw the lights in the eyes of each avatar dim: one by one, group by group, soul by handmade soul.

The entire world slowly dimmed, then went dark. Then she heard William, in the room, saying patiently, "You can come out whenever you're ready."

Slowly, she removed the mask, squinting instinctively even though she didn't need to: the dimming had pre-adjusted her to the duller settings of the world, which she realized was William's aim. To give her a minute alone in the world, and then to ease her out of it. A decompression chamber.

William in the room was looking at her. She couldn't quite shake thinking of him that way—William-in-the-room. "What do you think?"

Girlie looked down at the mask; inert, harmless. "As team-building exercises goes, I like it more than bouldering."

William in the room smiled; his eyes didn't crinkle.

"Is that your way of saying you'll come in for a last round of interviews?"

Girlie looked up. "You're not one of these start-ups that have no HR department, are you?"

William stared at her and then laughed, genuinely, seemingly for the first time: an uncalculated, unperformative laugh, a half-ugly bawk from deep in his chest, the lines around his eyes deepening. Aditya, whose presence she'd almost entirely forgotten, now joined in with the laughter; he was Aditya again, in the lilac polo shirt, zip-up Reeden sports jacket, khaki pants. But Girlie couldn't unsee this other limb of him now, the knight's mask he'd chosen to wear as his face.

"No, Ms. Delmundo. We have a Human Resources department."

"And full medical and dental. Three weeks' vacation."

There was a merry glint in William's eyes as he played along. "We match your 401(k) contributions at seventy-five cents to the dollar, up to six percent of your salary. After five years at Playground, you're one hundred percent vested."

She wasn't going to mention the Roth IRA she'd set up years ago, when she realized Reeden contractors got no retirement benefits. He was still talking. "Not to mention—given the nature of the tech, and the value of your expertise, you'll be working here, in this wing of the building. You'll have your own private space."

"Here?"

"Here. In your own office." William nodded down at the mask in her hands. "Well, here, in this building, and—there."

Girlie stared down at the mask in her hands, turning it over delicately to look at the small screens, the small nodules on each side where an electrode—was that the right word?—must be elegantly situated. Neural networks, deep learning algorithms, three weeks' vacation, but also: no more cupcake potlucks on Fridays, no more nine-minute wellness breaks, no more avoiding certain bathrooms when they smelled of cum or vomit, no more coworkers crying at the station next to hers.

Right on schedule, the world was ending yet again. She already knew content moderation for social media was a shrinking industry. She and Rhea and Vuthy and Robin and Maria Makiling and Bonifacio and José Rizal and all the rest of the self-named: they were all being observed and recorded and siphoned off, like gas from a janky car, so that their skills would eventually be automated. There was already talk of AI programs that could do content moderation at 99 percent accuracy. She was familiar enough with the precursors of apocalypse to know when it was time to jump worlds.

When she looked up, she saw William thinking *Got you*, the way she'd looked at him when she'd first seen his Reverso. To his credit, he didn't—visibly—gloat. "Shall we schedule that last interview, then?"

Girlie thought of the house in Milpitas, the persimmon trees in the garden that might still be fruiting, the carved-out crater in the living world. The question of how long this world would last; that, of course, she couldn't know. *Make me move!* Still. There were worse ways to be asked for a third date.

4

Pecunia non Olet

our first week will be for onboarding, just training simulations—you won't be moderating in the world just yet," William had said, when she'd formally accepted the offer. He was wearing a tie that day; rich navy silk. Sober and conservative; projecting a steady hand.

"We're lucky to have you, Ms. Delmundo," he'd said later, standing in the doorway of her new office, just a ten by ten room, a congratulatory basket of granola bars and potato chips on the desk. Girlie was turned away from him, moving toward the personal note, written by Aditya, COME BACK TO VISIT US ON THE FLOOR WHENEVER YOU WANT! CONGRATS AGAIN! There was also the issue of not wanting to look at William for too long, lest she permit the higher-level processing of her brain register that he looked—that navy was his color. "I'll let you get settled in."

The initial active moderation training exercises had been easy enough, programmed disruptions she saw a mile away: there were the obvious racial and genital slurs, of course, to mute and block, mute and kick; a young man in a toga making blowjob faces at an impassive gladiator, lightweight trolling; a big blue-skinned avatar repeatedly bouncing into the lap of a mute medieval maiden, one of the standard forms of sexual harassment that VR users had come up with.

She learned quickly that the rule of thumb in VR content moderation was, if anyone remotely femme was in the room, someone was going to find a creative way to assault her. If there was a hole, a face, a girl, all three, what was the difference; someone was going to try to fuck it. You had to keep your eyes open for the constantly renewing online language of assault, its font of resources, all the hundred-blooming-flowers of how to rape someone, how to let someone know they were about to be raped, how to let someone know they'd just been raped.

Sometimes a rape was just a case of letting one's avatar run headlong into another avatar, over and over and over again. Sometimes a rape was sticking so close to another avatar that no matter where they tried to move in the virtual space, the first avatar would remain superglued to their virtual body. There were a thousand, a million, infinite ways to assault somebody. At least one for every firing neuron in the brain. The moderators were highly discouraged from ever using the word *rape* to describe their experiences, so as not to minimize rape in the real world; rape with real bodies.

Not real bodies, is what Girlie told herself, the first time she surfaced from a training session in which an avatar with neon green fur had wrapped itself around her, so she could barely see the world she was meant to be moderating. This time it was just an easy Parisian tourist scene, rue Bonaparte, voice-over tour guide leading them to the Place Saint-Sulpice, one of the best places to kiss in Paris.

Only she couldn't see any of it, endeavoring hard, with all the bodies of her body, to push the avatar's body off her, feeling the faux fur slide slippery under her fingers, smelling its acrylic pelt, seeing its unchanging, pleased gaze bore into her, its warm damp hands grasping onto both of hers, so she couldn't move her fingers to navigate, didn't remember how to override the motion controls, until finally she logged out.

Girlie took the mask off her face; breathed out once, ragged. All the waste baskets were made out of easily washable plastic, no lining, eco-conscious. She didn't vomit.

"How are you doing," came William's voice, even, low, gracing her with enough dignity to not sound apologetic. He wasn't in her office, but in her ear, supervising the training from his own desk. "Why don't you take a break."

Girlie took one more breath. "No. I'm good," she said and logged back in. She waited for the flash of green fur to rear up in her peripheral vision, then, like a quick slicing strike to the trachea: mute and kick. On to the next.

. .

"Ready to make a skin?" William asked, on the fourth day.

They were standing outside the Viking scene, another one of the L'Olifant landscapes. The storyline was set in a village by a river, starting with an idyllic Gallic marriage, two soft pale sweethearts looking at each other under an arch draped with garlands of white flowers, until the whole thing was broken up by a siege of Viking warriors, leaping off longships in a stream of shouting—there was a lot of incoherent yelling in the L'Olifant narratives, probably because voice acting was time consuming and overly specific; easier to layer sounds to create the sense of a crowd. Poor little French monks were running around a monastery, Vikings striking them to the ground, dragging some of the younger ones onto the longship, holding aloft great gold tabernacles and wheels of cheese, along with the bloodied bride, hoisted over some Viking's shoulder.

"Is the training over? I thought I'd have to do more shadowing."

"Well, there's the shadowing, just to get your feet wet in the world, which you've excelled at—to no one's surprise." William's compliment sounded a little mocking, which made it sound a little personal, which Girlie couldn't decide whether or not she liked. "But getting used to moderating in-skin is obviously also an important part of the training, and it can take some time to complete the 3D modeling for your avatar, so we'd like to schedule that as soon as possible, to have you ready for launch. We've got the researchers on-site this week."

She gestured at their necks, chests. "Do I have to wear one of those?"

"The bodysuit? Yes. It's not required for users," William said, once again sounding like he was reading from a script, "a Playground customer can choose whether or not they want to buy the full set, for complete immersion, or just the mask and gloves, as a more entry-level option. And their suits aren't, of course, personalized to the degree that the employee suits must be; that would be quite costly to scale. But we do require moderators to fully saturate—the daily logistics of moderation are much more difficult if a moderator doesn't have full sensory access to the environment."

Girlie thought it was darkly clever how William framed it; that not wearing the bodysuit would be doing a *disservice* to herself; as opposed to a corporate obligation to expose herself, to make every part of herself available to the site, for the site's ultimate benefit.

William seemed to detect that, because then he said, somewhat too quickly, "I wear the full suit every day, myself. It's designed to be worn under regular clothing."

"That still seems uncomfortable," Girlie said. William shook his head. "You get used to it."

It was only at the skinmaking appointment that Girlie finally saw just who made the cut. There was Vuthy, and Robin, and some other of the moderators she never talked to; about ten of them, or maybe there were only ten of them scheduled for that particular block of time. No Rhea, none of the Marias. All the moderators were on the younger side, though not too young, maybe late twenties, early thirties; she was probably the oldest.

She was also, she realized with a faintly political jolt, the only woman in the room. She wasn't sure if she should see that as a red flag, or a badge of honor, or just daily life in tech. Since becoming a moderator, she'd only ever had one female boss, back in the Bay, an Asian American woman from a Midwest swing state, who quit after years of stomach ulcers, citing systemic toxic behavior from her own line manager, a white woman who'd been a bigwig at Microsoft, had been hired for her dynamic skills in streamlining, said things like *the sky's the limit*. There were a bunch of layoffs that year; Girlie survived.

This was Girlie's first time on the clinical floor of Playground's Content Moderation department, sitting on a midcentury armchair in what could only be described as a hospital waiting room. And sitting there with the rest of the patients for their prescriptions, she felt a peculiar sense of—rightness; like she was exactly where she was supposed to be, at this particular moment, at this particular juncture of the world's turning.

Vuthy was sitting next to her. She turned slightly to him. "What did Rhea say about your promotion?"

"That it should have happened earlier," Vuthy said, looking at once terribly shy and frighteningly ambitious, the way she often thought men his age seemed. He was still wearing the same friendship bracelets he'd worn during their first presentations. "And said congratulations to us both. And said that we're lucky." He looked around the room. "I don't know about the lucky part. We both worked really hard to get here. That's why we got picked, right?"

Girlie sensed Vuthy studying her, trying to figure out if he should befriend her and try to turn her into his new work mom, Rhea 2.0—or see her as competition, take her down, jostle for pole position. She tried to telepathically beam into his brain her preferred third option, which was to continue leaving her the hell alone. "Yep."

The process took longer than Girlie thought it would. They'd had to sign off on a full-body MRI (that, she'd approved when she signed the contract), but she hadn't realized they'd have an MRI in the fucking building, like a Hollywood actor with a home ultrasound. Their musculoskeletal data duly noted—"Any major tumors or brain bleeds?" Girlie asked the MRI tech, who said brightly, "Rest assured, you're in perfect health," though he didn't know how to react when Girlie responded, "Better luck next time"—they moved to an enormous room, a kind of mini-hangar-cum-soundstage-cum-operating-theater, wallpapered in what looked like hundreds of cameras.

"If you'll just let us," a young female researcher—the only other woman so far, also Asian, with a name tag that said *Kim*—said to Girlie, holding up a hand full of what Girlie later understood were small sensors, to be placed gingerly on her tongue and at different points of her teeth, so that the particular movements of her mouth would be faithfully understood and translated.

"Our haptic sensors for the lips and teeth are very powerful," Kim said proudly. "We're confident that water pouring over the face in the Playground universe will feel no different from water pouring on your face in the real world. And we have over three thousand flavor presets programmed, so eating in-game will almost feel like eating in real life—only calorie free! Some people even find they lose weight in real life, from being satiated in-game!" Girlie thought of Aditya, his handful of caramel popcorn.

"As for the touch, we use ultrasound waves to create the sensation; there are dozens of tiny transducers in the mask that turn ultrasound energy into electrical energy. You'll feel a bug crawling across your lip and want to swat it!"

"My dream," Girlie intoned.

Her baseline model created, she would then be outfitted with different costuming options, relevant to the various landscapes she would be moderating: medieval maiden, American tourist, Viking warrior, alien NPC, noblewoman in kimono, woman in blue silk brocade cheongsam pouring tea into a lacquered cup, museum security guard at the Villa Borghese presiding over the Berninis, waitress at the baroque Le Train Bleu restaurant in the Gare de Lyon, one of the main hubs where users came to change lobbies for their next destination.

After that, two people they were calling Tailors came to take her measurements; she didn't have to remove her clothes, as she'd thought, just stand in a room as the audience of sensors took stock of the shape of her body, then immediately 3D printed a black catsuit, which she was asked to try on in the provided changing rooms. There were no sensors or tech in the suit as yet, they explained; this was just to perfect the sizing, ascertain her comfort level. The full suit would be ready for her by the time training was over. The material would feel exactly the same, even with the sensors applied; she'd be able to wear the bodysuit under jeans, if she preferred. "Think of it like long underwear," they explained.

It zipped open at the neck, and then zipped apart at the waist, so moderators wouldn't have to strip naked just to pee in the middle of the day, which Girlie thought was a nice touch; she was afraid they'd just put a peehole in the crotch and call it a day. Breathable mesh sections in the armpits, so moderators wouldn't overheat. "You guys think of everything," Girlie said, and they said, "Thank you!," didn't pick up on her tone.

They said that she would have to remove the suit, mask, and gloves every day, of course; she couldn't take the materials home, they were highly valuable company property. There was a deposit chute on her floor where she would drop the full suit off after every shift—they'd give her the labeled packaging she was supposed to use to identify her suit from the others. The suits would be taken to specialized dry cleaners, and in the morning, the fresh set would once again be available in her office, fully charged (the suit and mask were dual voltage, internationally minded; if you ever ran low on power during a shift, you could ostensibly charge while in use, but this was usually avoided, if only for the moderator's comfort; the plug went in the lower back area). Where the suits went for cleaning, and whose hands, exactly, cleaned them or brought them back to her office, was not part of the orientation. They didn't even make a comment about using "green dry cleaning," or some other gesture at their ecological thoughtfulness, so she could only imagine the care that might be required to clean such technological wonders; lacemakers in Belgium, going blind for beauty. Every time she thought she was at the bottom, there was another bottom, yawning open below.

Like William had said, the integrated motion control was sewn into the gloves, so that it would require only the slightest movements of her fingers to shift directions, entirely avoiding the in-world accidents that so often happened with clunky VR headsets. Now her body in space was just a soft little pawn she could push around, a little boat she could row far and wide in the sea of the world, thumbing herself through it by turning left, then right, with a faint stroke; the motion control dismissible with a swipe of all fingers, so she could then reach out and touch something, use her hand with its original factory setting: as a hand.

It would have been a surgeon's idea, she thought; that the dexterity of the hand should come to express the dexterity of the mind. There were also two emergency physical controllers, optical mice, strapped to her suit in case the motion control in the hands malfunctioned for whatever reason, sitting in the kind of holster police officers wore in the '70s, making it easy to dual wield. That, on the other hand, would have been a weeaboo tech bro's idea: someone who'd seen *Bullitt*, jerked off to Asuka and Rei in *Evangelion*.

Girlie smoothed her palm along the turtleneck of the bodysuit, so it glided up her throat, kissing at the underside of her jaw, where it would meet the edge of the mask. Before realizing she was doing it, she stroked one hand up her forearm, wrist to elbow crook, peering close to glimpse each minute almost-hair, which must have connected at the root to millions upon millions of sensors, making up a downy not-quite-fur coat that she could arouse, like fingering a nap of panne velvet, up and down, so that the black of it shimmered into a brighter or deeper blackness, depending on the light. Her breath trembled the velli; she was giving the suit goose bumps.

She looked at herself in the mirror: well, it was a skintight anime catsuit and a copaganda-porn faux gun holster, she looked hot, who was surprised. What was she going to do about it, ask for a hairshirt? She did a couple squats, some arm rolls, bent backward. The stretch was solid. The socked feet were a little too big, the heel part was almost at her ankle, but that was the only necessary revision she could see.

She slid her jeans over the catsuit; it still fit comfortably, but wearing it under her clothes added a dash of kink—or maybe she just wasn't used to feeling fabric like this on her skin. The rare times she bought high quality clothes, they were usually vintage, battered; when she bought new clothes, they were polyester, hard-wearing. Now here she was, a couture client.

There was a sleek, languid eros to the suit, which was just the eros of—something fit to her. Made for her, she supposed. Moving in it, her body was at once supple and taut, ready as a nocked arrow; immediate, standing at attention, aimable anywhere. The erogenous readiness of it wasn't just sexy, but felt like sex—or rather, not the act itself, but the crackle in the atmosphere, just before the inclement stormfront of fucking; knowing a fuck, like rain, was coming.

Maybe it was just because the suit was the almost-Vantablack color she'd first seen on William. Maybe it was because the suit wrapped her tight, held her in; maybe it was because the suit slicked her down, opened her up. Maybe because it made her nude, covered her up, gave her freedom—then threw in safety too. There was one contradictory sensation for each follicle on her body, and each one: rang true, ran hot, felt real. "You get used to it," William had said.

Girlie took the catsuit off. She did not linger on her reluctance to do so. Exited the dressing room and said, "Just the feet are too big. I'm between a six and a half and a seven."

••

Nearly every day, she saw William. Sometimes it was William-in-the-world, in the parking lot after the workday, sometimes in the hallway, sometimes on his way out of the canteen with a cold bottle of Fijian water.

But more often: outside a London pub, waiting for a planned

NPC disruptor to start glassing somebody. In the Van Gogh exhibition in Amsterdam, everyone's pant hems soggy from the rain outside. In Le Train Bleu, ignoring the Mouloudji track or Gainsbourg's "La Javanaise" alternating over the speaker system on repeat, looking out for anyone trying to grope the waiters in their starched shirts and black vests.

William, drinking a Guinness with a perfectly poured head. William, waiting patiently behind the velvet rope with the other tourists, shadowed against the dark teal walls, reading a brochure with sunflowers on the cover. William, sitting in a deep-blue banquette, under a neobaroque fresco, eating a Rum Baba.

He was there to observe her at work, she knew, and yet whenever she looked at him, he wasn't looking back at her. She knew the lingering physics of having just been looked at, lifting the hairs at the back of her neck—her neck-in-the-world—but it was just a trace of a feeling, the atomic shadow of something that had been there once; gone now.

Once, she saw him in the Galleria Borghese in Rome. She'd been struck by the building the first time she came to moderate it, the touch of pink in its neoclassical white pillars and porticos, like a drop of blood in a vat of alabaster paint. She was shocked when she entered the first room of the museum—she'd never before been in a room in which absolutely nothing was saved from ornamentation.

The effect was clearly meant to be awe, and Girlie was, indeed, awed—awed by the gold, awed by whoever built the museum in the first place, awed by whoever recreated it here, for her, there. Girlie looked up at the ceiling fresco, though it would have been better to say that it looked down upon her; squinting, she tried to make out the figures painted there, men in uniform, two armies, fighting each other.

A tab popped up in the corner of her eyesight. A regular user would be able to learn more about whatever was in their immediate field of vision. She ignored it, but the tabs kept popping up; there was art everywhere, something to annotate, something to caption, something to tell the history of, the artist of, the date of, the inspiration behind. There was only seeing, never coming to the end of seeing.

Girlie had been looking down for a moment, trying to find a blank space, take a break from the museum's overly helpful guidance.

She realized she was standing on the mosaic of a woman's face: an assemblage of tiny tiles, or glass, or stone, each tessera delicately hand-placed, the constellation of disparate pieces so complex that the mosaic seemed almost to be moving, as fluid and mutable as water.

Girlie stepped back from the mosaic to look at it better; at the woman's fragile, limpid, almost transparent beauty, her dark eyes, her mouth, not quite closed; about to speak, already deciding against it. A look of resignation; a private look. It took Girlie a long time to realize that instead of hair, the woman's head was crowned in snakes.

What she'd been searching for, she got: there were no pop-ups, no tabs, no virtual placards giving any information about the mosaic; no title, no caption, no artist, no history, no claim.

She heard his footsteps first. Playground had captured the sound of dress shoes on stone very well. Again, like mercy, he came not from behind, but from the side.

"I like this area too," William said.

"Have you ever been to Rome?"

"Once. Spent less than a day there. Rail trip, after university." He looked down. "It's Medusa, right?"

"Yes."

"We've asked the Galleria Borghese. There aren't any informational tabs available for the floor mosaics, but they're art pieces in and of themselves, I know." William looked down at the mosaic; both of them kept their feet outside the tiles that framed Medusa's face.

"The information tabs are overwhelming as is. There are too many of them in this room. You can tell that to the UX team."

"Noted," William said, sounding amused.

"I don't mind that there isn't a caption on this," Girlie said, still looking down at the mosaic. "It's a nice break from having to know everything."

William couldn't help but laugh. "Is that something that often plagues you? Having to know everything?"

"Or what, just live and let things happen?" Girlie laughed next to him; not with him. "No, thank you."

Their eyes met. She saw a thought coming to him; saw him suppressing it. She knew then, with the clitstruck knowledge of someone who'd been a conventionally beautiful human commodity all her life, that he found her attractive. Which was strike one.

"Yes," William said, not laughing anymore. "I don't go in for that much either."

A Confederate soldier came hurtling through the museum, jostling past Girlie and William, running across Medusa's face, stabbing his bayonet in random directions, yelling incoherently about freedom. "Back to the mines," Girlie said.

She wasn't naive enough to tell herself: what had been found attractive wasn't actually *her*, wasn't actually *her-in-the-world*, but just the skin of her, rendered here by a team of researchers, technicians, and the vast churning engine that powered this world. Wasn't naive enough to tell herself that what had been found attractive was merely an appealing fungible resource, available for consumption, as nice to look at as a still life. The real, unfortunately, still had an intuitive smell. A specific, unrenderable chemistry. Girlie had known since she was seven what it looked like when she turned a man on.

She turned to give William a goodbye salute à la Aditya, but William wasn't looking at her, as she'd expected. He had his eyes fixed on the mosaic on the floor, brows tight together. When he looked up instinctively at the motion of her hand in the air, she saw him register the salute, then bat it away reflexively, like a dog shaking water from his fur.

..

At the end of the week, waiting in the stands for the lists, the next joust about to begin, Girlie was passing popcorn out to users and NPCs alike when she saw William coming down the aisle, now in a half suit of armor she hadn't seen before, his eyes trained on her, hand lifted in a hello.

She straightened, steadying the tray of popcorn buckets hanging from her neck. "Popcorn," she said when he approached. "It's regular salted, not caramel."

"Thank you," William said, accepting a small bucket. "You're almost done with your shift here, yes?"

"After this last joust. Sir Edouard may actually prevail," she said, grinning, like they both hadn't seen this story end a dozen times that week. "His lady's in the audience. She's allowed him to win this time."

"Poor bastard," William said, and she couldn't tell if that sounded weird because for once he actually sounded like he was from some-where, as opposed to a palimpsest of a hundred Londons, a hundred London men; fictional, therefore believable.

"Well, now that you're at the end of training, I'd like to introduce you to Perera, our local consulting physician; I mentioned him to you during our first lunch, do you remember?"

"I think so."

"He's a trained gastroenterologist, but at some point made the transition to the clinical virtual reality field, we met in London, dur-ing our collaborations with the NHS. He's now specializing in vir-tual reality for chronic pain, but he's also been supervising our therapeutic offset program, which you and the other moderators will be able to benefit from, should you so choose."

"Therapeutic offset."

William smiled. "We're workshopping the name. But essentially, much of the early contributions around content moderation for Play-ground, at the beginning, focused on the psychological effects of content moderation on the moderators themselves. I certainly don't have to tell you that content moderation can be extremely difficult work. Psychically."

He paused there, leaving her room to respond, but she remained silent, staring back at him, chin raised. He took that beat of silence, looking back at her. Then he cleared his throat, looking away. First chicken.

"Dr. Perera initially worked with us to treat patients—combat veterans, people with chronic pain—using virtual reality as a thera-peutic device. We found that it helped to ease some of the more stub-born pain symptoms that traditional medicine had been unable to resolve. And given how important content moderation was going to be for the success of the Playground space, it made sense to incorporate a version of our discoveries—made simpler, perhaps—for the use of our own employees. Nothing too demanding of your time; an hour a week in the therapeutic space will be made available to all moderators. With more time negotiable, if deemed necessary. But I should really let Dr. Perera do the explaining."

Down in the lists, Sir Edouard had—lost. His love made herself scarce, retreating in a brocaded retinue of ladies-in-waiting. Girlie looked down at him, genuinely surprised; she hadn't seen this ending before.

The knight looked small there, next to his horse, lance broken around his feet. "Poor bastard," she murmured, trying the words out in her mouth; almost tasting them.

"Pardon?" William asked, leaning forward, reminding her, once again, that he was taller than her; which, once again, she felt politically irritated by.

"I'll take the carbon offsets for my brain, thanks," Girlie said.

"Oh, excellent," William said, straightening. "Would you like to sign out here, then meet us on the clinical floor?"

The therapeutic offset sessions required a different suit, mask, and gloves than her moderator work, though she didn't have to give her body up again for modeling; they could transfer her biometric data. But it was nice to slip into this other suit, which looked identical to the one she used for work, and yet, the fact that it wasn't the one she used for work—made a difference, however minute.

When Girlie did meet Perera for the first time, he was standing behind his desk, smiling at her. His forearms were wiry but corded with muscle and covered in dark graying hair, shoulders very broad, legs long and skinny, the drainpipe shape of them visible even through dress pants; not a CrossFit guy like a lot of these rich white and Asian doctors in Vegas and the Bay, but probably a long-distance runner who bench-pressed; barbell rows and rack pulls, skipping leg day, skinny calves, big traps. The Seamaster Aqua Terra looked new; the wide gold wedding band looked old, too pale to be anything but 14k.

Warmly, with a South Asian–inflected accent more Britannic than British, his first words to her were: "Hello, Ms. Delmundo. Are you a forest or a beach person?"

Girlie startled. "Is that a trick question?"

"No, no, not at all—please, have a seat." Perera gestured at the plush armchair in front of his desk. Girlie sat down. "I just find it's a good icebreaker, that's all," Perera went on. There was a bottle of antacids on his desk, behind the old-fashioned nameplate that said THARINDU PERERA, M.D., GASTROENTEROLOGY.

He saw her looking at the antacids and smiled. "I know. A bit ironic for a gastroenterologist. Chronic heartburn. A hereditary condition."

Then he folded his hands over each other, leaning forward. "So. Forest or beach?"

"One-bedroom apartment," Girlie answered. "Quiet neighbors."

Perera laughed, leaning back in his chair. "All right. I see you're going to give me a hard time. That's fine. I'll start. I would say I'm a beach person. I grew up by the sea, it's what I understand, it's the background to my earliest memories. I prefer the openness of the beach, the limitlessness of the sea."

"I don't have any experience with forests or the sea."

"Didn't you—" Perera stopped. "The files I have from Reeden say you grew up in Northern California."

"Yes."

"Forgive me, I haven't been long in America," Perera said, "but even I know California quite famously has both forests and beaches."

"Suburb life," Girlie said. "Parents worked all the time. Never went to Tahoe, never went to the beach. Never been on vacation with my family. Or been on vacation at all, unless you count study abroad once."

She saw Perera starting to feel a little sorry for her, which was how people reacted when she said things like never having gone on a single family vacation, or eating mayonnaise sandwiches, or having to use white rice as glue for her school projects. She was old enough now not to shy from it; better to rush forward onto the sword. "Never been to Disneyland either," she added, with a touch of sadism.

"Ah," Perera said, seemingly having to recalibrate the fact that his ostensibly politically neutral question had in fact uncovered a little land mine around class and leisure time. Girlie smiled at him. He smiled back, uncowed. "But you do know what forests and oceans *are*," he ventured.

"I've heard of them," Girlie said. "They have them in California, right?"

Perera laughed, nodding, too good-natured to see offense where it was meant; William, she already knew, would have paused, a little calculating look in his eyes, thumbing through one or two caustic little couplets in his mind before finally choosing one. "That is what all the guidebooks say, yes. So if you had to choose, purely based on instinct, which would you choose?"

Girlie hated these types of psychological tests, the way she hated trolley problems and hypothetical scenarios—horse-size duck, kill one person or the whole of humanity, they were for small, hedging imaginations yearning to be big. "Forests," she bit out, finally.

"Any reason?"

"I don't know how to swim."

"Anything else?"

A one-bedroom apartment, in a faraway city, no history to her, no one to know her name. Not quite a cabin in the woods, but: a sense of remoteness. When she walked out of the imaginary door into the imaginary city, there was, sure, why not, a large park to visit, conveniently within walking distance. Dogs running around, two of them hers, a language she didn't know, couples she'd never meet, families she'd never been part of, not a single childhood friend. A dirt path she could walk down, that she hadn't walked down a thousand times before. A place full of ghosts that weren't her own. Slipping into the solace of the tree canopy like a thief, having stolen nothing less than her own life. The air on her face would be cool; haptics, perfect.

She folded the old fantasy up into its well-worn shape, weathered as an unsent valentine; tucked it away again. "It sounds peaceful," she said, telling the truth for some reason. "Restorative."

"Then let's start with the forest scenario," Perera said. "I know William briefed you a bit on the concept of therapeutic offset—we're workshopping the name—but for this first session, it's basically a bit like a guided meditation: you'll be in a forest scenario, very similar to the landscapes you've been moderating all week."

He smiled. "Only this time there'll be nothing for you to moderate! All you have to do is enjoy it." *All you have to do*, Girlie thought to herself, wry. Like it was a small thing.

. .

The only time Girlie had ever really seen a redwood up close and in an actual forest was in the sixth grade, during a week at science camp, in the Saratoga Mountains. It had to be required by a school curriculum, in other words. There was no other way she'd ever find herself in a redwood forest; maybe she'd see a redwood in Milpitas, here or there, one ornamentally planted in front of City Hall or something; a real redwood, but its placement, its purpose, had made it a kind of simulacrum of itself.

Now Girlie was standing at a mulch-covered trailhead, which led into a vast redwood forest, with one enormous sequoia, whose top she could not see, even as she craned her head back to peer at it. When she moved forward, she heard the ground beneath her crunch. It smelled alive.

She moved forward through the world that had been created for her; or, not for her, for someone like her. Birdsong, insect chirping, the breathy rustle of leaves in the air, leaves falling, mulch underfoot, somewhere the hushed distant gossip of a small creek—the sound—the sound design—was impeccable. She was starting to find she could tell the difference between a Playground landscape and a L'Olifant landscape; the shape of the mind that made it, the hand of its potter in the clay, the faint wind of a soul moving through the trees. Both landscapes were in the genre of the romantic, but the modes of seduction were not kin.

Here was nothing like the amphitheater she'd seen, that first day when William had shown her the dazzling carnival face of Playground, the castles, the towers, the great Viking longboats and Roman galleys. That had been the Coliseum, Versailles; a place designed to impress her, to be a living buffet, to overwhelm her with stimulation from all sides; a place designed to be overwhelmed by and triumphed in, not reflected about. A place like a grand hall of mirrors, every rich sparkling surface shining back at yet another.

This was different. There was so—little, here, comparatively, she realized: an easy hiking path, big trees, somewhere a river, somewhere a bird, she couldn't tell which one. Early afternoon in Northern California; some sunlight peeking through the tree canopy, but relieved of the worst of the midday heat. A stillness in the air, but not the stillness of awe, not the kindless quiet of the holy. She had the sense of entering a space in which she was not welcome but accepted; acknowledged but not respected. She tried to remind herself that each leaf, each blade of grass, each push of wind through a branch, had been painstakingly engineered, filmed a million times to capture as many iterations of wind-pushing-through-branch as possible.

She stepped forward, farther into the forest, and still tried to keep throwing her rope to shore, to catch on to the last peg, to say to herself: *not* in the forest, but on the clinical floor, in Vegas. But found she could not keep telling herself this so much less persuasive story. She simply couldn't hold on to the thought, couldn't keep the logic of it in her head, while here, immersed in it. The forest of it.

She moved into the shadow of one of the great trees, in whose indifferent coolness and shade she lingered. She felt herself inhaling, then exhaling. To her great embarrassment, her heart began to calm—and then, began to race.

Perera was tracking her biometric data, her heart movement, her eye movement; she knew the pink line that indicated her overall cognitive load would be rising. Still she couldn't stop it.

She heard him unmute himself to say, "You doing okay over there? Want to continue?"

The sound of his voice, the memory of his likely subpar bench-press, brought her back into the world.

"Yes," she tried to say, and found she could; her voice did not waver. "Yes. Let's keep going."

"Great, good. I'm here if you need me."

She started approaching one tree, wanting to reach up to it, to touch its gnarled bark with hers, though some part of her was afraid that the touch would break the spell. She tried to remember how sophisticated the haptic gloves were, that she could touch sticky caramel popcorn, that she could tear faux fur off a rapist at the Louvre. She tried to remember how advanced the suit was, that the uneven ground underneath her feet was being transmitted to all the sensors at her soles, that the wind she felt ruffling the hair at her back had been iterated for months.

She knew what she knew, but it had become so much less vital, its grip so much weaker. Why be afraid of touching, and being disappointed by the nothing that might make itself known beneath her fingertips? What was so disappointing, about nothing? What was so frightening, about being disappointed?

She stepped closer to one of the trees and reached out, and let her thumb, index, and middle finger brush slightly against the bark— and felt it. Felt its rough deathful skin, its soft lichen and moss; felt it flake, gentle, beneath her touch. It—felt like the world. Here she was. In it.

"Enough," she tried to say, and found she could not, her throat thick, and so she tried again.

"*Out,*" she said again, like a safe word.

The forest dimmed, then went black. She reached up, but Perera's cool doctor's hands were already taking the headset away, his familiar human face swimming into view before her, concerned.

"All right," he said. "The first time can be a little bit intense for some people, I know. You okay? Can I get you some water?"

She opened her mouth, ready to be a person again, but found the woman in the forest was still there; was still here; was still her. Mortified, she found her throat was entirely closed. She covered her eyes with her hands, forming a makeshift headset of them.

Perera, mercifully, backed away to grab a bottle of water from a nearby mini fridge. He placed it in front of her and said quietly, "Just some water here whenever you're ready. Take your time."

Girlie, who was not in the business of getting emotional about nature and certainly not in front of upper-middle-class men she didn't know, groped for the bottle with half-seeing eyes and found, to her ever-spiraling horror, that her hands were shaking and she couldn't open the bottle.

Perera took the bottle from her and opened it himself, said, "Sorry about that," like it was his fault.

"Thank," she said, couldn't go any further, and drank deep from the water like it was mortal food; like it would bring her out of the sweetness of Hades; like it would restore her to human seasons. Her throat cleared. "Thank you. Fuck. That was."

"These kinds of reactions are extremely common," Perera assured her again. "Absolutely standard procedure. For many patients, they're doing this because more conventional forms of therapy"— Girlie felt her insides jerk in protest—"haven't been successful in treating their conditions. It can be a very. A very powerful thing."

"How long was I in there, ten minutes?" Girlie asked, after finishing the entire bottle of water. Perera was already opening a second bottle for her. She took it, and sipped from it more delicately this time.

Perera nodded at the headset. "In there? Nearly the hour."

Girlie gaped at him.

"An hour—it felt like—"

"Blink of an eye?" He smiled with one side of his mouth. "That's what patients often say. There's a time dilation effect with VR therapy that often happens. Less so with active content moderation, because you have to be so alert to triggers. But as a user in the space, the experience of time can be quite different."

Girlie looked down at the mask, now in Perera's hands, with a strange churning feeling in her stomach she realized was—longing. She wanted to go back.

Like every doctor on earth, he was already assessing his patient. "The first time I did it, I died," Perera said kindly.

"In the VR space," he clarified quickly, as if he, like Girlie and everyone she knew, had another first death he could be referring to.

"It was the first time I'd ever experienced virtual reality before," he went on. "My clinic specialized in unexplained colon disorder, IBD, Crohn's, ulcerative colitis. Of course, like anyone, we'd heard the rumblings about virtual reality being used in the medical sphere. But it wasn't until I had an older woman come in with chronic abdominal pain, who had undergone one of the earliest trials and saw her pain finally resolve, that I started considering bringing it into my practice.

"When the Playground guys came into Kings to offer their tech to our clinic—we weren't the only clinic they were shopping the tech around to, of course—I volunteered to be the first guinea pig. I wasn't going to put my patients through something I hadn't experienced myself. So they came into my office, strapped one of those headsets over my eyes, and when I opened my eyes, I was sitting on the edge of Big Ben."

Girlie tilted her head. "Big Ben? The clock?"

"Well, I didn't know that at first. I just knew I was very high. I swear to you, I opened my eyes and I grabbed backward to hold on, because I felt it—I heard the wind. The wind sounds very different when you're high up versus on the ground. I felt and heard the air, I felt how shaky my position was on that narrow ledge.

"I told myself I was in a conference room, that I had an unfinished coffee on my desk that I'd spill if I kept reaching backward, but

I couldn't hold on to that knowledge." Girlie thought of herself, trying to remember that each blade of grass had been painted.

"Then what happened?"

"They gave me some time to process. I felt like I was having a heart attack. My breathing was shallow and rapid, my muscles and tendons were stiff from trying to hold on to what felt like a railing behind me—which was really the back of my office chair.

"And that was when they said, 'All right, Dr. Perera. Now we'd like you to jump off.' I said, 'Jump off what?' 'Jump right off the ledge.' I thought—you must be bloody kidding me. Excuse my language.

"I tried to get myself to reason with what was going on in my head, that I was still in my office, that nothing bad was going to happen if I jumped, that I was sitting in a comfy office chair and not off the ledge of this national monument, but I just couldn't get myself to believe it. What I was seeing, I believed. It had completely taken over my brain, my senses, my entire sense of the world. And I was very, very afraid."

Perera was standing behind his desk, one hand poised on the office chair in question, tapping it occasionally for emphasis, like an old friend who had gone through the same harrowing experience and lived to tell the tale. It couldn't have been the same chair, Girlie thought.

"The most shocking thing was how it was able to produce the overwhelming feeling of *immediacy*. Presence. I was there. I was there, on Big Ben."

Perera crossed his arms. "You know those theories of alternate realities? Multiverses, all that. People often still describe the VR space as such. That used to be interesting to me. But after working in VR on the clinical side, I've come to think differently. A lot of the research around VR—most of us in the clinical sphere are calling it immersive therapy, because of the stigma that's sometimes attached with a concept as old and well known as *virtual reality*—has shown us that, actually, our brains aren't equipped to live in more than one reality. Not neurologically. There may indeed *be* other realities—I don't know enough about quantum mechanics to tell you. But not to the body.

"My brain couldn't compute that I was in my office and on Big Ben at the same time. Just couldn't do it. Physically, psychologically, could not tell you that one was virtual and one was real. It wasn't an alternate reality; you might say it was an *also*-reality. According to my brain and body. Gut.

"And, yet, despite my fear, I was starting to want to jump. Have you heard of the concept, l'appel du vide? Call of the void?"

Mercifully, he didn't wait for Girlie to nod or shake her head; Girlie, who was still grasping the bottle with both hands.

"It's also called HPP, high place phenomenon. It's the compulsion some people report experiencing when in high places—that of being compelled, inexplicably, despite having no prior suicidal ideations, to jump off.

"They were changing, in live-time, how I experienced the world around me. And how I felt about it. What I wanted to do. And it was real; I was really there. On Big Ben. It felt more like teleportation. Like they'd conjured me there."

Perera smiled, an almost William-like smile; no joy in it. "Reeden invited all of us to a Cirque de Soleil show and dinner at the Stratosphere Tower when we first came to Vegas. I couldn't go to the tower."

"Afraid of heights, now," Girlie concluded.

Perera shook his head. "Not afraid enough, anymore."

Girlie looked at Perera. She didn't know what to say—how to

knead his story, the titanic, ego-dissolving heft of it, into a tiny little cube, a teaspoon of sugar, something either of them could swallow with no pain.

"When I was down there," she started, then stopped, trying to figure out how she was going to get the truth she needed, by divulging as little of herself as possible. She didn't know why she'd instinctively said *down* instead of *in*. "Yes. I felt afraid, a little. But also—strange."

"Mm-hmm," Perera said, active-listening. He made a motion for her to continue.

"Strange, as in—" Girlie didn't like stuttering. "I also had trouble— distinguishing between—remembering that the forest wasn't real. I was trying to remember that I was here, in the room, and I—couldn't, exactly. Or, more like—it wasn't the more convincing story. It was different from the L'Olifant landscapes."

"And how did that feel?"

Good, Girlie thought, then thought better. "It felt—it felt like there was potential there," she said, careful. "Like more things were—possible." She tried to huff out a laugh. "And, well, yes, the— therapeutic—benefits—it was relaxing. I mean, until I freaked out."

Perera, kindly, joined in with her, chuckling. "Listen, all of that is completely normal," he assured her again—she really wanted him to stop telling her this was normal, because each repetition only burnished the opposite. "The conclusion we came to, around VR in the clinical environment, was that virtual reality had incredibly powerful potential, not as a provider of alternate realities, but as a *behavior modification* technology—that it could truly change how we think, how we feel. About the world, about ourselves, about our bodies— *these* worlds, *these* selves, *these* bodies.

"Perception modifier might be a more elegant way of putting it; in that first instance, it quite literally changed how I perceived reality.

And it's able to do that because the effect it induces is so immersive, so comprehensive. Hence *immersive therapy*. Not *virtual reality medicine*. It's something more than medicine. To be made to feel, during a VR therapy session, that one no longer has any pain—this has consequences."

He stopped. "Do you have any experience with chronic pain? Any type of injury?"

"Old shoulder injury. From overhead lifting."

"Ah," Perera said. "How's the shoulder now?"

"Did some PT on it. Doing better. Just can't lift overhead anymore."

"Hm. Yes, overhead loading can be difficult over a certain age—"

"Can't lift with your ego anymore. Those tendons aren't getting any younger."

"I know what you mean," Perera said, looking down at himself, nodding like they'd established some vital rapport between them. "I've got a bit of the old bicep tendonitis, flares up every now and then—"

Girlie had the comforting sense of having a conversation by numbers, like talking to an NPC in a game—with fellow lifters you could trigger the same dialogue just by saying *shoulder injury*.

"Well, what I'm getting at is—you know how persistent those types of issues can be. They go away, then come back, and you end up, at best, essentially modifying your behavior *around* the injury. Not lifting overhead anymore, for example. But the immersion therapy seems to offer a different, deeper way of modifying behavior. Modifying, instead, the way your brain responds to pain. Injury-related pain is a little different from internal chronic pain, but the principle stands. How can the brain help us manage our own experiences of pain?"

"How did it help your—patients, clients," Girlie asked. "The ones with chronic stomach issues?"

"It's still quite difficult to pin down, exactly," Perera said. "I mean, in the early stages, I saw people's chronic anxiety improve in a single VR session, seen people stop smoking, cold turkey, after a single session, and keep *off* cigarettes for a little under a year, after which they started to report cravings, which abated with another session. A lot of it points to a kind of psychological relaxation, an easing of suffering, that is comparable in efficacy to some of the most abused opioids on the market. Without some of the obvious side effects. But most doctors will admit that there is still so much we simply don't know about our own bodies. Minds. Some of it indicates that, essentially, immersive therapy doesn't just work as a painkiller. It changes how you experience pain; or rather, changes you into someone who doesn't experience that particular pain."

For the first time he paused, and looked up, as if he expected Girlie to provide an answer.

Instead, she had a question. "Did you?"

"Did I?"

She tilted her head. "Answer the call of the void?"

Perera laughed sheepishly, running a hand over the wrinkles creasing his forehead. "Well, I cheated. Those VR headsets back then were bulky. And because it was bulky, it only half fit onto my face, so, well—I could sort of still see just a little tiny fraction of my office, just like the light out of the window here, since it was late afternoon, the light was low and coming in through the blinds. And because of that, it took me out of the immersion. And that was enough to help. To remind me, even for a second, that I wasn't really going to get hurt. I pushed my hands off the ledge and propelled myself feetfirst into freefall, plunging straight into death.

"When I took off the headset, I was standing up from my chair. All my muscles were rigid, like I was still falling, still waiting to hit the ground. But I also knew, somewhere, that I had jumped off Big Ben and survived.

"'Welcome back from the dead,' they said. We signed the papers to start working with Playground pretty much that day."

Perera sat down in the desk chair with a soft puff of air.

"It's—I didn't even realize, but it's—considering what happened later, it's a bit disturbing."

"What is?"

Perera looked up at her. "Well, with what happened with Edison Lau."

"Edison? The original founder of Playground?"

"Yes," Perera said. "He led the presentation, and he was—well, he was very convincing. He knew he had a revolutionary product on his hands. Not just product. Paradigm. That was clear.

"He kept talking about the revolution of virtual medicine. *Some people talk about alternative medicine. One day, we'll be able to prescribe alternative realities to people*, he said. I mean, the whole department ate it up. And me too. He was—he was the kind of person who made you believe in things."

"Was."

Perera frowned. "This may be indiscreet to say, but—it is in the public domain—he died, not long after Playground and L'Olifant merged, and Reeden entered the picture. They said he fell from the balcony of his flat."

Girlie didn't know what to say. She hadn't, actually, known that; had been trying to avoid googling Playground or—William, she admitted to herself now. She didn't know what to say; but she did, selfishly, know what she wanted to ask. "Who else was there for that first demonstration?"

Perera made a gesture with his hand, pointing to someone who was not there. "Edison led the presentation, but he had along with him his partner, a young man, I remember he still looked like a student, even though by then he must have graduated long before. That was William."

There was a piercing shock of pleasure, at being given so freely an answer she had already been anticipating.

Perera continued. "I heard William turned down the CEO position after Edison's—after Edison. I would've thought he'd have left by now. He's really the only day-one employee left in the company. Besides me, I suppose. It's all L'Olifant's people now, I hear. And, well, then the Reeden buyout—"

Now he gestured at Girlie, as if she represented the entire company in absentia. He looked somewhat chastened, all of a sudden.

"Though of course their involvement has meant—leaps and bounds," he course-corrected. "The possibilities really do seem to be—endless."

Girlie was aware she was having a feeling for another human being; thankfully, the feeling was pity. She marveled at it, looking at it from all facets like a newly found and as yet unrefined jewel, examining the size and weight and carats of her pity. She pitied the doctor, because he was clearly in an uncomfortable relationship with a company that he—like most people on the planet except perhaps the most brainwashed of boomer aunties and uncles—obviously viewed with, at best, queasy suspicion and a kind of resigned, ambient hatred. Sure, they were allowing troll farms to win presidencies for sons of dictators, carpet-bombing the mental health of children, carving at privacy laws like a too-small cake at the corporate potluck, but: the money. Without their financial backing and provision of resources, none of his research, none of these human advances, would be possible, at least not to this degree; not to this level of sophistication; not at this speed.

"I know it's only my first time," she said, smiling helpfully, "but so far I can say I'd leave a five-star review."

Perera smiled back at her, easy.

Then he said:

"Your file mentioned you very rarely made use of some of the wellness tools that Reeden's contractors made available for content moderators. Yoga classes, meditation workshops, that sort of thing. All at your disposal. But your record says the last yoga class you attended was the first one, over ten years ago."

Girlie felt saliva in her mouth, a knot in her throat. It would be too obvious if she swallowed now.

"That's right."

"Not a fan of yoga or meditation?"

"Not particularly."

"Hm," Perera said. "There have been studies that have shown that yoga and meditation can be contraindicated for people with CPTSD. It activates their fight or flight: the stillness, the poses, being trapped in space, told to listen to their breathing. Or even being physically corrected without consent, as by a yoga instructor."

All this he said with a calm, clinical lucidity, like bright sun moving through clear water. Girlie couldn't speak.

"Talk therapy, as well, has been found to be harmful in certain cases," Perera added evenly.

Suddenly, she realized he'd probably also clocked her from the beginning: hobbyist lifter, probably never pulled more than two times bodyweight and that had to have been years ago; fucked shoulder, heavier lower body, couldn't lift overhead anymore; stiffness in the body said she never stretched, rarely foam-rolled, didn't drink enough water. The kind of lifter who pushed and pulled until something broke. Deflects personal questions with borderline rude evasions; has a performatively officious, near-insubordinate nature, yet in the field displays extreme professional compliance to the point of compulsion. Wouldn't tap out of a chokehold; would rather pass out. Never been to Disneyland, never been in a forest. Had a panic attack in front of a tree. Went to therapy for two weeks after her father's death then ghosted the therapist after she'd recommended her a book by a Filipina American novelist, something something something three generations of Filipina women, saying, "I think this'll really help your healing." Left a class after the yoga instructor that first session a decade ago had corrected her form by standing behind her during downward dog, grasping both of Girlie's hips firmly in her hands, saying in a soft voice, "Like this."

Now Girlie saw that she, too, was a person who could be known, that her body had a dozen run-of-the-mill tells, that it had not been quiet. There was an impersonal, everyday kindness in Perera's expression she hadn't quite let herself see or believe at first, but she was starting to realize that was just her chronic condition talking. Not everywhere a spike to dodge, a boulder to clear. In some places, a redwood.

"It's promising, then, that we're making advances in the sector. Finding more inclusive alternatives. In any case, I'm grateful for your five stars," Perera said, with actual warmth in his voice. "Same time next week?"

· ·

At home that night, she finally did something she'd been resisting since coming back from that first job interview, weeks ago. She googled William.

First she let herself google the Playground device, saw Aditya's paywalled interviews for the *Financial Times*, even saw a mention of Playground on Aditya's semiabandoned utopian tech-bro Twitter account, which he hadn't posted on in years, since the whole caste-discrimination scandal. Privately, she'd sort of hoped that William would simply show up in the material of these searches, and she would have plausible deniability—she hadn't been searching for him, just searching in his vicinity, and there he was, by happenstance—but he wasn't mentioned in any of the articles.

Just endless interviews with the president of the L'Olifant parks, Maurice de Coligny, son of Jean-Jacques de Coligny, the original founder of the parks and a former cabinet member in both the d'Estaing and Chirac administrations, now a member of European Parliament. He'd originally been Parti Républicain before later going on to found his own political party in the mid-'90s, campaigning on a Eurosceptic conservative platform; the party's stronghold was particularly concentrated in Alsace, and their primary raison d'être was opposing the Islamicization of France, most notably by rejecting the possibility of Turkey entering the European Union as a member state. In the 1995 election, Coligny père had received a million votes; less than 5 percent overall. But Turkey never joined the European Union.

Their party's greatest like-minded political competitor, Rassemblement Nationale, formerly known as Front National, had just this past year won eighty-nine seats in Parliament. Pictures of Coligny père shaking the hand of Claudine Le Conte, Rassemblement Nationale's party leader, were all over the internet, because it was rumored he'd said to her, "Merci, madame la présidente," in a nod to their allied institutional ambitions.

Meanwhile L'Olifant, the theme park selling French history to the French, thrived. There were debates on French television about the conservative—neofascist, some declared—spin of the theme parks, but every L'Olifant YouTube video Girlie looked at online featured thousands of (moderated) comments penned by raving visitors from all over Europe who'd loved their experience and were more than happy to defend it fiercely from killjoy critique, top comment being: "Je suis sénégalaise, residente en France. Nous avons passé une journée a L'Olifant en famille et c'était génial. Il faut préserver la culture française coûte que coûte. Bravo, et j'éspère que du côté de l'Afrique des pareils projets soient aussi entrepris!!"

Now it was Coligny fils, current president, who was the one pictured in all of the park literature; a clean-shaven, blockjawed Frenchman in a red tie. Maurice and his father looked very similar: the same bone structure, with only the hair really setting them apart; sandy blonde versus thinning white.

But Maurice was noticeably more dynamic, more internationally minded than his father, Jean-Jacques, the articles remarked approvingly; for some years Maurice had worked closely with Samsung's strategy and innovation center in France, praising the values of Asian work culture, made friends with everyone from public officials to venture capitalists. Google even offered up a series of *Business Insider* pictures of Maurice posing next to the Chinese crypto CEO who lived in Paris and who had been sucking up to de Coligny and the French technocracy for years, calling France the new European financial hub of the future, saying things like "Knowledge is only worthwhile when it's shared," and who had recently been sued by investors and convicted for money laundering, serving just four months in prison, term nearing its close; de Coligny downplayed their friendship in subsequent interviews.

Featured in many of the articles Girlie found about the Playground acquisition were also photos of Reeden's own founder and CEO, Tim Reed, looking chronically indoors-pale and dissociative as usual; supposedly he was massively investing in the burgeoning hallucinogen industry.

In their few photos together, de Coligny and Reed looked comically mismatched: one square and proud as a superhero, the other wan and anxious as a starving poet. That the former was the European, and the latter the American, struck not a few clever listicle-journalists as ironic.

As far as Girlie could tell, there were only two photos of William that existed on the internet. One was a corporate portrait of him taken at the acquisition of Playground. WILLIAM CHEUNG, HEAD OF CONTENT MODERATION was printed beneath his crossed arms.

He was dressed in a pale-gray suit here, too, but it didn't fit quite as well as the suits of today. It was off the rack, polyester blend; not yet bespoke, not yet virgin wool. He looked much as he did now, his smile very faint, like he was replaying an inside joke to which the photographer had not been made privy.

Maybe he was shy about his teeth, Girlie thought. They were quite long. The telltale eyebags were there, eye-bagging; the lighting in the photo emphasized the depth of them. He looked—when she peered closer—exhausted.

The other was an uncredited, uncaptioned photo, and she couldn't be 100 percent sure it was him in the shot. It was a photo of young Edison Lau, for a profile about the promising young face of virtual reality medicine. The photograph was taken at Imperial College, the article said, surrounded by friends, smiling students, all unnamed.

Edison was handsome, in a more open, generous way; his skin tan and luminous, with a wide shining face, the same huge, toothy, double-dimpled smile in every photo of him, at every age.

In the corner of the photo was someone who might be a young William, only his profile visible, looking off to the side. His hair was longer, thick and floppy, with the '90s center part every other boy in the photo sported, curling slightly at the ends. He was wearing sunglasses, which obscured his eyebags, or maybe he didn't quite have them yet. His lips were thin, his cheeks red. She didn't know for sure if it was him. But—it was him.

In the article, Edison Lau was being touted as one of the most exciting young names changing the future of medicine in the United Kingdom, not to mention the world. "I think we're at the forefront of a watershed moment," Edison said in the article, sounding very young indeed. "Where everything we think and know about pain and healing is going to be reconsidered."

The article went on to describe the early clinical experiments: a low-income patient with depression who'd expressed fond memories of visiting Niagara Falls with a dead spouse, who was given a virtual Niagara Falls to visit; a former surfer with chronic pain who could choose between beaches in Fiji, Indonesia, and Thailand to relive his glory days; a trans woman whose suicidal ideations and dysphoria had been eased by the transformative freedom made possible by the newly discovered solace, and then limitless play, of being herself in their world; a former combat veteran who needed a virtual war zone, tailor-made to his memories, so that he could experience the very nightmares that plagued him at night, only in a controlled environment, with a reliable way out.

"One day we'll look back at the ways we dealt with PTSD like we look at Stone Age weapons," Edison was quoted as saying.

There were almost no articles about Edison's death. The ones that remained were brief, perfunctory. Former CEO of Playground found dead outside of his apartment building, no foul play suspected, once a hotshot in the virtual reality world. She could imagine the work that must have gone into scrubbing the story from Playground's history, from any of the search engine results; Reeden would have been thorough about their acquisitions.

Girlie looked at the more recent photo of William, the hard, lacquered smiling skin of him, the luminous gray tie, the featureless background. Too far away to see the mole at his lip, under his eye, the freckles under the bags.

Her cells felt like they were vibrating in secret, muffled pockets all over her; the base of her fingernails, the meat of her earlobes, the very tip of her tongue. He was just good-looking. That was it. She didn't know why she felt like someone was watching over her, seeing everything she was searching for: the great memory of the net, or all her dead in the next world, the ancestors she hadn't met and wouldn't even like, every invisible judge the age of information could summon forth, all giggling at her search history. She shut down the tab, made sure once more that she had been in incognito. Deleted all her browsing data for the day, just in case.

5

"The Only Known Pair of Matching Singing Bird Pistols, Attributed to Frères Rochat"

hen there was Girlie's first time being stabbed. Weeks in, they'd soft-launched, with the official launch happening at the end of February—culminating in a big launch party-cum-presentation happening at the Bellagio, which Girlie was still figuring out how to skip—but now the users weren't just programmed disruptions, employees just like her, doing a job, meant to train her in all the ugliest possibilities of crowd control, user submission. Now she was in the field, with civilians.

Most of her days were spent making easy rounds between the medieval landscapes and the tourist landscapes: the amphitheater, the lists, the castle, the museums. Her main beat consisted of the L'Olifant sites, then French and Italian tourism; contemporary (sanitized) Paris, sixties (sanitized) Rome.

A few times, early on, when she was just getting to know the space, she'd trial-moderated the main cyberpunk landscape: pan-Asian city, very *Blade Runner*, very *seedy underbelly of the world*, except that it was all a bit binary and juvenile, the whole seedy underbelly thing. The idea that crime, sexual danger, or even evil, was spatial: a question of surface and depths, heavens and hells, penthouses and basements. Instead of, as Girlie thought of some things in her life: merely another one of the internal components of a watch—mainsprings, balance wheels, regulators, escapements. The entire mechanism working together, to tell the time.

L'Olifant wasn't very good at sci-fi, really. You could tell the landscapes had been thrown together to placate a diverse set of test audiences, but there was no heart in it, the storylines imprecise and flat. The neon signs, the wet concrete, the men in two-tone Datejusts waving Berettas, the moody women, aloof and sad. They'd said a famous Asian director had consulted on the cityscape, but it was as a perfume commercial directed by an auteur: the point was to move units.

William told her it was possible to request a transfer if she found a landscape more amenable to her skills. She said she was fine where she was, in the Middle Ages. As far as she was concerned, the feudal era had never ended.

Most of the days were slow, felt easier, even, than the training sessions—certainly easier than her years on the moderator floor—with the worst disruptions being someone spamming the info chat box with smiley faces, or demands about where the armorer and the trapper were located that day (they changed location daily). A rape or two was usually on the agenda—there was so much frantic humping in virtual reality—but for the most part, the users seemed curious, enthusiastic, open to wonder, even helpful. People waited in line at the Musée d'Orsay, worked together to help a fallen villager from a marauding Viking (a planned interaction, like so many in the L'Olifant spaces that received rave early reviews on the Playground subreddit), notified each other of loot piles when they came across one (gold for purchasing cosmetic refinements to their avatars, hidden doors leading to secret bonus missions with Roman collaborators).

There was an unmistakable queer undercurrent to many of the interactions; people availing themselves of the benefit of experimenting with their avatars' many-gendered bodies, the everyday possibilities of imagining a coherent, unruly, sovereign self. Or, equally: the everyday possibility of imagining themselves ever-differing: changing their minds, shifting skins from one day to the next, each deviating self therefore at last being true, every time.

So when the user came up to her just outside the lists, dressed like one of the tournament competitors, chain-mail hauberk over his tunic, basinet helmet obscuring his face, she prepared herself to be humped, already ready to flag, mute, block, kick.

Instead, he pulled out a short single-handed sword from his belt and, without speaking, brought it two-handed toward her chest.

Stabbing wasn't one of the more common forms of violence in the Playground world; there wasn't any real feedback loop for it. You could put a knife in an avatar's body, sure, but unlike a video-game engine programmed for in-game combat, Playground only allowed for violence against specifically designated characters, within specifically designated sites. Combat was disabled entirely in Paris, Rome, all the tourism sites; it was the only time you could wear a Daytona in London and not risk being macheted over it. You could axe virtual Roman soldiers, Viking warriors, even French villagers if you'd sided with imperialists and marauders, but fellow users couldn't be targeted. This was to keep Playground a safe environment for all, the Playground copy said. PvE only. No PvP. Hence the recourse to humping and bouncing as a creative improvisation on rape.

The sword slashed at her untouchable clavicle, the plot armor of being a fellow user or content moderator protecting her quite thoroughly. She tilted her head, curious. The plot armor didn't, however, protect her from the look in his eyes behind the helmet, or the words he spoke, with a voice reedy and young and high: *Die, bitch. We'll take all of you down.*

He reared his sword back, brought it down on her again, frustrated, like trying to break through a force field. *You're one of them*, he was saying, not quite to her. *You're one of them.*

He tried her belly, then tried to grab for her hair—that, he managed; you could hold hair because there were hairdressing options in game, so hair-touching was one of the main rapey strategems.

He brought his hand up to her throat, blade held horizontally, taking the telltale posture of someone about to slit the aorta. She could feel the tension of her hair being pulled, right at the sensors at the edge of the mask and strap, felt the responding stiffness in her upper back.

Then he went still, arms up in the air, her hair clutched in his fist, now spilling out of its slackened hold, the light going out of his eyes. She stared at him for a moment longer, before he blinked out of existence.

Behind him, there was William. "Please, don't thank me," he said.

"I was going to kick him."

"I hope so, as it's your job," William said. "He just came to slit your throat? Out of nowhere?"

"No, he tried stabbing first."

"Oh, all right then," he said warmly, patient and polite, which was how she realized he was furious.

"He'd been talking—"

"Been—" A muscle in William's jaw ticked. "I just got here. How long was that going on for?"

"Not—" At the warning look on William's face, she changed direction. "A few minutes."

"A few—" Most moderators could kick a user within seconds of bad behavior. Girlie, for example, prided herself on the one-second block. Once a week, they even gamified it for the moderators; Girlie was top of the leaderboard. Not that she was keeping track. "And you were just—what—having a chat?"

"He said something to me," Girlie said, transmuting her defensiveness into pissiness, as per custom. "I got distracted. It happens."

"He did look gifted in the art of conversation," William said shortly. "What did he say?"

"I don't—it was hard to make out. Something—something about taking us all down. He—"

She grimaced, trying to decide whether or not to listen to her gut. "I think he was—trying to figure out who was a user and who wasn't. Or—who was a moderator, and who wasn't. He was trying to get around the PvP block. Maybe trying to install a mod."

William looked to the side, jaw still tight, thinking. A hand came up to rub at the bridge of his nose. In her mind, she saw him, William-in-the-real-world, somewhere in his office, rubbing at the nose of his mask. She could smell cigarette smoke, burning at her nostrils. Those were just the olfactory hallucinations.

"Right. That's not—there can be bad actors like that. Looking to smoke out the moderators." He let out a sigh. "I suppose they would get more creative."

"It felt—" Girlie paused. William shot a glance at her, hard. Then, indicated for her to continue with a twitch of his eyebrow. "It felt almost more than him just acting like one of the characters in the storyline. Like—that he was really treating me like I was one of the Vikings, or something. He was—" She second-guessed herself but said it anyway. "It felt like siege mentality. He was really protecting the castle."

"Right," William said. He let out a sharp gust of air from his nose. Then, to himself, a low: "Bloody hell."

He looked over at her, said brusquely: "Are you all right?" It came out of his mouth too fast. She saw that he hadn't had the time to cycle through the first, second, third thought, to give her the more measured, more calculated fourth thought, as usual. She was getting the first, greenest thought.

"I'm fine," she said. "It won't happen again. I'm sorry you had to intervene."

"What I'm here for," he said, after a moment. She could see his face trying to work out a closing kind of smile, his mouth buffering, not quite making it.

"It isn't," Girlie said, brusque herself. She wasn't buffering. "I don't need a babysitter. I'm on it. I'll know what to look for now. It won't happen again."

"Thank you," William said. He had a constipated look on his face. "Your work is—has been—exemplary. I don't want to give the impression otherwise."

"Thank you, I appreciate it, that means a lot."

"I mean it," William said, dismissing her out-of-office auto-reply. "You—"

He started counting off on his fingers. "Commendable speed in the field, extremely high rate of accuracy, far above-average recovery time. Calm under pressure."

He stopped, then said, carefully: "Longtime moderators are uncommon. Most leave. Get nightmares. Retention rate is low."

Girlie narrowed her eyes, drawbridge up. "You see a lot on the job. Yes."

"It's not work everyone can do. It's not work everyone understands. So I mean it, when I say I know a good moderator when I see one."

"Like Justice Stewart."

"Sorry?"

He wasn't American. "Never mind," Girlie said. "Old joke about knowing things when you see it."

"You mean *The Hound of the Baskervilles.*" At her blank look, he said, "Sherlock Holmes. 'I know what is good when I see it.'"

She smiled helplessly, then shook her head. "Never read it."

"Oh," William said, looking perturbed. "I just meant—you've been excellent. Which you know. You're—" She saw him wince, then school his face; saw him second-guessing himself, then saw him say it anyway.

"It's rare, what you can do," he said finally.

"Thank you, English," Girlie said. She didn't realize she was showing off, making up for not having read Sherlock Holmes, until she saw his face light up, some of the tension bleeding out of his shoulders. The tendons in his neck flexing, then relaxing—then flexing again.

That night, rewatching the scene on YouTube to verify, she saw that she'd gotten the Omar Sharif line wrong; should have said, *God be with you, English.* But even the wrong line had its own effect. He didn't look like anybody had called him English that way before.

• •

"Is there anything you'd like to learn?" Perera asked after a couple of hiking sessions. Perhaps he'd noticed that she was getting used to the forest scenario, had come to expect the level of relaxation she could get out of it; reading her biometric data like a well-thumbed pulp.

She knew there was a baseline of doctor-patient confidentiality that guided their sessions, but the conclusions drawn from the data itself belonged to Playground, and therefore Reeden, looking for the most downstreamable takeaways, to turn a user's problems into profitable solutions. Girlie had a sense of herself like thick black oil, being drawn up from the oozing heart of the earth, surging through the pistons of a pumpjack, some great thirsty bird, nodding and pecking, only to eventually be delivered, crude and whole, to the distilling tower, where she could be burned, boiled, and turned into something useful.

"Learn?"

"It's a great learning tool, the VR space—I wish I had practiced laparoscopic surgery through VR, when I was younger. Some people"—the other moderators during their own therapeutic offset sessions, she guessed—"use this opportunity to learn a new skill that might be difficult or inconvenient to learn in their daily lives. Learning a language with a personalized teacher, for example. Perhaps a new sport, or even an instrument. The virtual piano lessons, I've heard, are quite good."

"I haven't given it any thought. I—"

Then she stopped.

Perera saw this, perked up. "Yes?"

"Just one thing."

Perera nodded, folding his hands over each other in interest. It felt unbearably naked to say this. "I'd like to learn how to swim," she said at last.

"Of course," he said without missing a beat, like it was obvious.

"Well, I'm happy to say we have quite the selection of swimming instructors. Swimming—I'm sure you remember this from your avatar creation—is one of the more complex virtual experiences, just because of the water aspect. Though Playground's proprietary water sensory experience is superior to anything else on the market, obviously."

He tapped his chin, thoughtful. "Some of the swimming lessons are structured like your forest sessions, you seated there, entering the virtual landscape. Some of the swimming lessons are multisensorial, and can even include actually being in the pool—as you know, we have a twenty-four-hour rooftop pool and gym that's accessible to all Playground employees with your fob."

Girlie knew; she'd signed the disclosure form absolving Playground from any responsibility should she drown in the pool or drop a dumbbell on herself. Loyal to Barkada, she'd never set foot in the gym. "I don't think I need the multisensorial experience for now," she said.

"I think that's wise, especially for a beginner," Perera said. "In fact, why don't we just dip a toe in—if you'll forgive the pun. We can do something simpler; you remember I gave you the beach option, the first day? It's a good course to start with, and you'll be able to enter the water should you so choose. In the meantime, I'll prepare some swimming module options for you. Sound good?"

Girlie found herself sitting on a striped lounge chair on a white-sand beach, her knees bent slightly in front of her. A great kaleidoscopic pink and purple mandala floated in the air in front of her, moving forward and backward, getting larger and smaller according to her breathing rates; a soft, relaxing synth strings tune played in the background, its tempo designed to regulate her breathing.

She inhaled, and the flower bloomed, again and again, every

lotus-like petal uncurling into another; she exhaled, and the flower receded into the distance, like she was blowing its bud away. Thankfully there was no meditation voice actor taking her out of immersion by whispering wetly into her ear, so she could just enjoy the flower, blooming and retracting, blooming and retracting.

She did this again and again, for how long she could not remember, then heard herself saying aloud: "Can I go into the water now?"

Perera responded promptly. "Yes, of course you can. Feel free."

The sand sank beneath her footsteps; she felt the weight of herself, the gravity of her body; each step was heavy, just the way it felt to walk through sand on a beach. Not just the way it felt; the way it was. She approached the edge of the sea, momentarily unsure.

The waves came up but the tide was low, so she had to move forward if she wanted to feel them lap at her feet. The sand beneath her now was wet and compacted, with piles of seaweed strewn here or there. She stepped forward, then forward, until the water was at her ankles—warm water, Mediterranean maybe, and she walked herself forward, and forward, until her knees were wet, and her chest was wet, and the water began to take her, and she raised on her tiptoes to go as deep as she could while still touching the ground, but the wave pulled her in and she said abruptly: "Out."

The screen blinked, dimming. She took the headset off, left the gloves on. "How did that feel to you?" Perera asked.

"The beginning was very good, I felt—it was very relaxing."

"Your heart rate slowed down, your cognitive load went way down. Pupils were much less dilated. These were all signs of deep relaxation. At the end, as well, until maybe just the very end—did you feel uncomfortable then?"

"I remembered I don't know how to swim."

Perera nodded. "Makes sense. Why did you want to go in?"

"I don't know," Girlie said. "It just felt like I could. Until I remembered I couldn't."

"You could, though," Perera said. "Next time, you could remember that you can."

Girlie looked down at the headset and tried to solve that puzzle, untie that Gordian knot without the brute force of a sword: remembering that she could do something she knew she couldn't do.

When she looked up again, Perera looked almost apologetic; maybe he thought he'd been too flippant. "It might take a while though," he said accommodatingly.

There were so many options when it came to the swimming lessons. One session, she could be taught by former American Olympic gold medalists, and another session, switch to half the Swedish national team—Sweden was particularly involved in the VR swimming scene, since apparently one in five Swedish children reported a fear of the water; urgent, in a nation so abundant in lake and sea. By and large, the VR swimming scene was focused on phobia reduction in children.

The first lesson was simple: immersing the face and ears in water. Simple, or so Girlie thought, but it took her the entire session to stop sputtering and choking, dragging her head up from the water that wasn't drowning her, crying out "fuck," then "sorry, sorry, one more time" for what would not, demonstrably, be one more time.

"Before you move forward in your life as a swimmer," the Swedish national Olympian said in perfect West Coast English—they'd dubbed him, surely, he sounded too Californian for it to just be the sound of a Swedish person proficient in English, but the dubbing was imperceptibly done, the vocal posture having been so faithfully captured so that even the place where the Swede's tongue sat in his mouth was San Diegan—"you'll need to master the skill of putting your face in the water without water going up your nose, and without swallowing the water. This can be a very tricky thing to learn, so take your time, and be patient with yourself!"

That there was no water to go up Girlie's nose or down her throat, into her lungs, was something not apparently obvious to Girlie's mind, which was being a real fucking pill about the whole thing. She tried to use Perera's trick of finding some bit of the real world to peek at, to remind her terrorized head that there was no water waiting to drag her into Poseidon's great embrace, or whatever the hell it was that she was fearing—but the headset was on very, very securely.

Then, suddenly, she remembered what else Perera had said about jumping off Big Ben; what he'd called l'appel du vide. And if she did drown? And if she had thrown herself in front of the train at MacArthur Station? And if she did pull the plug? The answer to none of these questions seemed mysterious at all. At that, slowly but quite definitively, the terror in her body gave way to surrender. Girlie put her face in the water, prepared to die. Instead, she passed her first lesson.

..

All things considered, most of Girlie's days on the job were pretty easy. All things considered; past job experience in particular. But when a day went badly, it—well.

The afternoon had gone normally, all disruptions well within expected limits; she'd even seen a party of experienced users chop down an oak tree then turn its wood into basic bows and arrows for a bunch of unarmed newbies who hadn't yet figured out how to trigger the mission to get their first axe at the armorer's.

It was with this sturdy, pleased sense of the magnanimity of the world that Girlie happened upon William, on the shore of the river where the Viking longboats usually came out, bent down on one knee, talking to a woman in a damask gown with fluttering sleeves whose hair was mussed, covering her face. Then she turned, shaking her head, and Girlie recognized in the tear-covered, crumpled-up expression, a woman who'd been on the moderator floor with her at Reeden.

William was kneeling down, talking to the woman, but not touching her; the woman was shaking her head repeatedly, hands digging into the soft wet earth of the shoreline. William looked up sharply, had sensed Girlie looking at them. He didn't say anything, just looked at her. Thinking. Girlie diverted from her route before she knew she was doing it.

"Is everything—" She stopped; she could hear the woman's breathing. She was having an anxiety attack.

"She just started this week," William said tersely. "She's—a group of users who'd been playing on the Viking side stayed hidden on a longboat, came out and attacked her. I saw the attack and kicked them immediately; I don't think they—got to her. But she's—" He stopped, looking down at the woman.

"We have to get her out of here," Girlie said.

William nodded. "I've been trying. She won't log out. She's stuck. I don't want to override her login myself if—"

He didn't want to just kick her out of the world like a banned user, Girlie concluded, and have her wake up in her own office, behind a mask, still midattack, with no one around to help. Or worse: to wake up in her own office, in the real world, alone with a man, if William decided to log out himself and help her.

They exchanged glances, a silent negotiation. "I'll go to her office," Girlie said. "What's her name?"

"Jess," William said. "Acevedo."

Girlie knelt down. "Jess?" The woman barely looked in her direction, face ruddy, pupils blown. "Hi, honey," she said quietly. "Jess, do you know where you are?" The woman didn't register the question, looking down at the patches of shore; she was pulling out wet fescue by the handful, staring at it. "Jess, my name's Girlie. You're in the Playground virtual reality site. You were moderating today, and something difficult happened to you. I'm a moderator too. I'm here to help. Is that okay?"

"You can't," Jess said, and started crying again.

"I think I can a little bit," Girlie said. "Let's try—can you hear my breathing? In—out. Breathe with me, Jess. Follow this pattern."

"No—" Jess cried out, shaking her head, chucking her handfuls of grass and dirt to the ground, left and right, all around her.

Girlie didn't move. "You can. In—out," she said again. Finally she saw Jess's chest starting to move; pairing her breathing pattern to Girlie's.

"That's good," Girlie said. "You're doing really good." Girlie met William's eye over Jess's head. He was still kneeling, dressed in the Viking's tunic he usually wore at this site; matted fur mantle over his shoulders, wooden shield to the side, a long beard and a ponytail, tattoos under his eyes. One threadbare knee dipped in mud.

After they'd been breathing together for a while, Girlie asked: "Jess. Can you remember something for me? Is your office door locked?"

"—. No," Jess whispered, the first sign she was actually understanding them.

"Do you give me permission to come by and enter your office? So you can leave here? You won't be alone when you leave. I'll be there, in your office."

"—. Okay," Jess whispered, again.

Girlie looked up at William. "I'm going to take my mask off so I can see my way there," she told him. "I'll keep it on by my ear. Stay with her." She didn't wait for his response.

Girlie removed her mask, leaving it balanced on top of her head like a fencer; blinked a couple times, because she hadn't dimmed the world to ease herself out and had to visually adjust to her office. Stalking down the hallways, she surveyed each office, identical to hers, looking at the nameplates; saw Vuthy's, saw Robin's, saw names she didn't recognize, until finally she saw J. Acevedo.

She knocked on the door, then opened it—Jess was there, in her moderator's chair, same as hers, mask on, wearing big baggy jeans and a Thrasher sweatshirt, sleeves rolled up so Girlie could see the moderator's black suit sleeves gleaming down into her gloves. She was curled into a ball, hands twitching, pulling at something.

From the speaker in her own mask, Girlie could hear William's voice, taking over.

"Jess, it's William here again. Girlie's just going to your office now, she'll be with you soon. And I'm standing guard here. Nobody's going to hurt you. You're safe."

"No," Jess was saying; in the world, in the room.

"I'm here," Girlie said, and put her mask back on. Jess was pulling apart the blades of grass, staring.

"Jess? It's Girlie again. I'm in your office. I'll be there when you get out. Will you let us get you out of here?"

To William, she said, "Tell Perera I'm bringing her straight to his office."

"He's already waiting, his afternoon has been cleared," William replied. He hesitated. "And—yours."

"Jess?" Girlie asked. Jess lifted her eyes up to Girlie; she was very, very young.

"It wasn't what I thought," she said softly.

"I can see that, honey," Girlie said, steady. "Will you let us get you out of here?"

Jess started to cry again. Then she nodded, desperately. Girlie looked at William. He met her gaze, didn't hesitate; kicked them out.

When the screen went black, Girlie lifted her mask first. Jess was in front of her, struggling, having somehow decided to take the gloves off first, mask still on. Girlie didn't know whether or not she should touch her, so just said, aloud, so Jess would know she wasn't alone, "I'm right here. Take your time."

Finally Jess took the mask off, tugging the neck of the bodysuit down; her entire face was rash red, going down her throat into her chest, like she'd broken out in hives, and her eyes were watery and bloodshot. She finally seemed to register Girlie's presence; that she was there, in the world. "Hi," Girlie said. "You don't know me, but—"

"I know you," Jess said blurrily. "We worked together."

Girlie nodded. "Yes, of course. We were on the floor together. That's right. Just never talked before, I mean. Hi."

Jess was still blinking like her vision wasn't in focus yet. "Vuthy said the job was easy. I'm Maring's friend," she said dully.

Girlie stared back at her. That should've been on her file, she thought grimly; she never should've passed any of the assessments. "Yes," Girlie said, lying. "I remember."

"What happens now." Jess's voice was toneless.

"I'd like to bring you to Dr. Perera's for an offset session," Girlie said, "if that sounds all right to you. You've had a shock and you don't have to deal with it on your own. You've started those, right?"

"Only two," Jess mumbled. "Beach person."

Then she sniffled. "I was gonna—cello."

"Okay," Girlie said. "What I'm going to do is walk you to the elevators, then to Perera's office. I'm not sure I can stay in the room while you're having sessions, for privacy reasons, but I can stay just outside. After that, we're going to call an Uber and have you take the day off early, unless there's someone who can pick you up?"

"My brother. He's my—emergency contact."

"Okay," Girlie said. "We'll contact him while you're with Perera. Does that sound good? Or do you want to just go home right now?"

Jess hesitated. Then: "Dr. P first," she whispered. "Will—you'll stay outside the door?"

"That's right."

"—. Okay," Jess said, and Girlie stood, holding out an elbow, thinking maybe a hand would be too intimidating. Jess looked up at her, at the bend of Girlie's elbow, then took hold of it tightly, dragging herself up.

As Girlie waited outside of Perera's office, she realized only after she'd instinctively tugged her own turtleneck down that she was still in the bodysuit, mask still hanging around her neck, just jeans covering the legs of the suit, her normal boots on. She crossed her arms, feeling suddenly half naked. Then Girlie heard someone's footsteps jogging around the corner and tensed.

William, out of breath, appeared. Black dress shoes, gray slacks, white dress shirt, open at the neck, mask hanging. He skidded to a stop, cartoonish, at the corner. He'd tugged the neck of his bodysuit down as well, so she could see his throat bob when he caught sight of her.

She registered that this was perhaps the first time he was seeing her in the bodysuit. She registered also that she'd never seen him without a jacket on.

"She's—"

"In there now, with Perera," Girlie said. "Her brother's coming to pick her up. I'll wait until she's left with him."

William nodded. His feet seemed rooted in place.

"Right. Then I'll—"

Girlie nodded; she didn't want him to come any closer either. "Go. I got it from here."

To no one's surprise, Jess turned in her resignation the following day. Girlie shouldn't have been surprised that they were still hiring; that the original ten ronin, or however many there were, wouldn't have been enough for the world that was being built and populated right beneath their feet. But it was only confirmation of what William had said about moderation; not everyone was made for it.

After she watched Jess get driven away by a worried-looking older brother in a Hyundai Sonata, Girlie went back to her office, put the mask back on, returned to work. She had about an hour left on her route.

When she logged in, a pop-up appeared; a message from William, who probably thought she'd left for the day. **Your help was indispensable. Thank you.** She clicked out of the screen, too quickly.

But a tab asked: *Save this message to your archives?*

No, she went to respond, but then: *Yes*.

When she was back on her usual route, passing by the shoreline where the new Vikings were on the attack again, she saw William, standing there, staring at her. His knee was clean. On his face was a naked look of surprise, and then, underneath that, an unmissable easing—she knew, because she'd felt something ease in her just then, at the sight of him. Just a simple, sharp relief, a helpless lightness in her chest, a quick slicing strike to the trachea: that he was there. He nodded at her. She nodded back. Got to work.

The evening after Jess had gone home early, Girlie had been, un-derstandably, somewhat distracted by the entire turn of events, and thus ended her own shift in a state of mind amenable to something resembling self-care, so she'd decided to buy herself a steak at the twenty-four-hour Walmart—and just as she was internally debating as to whether or not she wanted it covered in garlic salt and sugar and grilled well done, per her father's recipe, or simply salted and peppered, medium rare, then slathered in steak sauce, her own adult-hood preference, just as she was ruminating over the minute details of how to turn bleeding meat into serviceable caloric energy, she ran, quite literally, into William.

William-in-the-world; William-in-the-parking-lot; the bony wall of William's turned back, around a corner, that she only just stopped herself from fully knocking over.

"Jesus, fuck, sorry, sorry," she said, backing up, one hand over her face, the other on her chest—her heart was racing, Jesus, she'd actu-ally been startled. When she looked up at him, his eyes were wide with shock at the brief impact; she'd startled him too. The second thing she noticed was that he was, improbably, sucking on a very small lollipop.

"Sor—hi. Hello," she said, wrongfooted by the absurd picture of him.

Not the picture of him. The him of him; here. The third thing she noticed, besides the lollipop, was that he looked—terrible.

"Long time no see," she joked weakly.

William smiled without joy around the candy; that angel of his-tory smiling, tilting his head toward her as if tipping an imaginary hat.

"It's been an age," he agreed, playing along. "Thank you again, for today."

He pulled the lollipop out of his mouth; grape. The center of his mouth was blackened. He saw her looking at it; he seemed to be looking at it for the first time himself, realizing what he was doing. Then he closed his eyes briefly, as if to ask God to give him a break.

"I'm trying to quit smoking," he explained.

"Ohhh," she said, with a tone that suggested that this explained everything; everything being his haggard face, the bags under his eyes, the red veins in them.

He raised his eyebrows. "*Ohhh?*"

"I keep smelling cigarette smoke," Girlie said. "Must have been you."

She didn't say that she'd been having those olfactory hallucinations since long before she met him. She also realized belatedly that she was admitting to having smelled him, which felt like a misstep.

"Possibly," he said. Then: "Smelling smoke? Isn't that—a sign of something. Serious?"

"Might be," Girlie shrugged. "I've had it checked out by my doctor. Supposed to just buy Flonase."

"Surely there must be other tests."

"Probably."

"That's reassuring," William said darkly. Girlie shrugged again. "Why don't you ask Perera, he might know a specialist in the area, or—"

"Do you think I'm incapable of getting a referral from my primary-care physician?" Girlie asked, very calmly.

William blanched. "No. Sorry—sorry."

Girlie waved it away, but now William was the one looking embarrassed. "That was over the line. You're right. I apologize."

"You're fine," Girlie said, even though it didn't look like he was.

William nodded, put the lollipop back in his mouth absently, then seemed to think better of it and took it out again. "Speaking of Perera," he said. "Your offset sessions. They've been. Adequate?"

"More than," Girlie said. "They're—fun. Good," she corrected, trying not to so obviously downplay the thing, thereby making her sound even more serious. "I'm learning how to swim," she said finally, trying again with the truth.

William nodded, still holding the lollipop, somewhat away from his body, awkwardly, before flipping the stem between his fingers to hold it more like a cigarette, his fingers relaxing naturally.

"He's been incredibly helpful," he said. "We're lucky he decided to stay with us after the acquisition. And that he agreed to come to the Las Vegas site, especially given how many years it all took to launch. It's nice to have someone—from the old days."

He tapped the lollipop, like he was absently ashing it. "Even at the beginning, some of his clients found they didn't need to renew their sessions for as long as a year. Sometimes ever."

William laughed, still mirthlessly. "Someone at Playground, right after the acquisition, reminded him that wasn't a very good business model."

Then he sat down hard, on a concrete stump, placed to delineate a parking space, to stop a car left in neutral from crashing into the building. He let out a little unconscious grunt of middle age.

Clients, he'd said deliberately; not patients. Girlie didn't know if that was for her benefit.

"I'm sure I speak for all the moderators when I say, we're very much enjoying our guinea pig privileges," she said, trying to sound overly formal, to match William's formality.

"I used to have guinea pigs," William said suddenly. "Very amiable animals. Surprisingly affectionate. One of mine used to drink out of my water glass as a child. My parents couldn't stand that."

Girlie stared at him. He wasn't looking at her. She'd realized it had gone dark all around them; she'd been one of the last to leave the building, her own session with Perera having gone longer than she'd anticipated, probably because of the whole Jess thing. Only a few cars were left in the parking lot. The tail end of January, the days still short, desert chill biting at her sore ears. There was a calm, sedate wrongness all around them: in the sharpness of the fluorescent lights shining down on their faces, in the alien feeling of a corporate park after hours. A feeling of the world gently coming apart at the seams. She didn't have to look up at the sky to know she wouldn't see a single star. "Because they weren't clean or something?"

"Because they were animals," William said. "Clean or not clean: does that matter, when you care for an animal? I've never thought so. It's your job to clean them."

"Well. If you loved a rat who carried bubonic plague—"

"Yes." William suddenly was staring up at her, more closely than he ever had, with a piercing attention in his eyes. "If you loved a rat who carried the bubonic plague. Then what?"

Girlie stared back at him. There seemed, suddenly, to be lightning at the ends of her hair, at the ends of her fingertips, at all the ends of her, all the places where she supposedly ended, and the supposed world surged up between them. The sensation she'd felt before, of reaching out to touch the tree, expecting nothing, and feeling instead its bark, now roared back at her, churning up from her blood, like water into an arena, flooding her vessels, rushing up against the underside of her skin, changing entirely the landscape around her.

She realized William, seated, had been leaning down, almost bowing over, so now she was taller than him, hovering over his frame. He was looking up, holding himself in the coolness of her shadow, thrown by the parking lot floodlights. His mouth dark, and wet.

She took a step toward him. "William," she said into the stillness that was not holy. "Are you okay?"

He stopped smiling. There you are, she thought, and she saw him as she'd seen him the first time they'd met, knowing without knowing that there'd been a tie, silk, crumpled in the cupholder of his car—why was she so sure of this—and almost took another step toward him, almost reached out with her hand; expecting to feel nothing, but knowing that there would be bark.

But then, just the way that she, in that first unreal sea, had known for a long unfettered moment that she could swim—until she remembered that she couldn't—she saw herself pull back; step back; safe word out. William's eyes crinkled again in a smile. He was gone.

"Right as rain," he said evenly, sounding like he was quoting something else she'd never seen, turning away from her. Like he couldn't look at her; like it hurt to try. Or: that was her, turning away. Couldn't look at him; hurt to try. "Get home safely now."

. .

If she were twenty-one, there would at least be the mercy of stupidity. At twenty-one, you could be green enough to play games, ignore your nose, mute your cells, unknow the signals, snub rarity. A young person didn't have to know what it meant, when your chemicals felt like they knew someone. But she wasn't twenty-one.

Girlie hadn't felt anything resembling true desire in so long, now the old reaper hit her like the first drink after a hundred sober years. Quick, silken, lethal. It was early onset, at least. She'd caught it at stage one. But worse than desire was the other feeling—which, again, if she were younger, she could pretend to be dumb to; she could pretend not to know what it meant.

Recognition. She recognized—something in him. No, that was prevaricating. She recognized him. Alien to alien. Attraction was one thing; free, silly, ancient. Evolutionary biopolitics. Recognition, though. Recognition was something else.

Girlie had been followed around by strangers in grocery stores, gyms, hiking trails, her whole life, so she knew what it looked like when a man stumbled on her hotness; how someone's face lit up when they saw hers; how people got stupid, or flustered, or mean, or solicitous; how they looked when they shot their shot, or gave up on the dream. Beauty made people stupid: neurologically, historically, globally. But recognition was—not that.

Squeezing her eyes against it in bed that night, willing her regular five milligrams of melatonin to kick in, still Girlie saw him—the look in his eyes, before he kicked her and Jess out; the look in his eyes, seeing her in the bodysuit; the look in his eyes when she'd shown up back in the field; the look in his eyes the first time he'd complimented her watch. She banned those visions, closed every single pop-up. But now it was him, early on, in the Villa Borghese, standing over the Medusa mosaic. Not the moment she'd realized he found her attractive too; the moment she was ready to dismiss him, indict him, the way she did any man who showed attraction to her. But the moment just after: his body closed entirely against it, gaze drilling down into the ground. He'd looked at her like he recognized her, too. And didn't like it much, either.

It was better, she thought, to admit the desire herself here, now, to more cleanly nip it right at the base of the bud, knife through the stem. To study the workup, sift through the likely dominant pathologies, before going in with the scalpel. To look at it, like a newly cut gem, observing its facets from all sides, before crushing it to powder. Better yet, to stop thinking about what it was *like*, and just face what it was.

She'd once overheard Rhea giving Vuthy a long lecture on crossbow injuries during his ballistics identification training: there'd been an increase in archery recreational clubs in certain regions of the United States, which meant modern videos to moderate of men accidentally shooting a crossbow bolt into their laughing friend's gut. *The arrow has killed more people than any other weapon in human history*, she remembered Rhea saying, with a very Rhea sort of maternal pride in something she'd had precious little to do with.

So Cupid's arrow had come for her. Fine. Not just a tangential graze, but: full penetration, no exit wound. She wasn't bleeding out, so no major organs hit; she wasn't paralyzed, so not lodged in bone; the trauma was just to the deep tissue. Untreated, untouched, it was buying her precious time; serving as tamponade. She wasn't going to bleed out, but she had to assess the damage, act quickly. Now the question was forensic: imminent infection, requiring removal. Now the question was method: to pull out, or to push through.

She chose extraction. All she had to do was feel for the arrowhead and shaft, grasping both at the same time so the arrowhead wouldn't break off inside her and fester, turn into something terminal. She had to probe around the wound, cutting through the skin surrounding the shaft, to give herself space to work.

Cut number one: boss-subordinate was not her particular parish of kink, she was a masc4masc service top at best. Cut number two: she wasn't a dumb kid, she knew right from wrong, she was an eldest daughter and an earth sign. Cut number three: she didn't need a sexual harassment lawsuit, on top of everything else. Cut number four, final one: she didn't have enough money to afford this feeling. Girlie's bloody fingers had a firm grip of the arrow now—the only thing left to do was pull.

6

Mona Fong Meets Carding Cruz

irlie was not, in the end, able to get out of the launch event extravaganza at the Bellagio.

Aditya had even come up to visit the Playground floor, laughing in his bright white Allbirds shoes, resplendent in his new bright-blue Reeden–Playground fleece, gesturing regally at all the moderators whom he'd gathered into the break room under the guise of a quick chat, saying, "I expect you all there!" then specifically pointing to her, to Robin, to Vuthy, to the moderators she hadn't even really met in person yet, though by now recognized as *guy with the big mace who's especially good at flagging and blocking streakers, fourth on the leaderboard* or *girl who permabanned a group of users who'd gotten around the hate crime restriction by wearing all white clothes and white baseball caps, went around calling everybody tiggers.*

Packed into the forty-five-thousand-square-foot Grand Ballroom of the Bellagio, Girlie hadn't been around this many people since her college graduation, when she'd been one of her graduating class's five University Medal finalists (the University Medal winner had been some EECS graduate who'd founded a charity start-up in Kenya;

was not, himself, Kenyan), the five of them in chairs on an elevated dais on the stage in the Greek Theater.

All Girlie could remember from that day was that when they'd handed her the diploma and the certificate verifying that she'd been one of the top five members of her graduating class, she'd grabbed the papers so quickly, hurrying off the stage, that the official photos Berkeley had sent back of her graduating moment just showed the dean staring after her, hand outstretched in the handshake she'd dropped like a hot iron, only the shadowed profile of her visible as she rushed away. That photo was the only googleable photo of her that existed on the internet; it was still up there, over fifteen years later.

The food was terrible, some type of skate wing. The people who'd chosen the chicken fricassee weren't faring much better, from the looks of it. The starter was tequila jelly and sustainable caviar bumps, everyone tittering as they licked the crook of their thumbs, precisely the kind of faux-decadent appetizer thought up by charisma vacuums who only ever partied with their employees. Girlie kept the mother-of-pearl spoon; nobody said she couldn't.

She was seated at a table with Aditya, Vuthy, Robin, and some of the other moderators. William was seated at a table with Perera and some men she vaguely recognized from the Playground corporate team, along with Reeden's Tim Reed and L'Olifant's Maurice de Coligny, each of the latter two with their individual right-hand man next to them, surrounded by an orbiting system of bodyguards and assistants and yes-men, each retinue obviously competing for who had the most people, who needed the most security, and therefore who was the most important person in the room.

They showed several video presentations on a gigantic screen, mostly Marvel-style trailers of the delights to be found in Playground, grand sweeping shots of the medieval castle, the jousts, the dead

Vikings, set to a soundtrack scored by the person they'd hired when they couldn't get Hans Zimmer. Perera spoke briefly about "the next stage in virtual reality medicine," but the mic was faulty during his speech, and so after giving up on shouting—his voice did not have a comfortably loud register—he sheepishly gestured toward the screen, introducing the prepared video presentation, called VR Therapy: Boldly Going Where No One Has Gone Before. Girlie smiled for him; even meant it, when she clapped.

Next up, a pair of venture capitalists who'd invested in L'Olifant's VR ambitions early on, Srinivasan and Chan, who clearly hadn't prepared a presentation, just riffed a lot about other VR companies getting "dunked on" by Playground and Reeden, the only companies actually willing to "go hard in the paint," and how the tech landscape had long understood that, in comparison to the advances being made by international companies like Playground or L'Olifant, America was in danger of becoming "the Microsoft of nations" if they didn't keep up with the times. One wore a rose-gold Nautilus, the other a Daytona; Girlie could see both on the large screen behind them, projecting their magnified bodies to the cheap seats.

Then Maurice de Coligny took the stage. He was wearing a dark-blue suit, crisp white shirt, and the same red tie he seemed to wear in all his official portraits, videos, and interviews; still clean-shaven, still ash blond—perhaps he dyed it—still smiling with very straight white teeth. His English was the confident, capable, somehow simultaneously obsequious and disdainful English of the French political elite (still she'd never heard a single French person of any class say the word idea instead of idée) but with a performative Asterix and Obelix accent that he seemed to be emphasizing on principle— the Sciences Po/London School of Economics in the voice only jumped out from time to time—which then made him speak in a strangely staccato pattern, as if every clause was being frisked before it left his mouth. The result of this peculiar rhythm was that everyone, especially the monolingual Americans in the room, had to lean in to understand what the hell he was saying.

"In 1989, my father came up with an idée," de Coligny began, surveying the audience in the Grand Ballroom. "What if you could build a theme park that didn't have one single ride?"

He held up his right index finger. "What if, instead of the commercialism and cheap thrills of other, more famous theme parks, you could imagine a different way to connect with visitors—a different way to connect with ourselves, and our history?

"My father, despite his very busy career as a politician and diplomat, has for a very long time been a passionate lover of history. He taught myself, my two brothers, and my sister our family's entire genealogical tree before we learned how to ride a bike. And seeing the excitement we had over these stories—which were about our own past—he had the realization that *our own history*, that is to say, *French history*, was just as exciting, just as thrilling, just as deeply moving, as anything made by a cartoon mouse—no, I'm joking, please! I don't want to offend my very generous American hosts!" He laughed, with his endless rows of white horse teeth; the rapt audience laughed with him.

"Two and a half million unique visitors a year," he continued. "We became, very quickly, the second-most popular theme park in Europe, after—well, after the one occupied by a certain mouse. We were very proud of our accomplishments. We didn't offer people roller coasters, or cotton candy, or plastic toys to be thrown away in six months. We offered something different. We considered ourselves, at heart, storytellers.

"This is why I said *lover of history*, and not historian. You know,

historian is a very dry term, very academic. My father was never academic when he told us our family history: he was telling us a grand
epic, with heroes, villains, intrigues, blood, tears. We were giving
people an opportunity to connect with a glory bigger than themselves, to connect with a sensory experience that spoke not just to
their minds, not even just to their bodies, but to their souls. That
was who our true audience was, my father said. The soul of France.
L'âme ancienne de la France. Which, he felt, was a soul in danger of
disappearance; a soul in need of revival and renewal.

"And it was when I took my father's place at L'Olifant, after his
very much deserved retirement, that we began to dream even bigger," de Coligny said, starting, now, to pace down the stage, each
move carefully choreographed. "We successfully expanded in Spain,
with a thirty-hectare site in Toledo. Now in Spain, you can go on a
voyage with Christophe Colomb or follow along with the adven-
tures of El Cid! Finally, we successfully expanded to China, with our
Hero's Saga site in Shanghai, still expanding: a two-hour live-action
show, with the greatest actors and dancers in China, over forty thousand square feet of performance space. Our total investment in the
heritage of the Xuhui district in Shanghai has been over seventy-six
million euros.

"Evidently, for us, the pandemic was a challenge, like everyone
in the world," he continued. "At the time, we had two options: we
could either be paralyzed by this crisis, or we could see it as an opportunity. We could imagine a way of bringing the magic of L'Olifant
to the world, a way beyond countries, beyond even the physical.
How to not only bring visitors into *our* world—but how to bring *our*
world, our vision, to the people. In their phones, in their homes, and
most importantly, in their hearts and minds."

Now he held his hand out, palm up, gesturing toward the table with William and Perera and Reed. "And this, this, is when we first encountered the brilliant minds at Playground and Reeden." He put his hands together in a sort of gesturing prayer, the tips of his fingers pointing sharply at the table.

"Now, our joint future looks brighter than ever. Virtual reality, the true next frontier, not just in entertainment, not just in health care, not just in social media, not even just in technology, but in the most important, most ancient of all things: storytelling. Together with Playground, and with the exciting support of Reeden, we are truly at the *avant-garde* of a global revolution.

"And yet, at the heart of all this, is still the belief my father held dear: that no matter the medium, it is all about how you take the hand of the visitor: to bring them deeply into the story you want to tell, to connect with them and make them connect with you," de Coligny intoned.

"For those of you who don't know French, *l'olifant* is the name for a horn—that's why the previous English name for our parks is Hero's Horn. It is an instrument from a French epic called *La Chanson de Roland*—which, if you want to know more about such epics, just go to our parks, we're open nine a.m. to nine p.m. in France, Spain, and China, twenty-four hours a day in Playground!"—he laughed, the crowd laughing with him again; he had them in the palm of his hand—"and this instrument is used by a hero, named Roland, to call for support from his fellow soldiers during a very great, very important war.

"Because of his pride, Roland does not want to blow the horn until it is too late, despite his very wise friend, Olivier, urging him to call for help. It is only when many of his fellow men have died that Roland realizes he must blow the horn.

"For us, *l'olifant* is the call of a very important story—and, this time, we do not want to be too late. We want everyone to hear the call. Merci beaucoup."

Around Girlie, the audience broke into applause, with some of the tables—notably a French contingent, a Spanish contingent, a mainland Chinese contingent—even calling out, with hoots, air punches (how much coke was at this thing?), and cheers. Girlie touched her hands together without creating enough impact to make a sound, just enough motion to avoid drawing attention at the table for being the only one not clapping. Her eyes were fixed on William; was he going to have to follow that? He wasn't moving. She couldn't see his expression, just the very still back of his head, half hidden by a bodyguard: unmoving, his hands folded in his lap, out of sight.

"How fucking inspiring was *that?*" Aditya was saying, as everyone else ordered or refused the pots of espresso being offered to them by grad student servers in starched shirts and bow ties, black aprons. "I feel *hyped!*"

Girlie wondered how long she had to stay to log the requisite team-building points before she could sneak out. Maybe when the much-publicized mini concert started—reportedly featuring one of those not-quite-so-young pop goddesses who'd sung empowerment anthems for Gaddafi and Bezos—and everyone was distracted on the dance floor.

The warmup DJ had started, playing listless Top 40 Spotify pop, but most of the people were still seated, except for the crowd milling around a chocolate fountain in the shape of the Bellagio fountains, spread out over one enormous table to the side. That was her transition spot. Good enough to use as a lobby.

She waited for a few minutes, bopping her head vacantly, finishing the last of her lemon cake. Then got up, nodding toward no one in particular, saying, "I'm just—"

As she got up, she saw, out of the very corner of her eye, that Vuthy's hand was in Aditya's, under the table. She blinked, thinking she was just seeing things, but—they were, in fact, holding hands, Aditya's thumb stroking Vuthy's.

Then Aditya pulled his hand away quickly, Vuthy's hand dropping. She glanced at Aditya, but he hadn't seen her looking at him; he was staring resolutely into his own untouched cake, having been spooked by something that wasn't her, maybe just the universe at large.

Vuthy's expression was soft—but that was just him, Vuthy was a soft person—or, she didn't actually know Vuthy all that well, he also seemed to her a ruthless social climber, the kind of person who could play a stabbing video, throw up pizza into a wastebasket, finish his presentation, nail the job.

Girlie shook her head, making an executive decision to ignore what she'd seen. Made her way to the chocolate fountain, trying to muscle her way past the apparent blockade of dessert fiends waiting to dip their bananas and waffles in the ribbons of syrup, white, dark, milk. She was loading her plate with pretzels, dipping them in milk chocolate, still distracted by what she was actively ignoring having seen—she'd really seen it, hadn't she; it wouldn't be something her mind would just invent—when she heard, Jesus actual Christ, fucking Maribel, saying: "Ate?"

· ·

If one was the type of person—the only sensible type of person, in Girlie's view—who separated out with martial discipline the distinct, incoherent parts of one's life, so that work colleagues never had to meet family members, and family members only rarely had to meet friends, and childhood friends rarely had to meet adulthood friends, and so on, and so forth—any unexpected collision of those parts was the stuff of unmitigated disaster, as with any clash of worlds.

Maribel was standing behind one of the chocolate fountains, dressed like the rest of the servers in a white starched shirt and bow tie, black apron, directing people on how to dip their bits of pineapple into the stream.

Or she had been; now she was staring at Girlie, eyes wide in shock, a helpless smile already forming on her face, so happy to see her, like a kindergartner finally being picked up at the end of the long school day.

Girlie, for her part, was not fucking smiling. "What the fuck are you doing here?"

Maribel held her hands up. "Somebody this morning texted me about a server dropping out of the event at the ballroom, and could I come in. I didn't even know it was a Playground thing!"

Now Maribel looked upset that Girlie was upset, which was just what Girlie needed. "I told you I would try to work more days," she added, wilting.

"Oh my god, who's *this*?"

Aditya was behind her now, with Vuthy and Robin and—Christ—William, all of them with their little plates and their little bananas and their little strawberries and their little pretzels. "Is this a friend of yours?" Aditya asked. Then grinned. "More than a friend?" Girlie could not physically prevent her eyeballs from darting to William's face at that line, which was now studiously blank.

"This is my cousin," Girlie said, ripping the Band-Aid off. "Maribel.

Maribel, these are some of the people who work with me. This is Aditya, Vuthy, Robin, and—William."

Maribel waved, beaming. "Hi! I'd shake your hand, but, you know. Food service. It's so nice to meet you! I've heard lots about you," she added, which was empirically untrue.

"*Wow*, how awesome to get a peek behind the curtain," Aditya said. "Your cousin's so private. I thought maybe she was raised by wolves."

Maribel giggled. She was dead to Girlie. "We think the same, sometimes!"

"So you work here?" Vuthy asked, politely holding out his strawberry toward a waterfall of chocolate. *Don't say where you work don't say where you work don't say where you work.* "Oh, no, I'm a bartender over at Dram," Maribel chirped. "Right by here! So still *in* the Bellagio but not *here here*, not in catering. I just took this job to help raise some money for my thirtieth birthday party—"

"Oh, happy birthday," Aditya and Vuthy said in union, which was making Girlie realize things she hadn't realized before, namely 1) they were fucking, and 2) they'd been fucking for a long time. Her brain felt like it was sliding out of her ears. Robin wasn't saying anything, just quietly holding his sliced kiwi under a stream of white chocolate. Girlie had never thought more highly of a single human being ever in her life.

Maribel blushed. "Haha, not yet, not yet, but—" Then she lit up. Girlie had a prey animal's sense of imminent disaster, just the fine hairs at the back of her neck, telling her danger approached.

"Oh my god, you guys are more than welcome to come! It would be so nice to have some of your coworkers there." This, she directed to Girlie, as if they were still family.

"Oh, awesome!" Aditya said, shoving a chocolate-covered biscotti slice in his mouth and crunching down on it like bone. "For sure, for sure, for sure, we'll be there!"

"It's in a couple weeks, March fifteenth! Starts at six p.m., at Rocky's, downtown," Maribel said, smiling with celestial munificence.

Aditya whistled in approval. *"Love* that place! *Love* that guy!" He said this to no one in particular, not to Maribel, not to Girlie; just declaiming to the universe, so the universe could keep tabs on just what poor soul Aditya did or did not love.

"It's so nice of you to invite us," Vuthy said. He and Maribel must have been around the same age. They had the same dewy beatific look, that luminous, soft-skinned, trusting gaze of people who believed the best in others because, at heart, they wanted to believe the best of themselves. Innocent people were capable of anything, Girlie thought again, murderously.

Now she dared a look at William. He was already looking at her. The sense of her own body, here, her body-in-the-world, her body in the Grand Ballroom at the Bellagio, standing next to her baby cousin and eyes locked with—her *boss,* Jesus—was time dilating. She closed her eyes for just a nanosecond, and when she opened them, William was still looking at her, trying a smile of commiseration. It wasn't exactly pity on his face—if it had been pity, Girlie would have sunk into the ground on the spot—but something like powerlessness; like he, too, couldn't believe they were in this moment and couldn't do anything to stop it either. Couldn't just kick her out of the world, this time.

On the plate, all his fruit was still bare. "Are you going to dip those?" she lashed out.

William looked down at his plate, like he'd just remembered it existed.

"Yes," he said. "Thank you."

Now William approached Maribel. "It's lovely to meet you," he said, careful and gracious. "And very kind of you to invite us. Unfortunately," he added, slowly covering his strawberry slice in milk chocolate, "I don't think I'll be able to come."

"Oh, no!" Maribel said, with more feeling than was justified, for someone she'd known for twenty seconds. "You're busy that night?"

Girlie knew what it looked like when someone was considering a lie. "No," William said, halting; Girlie also knew what it looked like when someone was choosing to tell the truth, and was unhappy about it.

"Don't say you can't come because you're coworkers!" Maribel interrupted. "We've got people from all over coming, coworkers, old friends from the Bay, we're all family here—" If that undiagnosed stroke wanted to come and take her, now was the time, Girlie thought, pinging any unoccupied gods within range.

"No, no, it's just—"

Now William was coloring, high and vicious on his cheeks, visible even in the dim light of the ballroom.

"I have a senior dog at home, and I don't like to leave her alone in the evenings," he said at last.

There were too many things in that sentence to process. Not least of all the fact that Girlie saw Maribel, wide-eyed, in live time, internally moving William from the category "Girlie's handsome polite boss with the sexy accent" to "Extremely hot dog dad Girlie happens to work with, no power dynamics registered!!!" Girlie—unkindly, and with a great deal of admiration—told herself that William was probably lying, which compelled *her* to internally move William from "decent, somewhat inscrutable boss whose hotness level was never to be revisited in any capacity" to "the kind of person who would make up an imaginary dog to avoid an uncomfortable social situation, and therefore: kin."

"Oh, *god*, I love that," Maribel said. "Is she alone right now?"

"Well—no—she—"

William looked like he wanted to have a stroke of his own. He looked at Girlie briefly, then looked back down at his plate, all the fruit chocolate-enrobed, no more tasks to fulfill.

"During the day she goes to her senior doggy daycare. There's a nice woman who—she runs it out of her home—it's—sort of a retirement home for senior dogs. All the dogs are vetted, because— they can get—in their old age, they can get a bit—stroppy, so. She enjoys it there. But she really prefers to be around people. Well: person. Me. She can get a bit depressed if I'm not around in the evenings or if I have to kennel her at the daycare, so I don't like to leave her alone when I can help it."

Girlie wasn't sure she'd ever heard him speak this long about himself, and certainly never addressed to a sliced banana.

Maribel was doing the Pixar eyes. "But you know, the restaurant— the place we reserved"—*I* reserved, Girlie thought sourly—"it's an outdoor patio! So it's open-air, totally dog friendly—"

"You don't know if it's dog friendly," Girlie said.

"All outdoor patios in restaurants are dog friendly," Maribel informed Girlie with great grave patience, looking to William for corroboration; he half nodded, saying, "Most, it depends," shooting a glance that almost looked like apology to Girlie.

"And Avery's friend Sarah and her wife are bringing *their* little dogs, I'm sure of it, they don't go anywhere without them. So there's already gonna be nice dogs there!" Girlie had met those dogs; they were not nice.

"She's a larger dog," William warned.

"Oh my god! What kind?" Maribel asked, helping a lady who'd been waiting for too long with her little baguette slices.

"German shepherd," William said, like he was giving up information under torture.

"Awwwwwww," Maribel and Vuthy said at the same time. Aditya looked mildly disturbed by this revelation; perhaps he thought that William didn't seem like the kind of man to own a German shepherd, which shifted something in whatever internecine sigma male competition was going on among upper management, which William was clearly winning, by virtue of being utterly oblivious to it.

Girlie nearly dumped her chocolate-covered pretzels to the ground with the force of her fingers squeezing the rim of the plate in impotent rage. "You should still call the restaurant to make sure—"

"What are they going to do, turn away a fifty-person bill?"

"The capacity for the space is thirty-four," Girlie murmured, life force draining.

She turned to William finally. The word she'd give for the expression on his face was: *shy.* Jesus—Christ.

"Of course, you're—" Girlie was biting her words out, then faltered, seeing the flash of a look on William's face, unnameable.

"You're welcome to come," she finished finally.

"Oh—well. Thank you," William said, mercifully directing this at Maribel so Girlie didn't have to hold his gaze for long. "It's such a kind offer. Truly. I'll think about it."

Maribel nodded. "We'll expect you there! You guys too," she said, pointing at Aditya and Vuthy and Robin, who was still Girlie's current favorite person in the world, for having not said a single fucking thing. This guy had cousins. "I better—" Maribel gestured toward the crush of people waiting behind them, being helped by the other servers, who'd been shooting Maribel irritated looks for the past fifteen minutes. She was going to be fired before the end of her shift.

"Okay, bye forever," Girlie said.

"Huh?" Maribel asked, looking down at some guy's mini chocolate chip cookie.

"See you later," Girlie said. Then:

"I'm really sorry," Girlie rushed out to William as they walked away. "You don't have to—obviously—she's just like that, she's like that with everybody, she's too friendly, but you don't have to feel obligated at all—"

He held up his right hand, balancing the plate on the open palm of his left hand.

"She's very kind," William said. "Tell Maribel thank you again for the invitation."

Then he stopped trying to smile with his mouth, his eyes still settled on her.

"It—you don't look that much alike, for cousins."

"No," Girlie said.

"You're—shorter," he said, a little stupidly.

"William! Aditya!" Someone Girlie recognized as a suit at the table with Reed and de Coligny and Srinivasan and Chan was gesturing at the two of them, beckoning them over. Aditya brightened at this summoning, while William went very still.

"I'll just—" he said. "Sure, sure, go," Girlie said.

She watched him walk away from her, watched him approach the table and its perimeter of guards, hold himself just slightly apart. Maurice de Coligny walked directly up to him, all his straight teeth on show, hand outstretched. He had to take hold of William's hand himself; William hadn't reached out for the handshake, still balancing his plate of chocolate-covered fruit with the other. Maurice grasped

William's hand with both hands, shaking it firmly, one hand sliding up to William's forearm, not in intimacy but complicity; a warrior's clasp, lord to vassal.

Maurice's face was radiating confidence and certainty—he seemed aggressively attuned to the value of his own handsomeness, making sure it could be seen from all angles. The way he saw through the crowd, the way he moved in the world—or rather, how he moved the world out of his way, pushing its mass aside so he could stride forward unencumbered—gave Girlie the dulling sensation of being an NPC, blandly navigating through waypoints along her route, three seconds away from getting sniped in the head because she was blocking the road during someone's main storyline quest. It was how she usually felt during senior management visits; until.

William's back was turned to her; she couldn't see what his face radiated. Someone started taking photos of them with a fancy-looking DSLR; a machine-gun sound of flash-flash-flash.

Girlie saw her narrow avenue of escape opening, and hurried toward it, making her way to the exit. An Asian woman in a burgundy power suit, not that much older than Girlie, upon seeing her walking past, raised an empty champagne glass toward her expectantly. Then, upon realizing that she wasn't a caterwaiter, the woman pretended that she'd just been waving, "Oh, hi—sorry—you looked like my friend! Ha!"

Then, right before Girlie reached freedom:

"Whoa, whoa, whoa—" Fuck. Girlie briefly considered making a run for it, then turned around to face Aditya.

"You're not going yet, are you? The concert wasn't canceled, that was just a rumor! Twitter cancellation isn't a real thing."

"I'm just going for a smoke."

Aditya frowned in what Girlie realized, to her dismay, was something like brotherly disapproval. "You didn't smoke before."

"Uh," Girlie said. "Just fell off the wagon."

Aditya stepped forward. There was a cloud of importance gathering around him, an austere gravity Girlie hadn't ever felt from him before. Only out of pride did she not step back.

"Look," Aditya said, patting the vape that was in his suit's inner pocket. "Take it from me. If you managed to quit, stick with it. I've tried everything. I've got it down to one cartridge every three weeks, but I'm trapped, man."

He shook his head. "How'd you quit the first time? Patch? William's doing the lollipops, lozenges. I'm thinking of going hypnosis."

"Cold turkey," Girlie said.

Aditya whistled. "Man. You're a grown-up, you do what you want. But if I could quit cold turkey, I'd keep it up. It's ugly business, bro."

Girlie stared at him, the wholesale American vision of him: ducked a class-action discrimination lawsuit, fucking a younger subordinate, concerned about her smoking. "Thank you," she said tightly. "I appreciate that."

Aditya clapped a hand on her shoulder, shaking it a little. "You got this," he said, with feeling.

··

Girlie made her way out of the Bellagio, facing the fountains. The sun was starting to set, and the water in the lake was still, placid.

She had the urge to buy a pack of cigarettes, just to make her alibi airtight, but that was serial killer behavior. She was too distracted to remember not to be an uncertain woman in public, so two white guys in Yeezys passed her on their way in, said, *Oh, hi beautiful*, then when she pulled her jacket around her tighter and turned away, digging for her phone, *Okay then, bitch.* She was trying to decide whether or not she should just swallow the cost and take an Uber home; she couldn't face the bus right now.

She looked at her phone; it was a brick. The thing was four years old, but in a self-defeating protest against design obsolescence, she'd been refusing to buy a new one. Now she wished she'd just gone to Best Buy, like Avery'd been telling her to do for two years. Then: everything in her stopped.

There was a man coming out of the Bellagio, just to the right of her. She couldn't even quite see his face, just his moving profile. Caucasian, average height, brown hair, a little paunch, rounded shoulders, between forty and fifty.

She froze in place. Her ears were ringing; nearby, the sound of a car sliding up to the valet station, its horn beeping brightly in hello, sounded as if it were coming at her underwater, through a copper diving helmet.

The man was moving, crossing in front of her, past the guardian lions, toward the footpath on Bellagio Drive where tourists and hotel guests were walking, to get a better view of the fountain show, which—she wanted to look at her watch, but couldn't bear to take her eyes away—was likely scheduled to start soon, if the crowd gathering was any indication. She started following him.

As they walked, twenty or so people between them, she kept her eyes trained on him, tried to note what he was wearing, anything identifying in case she lost him, blue sports jacket, khaki pants, a polo shirt, no hat so his hair was visible, it could be anyone, there were at least five other white guys dressed the same on the footpath.

In the distance she saw the Eiffel Tower, the giant hot-air ballon of the Paris hotel; there were too many people on the path. More than once, she had to dart out onto the strip of green turf, then the street, around the Italianate street lamps and huge terra-cotta planters meant to give a continental feel. Trying to get back onto the path, keep him centered in her field of vision, she ended up jostling a tourist couple, murmuring, "Sorry," the woman giving her a dirty look.

The fountain show began. The man had a phone lifted to his ear now; she still hadn't seen his full face. But then, she'd never really seen his full face to begin with.

The man was looking around, standing on his tiptoes, then plugging his other ear when the fountain jets exploded to the music. He was looking for somebody. The shape of his forearms, the curve of his belly underneath his shirt, how it went into his hipline. A girl's braid, wrapped up in his fist, the angry wet tip of his circumcised dick.

But now the forearms looked too thick; the torso too long; the hair too dark brown, not chestnut, no gray in it. It wasn't him. Then he turned again, and—it was him. It might be him.

The man was still on his phone, looking around, starting to look a bit concerned. Then, he started waving, his fingers stretching as high as he could. Girlie couldn't see the person, or people, he was waving at. She stood on her own tiptoes, trying to get a better look. She started moving forward again, but the crowd was denser here, where there was a full-on view of the fountains.

She was going to lose him. She was aware that she was holding her breath, that sweat was running down her temple. It was Vegas, it was just hot; no, it was late winter, it was cold; she was mistaken; it was him; she didn't know.

Then she heard it: William's voice. Calling her by the wrong name—cutting through the deep water and pulling her to the surface.

"Ms. Delmundo?"

She stopped at the sound of him; didn't turn around. The man was still in her sights. William came up to her: once again knowing not to come at her from behind, but the side.

When she didn't acknowledge his arrival, William moved to stand in front of her. His body half blotted out the view of the man. William was very tall, she thought numbly.

"Hey," he said sharply. "Is everything all right?"

She could push past him, keep going, maybe see what was at the end of the road this time. Instead: she gathered up her gaze, like deadlifting a heavy weight. Held it for a long blighted moment, that might have lasted forever. Then set it down.

She turned to William. "I'm fine."

"Where were you—were you following someone?"

"I thought I saw somebody."

"Someone you know?" William's face was blank again, with a neutral sort of pleasantness on it.

Girlie could lie. She should. She didn't. "I don't know them."

Now William's eyebrows came together. "You thought you saw someone you don't know," he repeated slowly.

Girlie looked back at where the man had once been; now, gone. She kept her eyes on that place; the hole in the world where he'd disappeared, again.

"Someone I've moderated," she said.

She felt something dawn on William's face, even though she still couldn't bear to look directly at him. Girlie continued:

"There's no way for me to be sure. I don't know. It happens some-times."

William was still staring at her. The line between his eyebrows; deep. "Hate crime ban?"

She met his gaze now.

"—. No," she said. They both knew her old specialty.

William turned very quickly on his feet, posture stiff. "What was he wearing. Maybe there's—"

"He's gone," she said, tired. "It was my imagination. I never even saw his face. Not before either."

William didn't turn back around, still scanning the crowd. "Hat? What color hair?"

"Drop it," she snapped. "It was my imagination."

William still didn't turn around. "'It happens,' you said."

Now he turned, but just his head, not looking at her, gaze angled downward. "How often?"

"Rarely."

"How often."

She looked away. "Couple of times a year."

"And how long has that been happening?"

Again she could lie; should; didn't. "Since the beginning," she said.

William whirled around then, aghast. "Since the—"

"It was more often at the start. Less, now."

"That's—" The lines were gone from his forehead, face slack with shock. He looked—young. Innocent. "Unacceptable."

"It's extremely acceptable," Girlie said. "Proof being: I've ac-cepted it."

She looked down at his hands, and realized they were clenching around something; her handbag. A brown vintage Hermès Gao, little-known and undervalued early 2000s model (leather: Chèvre / cadena:

handmade Touareg silver / source: Japanese eBay). He saw her looking down at it.

"Aditya said you'd gone out for a smoke. He was very—worried about you," William said. "I assumed you'd just left. But your bag was still here, so I thought you'd—. I thought I might still catch you."

Girlie nodded, held out her hand for the bag; he didn't move. "I forgot it. Thanks."

"Can I—"

Girlie shook her head at the beginning of his question, which had no real ending. Can I: help, change things, make it better, make a difference. There was only one answer to be given, from this partic-ular paper fortune-teller. A child's game; an adult's answer.

"No," she said.

She took the bag out of his hands; he released its strap at the slightest pressure.

"Good job on the launch today," she said finally. "You did great."

William nodded, face still blank. "On a scale of one to total fas-cist, how did you find Maurice."

"Very Reichstag-core."

William let out a laugh then, dirty and choking, breaking the spell. She went on: "I thought the French were above veneers."

"It's downright American of him," he agreed. "Though I feel some-one with teeth as straight as yours shouldn't talk. Braces, I assume."

She shook her head. "Five teeth knocked out. Solved the crowding."

"Knocked out."

Girlie felt her mouth starting to smile. "Consensually. By a pedi-atric dentist." William relaxed a little.

Then she continued, "Really. You guys did great. Perera too. The presentation—it looked beautiful up there. The world-building of it, I mean. The vision of it. The forests."

She thought about it with care, how she wanted to put it, what she could say to: help, make it better, make a difference.

"It is—beautiful, what you've made," she said, looking him in the eye.

"—. Thank you," he said.

The fountain show was long over; the tourists were starting to disperse again. Neither William nor Girlie seemed ready to disperse with them.

"Do you know what L'Olifant calls a content moderator?" William asked suddenly.

"Modérateur de contenu," Girlie said promptly. She'd looked it up.

William shook his head. "That's what it's called in French, yes," he said. "But L'Olifant calls them les passepartouts."

"Go-everywheres," Girlie translated. She had to stop fucking showing off for him.

William looked at her, that internal light of his flickering on. He smiled, faint.

"Yes. I think it's a Jules Vernes reference. But it's also the word for a skeleton key," he said. "Or perhaps you'd say: a master key."

"Oh," she said; she hadn't known that meaning.

She saw William, unreadable, watching her face as she registered a new, curious piece of knowledge; examining it from all sides then tucking it away somewhere private in her mind.

"They're a sort of old-fashioned—they're not really in use anymore, I think, with our contemporary locks, pin cylinders, all that sort of thing," William continued. His smile became less tentative. "Trust the French, even in tech, to come up with something approved by l'Académie Française."

"I like it, though," Girlie said. "Skeleton key. Sounds—spooky," she said, just to make him laugh. "And—dignified."

"—. Well. Some things they do all right," William said, low and personal, like conceding Calais.

Then he turned around once more to face the Strip, his eyes on the Eiffel Tower. Nodded at it. "I think this one's nicer than the one in France."

"Vegas is very virtual reality–coded, yes," Girlie said wryly.

"Well, they've got a twenty quid all-you-can-eat buffet breakfast at this one."

"Yeah," Girlie said, puckish; it was too easy to smile, there was an effervescence in her chest that she realized was—fun. "You seem like a big champagne brunch guy."

William smiled down into his own chest, shaking his head slightly again like that one time she'd watched him shake her salute off his body; like he, too, was having fun, and had to cut it out. He seemed to be remembering why they'd come out here in the first place. "Can I—call you an Uber, or—"

"No, I—" Then she thought about it. "Actually. My phone's dead. So. Yes. Sure. Thank you."

She didn't think about it on the way home, that she shouldn't have put in her real home address, but of course he would have it on file anyway, Reeden had it, Playground would have it. She wasn't thinking about that yet. She was just in the car, the driver much younger than her, five-star-silent the entire drive. She was just in the car, her dead phone on her lap, thinking instead about what William's face would look like, when the notification came that she'd arrived at her destination. If he'd look at the message quickly, then have to put his phone back in his pocket, carry on with the rest of the launch event. Or if he'd linger on it, zooming out the map, to peer at the swirling tattoo of her neighborhood's streets. Or if he'd already had his phone out, had already been looking, waiting, didn't need the notification at all. If somewhere she couldn't know, couldn't see, couldn't be sure, he'd been diligently tracking her journey, watching the dot that represented her body in the world, seeing that she'd got home safe.

. .

PLAYGROUND'S NEW VIRTUAL REALITY INITIATIVE: FAR-OUT FANTASY OR FAR-RIGHT NIGHTMARE? KNIGHTS IN SHINING ARMOR: WHO ARE THE BRIL- LIANT MINDS BEHIND REEDEN'S LATEST VIRTUAL REALITY TRIUMPH? UNTIL THE LION LEARNS TO WRITE: ACCUSATIONS OF REVISIONIST STORYTELL- ING FOLLOW REEDEN'S NEW PLAYGROUND LAUNCH. MAKE THE WEST FUN AGAIN: HOW I SPENT A WEEK IN PLAYGROUND'S NEW VIRTUAL WORLD AND LEARNED TO LOVE THE BOMB.

. .

She'd progressed fairly well for a beginning swimmer. Floating, for example, Girlie was very good at. The floating part of the swim- ming lessons with Perera consisted of letting one's ears be sub- merged while she laid face up in the water, or indeed face up on a reclined lounger in Perera's office. Then, the same position, but re- versed. This was her favorite lesson yet: floating in the Olympic swimming pool, suspended in the water, buoyant as an otter. Fittingly, she'd learned it was called the Dead Man's Float. Fitting, considering she'd had to die in order to pass the first lesson. Now dead, she was carrying on with the rest of the curriculum. That felt familiar.

There was the skill of getting into floating positions on the front, then the back, then returning to a standing position; no arm or leg movements allowed, no swimming strokes yet. The point was to get over the feeling—the instinctual terror—of sinking; learning how to release one's body weight, how to rely on the support of the water. Stationary floating was very difficult at first; though there was a pleasure to it, especially the back float, once she finally let the buoyancy of the water do its job, let her body be submerged, arms loose at her sides, face out of the water except for her ears, so the sound of the world she knew fell away, and she was wrapped in the slow, tranquil pulse of this other world; a world which, it almost seemed, knew her.

"The water's very cold up in Northern California, isn't it?" Perera said at the end of one session, after she'd come up for air, taken off the mask, smiling before she was aware of it, a little out of breath. "I looked it up."

"Alaskan current," Girlie said. "People don't really swim in the water, except for surfers in wetsuits."

"Ah," Perera said, nodding. "In Negombo, the water's very warm. Browns Beach." That was why he had such broad shoulders, wingspan, she thought; not a bencher, a swimmer. He considered. "So is the cold why you don't know how to swim? I still think most people have an image of all Californians swimming like tadpoles from birth."

"That's Australians."

"Oh! Never been," Perera said, affable.

Then, for a reason she could not comprehend, and with a momentum she could not thwart, with a vague, almost mystic calm,

Girlie heard herself saying: "No, I started swimming lessons when I was about five or so, but the swimming instructor—he must have been a college student—kept unzipping my swimsuit every time I went underwater, so I stopped the lessons. And then I—didn't have anyone else to teach me. Beach was too far, and—like you said. Water was too cold." She shrugged, as if the Alaskan current were the subject here.

Perera was staring at her. He put his coffee cup down on the coaster on his desk. She could see that he was making each movement with the greatest of care, and in response she felt a sort of kindred impulse to the call of the void; a desire to lurch forward and push at his hands, crashing the coffee cup on its side so that the liquid would spill everywhere, all over his desk, onto the floor. She did none of these things.

"I'm sorry," Girlie said immediately. "I don't know why I said that. That was inappropriate."

"No," Perera said very evenly.

"Yes. I'm sorry," she said again, firm. "I never should have said any of that. I don't know why—"

She stopped, collecting herself, staring at a speck of dust on his desk, homing in on it. "I don't bleed on other people. I make a point of it."

"I believe you," Perera said. "I believe that."

He paused, choosing his words very carefully, hands flat on his desk. The black and gray hair on his knuckles seemed to Girlie unanswerably mortal.

"I'm not sorry you spoke. I won't flatter myself into thinking it's because you trust me. You have the right to take back what you said. But if I tell you very simply that I don't regret hearing what you had to say, and you have no reason to feel embarrassed about it, will you believe me?"

Girlie stood up from the reclining lounge; they were long past the end of the session.

"Yes," she said. "I can believe that."

Perera nodded. Girlie started to gather her things, putting on the old flight jacket, turning the collar up to warm her neck, which was not at all cold, even in this early March weather, but burning with heat.

"I've been enjoying my swimming lessons," she said, realizing she hadn't yet told him this far more important, far more relevant thing.

Perera smiled. "It's very good to hear that."

"It's just like what Michael Phelps said in the first lesson," Girlie said, couldn't stop fucking talking, trying to white out what she'd said before: why had she even brought up that particular incident, that had been the smallest of them all, a nothing thing, it was just because of all the swimming. "'It's never too late to learn,'" she quoted.

She gave Perera a thumbs-up, in her best Olympic gold medalist impression. She had no idea who she fucking was, or what she was doing.

"It really isn't," Perera said, a sorrow in his face so palpable and sober she couldn't even recoil from it. She had the slightly demented desire to mute, block, and kick him; to evict him from the space, and with him, her embarrassment. But they weren't in the Playground; they were here. In these also-bodies, in this also-world. "I hope you actually believe that one day."

••

The space had gotten buggier since launch; more traffic than anticipated, not enough server capacity to keep up. It was hard to be an unprecedented success. The rapes tripled; assaults too. That was normal.

There were, to be fair, still plenty of nice, friendly users, veteran and new; people happy to link up in a party, play cooperatively, share resources, call out loot piles, exchange tips for taking down programmed bosses, encourage old-timers not to spoil storylines for newbies in the chat log. There were role-playing parties, people who'd taken up the role of traveling bard, or afternoon jester, or village idiot, lifers who were at home all day recovering from chronic injury or illness or unemployment—the chat was rife with oversharers—and spent hours in the park, or underneath the Eiffel Tower, or sitting on the Spanish Steps, just hanging out, giving advice, encouraging people on how to catch that one rare fish in the lake, not be disheartened by the cruelty of the RNG gods.

Sure, there were nests to clear, like the child trafficking ring exchanging descriptions of grade-schoolers like personal ads, who'd been kicked and blocked and reported time and time again until the FBI got involved. Or more recently, the alarming number of people trying to have cybersex—the term felt very '90s, but the '90s were back on trend—in the Fontana di Trevi, apparently as part of some type of online challenge, the people for whom actual VR porn was too vanilla. There was exhibitionism kink, and there was fuck-virtually-in-front-of-avatars kink, a cut scene from *Eyes Wide Shut*, surely. The entire server hadn't consented to be party to this particularly jolly orgy, so Girlie had to permaban them all.

"La dolce vita, indeed," William said, when all their naked bodies finally blinked out of the fountain. The site was still too laggy, they needed to get on that. A ban prelaunch would've taken seconds at most.

"I knew I hated Fellini for a reason," Girlie said stonily. She felt him shiver into a smile next to her; he was dressed in a white waiter's tuxedo, she in a sixties-era cheongsam, both based on background Asian characters in the party scenes of *La Dolce Vita*.

They weren't looking at each other, but together, at the empty Fontana di Trevi at dusk. At the sky, pink as a lip; at the creamy marble body of Oceanus upon his chariot. At his two horses, one wild, one tame; at the calm green waters, glowing with wishes.

"Have *you* ever been to Rome," William asked, continuing a conversation she'd started, with a question she'd asked him, a long time ago.

She smiled next to him, so he could feel it too. "Of course not. Americans don't have passports. Or take vacation."

"Of course," William said. "You just—stay at home, eating—barbecue-flavored crisps."

"How'd you know what I did last summer," Girlie asked. Now she felt William laugh next to her; felt the breath of it all along the side of her arm, though they weren't touching.

In silence, they watched as a group of new visitors approached the fountain; Girlie's antennae went up, but they looked like a regular family of tourist users. They'd collected some of the complimentary coins (one coin per user was free, any further wishes came at an extra fee) at the entrance, so they could perform the ritual of tossing a coin into the fountain to make a wish. It was, after all, one of the main Rome site attractions.

Next to her, William's shoulder radiated heat, which was, again, just her imagination; just another trick of immersion. But she, too, felt hot all over—like she, too, was radiating, burning out of her skin.

Together, they watched the family of four turn their backs to the fountain, then toss the coins in over their shoulders, giggling. One of the kids stuck her feet in the water, then squealed. "Mom, it's really cold!"

"You ever make a wish here?" Girlie asked suddenly, voice lower than she intended.

William didn't say anything for a long while. She listened for him breathing; heard it. Here; there. The little muffled human sound his breath made, against the mask. "I never carry any coins," he answered finally.

••

The problems with parties generally, and family parties specifically, were numerous, numinous, existential: all the philosophers and virtual reality theorists might have disproven the Cartesian mind-body schism of *I think, therefore I am*, but no great luminary had yet disproven the truth: *Have family, will fight*. Why the fuck anyone would willingly choose to put all these people in an enclosed space was beyond Girlie's comprehension, but she chalked it up to just another generational rift. Maribel and Avery, bless them, still believed in the noisy old engkanto called community. But that belief, the hereditary disease of it, had skipped Girlie's generation; Girlie, at least. She'd evolved past that. But another problem with parties generally, and family parties specifically, was that evolving from them was not the same thing as escaping them. Now they were starting with the line dancing.

"VST & Company, put on VST & Company," someone was shouting from the far end of the banquet room to the DJs, two ex-Hayward kuyas around Girlie's age or just a little older, early forties, one in a

Warriors jersey and the other in an old Bape sweatshirt. At some point during the party they tried to hype the crowd by playing Richie Rich's "Let's Ride" over the speakers, but nobody else reacted the way the DJs were clearly hoping for—should have just gone for the easy "California Love"—because nobody else at the party was from the West Coast in that song. Only Girlie's chest had caved in, hearing the opening lines; she'd turned to look at Maribel, who was chatting away to a friend, too young for the song, grew up on Blink 182. There was no one to share a veteran's glance with. She made a mental note to Venmo a generous tip to the DJs.

The food had been laid out on long buffet tables: lumpia, ukoy, skewers of pork and chicken and even tofu barbecue, for the vegans in the crowd. Eggplant afritada, bangus poke bowls. Performative modern Indigeneity, garnished with scallions. The party was very clearly divided into distinct tribes: Avery's friends from Berkeley, mostly white and East Asian women, one Black girlfriend, one Palestinian girlfriend, both femmes. Danny and Deb, the couple who owned Puha, the Paiute-run weed lounge, looking polite but also looking like they were figuring out the best time to leave, having secured Maribel's return custom. Plenty of aunts Girlie barely recognized, must have been from Uncle Dodo's side, most of them up and dancing, somewhat loudly drunk on margaritas, with their husbands seated together, more quietly drunk on Coors Light. Neither of Maribel's brothers had been able to get leave to come to the party.

Auntie Stella and Uncle Dodo were at a table with the drunk aunties, sharing a piece of cake. Girlie's mom, Flo, was at the same table, not really talking to anyone, wearing the Chanel bag Girlie had bought for her a few birthdays ago. She'd driven there in the Model Y Girlie was still paying off; Girlie had seen it in the parking lot, freshly detailed for the party.

There was a time when Girlie went to a Filipino party, it seemed, every other week; there was a time when these parties felt like the very foundation upon which her entire world was built. Every one of her early memories was punctuated with the sense-memory of being in the back of someone's car while the adults in the front made their stupid little decisions; fucked someone over or forgave them; broke things apart or soldered them. Girlie, the first of the third-culture children, before Maribel or any of her brothers showed up, was long used to being a kind of child-baggage, someone at everyone's disposal, along for the ride: a decoy, a hindrance, a good excuse; a light at the end of the tunnel, or a way out. She'd been around adults more than children; that was the way of things. Like a child actor who'd blossomed early, ripened like a hothouse flower under the glaring artificial light of adult attention, Girlie still had trouble around people her own age.

And then, of course, by the time Maribel and her brothers and any of the rest of the younger cousins showed up, Girlie was expected to raise them, parent them by proxy, while everyone else was employed to take care of other people's peoples. But now, she thought—looking for the first time at the terrace full of the people she'd somehow managed to build her life around, subsidize, work herself to the bone for; all while not, really, ever speaking to them—now everyone was grown up.

"Oh my god," someone was whispering. "Look at that dog."

Girlie whipped her head around. William was standing in the glass-paned doorway, nodding to a server, who had clearly led him to the terrace.

It was the first time she'd seen him wear something other than a suit in real life—she'd seen him in knight's armor, Viking fur, tourist chinos, a waiter's uniform at Le Train Bleu—and if anything, he looked less relaxed in this skin: a dark-blue sweater, brown pants, a kind of greenish mackintosh, the cut alien to noncoastal American fashion, dark Adidas sneakers that seemed purposely designed to de-emphasize the size of his feet, a thought that Girlie did not allow to come to completion.

In his left hand was a leash, front-clipped to a harness that said DO NOT PET, worn by a lean, petite, sable German shepherd, black and tan and gray, her face sharp, with ears pricked high and large, face stern, gaze distant.

William, who was nodding to the server, saying *Thank you*, turning his face slightly, and almost immediately meeting her stare.

He blinked at her, standing there. They stared at each other for a long minute; two strangers meeting on the surface of the Moon.

"Hi," he mouthed.

"Who is that?" Girlie could hear one of the aunties say behind her, as she made her way to the entrance.

She stood in front of William. "You came," she said idiotically.

"I—yes," William said, his hand flexing on the handle of the leash. "Is that all right?"

"Hey!" Maribel had caught sight of them. She was holding a glass with an umbrella in it—a mocktail, Girlie remembered; she was trying to stay sober for the proposal. God, that was still happening. "I'm so glad you made it! William, right? And who's this? Hi, sweetie!" The dog ignored her. Even Girlie thought the energy was a bit much, and she wasn't even a dog.

"Yes—and this is Mona," William said. "Thank you for inviting me."

Still holding the leash, he reached inside the pocket of his mac, pulling out a small blue package, gold illustrations on the lid, a red bow around it.

"This is for you—it's just a small thing. Happy birthday."

"Oh my *god*, I said no presents!" Maribel was squealing, clearly forgetting that no one would have informed William of this policy, considering he'd been invited two seconds ago. "That is so nice of you! Oh my god!"

"Please, don't—it's nothing," William said, looking severely ill. "Really."

"It's not nothing to me," Maribel said, clutching the gift to her chest. Girlie was enjoying seeing William so harassed.

"It's not nothing to her," Girlie agreed. William flashed her an aggrieved look. She felt something giddy rear up in her stomach. "It's *so* nice of you," she added, just to see his deepening glare.

Maribel looked between them, then said, "I'll just go tell Avery you're here—thank you, William! I'll be right back! Wait, let me get you something to eat, so you can just sit down! What do you eat? Do you have any allergies? You like chicken barbecue? Can Mona have chicken?"

"Oh, no, please, she's already had dinner—"

"Just a little treat! Chicken? Shrimp? Does she like steak?"

"Not steak—!" William nearly cried out. It was the loudest Girlie had ever heard him raise his voice. Then, he explained, sheepish: "Mona can't have beef."

Maribel nodded. "No beef! Okay, let me get you a plate! Just stay here. Ate, will you introduce him to everyone?" William stared at Girlie as Maribel retreated. There was abject fear in his eyes.

"I will not, in fact, introduce you to everyone," Girlie said.

"Your kindness will be remembered," William vowed.

Mona, having thus far observed all of this from William's side, initially uninterested in everyone that wasn't him, now approached Girlie's hand curiously.

Girlie remained unmoving; she'd eaten two sticks of chicken barbecue, earlier. Mona sniffed the hand, assessing, then started licking delicately at Girlie's fingers.

"Mona," William admonished, but didn't pull her back. "Sorry. This is Mona."

Girlie looked down at Mona's shrewd face, her eyebrows—dogs had eyebrows?—drawn together, still sniffing and questioning, trying to figure out what had been on Girlie's hands. "It's chicken and barbecue sauce," she told Mona. "Hi."

Then she looked up at William and said, "I think I've seen this dog."

"Ah—yes. You might have. A very young version of her."

"In the lobby, the first day you showed me around Playground."

"Yes. That was her." Mona came back over to William, and he started rubbing, soothingly, at the top of her head, gently pulling and massaging at her ears, which she seemed to enjoy, from the panting grin that revealed all her sharp white teeth. He regularly brushed those, Girlie realized. "Early days. She wasn't even one then."

"How old is she now?"

"About to turn thirteen." He pulled something else out of his pocket—who the fuck was he, Mary Poppins—which turned out to be a small silicone bag of brown chunks. "Do you want to give her treats? There are her favorite. Venison liver. It helps her warm up to a person. You don't have to."

"Okay," Girlie said.

"Hold out your hand," William said.

Girlie held out her hand, careful not to hold it over Mona's head; she had a feeling, rooted in self-preservation, that dogs didn't like that. William smiled at the gesture, then opened the bag. He gestured for her to bring her hand a little closer, so he didn't have to move around Mona. Then, one by one, he put five pieces of venison liver in the center of her palm, careful not to steady her hand, or touch it at all, with his. Mona's head was craned up, eyes bright, very interested in the proceedings.

"Don't touch or approach her," William said. "Let her decide to come to you, smell you, and you can ask her to sit when—ah," he said, because Mona had already approached, and was eating all of the liver out of Girlie's hand in one voracious lick, her lips pulled back in a panting grin.

They both blinked down at her. She seemed exceedingly pleased with herself.

"Normally I give them to her one by one," William said, abashed.

"I think she prefers this method," Girlie said. "Hi, mama," she said to Mona, who wasn't paying much attention, more than preoccupied with her delicious hand. "You're pretty, huh."

To William, she said, "She doesn't look thirteen."

"She's a young thirteen. She has good bone structure. Healthy hips. She was bred as a working line dog. But her age shows in some ways. She doesn't like younger, pushy dogs—she's become warier of strangers—" William trailed off, flushing.

"She does seem very wary," Girlie said, looking down at Mona licking her entire hand clean, from fingertip to wrist. William's mouth twitched.

Mona started smile-panting again when she was done with her ministrations; Girlie's hand was extremely wet. "Old flirt," William scolded.

"You're probably hungry too," Girlie said. "Can I get you—"

"Maribel's coming," William said, nodding into the terrace. They hadn't even really left the entrance yet. Maribel was, indeed, coming, holding aloft a biodegradable plate of chicken barbecue, shrimp and pork pancit, eggplant afritada, and four rolls of vegan lumpia, half swimming in sweet and sour sauce.

"One plate coming up!" Maribel said. "Sit-sit-sit!"

"Thank you," William said, taking the plate with the hand that wasn't holding Mona's leash. Girlie beckoned him into the party, to the nearest empty table, its previous occupants in the middle of an improvised cha-cha, having created an equally improvised dance floor in the center of the terrace by shoving the formerly carefully arranged tables against the walls. The restaurant servers looked tortured. They knew not one of these fuckers was going to tip well.

When William sat, Mona started sniffing intensely at the tabletop; everything on William's plate seemed to be of utmost relevance to her abruptly narrowed field of interest. She began whining: a high-pitched whistle-register squeak from the back of her throat, *hnn-hnn-hnn.* "Mona," William murmured. Then, of her own volition she sat, the picture of obedience, with all the dignity of a union leader, clearly expectant of fair compensation for her labor. "Monasaur," William said, with a note of quiet desperation. She whined again. Her front paws were starting to stamp.

Then: "Could I—would it be possible to get a bottle of water," William said. Maribel looked horrified. "Oh, I'm so sorry, I didn't even ask you what you wanted to drink—"

"I'll go," Girlie said, raising her hand.

She made her way to the long buffet tables, looking for the table with the ice buckets. She barely recognized anyone, but could discern the high voice of her mother, showing off the Chanel bag. An aunt she didn't know was saying, "Flo has such a good daughter"— and then, catching sight of her, called her over, saying, "We were just talking about you! When is my daughter going to buy me one of these," the aunt sighed. "She goes to Paris, you know—that's how she gets these nice handbags," declared Auntie Stella. Girlie had been to Paris literally once, more than fifteen years ago. She'd bought the Chanel for her mother on Fashionphile. "Next time, get handbags for me too! I'll give you money!" Auntie Stella giggled. "Next time I win at Orleans!"

"I want one too! Flo, let me feel yours." One of the aunts reached out, covetous, to touch the luxurious quilted lambskin of Flo's bag, the braided 24-karat-plated chains. The new Chanel bags only used gold-tone brass, had wonky stitching, leather quality notoriously guttered. Flo glowed at the attention.

"What bag are you going to get next, Flo?" The aunts were now talking among each other. Girlie recognized one of them, someone's sister, related to some kids who were Flo's godchildren, two in Pangasinan, one in Jeddah. Girlie had discovered shortly after they'd moved to Vegas that her mother had opened a credit card in Girlie's name to pay the monthly tuition for several of those kids, whose parents regularly sent Flo messages of gratitude on Facebook, *our fairy godmother!! Salamat po!!* It took Girlie two years to raise her credit score back up. She started regularly tracking it, after that.

"Let me guess, let me guess—" one of the aunts was giggling.

Auntie Stella pointed directly at Flo, said, "I know."

Then, with a tone of finality: "Birkin."

All the women erupted in agreement. The aunt who was feeling Flo's Chanel turned to Girlie. They were, at this point, fully screaming at her. Girlie knew the word *shrill* was misogynistic, but it was also a valid descriptor of a real sound, in the real world. "You heard that! You know what to do! For her next birthday!"

Flo looked at Girlie, smiling, proud; proud that her friends expected her daughter to buy her a Birkin, and soon. Her mother didn't argue with them.

The last time they'd spoken alone, it'd been almost a year ago, late at night, when Girlie had come back too late from Barkada, Maribel and Avery out on a date. Girlie had walked into the house to see her mother sitting on the floor of the entranceway, one shoe off, one shoe on; she was staring at her phone. The tinny sounds of a slot machine were bursting out of it; there was a gambling app she'd become addicted to, even though thankfully she wasn't playing for money, just points that she could redeem at various mediocre Vegas restaurants, the cheaper hotels off the Strip. Flo had transitioned seamlessly from her '90s Gameboy to the smartphone age; hundreds of dopamine-serving friends on Facebook, got all her news from the feed. She'd looked up at her daughter, startled, as if set upon by a burglar. Then said: *Auntie Thelma brought Goldilocks to work*, pointing toward the kitchen. Removed her other shoe, stood up. *Have some.*

Girlie had said, *Okay, thanks*, gone into the kitchen. When she came back, Flo was gone. To be fair, it was an improvement on coming home from a sixteen-hour shift then screaming for three hours straight because someone had forgotten an umbrella at school—one of the more positive post-traumatic behavioral outcomes following the 2008 financial disaster was that the inveterate shouter in Flo had finally been shocked into something like chastened silence. Or Girlie was just taller than her now. Girlie took the food back to her room. That'd been the end of that.

"I'm just going to—" Girlie extracted herself, hearing them debate Birkins versus Kellys, reaching over the buffet table for two bottles of water, looking for the stack of bowls. But she felt Flo come up from behind her.

"Sino yan," Flo was saying now.

Girlie looked at who her mother was looking at. Obviously, because she was unloved by the universe, it was William.

William, who was, horrifically, being talked to by a gray-haired uncle Girlie didn't recognize. William, who was removing little bits of chicken from a wooden skewer, delicately sucking the sauce off, then tearing the denuded meat into tiny bits, feeding the morsels to Mona under the table.

"Someone I work with," Girlie said. The idea that her mother and William were in the same physical enclosure together was giving her inner ear dysfunction.

"Payat," her mom said, disapproving. Still: "Is he single?"

"*Mom*," Girlie said. "God. We work together. He's my boss."

"So? Your dad and I met in the nursing station."

And now he's dead and you're alone, so how'd fucking your superior work out for you, Girlie could have said. "I don't know if he's single, and I don't care," Girlie said instead.

"You're not getting younger," Flo said. "Especially for kids."

Girlie didn't know if this was the venue in which to tell her mother she had absolutely zero plans to subject a new human soul to the vinegar-dipped calamity of this family: financial illiteracy, parentification, brushing systemic abuse under the rug, short calves? She imagined telling her mother all that, throwing it all in her face; imagined walking out of the party, the house, their life; imagined something happening; imagined them losing everything again; imagined heart attacks, cancer, car accidents; imagined the deathless guilt; imagined having left; imagined having to come back.

Girlie's mother had almost died once. A drawn-out medical ordeal when Flo was in her early forties, which began with a routine procedure to remove a grapefruit-sized cluster of ovarian cysts: unilateral salpingo-oophorectomy, removal of one ovary and one fallopian tube. After her discharge, she started reporting debilitating post-op pain, but her OB-GYN, an older white male doctor, was slow to respond, and when he did, remained openly skeptical of her symptoms. He told her to just take a Motrin. When Girlie's mother replied that the Motrin wasn't helping, that indeed she could barely walk, he replied: "Well, then, it's a pain you'll just have to live with." Girlie's mother said plainly, if that were the case, she was going to kill herself.

Only then did the doctor grudgingly allow Girlie's mother to come back into the clinic for a visit. The radiologist's face went ashen when the results of the intravenous pyelogram came through: the OB-GYN had nicked Girlie's mother's ureter. She was on the point of death from septic shock.

Girlie's mother was immediately admitted to the hospital, where she remained for months, and eventually underwent two more surgeries to address the botch. She refused to allow the original OB-GYN to touch her. Instead, a very young Lebanese doctor with acne across his cheeks performed the surgery. He came to see her beforehand, spoke gently to her. Instead of saying, *Please save my life*, Girlie's mother said only: "I have a daughter." The Lebanese doctor took her hand and said: "I'll take care of you."

As a result of the surgeries, one of which included the reimplantation of her damaged ureter—post-op scar tissue now narrowing the duct that transported urine from the kidneys to the bladder—Girlie's mother would have recurring chronic kidney infections for the rest of her life. They tried a stent in her ureter for several months, which caused unbearable pain until it was finally removed. For over twenty years, Girlie had never known her mother to go more than a few months without being on antibiotics for a UTI.

Later, Girlie's mother described the moment she knew she was going to die. She'd had a vision of herself, in a coffin, dead. There was no pain, only peace and joy and comfort—except she could see the young faces of her daughter and her husband, leaning over her open coffin, weeping. Then she began to smell flowers, the sweetest, most fragrant flowers she'd ever smelt, and there was a woman there whose face she could not see—but she knew it was the Virgin. Girlie's mother, then, decided to surrender to the Virgin's will. She followed the smell of the flowers, deep into the cloud of their vast benevolence, and—woke up.

That day, the nurses told her that her infection had healed; that she would survive; and also, that the entire hospital floor had smelled of flowers that morning, but they didn't know where it was coming from. You couldn't convince Girlie's mother out of miracles after that.

One of the last times she and her mother had spent time together was back in the Bay, on the Fourth of July, only a few weeks before they were going to leave Milpitas. The house was sold; their things were in boxes. It was the first time Girlie could remember her mother taking the Fourth of July off in—years. The last time they'd gone to see the fireworks was in the '90s, at Great America; her father was still alive, and there was a picture of the three of them, taken by a stranger, bundled up under a blanket on a hillside. They'd never gone to see the fireworks in Milpitas.

Her mother drove them to park the car in the Golfland parking lot off Jacklin Road, next to the old liquor store where her father, grandfather, and the relatives who taught her how to kiss with tongue at seven used to buy their weekly lotto tickets and menthol ciga-rettes. Their destination was Cardoza Park, but there were already so many people on the street, walking—there wouldn't be enough parking in Cardoza, they reasoned.

Once parked, they then began walking the half mile it took to get to Cardoza Park—along with seemingly every other soul in Milpitas. And as they walked, it was clear that anyone in Milpitas who wasn't already part of this sidewalk procession to Cardoza Park was sitting in the driveways of the houses along the way: garage doors open, mahjong tables set up, garden loungers unfolded, beers clinking, vantage points settled. In the air, everyone's voices floated: in Tagalog and Spanish and Vietnamese and Cantonese and Taiwanese Mandarin and Hindi and Urdu and English.

Girlie remembered it took a long time to walk that short half mile to the park; not just because of the crowd. It took a long time because she and her mother were clutching each other so closely that they could only take tiny steps at a time; her mother's arm tight around her waist, her arm tight around her shoulders, their free hands clutching, her mother's head nestled into her shoulder, her hair against her mother's cheek.

Girlie could not remember how, or when, they started holding each other—if they'd reached for each other after getting out of the car, or if one of them had caught the other along the way—but hold each other they did, as they had never done before and would never do again. Like the shipwrecked on a makeshift raft, they held on to each other for dear life. There was no smell of flowers in the air that night. Not long after that night, they all left the Bay. Never went back again.

"I'm not dating my boss," Girlie muttered. "I have to go bring him some water."

"Wait, wait," Flo said, holding out her hand. She started posing with the bag, a little coquettish. "Cute, huh? Matches."

"—. It looks good on you," Girlie said finally. "You should wear it more often."

Flo's mother shook her head, resolute. "No, no, no. Only special occasions." "It's a waste to save it," Girlie said. "It's a waste to use it," Flo countered. It was an old argument. Girlie left with the water.

..

The gray-haired uncle was saying, "In the Thunderbird Lounge! It's very near here, just down the street! The Fabulous Echoes performed there—lots of famous people. They were on *The Ed Sullivan Show*. You know Ed Sullivan?" William was shaking his head, no, he did not know Ed Sullivan.

Girlie approached, balancing the water bottles and bowl in her hands. "I'm back," she said to William.

"Welcome," he said, then watched her as she opened both water bottles, put one in front of William, then poured half of the other into a little bowl and put it down next to Mona, who was lying down at William's feet. "Thank you," William said quietly.

Mona got up and looked down at the bowl, ears pointed, investigating. "Go on," William encouraged. Mona took a few polite, cursory sniffs at the bowl, then settled back down without drinking, ignoring it.

The uncle was talking to her now. "You know the Fabulous Echoes?" Girlie shook her head. "Oh, you're too young. He said he's from Hong Kong! I said, he should know—bands like the Fabulous Echoes, like Kong Ling and Celso Carillo—there were a lot of Filipino musicians in Hong Kong, back in the day. Like me! I used to play bass in the Hilton Hotel there. Two Queens Road. Wala na," he said to Girlie. "They demolished it now."

Then, turning to William: "'Sukiyaki'? You know that song?"

"It's a famous song," Girlie cut in. "Lots of people have sung it."

The uncle waved dismissively. "Or—'A Little Bit of Soap'? That's famous." William smiled apologetically.

The uncle shook his head. "Your mom would probably know," he said.

"—. Yes," William said after a long moment.

"But Mona Fong, you know!" The uncle sounded accusatory, pointing to the dog.

"I didn't name her," William said. "My friend Edison did. She was originally his dog. His dad liked Mona Fong."

"Mona Fong and Carding Cruz," the uncle mused, starting to hum to himself. "Teresa Carpio! You know?"

"I know," William said. "We had her records."

"Yes, she's younger. Very beautiful singer."

"Yes," William said.

The uncle pointed at William's plate, looking at Girlie. "Look at him! He eats a lot!"

Girlie looked down at William's plate, which was, indeed, empty. That was a rookie mistake. Another older woman was coming up to them now, the uncle's eyes lighting up: his wife. "Tignan mo, na ubos na," he said to her proudly.

"She's the one who made the pancit," he told William and Girlie. "We brought it. We didn't know what they were going to serve here." He looked around the room, all the happy vegan lesbians and their tofu barbecue, with unchecked disdain.

"It was delicious," William said, which was mistake number two.

"Oh, you like it?" The woman looked at his empty plate in horror. "I'll get you more! What else do you want?"

"Oh, I'm sure he's—" Girlie cut in again, trying to save him. "I could have more of everything," William said instead. "Is there dessert, as well?"

The auntie started giggling. Of course they were naturally inclined to treat foreign men with hospitality, Girlie thought viciously, it was precisely the trait that got us all fucking colonized for hundreds of years.

"Oh, you can eat! What kind of dessert do you like? I brought roll cakes. Mocha? Chocolate? Strawberry?"

William said the magic words: "I'm not picky."

The auntie beamed, then turned to Girlie. "Ikaw, what do you want?"

"Mocha," Girlie answered glumly. The auntie nodded. "I like your boyfriend!" she said, before departing on her sacred mission.

Girlie's face was going to melt off. "He's not—I'm *so* sorry—"

"It's really good," William said peaceably to the uncle, who looked absolutely delighted.

"You don't have to eat to be polite," Girlie said, her voice pitched so only William could hear. "I can throw away what you don't want. Don't feel obligated."

William frowned at her. "I don't feel obligated," he replied.

They looked at each other. There, on the surface of the Moon. Her ears were ringing.

"Thanks for coming," she said finally. "It was nice of you."

"I hope it wasn't—I hope it's all right that I did," William said.

"Yeah, no, of course," Girlie said noncommittally.

"You have a very big family."

"Everyone in my life is there against my will."

William laughed. "It's nice."

Girlie inhaled, nodding at the nothingburger of it, sure, sure, *nice.*

"It's nice for me, I mean," William amended. "I understand that's easy for an outsider to say. But I don't have—my family's not like that."

"In London."

"Mm. Big—parties, things like that."

"London's known for its quiet small-town vibe, it's true."

"My ground-floor garden flat in Crystal Palace isn't exactly the epicenter of rave you might think," William said drily. "I meant— this." He gestured around. "Lots of people, different generations. Community."

"It's overrated."

William looked down. "I wouldn't know," he said, too lightly.

Finally, she let herself ask it. "Why did you come?"

Now William let out a strangled chuckle, still looking down. "Oh, I don't know—no life, probably," he said, giving her the second and third thoughts.

Then he returned to her gaze, holding himself still. She watched him choosing to give her the first thought.

"You said—I was welcome," he answered softly.

One thought, arrow too swift, couldn't dodge it: I want him to lick me open. She nearly doubled over with the horror of it, the jerky as a heart murmur horror-horror-truth of it. She was thinking, right there, in the modern fusion restaurant terrace: I want to see the tendons in his neck straining when he's trying not to come in his pants while I'm jerking him off.

It was the acute specificity of the desire that made its horror. It wasn't just the garden-variety horniness of someone who hadn't fucked for at least six years, hitting her like a two-by-four across the temples; wasn't just the baseline stupidity of the as-yet-unorgasmed thinking—knowing—that they'd be good together, that it'd be— good with him. Knowing it without knowing it, knowing it just because. Which was the stupidest way in the world to be wrong—and at this junction in history, the stupid ways to be wrong were, to say the least, legion.

It wasn't just: I want to see what his face looks like when he's fucking me. But unambiguously: I want to see his eyebrows tight together when it's that good inside me he's about to die from it; I want to hear that telltale shaky *oh fu-uck* when he's trying not to come in two seconds; I want to see that glassy wet rapture-shock in his eyes the first time he fucks up into me and can't believe it; I want to feel him on a live wire, clawing at then pushing away his orgasm like a needy animal, tensing up, being careful, holding back, wanting to make it last, make it good; I want to feel the word shudder all through his bones when I say *more*; I want to hear that agonized *oh—fuck* when it's devouring him at last, burning in his blood, want to feel him trying to be valiant, hold on, give me fair warning, I want to laugh a little just to make him relax, then laugh a little more just to hear him cry out at the sweet teasing squeeze of it, tender all around him, *ah ah*, I want him going to pieces inside me, pulsing apart, straining for it, holding on too tightly, wild for it, hard for it, afraid of it. I want to give him permission; I want him to let go; I want to let him. Then I want him shattered under me after, shaking, depleted, eyes wide, face new and gleaming like he's been slapped, shock-laughing from the good of it, the *good-good-it's-good* of it.

She couldn't stop thinking, like she'd been holding back the thoughts for so long they'd mutated inside her into something all-consuming, city-destroying, alarmingly narrative— No, before all that: I want him on his knees; I want him kissing up my tattoos; I want his tongue honey-wet and sure on my clit, I want to come at least five times on the flat of it; I want to be gasping for air, bucking up into the wave; I want to come too much, too quickly, and still not be done, hot as an over-sharpened knife, angry about it, the still-not-enough of it, arching up into the seal of his patient searching mouth, licking down to the core of the comb. I want to be desperate to come for him again but too sensitized to get back there so soon; scraped-down and thrashing with need, crying out finally from the hungry harrowed tongue-tip hurt of it, the more-more-more hurt of wanting it, the mine-mine-mine hurt of having it. I want to be panting, clutching, electric; I want to finally have to ask him to *stop, wait-wait*—and I want him to stop when I say.

And then I want him to look up and ask, very patiently, in that soft, low, restrained voice of his: *red, yellow, or green?*

She thought; couldn't help it, hurt to try: I want to say *green*. I want to; will want to; I know I will. She couldn't shut it the hell up—the wet, wrecked, almost-dead heart of her. Murmuring *green green green green green*.

• •

The restaurant started kicking them out after the three hours they'd reserved was up, right on the dot. "But you're more than welcome to continue the party at our bar next door," a Pinay woman who seemed to be a floor manager was saying, smiling at everyone, at the open wallets of all their faces. "And happy thirtieth birthday again to the birthday girl!"

There was a wave of people making their way from the terrace into the bar; the older crowd was leaving, but Maribel's and Avery's friends were partying on. Avery was still lingering, giving a long meandering sendoff to aunties and friends who couldn't stay for drinks. The floor manager was smiling at them, clearly trying not to succumb to her intrusive homicidal thoughts.

Even Sam was there, on her way out with her brother, Rocky, who'd come out of the kitchen about an hour ago to join the party and let himself be waylaid into several dozen different selfies: **Me and @chefrockydimasupil! Michelin-trained! Proud to be Pinoy!**

Sam caught Girlie's eye, then gestured at William, not even trying to be subtle about it. *Happy for you,* she mouthed, with the smugness of someone who'd finally stumbled upon some decent leverage. Girlie pointed at the doorway and mouthed back helpfully, *Exit.*

Girlie had almost forgotten about the proposal until she felt a bogey coming up on her six: Maribel, now throwing herself into the empty chair next to Girlie, face a rictus. "Ate—"

Girlie looked at her, then sighed. "What did I tell you about public proposals."

Maribel was shaking her head. "I know, I know, I know—but—fuck, fuck, fuck, fuck fuck, *fuck*—"

Then she glanced over at William. "Hi again! Sorry! I'm fine, I'm just having a breakdown!"

Girlie snorted; public display of emotion, that was going to mix well with what she'd come to know as English reserve. But William was looking at Maribel with amused concern. "Don't mind me," he said.

"Ate, I can't do this, I can't do this, I can't do—"

"Then don't do it," Girlie said. "Very easy solution. I'm going home now."

"NO—" Maribel grabbed Girlie's elbow, which meant things were grave, because Maribel usually didn't just paw at Girlie like that, knew better. "*No.* Please. You can't. I—"

Avery was sailing up to them with the friends who remained, grinning. The floor manager was trailing them like a border collie herding sheep.

"Baby, should I get you another mocktail? The mango one?" She looked down at Girlie and William. "Hi! Come to the bar!"

Then Avery reached out to pat William's fucking shoulder. "You're really hot! We were just discussing it!" Girlie's life was officially a movie; genre: Asian horror.

"I'm overcome," William said benignly.

"Yeah, we're right after you, baby," Maribel said, staring fixedly at Girlie. "Mango again's good, thank you!" She waved Avery away, toward the bar.

William looked between the two of them once Avery had left. "Am I allowed to ask—"

"I want to propose to my girlfriend tonight," Maribel blurted out. They were the last people on the terrace besides the floor manager, who started directing servers to clear the tables.

"Ah," William said; his voice sounded like he couldn't decide what intonation to put on the syllable.

Girlie elaborated: "But she's a scaredy-cat, and as I've already told her, public proposals *are coercive*—"

Maribel was pulling on her own hair. "But *she said she thinks they're romantic!*"

"Propose, on your own birthday?" William asked. "Isn't that—"

"Today isn't my actual birthday—" "Today isn't her actual birthday," Maribel and Girlie answered in unison.

Maribel grinned, happy about that, in spite of herself, like an idiot. "No, it was end of February, but we had to find a date that worked for everybody that was coming in from—"

Then she sat up straighter in realization. "Oh! *Oh*, no-no-no-no-no, I would never do it on my actual-*actual* birthday, that's—"

"Serial killer behavior, yes," William finished. Girlie snorted. Happy about that, in spite of herself, like an idiot.

"Fam, you're going to have to take it to the bar, I'm so sorry," the Pinay manager said, smiling brightly at them with apex predator teeth. "It's really nice in there, I promise!" Then she saw Mona. "Oh, but dogs aren't allowed inside, is the thing—"

"She's a service animal!" Maribel shouted.

Now both Girlie and William were staring at her, scandalized. "She's for—seizure alerts," Maribel said.

"Oh my god, I'm *so* sorry," the floor manager said, then clocked the DO NOT PET signs on Mona's harness, nodded. "Right, right, I see, sorry, I didn't even read what it said. Please, go ahead. Accessibility is a big priority for us! We want to make sure everyone feels welcome."

"You are a fucking demon," Girlie hissed to Maribel as the four of them moved out of the terrace, toward the bar. "A service dog is a real job, you can't just lie about it—"

"It's fine, it's fine," Maribel was saying—Girlie looked over at William, whose nauseated face said it most certainly was not fine.

"Many people do claim to have fake service dogs," he said, trying to keep the judgment out of his voice. "I don't—agree with it."

Maribel gestured. "Why does she have all those DO NOT PET stickers on her, then?"

William looked down at Mona's harness. Mona, who was unfazed by the human drama happening around her, like so many of her intrepid ancestors—the old wolves who'd made their dubious choice of friend, and had to live with it.

"So people don't pet her," he replied mildly.

They entered the bar-lounge area. The whole space was a kind of upscale Asian-cocktail-lounge-cantina, a vaguely Chinese Mexican Hawaiian speakeasy theme to everything in it—which, if Playground had dreamt it up as a landscape, would have read corny and tryhard, but instead, here, felt lush, textured, carnal: the red-velvet booths and green-marbled surfaces, the hanging brass chandeliers, the sound of Trio Los Panchos singing "Corazón de Melon" on the sound system because it had gone TikTok-viral of late, the framed pictures of Anna May Wong on the walls, which Girlie had known Maribel and Avery would love. It was better than the photos online; the vibe was too sexy; Girlie cursed her good taste.

Maribel bullied and dragged them both into a booth, sitting between them, while Mona settled again at William's feet. "What do I do," she whispered. She pulled something out of her crossbody bag, keeping it hidden by her hand. Girlie recognized the velvet corner of the box, and pushed Maribel's hands back, looking out for where Avery was. "Be careful! Fuck."

Maribel pulled the box out again, this time more discreetly, opening it under the table. Thick, old silver band, with a large opal cabochon, shining blue-green-violet even in the dim light. "Her favorite," she said.

"It's very beautiful," William said.

Maribel now turned the Pixar eyes on William, hopeful. "You think so?"

"I do."

"Avery hates diamonds. Same as her," Maribel said pointing at Girlie. William looked sidelong at her. Girlie ignored both of them.

"So what is the problem," Girlie said impatiently. "You planned a public proposal. Now you're chickening out. There's no shame in that. It's scary, and there are a lot of things that can go wrong. What's wrong with just waiting until you're both alone?"

"Nothing," Maribel conceded, eyes dropping, voice glum. "No. You're right."

"Or," William said.

Girlie snapped her head up to glare at him. He wasn't looking at her. "Or," he said again. "You said—she likes public proposals?"

Maribel nodded. "She—there were all these TikTok videos of queer couples getting engaged in public, and I think she—. I think she wouldn't—she's been in relationships where—maybe she was the one who was expected to do the proposing. And she—I mean at the beginning, it was a thing, that I hadn't been with any other women before, she'd been burned, and it took time to—gain her trust. I wanted—" She took a deep breath. "I want to be the one who sweeps her off her feet this time," she said, wistful.

"Then—and this is obviously coming from someone who doesn't know either of you at all—I think you should be brave and do it," William said. Girlie's mouth fell ajar.

The light was coming back to Maribel's eyes. "Yeah? You don't think public proposals are—coercive?"

"Oh, no, public proposals are coercive," William said calmly— "*Thank you,*" Girlie spat out, but they were both at this point completely ignoring her—"but in this case, we've established that the other party actually likes, and in fact has expressed a desire for, a public proposal. So."

Maribel was nodding, her hands tapping on the table. "Okay," she said. "Okay, okay, okay, okay, okay—yes." She turned to William, stared him in the eye. Girlie saw something make itself known in Maribel's face, then; something hard and ancient and determined. A firing-line gaze; a headhunter's gaze, just before the first kill. Something that reminded Girlie of herself; reminded her that they were related. She caught William's eyes widening a fraction—saw he was realizing the same thing.

"You're right," Maribel said. "I'm gonna be brave. Thank you."

She went to climb over Girlie, to get out of the booth. "Wait," Girlie said.

Maribel turned around, dread in her eyes. "Ate—"

"Calm down," Girlie muttered. She pulled a box out of her bag. "Here, before I forget. Happy birthday. You can open it at home—"

Maribel was already tearing the wrapping paper off. She opened the telltale red box: vintage Cartier Panthère Ruban, sinuous stainless-steel bracelet, mother of pearl dial, original box and papers. Girlie thought birth-year watches were stupid, but she'd saved the search terms on Chrono24 a year ago. She didn't even like the standard Panthère, unserious sugar-baby-ass quartz watch, she was a 1978 two-tone automatic Santos Carrée (*not* Galbée) person through and through, but when she considered something with a proper mechanical movement, maybe a nice little 26-millimeter Rolex OP, she realized that she would have been appeasing her own taste at thirty: Maribel would never keep up with the setting or the service. Maribel should have carefree it-girl femme.

Maribel gasped. *"Ate—"*

"I just need you to stop wearing that ugly-ass Apple Watch now that you're thirty," Girlie said in a rush, more embarrassed than she thought she'd be; she hadn't imagined William would be there when Maribel opened her present.

"Ate, thank you!" Maribel leaned down to hug her, Girlie having to stretch up from the booth to meet her halfway. "Thank you," Maribel murmured again, closer to the skin. "I'm not gonna fuck it up."

Girlie pulled away, but held on to her shoulder. "It's okay if you do," she said, quiet. She wasn't sure if that was true—but it was her job to make it true. Maribel shook her head, smiled. "I'm not gonna."

And then they were alone in the booth. "Well," Girlie began. "Well," William replied.

"I'm sorry she took you hostage," Girlie said, not knowing where to even start. "You can obviously leave whenever you want. Everyone in this family is clinically insane."

"That is ableist language," William said superciliously. "Which you would know, if you'd attended any of the diversity and inclusion trainings when you first started. They were mandatory."

His eyes flicked to the side, impish. "I can't miss the proposal now. I feel a sense of responsibility."

A server was coming up to them, putting down two glasses on coasters and a bottle of icy tap water. "Hey guys, what can I get you—"

"Do you have any nonalcoholic beers, by any chance," William asked politely. Girlie saw the woman's eyes widen a fraction at the accent that came out of his mouth, the disconnect between his face and his voice, at least to her, and perhaps even the erotic value of it. It was past Girlie's bedtime, Jesus.

"We got Asahi Super Dry—"

Girlie perked up. That was one of the better nonalcoholic beers, she didn't need to hear the rest of the list. "I'll have one of those," she said.

"Two, please," William said.

"You got it," the server said to William, looking down at Mona, who had just gotten up to rearrange herself, turning around and pawing a little at the carpeting, to perfect her den. "Oh, aren't you a pretty girl—yes, you are—yes, you are—can I pet your dog?" People simply could not read, Girlie thought, getting annoyed on Mona's behalf.

"No—I'm terribly sorry," William cut in. "She's—"

"Oh, shit, of course," the server said, reading the harness at last. "I didn't realize she was working! I didn't even see. Thank you for your service!" This last, she said to Mona. "I'm so sorry!"

"Quite all right," William said.

"*Quite all right,*" Girlie repeated in disbelief, when the server had finally left.

"I find people in America are inclined to be nicer to a foreign man when you sound like you shoot pheasants or something," William said, plucking the food menus out from a stand behind a little raffia lamp.

"I also like how quickly you abandoned the whole 'I hate people with fake service dogs' thing," Girlie pointed out. "Needs must, sir," William replied.

Then he pulled a foldable silicone bowl out of his mackintosh pocket—how deep were these pockets, genuinely—and popped it open. He took the water bottle, poured one glass full and pushed it toward Girlie, then filled the water bowl, and put it down in front of Mona, who now vigorously drank from the water. A suspicious, monogamous soul; Girlie liked that. Then Mona settled back down, head on her front paws, her substantial butt now bumping up against Girlie's leg, haunch warming Girlie's foot, warm and heavy and alive. Girlie liked that too.

"She doesn't accept water from strangers," Girlie said.

William chuckled. "Noticed that, did you."

"Is that normal?"

"She's just a bit of a diva, really," he said, with no small amount of servile fondness.

"How did you get her to Las Vegas from London?"

William squirmed in his seat. "I—well. There's a service—"

"Was she in the cargo hold?"

"*No*," William said, appalled. Almost every single expression on his face tonight was an expression she hadn't seen before. "No. I wouldn't. Not at her age. No, there's a—a service—it's a kind of, well—a chartered jet."

"You flew your dog over in a private jet."

"*Not* a private jet," William said. "No, no. No. There's a company that does chartered flights for people traveling with—animals—non–service animals, I mean—and you can share a cabin with—other people in the same predicament, and split the cost. Obviously it's still prohibitively expensive. But it's nowhere near as costly as a private plane. No."

"Not as costly as a PJ," Girlie said. "Got it."

William was flushing again, red at the tops of his cheeks, his neck. "Well. At her age, I thought—it was a necessary expense. Certainly she was more comfortable. And it put my mind at ease. So."

They were too close together, in the booth; his cologne smelled too nice. It wasn't old—he'd applied it for the party. She thought: he'd had to have stood in his house, apartment, hotel room, wherever he was living, looked in the mirror, shaved his face, put this sweater on, sprayed cologne on himself. His neck, his chest.

"You realize if they do get engaged tonight, that's on you," Girlie said, gazing out to where Maribel was chatting to Avery's friends, biding her time, clearly shitting herself. "Avery might be a real dick-head. Is one, in fact."

William smiled wanly. "A teacher used to say I was prone to occasional impulsive behavior. Called it my 'mad five minutes.' Edison said so too. But then he said it was a good thing, because it showed I could follow my gut."

A silence came over them at the mention of Edison.

Girlie hesitated. "You said Mona was his dog," she said.

"Mm. We were doing—it was early days. We were still working with combat veterans, the PTSD studies. One of them brought in his service dog, a German shepherd. They'd been in Afghanistan together, then when he retired—the dog, Maverick, beautiful dog—he went home with the veteran. It doesn't always happen, apparently. That the dog gets to retire with the handler.

"Edison was fascinated by their bond. He'd been wanting a dog. His parents never allowed him one as a child. He asked the veteran for advice on a good breeder. And that's how Edison got Mona. I think her kennel name was something quite—German, though. Hildegarde von Wolfenhaus or something quite—Aryan. Edison misplaced all her pedigree papers, of course."

William shook his head. "God. She was destructive, as a puppy. Once chewed up half a door. But she was fine afterward. Bit indestructible herself, really."

Then he laughed a little. "It's funny, that—that man knew about Mona Fong. Small world."

"In that room, you could've tripped and fallen on a dozen musicians with the same story," Girlie said. "~*Diaspora*~," she added, making a sparkly hand-wave motion.

William snorted. "Yes. Well. Edison's mother was a singer. Not Mona Fong, obviously. But she was a singer—a bit like the man at the party, at hotels in Hong Kong. She worked with a lot of Filipino bands, big band, that sort of thing. As he said. It was the time. She was locally known, not nationally famous. Met a visiting Chinese American businessman, fell in love. Edison was born in Hong Kong, his father would come to visit every six months, that sort of thing. Eventually they all moved back to the States. Missouri. Right near the site where the St. Louis World's Fair was. He was obsessed with it, growing up. Then they moved to London, when he was fourteen, for his father's job; Edison's mother had family there, it all worked out nicely. But then his father left them in London. Disappeared from their life. His mother had boyfriends he didn't get along with. She remarried. He'd mostly stopped talking to her and his stepfather by the time we met." William looked down at Mona. "He said his father idolized Mona Fong. So that's why he named the dog Mona."

"What did your parents do?"

William startled; it was easier to tell Edison's biography, she saw, than his own. "Oh. White goods salesman and—homemaker."

"White goods?"

"Washing machines," he clarified. He was stiff in his seat.

"Do they still live in London?"

"Bromley, yes."

"Are they happy you're here?"

"Oh," William said blankly. "They—they're not people who—do, happy."

"Divorced?"

"Catholic," William said shortly.

Girlie paused. "Oh. Were you—"

"Raised Catholic, yes. And Edison. More House was a Catholic student residence. And Perera."

"And me."

"I figured."

Girlie looked at him. "Do you still go to church?"

"I'd rather be set on fire," William said pleasantly.

"I think they can arrange that," Girlie said. She tried not to look obviously relieved by his answer. "I think that's one of their main—areas of expertise."

William finally let himself smile. "Yes. Well. When I was a child, I thought heaven was a place where I'd finally be allowed to pet a tiger and play basketball with Michael Jordan."

At her perturbed look, he said, "I used to play a lot of basketball in—I suppose what you would call high school. Because—" And then he raised his flat hand from his shoulder to his forehead, to indicate that he'd been tall even then; as if he were too modest to call himself *tall* out loud. "Played locally. Thought I might even go pro."

"What position did you play?"

"Small forward," he replied. "Good at midrange jump shots."

"I don't think of England as a great basketball country."

"It isn't." Then he looked over at her. "Your parents?"

"Nurse, security guard. Well, he was a doctor, back in the Philippines. But security guard here."

"And they're proud of what you do?"

"One doesn't know what I do, the other's dead," Girlie said; his face didn't move—he knew that.

Still, he asked, "When?"

"Six months before my college graduation ceremony," she said evenly. "Good thing I hate public recognition. If he'd been there I might have actually had to pretend to enjoy it."

She saw him start to smile, say, "Yes, you—" then he shut his mouth up, coughed. Said: "Right. That sounds very difficult."

But she'd seen it. The smile had been a private, easy sort of smile, the smile one gives to someone or something long known; a smile for an old picture, kept in a back pocket. She knew, then, that he had googled her.

"Any brothers or sisters?"

"One older brother. Theodore. Theo. He lives in Brisbane with his family. Australia."

"I know where Brisbane is."

"There might've been a Brisbane, Texas, for all I know," William said, somewhat defensively. "He doesn't really talk to our parents as much. He's very—focused on his own family. One daughter, one son. Julia and Malcolm. His wife's name is Sharon. Shazza. She's very—she's kind. Funny. She sends me these joke art gifts—" He shook his head, as if it were too complicated to explain. "I've been meaning to go over and see them. But I'm not sure if Mona can handle that long a journey, and then there's a ten-day quarantine for dogs arriving in Australia—"

"How often do they come see you in England?"

William looked down. "Oh—Theo hasn't come back to England since the children were born. Julia's—twelve, now." Girlie watched him watch Mona; the pair they made.

"And you? Still talk to your parents? Or—same as your brother?"

"I call every Sunday," William said with almost no inflection in his voice.

Then he cleared his throat. "And you. Do you have any brothers or sisters?"

"Only child of my parents. Eldest of the cousins in my generation. So I think of myself as the eldest child," Girlie said. She considered stopping there.

Then heard herself saying: "My dad had three older children from a previous marriage."

"How much older?"

"The eldest is twenty-five years older than me." Girlie saw the server coming, pinned her stare on the gold detail on her apron so she'd have somewhere to put her eyes. "I don't speak to them."

The server put two bottles of Asahi Super Dry in front of the two of them, opened Girlie's first, then William's, and skillfully poured the bottles into their Asahi-branded glasses, giving both a decent head. "There you go. Do you want to open a tab, or close out here?"

"Close out here," Girlie said, reaching in her pocket for her wallet.

"Wait—" William said. "Could we—is the kitchen still open?" Girlie balked at him.

The server chewed at the gum parked in her molars. "Just apps and sides now. Fries, Szechuan olives, chicken satay, taquitos, hoisin-sauteed mushrooms—"

"Could we have two sides of fries, please?" "Regular or sweet potato?" "Regular," William said.

He looked at Girlie. "Would you like anything?"

"I'm not having fries, so you don't have to order two," Girlie said.

He blinked at her. "Both orders are for me," William said. He turned back to the server.

"Could I order the sauteed mushrooms as well?" He handed his credit card to the server, despite Girlie's protests. "I insist," he said.

The server took it, glanced over at Girlie. "Sorry, hon," shrugged, and left.

Girlie frowned. "You didn't have to do that."

"In the long list of things I didn't have to do tonight," William said, his eyes closing briefly, but then didn't finish his sentence.

Girlie took a sip from her beer, brooding. William was studying his.

"I haven't had a lot of Asahi," he said. "My father's quite—anti-Japanese. Relatives died in the Battle of Shanghai. No Japanese beer, cars, movies at home. That sort of thing."

"My grandpa was like that," Girlie said. "He worked as a clerk for the U.S. military in Guam during World War II when the Japanese occupied it," Girlie said. "Also an uncle on my dad's side, who was in the Philippine Army. Born in 1920. He was in the Bataan Death March."

"Right," William said, exhaling. "And yet," he nodded down at the beers; she'd been the one to perk up at the Asahi.

Girlie shrugged. "I mean, not all of us were *pussies* as children—" and William laughed so hard he visibly choked into his beer. "What am I going to do, never watch Kurosawa?"

"You do seem like a *Yojimbo* person."

"All right, Criterion Channel. For the record, I'm a *Red Beard* person. *Yojimbo* is for college freshmen."

"I'm not exactly sure what a college freshman is, but I happen to like *Yojimbo*."

"Beautiful dog," called a very drunk, very bleary white man with a white beard on a stool at the bar across from them, the only person seemingly not with their party, or with anyone else in the bar. "Is that a German shepherd?"

"Yes," William said, his guard going back up. His hand tightened slightly on the leash. But the man didn't ask if he could pet Mona. "Just beautiful," he said again, wondering. He barely looked at William and Girlie.

"You must get that a lot," Girlie said to William.

"I'm just her PR."

"Why did you put her in Playground?"

William touched his thumb to the condensation at the base of the glass, smearing the moisture there. "Edison did," he corrected. "He was—well, he wasn't a very good—dog owner at first. Sort of classic—bit off more than he could chew. He loved the *thought* of German shepherds—loved seeing the bond between Maverick and Thomas—that was the veteran's name—and wanted that for himself.

"But the reality of raising an actual German shepherd puppy—he wasn't the best at that. She was a danger to people, other dogs, terrified them; probably terrified herself, really. Young and frustrated and misunderstood. She even got him banned for life from some pubs in South Ken. Edison was never very gifted at the—everyday, of things.

"When he was building the original world, the first Playground space—back when he was calling it Fairground—she was one of the first avatars he created. Six months old, she was then. Motion sensor tags all over her body." William snorted. "That was a day."

"What, he just wanted her in the world?"

"No, not just that—well, that was part of it, I suppose. To immortalize her. But the practical reason was, at the beginning, we thought maybe the moderators would feel safer, more comfortable, be more identifiable, if they had a virtual dog next to them. We were planning to create avatars for different breeds."

"That would've been fun." Girlie had idly thought she'd like to adopt a dog one day—but good luck with that, in the Vegas house, with her hours. The idea of a virtual dog, given those limitations: she saw the appeal. She'd gotten very attached to her horse in *Red Dead*.

William nodded. "Well, we thought so. Users like having pets, in game, generally. Adds to the immersion, the intimacy. But instead we found that it actually made the moderators more self-conscious— and it made them targets for other users. It broke the immersion for *other* people in the world. And perhaps felt a little ominous."

"I mean, I guess, it's kinda police-y, yeah," Girlie agreed. William held out an open palm, as if to say, *exactly*.

"And we didn't want people to feel like they were being actively surveilled. Users began to target them. Or avoid them. As you—"

"I remember," Girlie said, thinking of the short sword coming at her chest. William sensed her tone and moved on.

"It seemed as though it would be safer if the moderators could be—undercover, as it were. A bit more inconspicuous. So Mona's model ended up being the only more advanced dog model that stayed in the engine. And so that character still roams around the lobby. Which was part of the original Fairground."

"What was the whole thing supposed to be, originally?" Girlie asked.

William smiled. "Told Edison people wouldn't recognize it. It's supposed to be the St. Louis World's Fair. I told you he was obsessed with it as a child."

"Ohhh," Girlie said. "Right. Yeah, okay, that makes sense."

"You know of it?"

"I mean, I've heard about it a little bit. Ethnic Studies classes. Philippine Exposition and all of that."

"Right. All of that," William said dryly. "Well, that part, Edison wasn't really interested in, which, I suppose, is one reason why the world never really worked. As a landscape, that is. In terms of the politics: total minefield. And as for practicalities—far too specific. It crashed every server. You couldn't scale it.

"And even when we finally had the money and resources to properly do the hyperspecific, it still wasn't viable as an immersive landscape. Everyone was telling him that composite landscapes and limited tourism were what worked, that he had to make it less St. Louis, that even if he had to keep, say, the cultural exhibitions—if he was willing to weather the inevitable backlash that would come with that—then he should take a page from Lucas and Tolkien, make up fantasy races, fantasy nations. Or do it like L'Olifant, do historical specific, but find the universal heroic. But he was determined that everything had to be just as it was. Even if no one else understood it."

The waitress was coming with the two platters of fries, the plate of mushrooms, and a bottle of ketchup.

William asked, "Excuse me, do you by any chance have mayonnaise?"

"Mayo?"

"Yes, please."

"For—sure," the waitress said, looking perturbed. She turned back around.

"You're just—eating mushrooms, like that?" Girlie asked.

William shrugged, speared them into his mouth. "I thought it would be a good idea to have some vegetables."

She tried to calculate everything she'd seen him eat in the last two hours; after the strawberry cake, he'd gone back to pancit and vegan lumpia, then ended the evening chewing through various kakanin that the uncle had recommended to him, pitsi pitsi, kutsinta, puto, the entire meal proceeding in no discernible order whatsoever.

"You didn't eat this weirdly at that first lunch," Girlie remarked.

William laughed around the mushrooms in his cheek. "Well, I was trying to make a good impression, wasn't I? And I wasn't sure about the food. Your steak looked all right. My fish was terrible."

He swallowed. "I also hadn't quit smoking yet."

"Ahh," Girlie said. "Ahh," William agreed.

"Anyway," she said, shifting in her seat. He gestured for her to take a fry, which she did.

"You were saying—about Edison. And his ideas about—virtual reality landscapes."

"Ah," William said, looking down at a mushroom. "Yes. Well. Edison's original foray into virtual reality had been based on a single premise, set out in his graduating thesis, which was based on a therapy originally designed for people with dementia—something called reminiscence therapy, where the landmarks of a patient's memory, their personal geographies, could be totally reconstructed. Could you use the design engine of virtual reality to create specific landscapes, including historical sites, and combine it with virtual reality's immersive capacities and therapeutic benefits, in order to, essentially, construct lived events and memories that users could then believe—and by every perceptive measure, *know*—were true? Could you, not just rewrite your story, but, essentially completely rewire your own brain, how it took in information, and what information it took in?"

"Volumetric brain increase," she said again, less sullenly than the first time. The corners of William's mouth lifted.

"Yes. But with the added benefit that the expanded, overwritten brain's experiences, due to the specific perception modification powers of virtual reality, would feel so true, and so believably, viscerally lived, that there would be, for you, no psychic or physiological difference at all. The overwritten *would* be the original. And everything else would be like someone else, telling you about a dream they once had. Strange, maybe even familiar—but not your own. Not anything from you."

"I have, indeed, heard of brainwashing," Girlie said dryly.

William shook his head. "Not washing. Razing. Demolition and construction."

The server finally came back, put the squeeze bottle of mayonnaise down on the table. William took it, squeezed out a blob of mayo onto the plate next to the fries, dipped a handful of fries in mayo, then in ketchup, and ate it. He shrugged. "They're not chips, but."

Girlie loved Thousand Island dressing and animal-style double doubles, but had never thought to mix mayo with ketchup for fries. "I've never tried mayo on fries," she said. "Well, go on, get involved," he replied.

She followed his lead. He watched her face.

"You're the greatest mind of your generation," Girlie said gravely.

William snorted. "I'll have to go home straightaway and revise my Wikipedia bio."

Girlie chewed, thoughtful. "He'd already done therapy?"

"Therapy, medication, which was already a lot," William said. "Our parents and their generation weren't exactly—receptive to the idea of mental illness. My own mother—" He stopped short. "Well. She's—had some form of—what you'd call clinical depression for—since I can remember. Done nothing for it. Aunt visiting from Hong Kong once said it was a thing you only got in Britain.

"Edison couldn't just—he was the kind of person who needed big solutions. It wasn't enough to shop around a bit more for the right therapist, the right medication. He'd rather: build an entire artificial world to potentially remake his brain. He was auditioning actors to play—he had old photos of his father. It was—" William looked hard into his plate. "He was someone who could sweep you up in things. Charismatic. Big visions. Risk-taking. Tech loves those kinds of people."

She thought of Perera, talking about Edison. *One day, we'll be able to prescribe alternative realities to people* and *He was the kind of person who made you believe in things.*

"What did you go to college to study in the first place?" Girlie asked. "Computer science?"

William smiled, rueful. "Aerospace."

Girlie froze with a fry half in her mouth. "Aero—"

"I was very interested in the design of electrodynamic space tethers."

"What do they do?" Girlie asked, genuinely curious.

"Not provide a stable living, for one," William replied, taking a pull from his beer.

Girlie laughed. "I don't think someone from the lucrative industry known as the classics has room to laugh," William said. "Medieval French, you said?"

"It was 2002, we were all being told to explore our passions. How was I supposed to predict there was gonna be an extinction-level event for the humanities?" Even though she had, often, thought to herself that she should have predicted it—that being seventeen was no excuse. Then Girlie paused; she'd been wanting to ask for a while.

"Did you hire me for the medieval landscapes because that was on my file?"

He put his beer down. "In future, I'd advise not volunteering personal information to a multinational corporation if you don't wish it to be used at some point."

She looked at him, watched him register she was still waiting; that wouldn't be enough.

"It was a factor, among others. The knowledge of classics, the fact you spoke French and Spanish. As Robin's training as a vet technician helps his moderation of animal torture. He's considerably reduced the onsite horse abuse in Playground. I won't go into detail, but it was an issue."

"A factor among others."

"Are you fishing for a compliment you'll deflect the minute I give it?" William asked curtly, but didn't stop talking. "You were one of the best and most experienced content moderators in the country.

Your Bay Area site was the top-performing location in network until you left. Then this Vegas site took the crown. There was no possibility of not recruiting you." He picked his beer up again, put it to his mouth. "Sorry."

Now pre-empted, there was no snide comeback she could make. "I just wanted to know."

"What I want to know is, why did the best content moderator in the country study medieval anything to begin with," he said, leaning back into the booth—if he'd leaned forward, she would have crossed her arms. She crossed her arms anyway, at him leaving off the words *one of.* "What was the draw."

She shrugged. "I liked old worlds. Old words. Old things. Old people. The man who raised me was born in 1930. My morning cartoon was *Casablanca.*"

Girlie smiled, picked up her own beer and pulled from it. "Spiritually speaking, I'm silent generation."

"That—makes a lot of sense," William said, clearly understating the point.

Then he said:

"You were close to him."

She kept herself very still. "Yes."

He was looking at her, waiting; giving her time.

She averted her gaze. The inside of her throat felt abruptly raw.

"And—far from everybody else," she said, very low.

Next to her, he was quiet. She didn't want to look. But the force of her turned-away face was still attuned to him, to the steady rise and fall of his chest, his fingers on the cutlery.

She could feel he was studying her profile. Maybe he was realizing that she, too, had once been cared for, in the details. That she, too, had once been created lovingly.

"And that's why you prefer—" He nodded down to her watch.

"Vintage watches?" She cleared her throat. "Maybe—he had an old Seiko quartz dress watch he wore all the time, kind of a Patek Philippe 96 knockoff. I do—I like old mechanical watchmaking, it's true."

Girlie held her wrist closer to the lamp and watched William lean in to peer at the dial. His breath raised the goosebumps on her forearm. "If I hadn't been such a good moderator, maybe I would've become a vintage watch dealer."

She pulled her wrist back, took another fingerful of fries. William did the same. "And space, for you?"

William smiled, chewing. "Oh—well. I liked it, growing up. Never wanted to go into space myself, though. Always wanted to be the one on the ground. Or—building Mars rovers."

"Ground control to Major Tom."

William chuckled. "Yes. But there were too many old men in aeronautics, too much bureaucracy, military influence, red tape, buried dreams. Virtual reality seemed so much more—free. Alive."

"And more lucrative," Girlie supplied.

"Not at first."

"Not until Reeden?"

"Mm," William said, after a pause. He leaned down, started petting Mona's flank. She startled slightly at the touch, then, seeing it was him, licked the salt and potato bits off his fingers, then nestled up against him, so that her front paws were on either side of his leg, her snout buried in the hem of his pant leg. The weight of her butt was now entirely on Girlie's toes; she ran very warm. Girlie tried not to move, so Mona would stay where she was. Her left foot was staring to cramp.

"So what happened there," she said. "When Reeden came."

William didn't stop petting Mona, but Girlie saw his shoulders tense, the chords in his long, thin neck working. She'd realized something about his beauty, just now; why he wore it the way he wore it. Awkward kid, in his own head, no game, no charisma, too tall too early, dreaming of basketball and outer space, made a strange, charming, big-minded friend. Probably only became handsome in his mid- to late twenties, and had to figure out how to navigate around it, like a well-made coat he'd inherited out of the blue. He had no time-worn defiance around it, like her; hadn't had to turn it into a weapon, grasp its hilt in both hands, lest it be used against him. She was thinking too long about his beauty.

"Oh, you know," he said dismissively, trying to draw a curtain around the conversation, having realized he'd been talking about Edison for too long.

"Tale as old as time. We had the technology, we had the ambitions, but we were bleeding money. They had the story, but they'd reached the limits of their world. Our NHS funding was about to be cut. We needed a life raft. Reeden was already in talks with L'Olifant. They both wanted us. Or, they wanted our engine.

"Edison was optimistic, at first. He liked their stance on history; making the past fun, inspiring, seductive. The partnership started off positively. But it became clear they didn't care about Playground—Fairground, we were still calling it. They didn't care about the therapeutic angle, at least not how we were using it. They just wanted the space. And, well. As you see." William had finished one plate of fries.

Girlie gazed at him. "You loathe them," she said.

William blinked down at his empty plate. "Oh, loathing's the easy part," he said. "Loathing them and taking the money—that's the hard part." He forced a smile. "Fortunately, you can wipe tears with euros, dollar bills, *and* pound sterling."

"How did Edison feel about the buyout?"

William looked at her. At her; then through her.

"Well, he fell out of a high-rise in Canary Wharf, didn't he," he murmured. "And I inherited Mona."

"I'm sorry," she said, then winced; exactly the thing she hated hearing when people heard about her father. William nodded, received it with his majordomo face, tucking it away with the rest of the honest, useless condolences.

"To this day, I don't know—" William started, then stopped. "There was no note. Like I said, he had—he'd had depression, on and off, for as long as I'd known him. But there are times I wonder—" He trailed off.

"What?"

William hesitated. Then: "Edison was the one who thought up the Big Ben scenario," he said, low. "The one—Perera must have told you about it." Girlie nodded.

"That was his idea. Go for the gut-punch, when we were looking for buyers. It worked. It was powerful. Memorable. Everyone, everyone at the NHS, every other tech platform, journalist, they all loved it.

"But what if he—the whole aim of it was to show the possibilities of immersion, of perception modification. What if he—" William exhaled, a noisy gust. "Went in there too often, or—what if it made him—"

He swallowed. "I don't know. Was it in him before, or did the landscape modify him. Was it an accident, or—did he mean it. And if he meant it—. Did he mean to mean it."

They were silent. "My dad did something similar, at the end," Girlie said finally.

William's eyes flashed up to her; again, there was no surprise in them. "You've read my file," she said.

247

William didn't move, then nodded slowly.

"So. You know."

"I know what it says," William said. "That's all."

Girlie picked up her beer and sipped it; it had gone a little flat. "It says something like *unwilling to moderate scenes of suicide due to family history*. But I don't know. If he meant to go. He was already dying, it was cancer, maybe he didn't mean to. You can accidentally pull a plug. I don't know."

She put her beer down. "I don't know," she said again, quieter. "But—I think I know."

William didn't move. "Yes," he said after a long moment. She looked down at the plates; she'd eaten almost the entirety of the other plate of fries, which she realized he hadn't said anything about, and which perhaps was his design in the first place. "Rats didn't cause the bubonic plague," she said abruptly. His eyes shot up to meet hers.

"It's misinformation," she said. "They think it was fleas, now. I looked it up."

At the raw look on his face, she felt in her chest a sharp stinging, a thousand pins and needles, like something in there had been asleep for a long time—but now she was putting weight on it, and it was waking up.

She looked away, and picked up another extra crispy burnt bit. "I'm finishing this," she warned. William shook his head.

"I've got my mushrooms to fill me up," he said to make her laugh, and she did.

Then she raised her gaze to him again. "Did you love Edison?"

William jolted at that, as startled and doomed as a fawn. He looked distinctly too English for the American straightforwardness of the question. She was finding it was fun to tease him; though she wasn't teasing him now.

"Oh. Well. He was my best friend." He cleared his throat. "So. Yes. I suppose. I loved him."

"That's nice," she said. William blinked. "Loving someone, having a best friend," she clarified. "It's not nothing."

William smiled, but it wasn't his angel of history smile, no joy in it. Not a fictional Viking, not a maiden, not a knight in the lists, no angels here; but a living person. Someone with unhappy parents; a funny sister-in-law; a best friend who was dead. "It's not nothing," he agreed.

..

A scream came up from the other side of the room: Maribel was on one knee in front of Avery, who was covering her mouth with her hands, weeping. They were too far away for Girlie or William to hear the words clearly—Maribel, youngest daughter, baby cousin, hadn't had enough foresight or sense of organization to ask the bartender to turn off the music for her big moment, as Girlie would have—but. It didn't matter. Girlie could hear them bellowing, all the grand horns and trombones and toloches and requinto guitars of new sierreño, Eslabon Armado, all the everlasting klaxons of love, heralding the new generation. No—not just new, but: salvaged. Still here, and fighting. Avery was pulling Maribel into her arms, into her kiss, into her place in heaven, into all of her next lives. But this one first.

Everyone in the bar was whooping, even people who weren't part of the celebrations, even Mona, who'd stood up at the scream and was now barking, indignant, at the commotion; even the old man who'd called Mona beautiful without sparing them a glance—even William, who didn't quite whoop, but stood up, ramrod straight, and joined in the clapping.

Girlie didn't stand up; couldn't. She saw William slightly turn to look down at her, check what her face was doing—saw him notice; saw him face forward again; saw him keep clapping. Shifting slightly to the side, shielding her from view. It was her turn to be in the cool of his shadow.

· ·

"Okay, lovers," Girlie was saying to Maribel and Avery in the parking lot. "Congratulations, et cetera. If you hurt her, I'll kill you. Blah blah blah. You know the drill."

"Okay-okay, come with us to Puha next!" Maribel was saying, pulling on her sleeve.

William was off to the side, talking to somebody's English girlfriend, who'd realized that another Londoner was in the vicinity when William had to go to the bar to ask where the restroom was, trusting Girlie to hold on to Mona's leash. The girlfriend looked a little annoyed that another English person was there, as if it diminished the commodity value of her accent. William looked much the same, and yet they were continuing to chat, with increasingly hostile competing politenesses, about certain gentrified neighborhoods in South London.

Avery leaned into Girlie. "He's nice," she said quietly, catching Girlie in the act of looking at him. "I like his accent."

"Easy," Girlie warned.

"He *is* nice," Maribel agreed. Girlie stared at her ominously, warning her with her eyes not to tell Avery about William's involvement in the proposal. Maribel was wearing the watch; Girlie had sized it correctly. It looked good next to Avery's ring.

"I'm just saying, you've never brought anyone around like that," Avery said.

Girlie felt her blood pressure rising, abruptly at the end of her rope with their noblesse oblige generosity, the overflowing cup of their conjugal bliss, leaving a spray of couples wherever its blessing alighted. "One, I didn't bring him around—*you* invited him, dickhead," she hissed, pointing at Maribel. "Happy birthday again. May you live a long and happy life together. Two, I would never fuck my boss. And three, I would never fuck anyone in a position of power over me. Anyone not my equal."

"Cross-examination," Avery said. "You don't think anyone's your equal."

Maribel nodded thoughtfully. "And you'd never fuck anyone you thought was beneath you."

"Rebuttal. Final motions," Avery said gleefully. Maribel threw her arms around Avery's neck in pride, and they slipped once again into the leafy cool of their lover's bower; grinned at each other like idiots; kissed.

"Motions?" William asked, coming up to them. Mona was starting to look tired; she settled down back onto the concrete the minute he stopped moving.

"It's nothing," Girlie said. "I'll see you back at home." This, to Maribel and Avery.

"How are you gonna get home?"

"I'm just gonna Uber."

"But it's surge pricing!"

"We'll march about it tomorrow."

Maribel wouldn't budge, still in the circle of Avery's arms. "I don't like the idea of you in an Uber this late." Girlie tried to breathe in through her nose, out through her mouth.

"I can drop you off," William said, which Girlie knew was going to happen, and which Maribel had clearly been angling for.

ELAINE CASTILLO

"It's really fine."

"I wouldn't subject anyone to surge pricing if I could help it."

"Yes!" Maribel said, really milking the birthday–engagement good-will. "Thank you! I'd feel a lot better."

Girlie exhaled hard. "Come here." She took both Avery and Maribel into her hug, one arm for each. "Count your fucking days," Girlie muttered.

Maribel, sparkling, didn't hear her. "What?"

"I think what you meant to say is *congratulations, good night, get home safe, I love you*," Avery said.

Avery's lipstick was smeared from all the kisses; Maribel's face was covered in red streaks, as were the faces of all their friends, climbing into their cars. Girlie took hold of Avery's chin, pinching it. She could feel Avery's jaw move, the force of her stupid, lucky, shit-eating grin so strong it moved her hand. "Congratulations, ading." Avery squeezed her eyes shut; they both knew Girlie had never called her ading before. Then Avery kissed the tips of Girlie's fingers, hard, so she was marked red too.

Girlie turned to where William had been. Now he was at his car, a Volvo electric SUV—she thought of her early guess, close enough—popping open the trunk. Surreally, she watched him take out a miniature set of carpet-covered plastic stairs, then open the back-seat door. He positioned the stairs against the car. "Up-up-up, Mona," she heard him coo. Mona hopped elegantly up the stairs, into the car.

Girlie approached. The entire back seat was covered in a nylon hammock, plastered with dog hair. William leaned forward into the car, pulling out a little seat belt that was secured into one of the holders, then attached it to the back clip on Mona's harness. She settled her head down on top of her paws.

Girlie saw him crouch, smooth down the fur on the top of Mona's head, kiss her between the ears. He zipped up the sides of the hammock, so she was properly secured, then closed the back-seat door. Now he turned around, and seeing Girlie there, opened the front passenger door.

"Your decision entirely," he said, sounding sharp and professional for the first time that evening. Now he sounded like the William she saw at work, the one who could freeze a man just about to slit her throat, the one who knew to kick her out of the world before she had to ask for help. Not that soft, sexable William, looking lonely, separate, hungry, familiar: cleaning his plate, never taking his coat off, telling Maribel *be brave*. She got in the car.

..

In front of the house at Living Edens Court, the lights were off, as usual; everyone asleep, or not yet home from the party. Girlie had never once brought a stranger this close to her home. Six years ago, she only ever went to Sam's place, three orgasms in two months, none particularly strong, and she'd have never spoken to her again if the opportunity cost of burning a good retail and service connect hadn't been so high.

"Well," William said. "Thank you for—thank you."

"Thank *you*," Girlie said. "For making Maribel insufferable for the next month."

"Glad to have made a good impression," William said. Girlie swallowed. Wanted to say, is that what you were trying to do? Make a good impression?

"Well, thank you, then, for—indulging my—mad five minutes," William added. Girlie shook her head.

"It was—mad. But."

Girlie looked for the words. They were right there.

"Thank you. For—. Thank you for encouraging her. Avery— Avery's a good person. I mean she's a dickhead. But. She's—. They're it for each other. So," Girlie said. "It was the right call."

"It felt like the right thing to do," he agreed. He paused. "Doesn't that ever happen to you?"

"What?"

William didn't turn to her. His face was not far enough away. Girlie's heart, stupidly, started to race. She couldn't even look at that mouth; hurt to try. He was staring straight ahead, both hands on the steering wheel, clutching it very tightly.

"Feeling as though something is the right thing to do, and doing it," he said blankly, eyes fixed on a point in front of him.

Something in her was fluttering, frantic, panicky, young; she was sliding toward the precipice of something, and she had to kick her feet out, back-crawl up from its edge; there was an alternative reality here whose glowing warmth she could almost touch, and she had to back off, log out, mute, block. He slid his gaze to her then. His eyes were very dark; he looked—panicked, too, like he couldn't remember how he'd gotten here either. She had to cry; she had to kiss him; she had to get out of the car.

"I do the right thing all the time," she said, her voice bright, chirpy, corporate. "Thank you for the ride. Good night, Mona! Nice to meet you! Thanks for coming!"

At the mention of her name, William turned instinctively to look at Mona, sleeping in the back like a child. His hands relaxed briefly on the steering wheel, face softening, flooded with helpless love for her; so that's what it looked like. When he turned back to Girlie, she was already out of the car, already slamming the door.

7

The Wheel

he next week, it was clear they were avoiding each other. An elegant mutual détente, agreed upon in silence. That long, strange night on the Moon had happened; but now they were back on Earth. Like astronauts who grow taller in space, spines elongating, freed from their customary compressions, each cartilage-cushioned disc finding new space—now, restored to gravity, they were contracting once more, shrunk, sore, themselves.

Still their eyes met, once or twice: in the amphitheater, as she was handing out popcorn; in Paris, as she studied a line of tourists waiting to see the Eiffel Tower. Each smiled at the other, polite and deterring, each with a little electric nothing of a smile.

Perera, on the other hand, seemed weirdly nervous. On Friday, when she entered his office, ready to finally learn the front crawl, she found him behind his desk, scrolling through his phone, forehead wrinkled.

He startled when she came through the door, jumping to his feet as if he'd been looking at porn, upturning the empty coffee cup that had been balanced precariously at the edge of his desk. Immediately turning off the screen of his phone and shoving it in his pocket, he then righted the coffee cup, checking there had been no spillage.

"Ms. Delmundo," he greeted, clearly trying to sound normal. "Sorry, I—how are you doing today? Sorry. Come in."

"Did—am I early?" Girlie made a show of checking her watch; she wasn't, and knew it.

"No, no, no—sorry. It's been a bit of—just a stressful day. Week. Weeks. Since the launch. To be expected, of course. I apologize. Have a seat. I'll get you started right away. Front crawl today, was it?"

Girlie sat in the reclining lounge. "Late in the day to have coffee."

Perera looked at her blankly, the headset hanging from his hands; she had a brief concern that he'd had a sudden fit of amnesia, and did not know where he was, or who she was. He blinked, shook his head, then looked down at his coffee cup.

"Oh! Yes. No. Well. I used to be a seven-cup-a-day drinker, used to drink coffee well into the night—used to have a bedtime cup of coffee, even."

"Wow."

Perera laughed. "Yes. Well, you know. As it usually goes with doctors. Do as I say, not as as I do. Then the bad heartburn started." He pointed to the antacids on his desk, Rennie brand. Girlie decided to be kind.

"My dad took six Tums with every meal, and at bedtime. Also a doctor. I don't know that brand."

"Rennie. Much better than Tums, you don't have it here. British. Well, it's owned by Bayer now, I think. Tums is just calcium carbonate. Rennie has that, plus the magnesium carbonate, plus the alginic acid—I have to buy them on Amazon over here. But it's more than worth the hassle. God," Perera started laughing, scraping a hand over his face.

"Sorry. I don't know why I'm talking about heartburn medication. I'm not sponsored. I have no stake in Bayer."

"Rennie. I'll look it up."

"Please do," Perera said, somewhat too passionately. "All right. Phelps program. Yes."

He busied himself doing nothing, putting the mask back on its velvet pad, picking it up, looking through his desk for a pen, not finding one, finding one in his front pocket, then patting his chest for his glasses, patting the top of his head, before realizing he was wearing them.

From her comparably restful position, Girlie looked at him and said, "Do you need a minute?"

"No, no," Perera said reflexively, picking the headset back up and coming to approach her.

Then he stopped, standing in front of his desk, facing her, and his shoulders slumped. He leaned back against the desk, letting it take a fraction of his weight.

"Yes. Just. I'd like to talk to you about something."

Girlie sat up straighter. "Of course."

"Just—" Perera took his glasses off, rubbing at the deep indentations on either side of his nose bridge. "I'd just—I may be out of office next week. I've been considering a—sabbatical. And I was thinking—I was thinking maybe you'd like to take the therapeutic suit home. Just in case. Just to be able to continue your—lessons."

"Take home?" Girlie shook her head, slowly. "I'm not allowed to do that. I've signed—"

"I know what you've signed," Perera said, rough. "Yes. I'm just. If I'm not here next week, I'm concerned you and the other moderators may not be able to keep up with your—lessons."

"I can skip one week."

"My holiday may last longer than that."

"Two, then."

"Ms. Delmundo," Perera said. "When we're done with our session today, I'm going to ask that you take your suit and mask home with you. If you don't wish to, that's your choice, of course."

"I think it's better if I don't."

"Yes," he said, sighing. "Right. I thought you might say that."

"I'm—sorry," Girlie said slowly. "It's just—I did sign."

"Yes. Yes. All right. Very good," Perera said, sounding like he meant the exact opposite. He frowned. "It's just—I don't know how long they'll—I don't know if the funding for this therapeutic team will be renewed. I don't know how much support we have at the— upper levels. Anymore."

"Oh," Girlie said. She thought of Rhea, asking where the expensive candy bars had gone. *The first sign a start-up is going to fail is if the snacks are expensive.* "Is that—something that's being discussed?"

"It's just," Perera exhaled harshly. "Is it an entertainment device, or a medical device? They can't have it both ways. They've had ten years to figure this out, instead of—messing about with—Playground box sites to build reputation, doing study after study. If they're sell- . ing a medical device, there are FDA approval processes—a human factors and usability team, a regulatory team. There are questions about privacy. *You* signed away any data gathered by Playground when you started working here"—WITH REGARD TO HEALTH INFOR- MATION, YOU ACKNOWLEDGE THAT REEDEN IS NOT A BUSINESS ASSOCI- ATE OR SUBCONTRATOR (AS THOSE TERMS ARE DEFINED IN THE HEALTH INSURANCE PORTABILITY AND ACCOUNTABILITY ACT ["HIPAA"] AND THAT THE SERVICES ARE NOT HIPAA COMPLIANT, and Girlie had signed;

how else to get the job?—"but with a civilian user, who just buys a Playground device—what about the privacy of their medical disclosures on site? What about duty of care? Who's going to be doing the guidance for the sessions? It isn't—this isn't a sodding meditation app," he said, almost spitting while he spoke.

"I would've thought all of that would be well established at the time of purchase," Girlie said. "The way William tells it—"

"*William*," Perera muttered, as if to say *Don't get me started*.

"The way William tells it," Girlie continued, a little thrown by Perera's vitriol, "Playground was always supposed to be a bit of both. Therapy, via entertainment. Entertainment, via therapy. Immersion. With real-life effects."

"I don't claim to have privileged knowledge of what William Cheung believes or doesn't believe about Playground," Perera said darkly. "I know that since Reeden and the French showed up, the entire therapeutic team has been squeezed. I know they've let go of more than half of the PTSD research team, who'd been there from the beginning. I know they've just put some—ex-Boeing VP—as the new director of human factors. Boeing! Human factors! Design and risk management! They want psychology and engineering degrees and industrial designers and art school graduates to just get along, because it looks good in the press release. *The world's best engineers and artists, working side by side.* But those teams have been fighting every step of the way, arguing over every bloody usability study, and have been for years, and burning money while they do it. And we all know they want the medical data for—whatever they want it for. To learn how to—get in people's heads. Who bloody knows. You must've read the articles."

"Mindless peons don't read *New Yorker* think pieces."

Perera stopped short of rolling his eyes. "Oh, go on, pull the other one."

Girlie smiled meanly. "Are you going to tell me I have wasted potential?"

Perera exhaled, shutting up. He seemed to be wondering why he was even talking to her in the first place.

But Girlie would always tongue a loose tooth. Said, "Wonder what Edison would have said about it."

Now Perera turned burning eyes to her.

"Edison Lau," he declared, "was volatile, clinically depressed, and angry about everything, primarily at how brilliant he was, and how little that seemed to matter."

"You and William kept calling him an idealist—"

"All cynics are frustrated idealists," Perera snapped. He scrutinized her. "In that way, you remind me a bit of him."

"Rest assured, I don't have any ambitions to create a revolution in virtual reality."

Perera scoffed. "I meant, Americans with a chip on their shoulder." That found its target.

"That's a factory setting. I wasn't aware there were other kinds," Girlie tried to joke; but she was winded.

Perera grimaced. "There are other kinds."

Then he let out a deep exhale, wet and gurgling, like he was sighing through a slit throat. He shook his head; pasted on a smile. "Lord. I've gone on for too long."

The disappointment she felt radiating from him felt as personal and intimate as a slap: she'd made a choice he'd predicted she would make, responded in a way he'd predicted she would respond, and in perfectly meeting his expectations, she'd let him down. A soreness came to Girlie's chest. Her hand almost lifted, to cut some gesture into the moment and halt it, take whatever she'd done back, but she didn't know how to—do that.

Perera smiled again, suitably enough, holding up the headset it would be illegal for her to take home. "Front crawl. Shall we?"

..

REEDEN BESET WITH ACCUSATIONS OF SELLING US-ER'S MEDICAL DATA. THE LARGEST SOCIAL MEDIA COMPANY IN THE WORLD IS BEING SUED FOR SUP-PLYING U.S. HOSPITALS WITH A DATA-TRACKING TOOL THAT ALLEGEDLY DISCLOSES CONFIDENTIAL PATIENT INFORMATION TO ITS SUBSIDIARIES, IN-CLUDING NEWEST ACQUISITION, THE VIRTUAL EN-TERTAINMENT JUGGERNAUT PLAYGROUND. I WAS RAPED IN VIRTUAL REALITY: THE EVOLUTION OF SEXUAL ASSAULT IN REEDEN'S NEW ALTERNATE UNI-VERSE. PLAYGROUND BLOCKS AND BANS USERS FOR SHARING NEW YORK TIMES ARTICLE SHOWING AB-ORIGINAL MEN IN CHAINS THROUGH GAME'S PUB-LIC CHAT ROOMS. THE PERSONAL LIFE IS DEAD IN AMERICA, HISTORY HAS KILLED IT: HOW TO NAVI-GATE PLAYGROUND'S NEW TAKE ON HISTORICAL REENACTMENT? PATIENTS CONSIDERING CLASS AC-TION LAWSUIT AGAINST PLAYGROUND AND PARENT COMPANY REEDEN FOR COLLECTING PROTECTED HEALTH INFORMATION. HOW VIRTUAL REALITY PROMISES TO CHANGE THE SHAPE OF OUR MINDS: AN INTERVIEW WITH MAURICE DE COLIGNY. FROM

REEDEN TO INSTAGRAM TO TIKTOK TO PLAY-
GROUND: WILL THE NEXT ONLINE FRONTIER MAKE
OR BREAK US?

..

Instead of leaving Perera's office, dropping her suit at the cleaning chutes, and going straight home, as she usually did, Girlie felt herself walking—down, back to the Playground moderator floor, the glass-ceiling nave just in her sights, past the hallway of closed wooden doors, the other moderators having already gone home. She was walking toward one door in particular: warm Californian oak, mid-century detailing. She didn't know what she was doing, until she was doing it. She knocked on William's door.

No one answered. She knocked again. Still no one. She leaned in, her ear to the wood, trying to hear whether someone was in there, maybe he was still on-site, mask on—but the door swung upon, and she nearly tumbled into his chest.

He stared down at her, looking harassed, frayed around the edges; then his face eased a little. "Hi—hello," he said.

She yanked her ear, and the head attached to it, away from the warmth of him. He wasn't wearing a jacket; he jumped back when she did, as if remembering that he should.

"Sorry," he said, straightening. "Hello. Can I—please come in. Please excuse the mess."

There was still no mess to be observed, except for an open laptop on his desk, a few print magazines, *The New York Times*, *The New Yorker*, *The Atlantic*, *The Guardian*, every outlet that had published something on Playground in the last month.

Girlie entered slowly, eyes darting around again, realizing she was now looking for Mona. But of course she wasn't there; senior doggy daycare. There was no dog bed; though she wondered, peering, if there was one under his large desk.

"How's Mona?" Girlie asked. The wild look in William's eyes subsided slightly. "Oh. She's—she's well. She—I think she enjoyed the party," he said. "I don't—she likes people more than I give her credit for. I don't socialize her as much as I should, probably. She does quite like the attention."

"Maribel says the chocolates were delicious."

"Oh," William said, giving up a damp sort of smile. "I'm glad to hear that. I was afraid they might have melted in my pocket."

"We'd never heard of that brand."

"Fortnum and Mason?"

Girlie shook her head. "I thought it was a Tiffany box, at first. Color's similar."

"Oh," William said, for the third time, which was making him sound unhinged. "No, it's—I suppose they wouldn't sell them physically here in the States, but they do ship internationally. It's a known sort of—slightly upmarket company, they do hampers—. They make nice Christmas and birthday gifts."

He looked mortally embarrassed at having been revealed to have made an effort. He was rubbing the knuckles of his left hand with his right, back and forth, in a nervous tic she hadn't ever seen him do.

"Are—you all right," Girlie asked, feeling her brow wrinkle.

William was looking at her like—she couldn't put a finger on it. Eyes wide, like he couldn't believe she was there, that she'd just shown up like that, the way you looked when you were thinking about someone and they came strolling around the corner at that exact moment.

"No—yes. I—well. Now that you're here. I was going to—I was going to come to your office sometime—"

He went to his desk, then hesitated. Finally he pulled out one of the drawers, tried to make a show of ruffling through the contents, but Girlie could see he was just pushing around air, had his eyes locked on exactly what he'd opened the drawer for. He lifted up a thick, multicolored volume of books, hardcover, gilt lettering, looked fancy.

"I just—I was going to give this to you," he said, his voice so hard it almost sounded like an insult, like he was keeping the sentence from cracking. He came back around to meet her in front of his desk, then shoved the volume forward. She took it from him carefully, as always, without touching him.

She looked down at the gift; *The Sherlock Holmes Collection*, it read. Deluxe six-book hardcover edition.

"It's got *The Hound of the Baskervilles* in it," William explained, sounding absolutely horrified at the proceedings in which he had found himself. "I just—you hadn't—it was supposed to be—congratulations—the company budgeted on something small for all of the new moderators, after the launch. Vuthy, for example—. We got him something from Le Creuset. He said—he's been learning to cook," he finished, miserably.

"I started reading it," Girlie said, still looking down at the books. "It's free online. Project Gutenberg."

"Oh," he said, a fourth time. Then, softer: "Oh."

She didn't trust herself to look up, see what his face looked like then.

"Thank you," she said, her thumbs pressing down on the spines, chest tight.

"It's—I don't—if you don't feel it's appropriate, please, don't hesitate, I wouldn't in any way want to—"

"I like it," Girlie said. "Thank you. It's not even my birthday."

"Right," William said. Then he blinked. "Your—when's that?"

"End of August. You?"

"End of January," William said.

Now Girlie looked up at him.

"What—*this* January? It passed? Here? You didn't tell anyone?"

"God, no," William said. "Why would I do that?"

"When was it?"

William smiled a little. "You remember that day, with—. The time you caught me with that—lolly?"

Girlie's eyes widened. "*That* was your birthday?"

William nodded. "Shared a takeaway with Mona that evening. She's partial to naan."

Girlie started laughing. Now they stared at each other helplessly, like they weren't sure how they'd gotten here again.

William rocked back on his heels, retreated for cover behind his desk, shutting the lid to his laptop. He'd stopped looking at her.

"Did you—you came in for something?"

"I can't remember now," Girlie said honestly, looking down at the box set, face soft.

William cleared his throat. "I—also—gave that to you now because—I might not—I don't know how long—that is—"

"You, too?" Girlie asked. "Perera was just freaking out in his office earlier. What, is everyone getting fired?"

William pasted a blank smile on his face.

"The official company script is that everything is going well, and any rumors of impending layoffs are completely unfounded."

"Jesus," Girlie said.

William squeezed his eyes shut, like that wasn't what he'd meant to say.

"Look—you—that's not—you'll be fine. I shouldn't have said that," he said, more to himself than her. "But you'll—you'll be fine."

"Easy for you to say, senior management," Girlie retorted. "Not all of us can run back to a country with universal health care."

William looked at her, hard.

"I'm aware of that," he said sharply. Then he turned away.

"You'd like England, I think," he said, all of a sudden. "It's very bleak. And repressed."

"Don't forget the weather's also supposed to be shitty."

"It has that to recommend it, as well," William said thinly.

Girlie snorted. William turned to his office chair, staring at the suit jacket there like he'd forgotten what it was there for, what he was supposed to do with it. After a beat, he picked the jacket up by the shoulders, started to shrug it on, his back facing her. When he turned around, he was smiling, full majordomo, receptive, placid—but there were corrupted frames in it, dead pixels.

"If I don't see you—" William began, then caught himself.

He was closer than she'd realized, had come around the desk to stand in front of her, eyes intent, his glance darting around every part of her face, her forehead, her eyebrows, her nose, her cheeks, the mole by her lip, an old scar on her chin, her mouth, like he was memorizing them; or, rather, like he was verifying something he'd memorized a long time ago, but wanted to revisit, to make sure he'd got it right. She felt—not naked under his gaze, not exposed, not laid bare at all, not assessed and evaluated and archived. But: tucked in, covered up, refuged, safe. When their eyes finally met he still looked desolate, hopeless, that old cozy death still in his face—but surging through it, bursting at the seams of its skin, the irrepressible hunger of the living.

"No. Never mind. I'll be on my way. You should get home yourself, Ms. Delmundo. It's getting late. Have a good weekend."

"William—"

"Don't worry about the door," he said, already walking out of it, taking the laptop in a tote he held by the handles, unzipped, broken in for years, old Bottega, didn't look like his taste, why should she even know what his taste looked like; was the bag, too, another beautiful and carelessly used thing he'd inherited from Edison, "it'll lock behind you."

● ●

She didn't go home.

She—she was walking—upstairs, to the topmost floor, past the employee gym, the rows of unmanned cardio machines, the racks of unused dumbbells, the doors to the showers and the toilets and all the bottles of Aesop soap, until finally she made her way to the roof, and thus reached a place she'd never been, never considered going, until she touched her fob to the entry sensor and smelled it first, its chlorine clarity, then heard it next, the hushed, blue, pelagic sound of it, and then, finally, walking forward, saw it: the pool.

She looked up, first at the corners of the glass roof—she couldn't immediately tell what might be a camera and what might just be a light fixture, but she assumed there was an unmanned video feed being recorded somewhere, to be deleted unseen after six months, unless a lawsuit required otherwise. Reeden had subcontracted management of the gym out to some other company, probably a subsidiary of a 24 Hour Fitness, or some boutique gym chain specializing in corporate clients. There might be video, but no one would be moderating it; she would be surveilled but not seen. She started taking off her clothes, leaving just her bra and underwear.

Facing the shallow end of the pool, she hugged her arms around herself, gingerly touching one foot to the surface of the water, bracing for a brumal chill, feeling instead the reliable warmth of round-the-clock wealth. She put her right foot on the first stone step that led into the shallow end of the pool, then her left. She stood there, still hugging herself, before she thought, *some of us weren't pussies*, and walked straight into the water until it reached just below her shoulders.

She got herself into position, back to the edge of the pool, touching the rough surface of the wall with something near to humility, like she was touching the surface of a meteorite. She was slightly crouched, her arms stretched out in front of her, prepared to slice through the water, one foot on the ground and one foot propped against the pool wall. She wasn't quite ready to fully glide underwater yet, but maybe she could try breaststroke with her head above water.

"The above-water posture is technically an incorrect version of breaststroke," one lesson had said, "but if you find it more comfortable to practice while you get used to being underwater, then that's perfectly all right. If it's good enough for dogs, it's good enough for all of us! And in fact, some people say it's even harder than the correct, submerged technique!"

She set off forward, trying to get the rhythm right, pushing the water away with her arms and legs, trying to keep her body balanced and her rhythm correct, so she would be propelled forward, not tilting left and right, or dragging herself down. She could manage to get a decent length away from the edge, until her arms and legs fatigued and she felt herself starting to sink again—trying to tread water was proving harder in this pool than in the virtual one, and she found her feet scrambling for the bottom of the pool more than once. She didn't have the strength or stamina to safely swim the deep end yet, that was clear. Still, she could get a decent way across the pool with her little hybrid froggy-doggy paddle, even if it was only in the shallow end, which was more than she'd ever been able to do before. A thought was intruding, calling for her attention, but she didn't give it safe passage yet.

She tried several times to put her face in the water, but every time she felt the water go into her nostrils, she splashed up in a panic, coughing and choking, shoving stray hair out of her face. She had in mind the stroke she'd been practicing, slinking her body underwater sleek and pointed as a fish, the way she'd done so many times in the virtual pool, but here she could barely keep her nose underwater for more than a few seconds before she sputtered back up again.

Frustrated, she clung to the edge of the shallow end of the pool, back to the water. Her knees were tucked up under her; she rubbed her nose along an old schoolyard scar.

She'd wanted to swim across the whole length of the pool, at least once. But she knew she wouldn't be able to do it with her above-water breaststroke; her neck and arms and legs clearly weren't strong enough yet to keep her afloat that way. There was perception modification, and then there was actual muscle-building. Then she remembered one of her early lessons. The pulse of the other world. She squeezed her hands on the lip of the pool again, back to the water, face pressed up against her knees.

The age-old dilemma came calling—float or sink, live or die—and she crouched there in the familiar fetal tension of it, the spiraling enclosing inevitability of it, until finally, fuck it, she shook hands with her death, patient in its old waiting room, and let go of the ledge, pushing herself backward into the water: expecting to sink, and probably die, and it was good while it lasted, or it wasn't, really, but there were bits of good in it, here and there, bright and defeating amid the more than minor hells—but as she surrendered, she felt the water, all around her, buoying her up.

Her heart was pounding. Floating had been one of the earliest, simplest lessons, but she'd wanted to graduate quickly to the more showy, technical, advanced stuff, the harder crawls and strokes and glides. But here she was: weightless, easy. It was child's play, no more difficult than swallowing a draught of cool rockwater. She floated there in uneasy repose, drifting like a current of oil atop the surface of the pool, for a long opulent moment that might have lasted forever. But then, remembering what she'd come there to do, she thought: why not. And started to move her arms.

The backstroke was sloppy; she hadn't really practiced it as much as the other, more impressive strokes, and when she finally brought her legs and feet in to help with the motion, the echoing sound of her flapping and kicking and slicing was so deafening and unruly it threatened to distract her from the more urgent issue at hand—that of not drowning. But on the whole, it wasn't very difficult, she was finding. It wasn't difficult at all, in fact.

All this time, she'd wanted to do it the hard way, the bootstrapper's way; as always, she'd been preparing herself to blunt-force it, grind through it, straight-A it, but—the easy way was right there. The easy way was hard enough.

When her fingers hit against tiled edge, she wasn't fatigued at all; she was almost laughing, loose and liquid in her skin, until she curled in, twisted her body so she was vertical again, and realized there was no immediate touch of the floor beneath her feet, and she started to sink. She scrabbled forward to hold onto the ledge, swallowing a mouthful of water then coughing, water in her nose, eyes stinging, waiting there for a moment until she got wind back into her lungs. Then, slowly, she lowered herself back down, one hand clutching the edge, one foot searching, until, submerged until her eyebrows, she found it: the bottom.

She popped back up, still holding onto the edge, breathing fast. She looked back at the direction from which she'd come: she'd crossed the entire length of the pool, floating over the deep end at the center, and made it to the other side. She stared across that expanse, for a long time.

And if she could do something about it? Repair the old tear in her brain, the rent in the world that had given her a personality? Walk into a fairground and rewire her circuits, carve virgin paths, build new hardware? Never again have to leave a room if people started singing karaoke, or wore Polo Ralph Lauren cologne? Sure; she would change it. Hadn't she already made a start? The hard reset she'd made of her life: her Roth IRA; her Excellent credit score; her new name; her good job. She hadn't gone full-throttle world-building, like Edison, but—hadn't she?

When they'd moved to Vegas, she used to have dreams: about losing this house, too, about there being some sort of mix-up, the house belonging to someone else. Dreams of the thirty-two-year-old who'd been her first kiss at seven: dreams she was older, he was desperate to see her, they were spooning in bed, they were married, they had to be quiet, she was beloved, she was forgetting something. After she bought her mom the Tesla: that there'd been some mix-up with her financing, that they'd given her the wrong car, had to start her payments from scratch. When she'd gone to Vanguard to set up her Roth: that she'd done the paperwork wrong, that she'd been paying her money into the wrong account, that the safety net she started building for herself, the little escape route for a day that would never come, had evaporated, gone to someone else, never been hers at all.

She hadn't had any bad dreams since Playground. She hadn't wanted to tell William that little truth, back when he'd hinted that moderators were prone to nightmares. The fact was, she hadn't had a single nightmare in months.

She thought of Perera, who couldn't go up to high places anymore. Not afraid enough, he'd said back then. There were things she found she couldn't quite do anymore either. Also: things she could.

At last, she let it in, the knocking thought, now a welcomed knowing. She'd wanted to know, and now she did. She could swim. She'd learned how to swim.

• •

The following Monday, all looked as it had been, except there were fewer cars in the parking lot; not Aditya's, not William's, not Perera's.

First she saw Vuthy, storming away from the building, toward his car. They met each other's gaze; she lifted her hand in a confused wave. "Door's not working!" he fumed. "I think—I'm going to Starbucks. I'll be back. Fuck!" He went to his car, immediately started typing something on his phone, the driver's-side door still open.

Vuthy turned again to Girlie, shaking his head. Yelled, "Check Twitter!" His phone started ringing. Then his head snapped up—

Aditya's car was squealing into the parking lot, stopping abruptly by Vuthy's.

Aditya, still holding his phone, jumped out of the car. Vuthy scrambled over to him, shoving his head against his chest. Aditya pulled him into a hug—then he caught Girlie's eyes.

His face froze, then he glared at her, something mean and daring in his face. She made no expression in return, taken aback by the strength of it. He told Vuthy something; Vuthy nodded, locked his own car again, let Aditya bundle him into the passenger side of his Tesla. They drove off, Aditya swirling the driver's seat to face Vuthy, letting the car take over.

Girlie stared at this departing car, then made her way to the entrance. A premonition started, just at the back of her neck, behind her ears, raising the hair on her forearms.

Robin was already there. He saw her coming. "Hey," he said. "Red for me."

"Shit," Girlie said. "You think it's just gonna happen like that?"

"Nuked 'em at Google that way," Robin said. "Vuthy almost broke the thing tryna get in."

She touched her fob to the entry pad, holding her breath, waiting for the light to turn red. But it turned green, and unlocked the door. Something under her ribs clutched.

Robin whistled. "Congrats. I'm 'bout to go donate some plasma."

She turned to him, holding the door open. "Are you—are you gonna be okay?"

Robin was thinking to himself, not paying attention to her, eyes distant. "Hey," she barked again, like throwing cold water onto someone's knocked-out face. "Are you okay?"

He looked at her, shook the fog from his eyes. Said: "I'm gonna go back to school and get my DVM."

"Oh. Sick. That's—great," Girlie said awkwardly.

"Yeah," Robin said, not really talking to her; she was just the stranger who was there to witness his whole life changing. "What a bunch of fucking assholes." Then he nodded at the green light on the door. "Good luck, fam."

Never the most populated of workplaces at the best of times—which had added to the feeling of being part of an exclusive team of elites, she supposed—and yet there was a palpable, unpeopled hush in the air of things now, in the lobby, the transept, the elevator up to her floor.

She had the distinct sense that she was trespassing, that she had entered a place she was not supposed to enter. But—the door had let her in.

Girlie opened the door to her office, waiting, somehow, for disaster; for it to be ransacked, for the little store of provisions she'd started keeping there, protein powder and bags of matcha tea, to be tossed hither and thither in disarray like the debris from a shipwreck.

But everything was as it was, nothing had been touched. Her suit, mask, and gloves were on the desk, freshly cleaned, fully charged. There was just that eerie silence in the air, that calm, sedate wrongness she'd felt, that one night, the day she now knew was William's birthday.

She suited up. Put on her gloves, the mask, turned the device on. It started up, as usual; the power hadn't been cut, her access hadn't been overridden. Everything was normal so far.

The login screen popped up. She entered in her identification information, but before she could enter the option menu to choose the landscape she was scheduled to moderate, as per her Monday schedule, the scene before her changed.

She was in the lobby—but no, it wasn't just the lobby. It wasn't just the antechamber to the rest of the Playground sites. There was an unfinished richness to the world she now found herself in, like a great horde of treasure left abandoned by pirates. It was the world under the world she'd seen, the first time William had introduced her to the Playground site. It was the fair.

The marble-white city, the palaces, here it all was again, familiar and unfamiliar, like a hometown she'd left and misremembered. The same crush of people in bowler hats and cravats and handlebar mustaches, the same voice saying, *But I don't want to miss the opening ceremonies, darling*; the gold-leafed dome, the ice cream vendors, the ear-splitting tumult of the Cascades pouring into the Grand Basin, and the shadow of the Ferris wheel. She was staring up at it, stupefied, like every other fairgoer there, until she realized someone was coming toward her, and the someone was Mona.

Or: not Mona, but the canine character who'd been based on Mona in her adolescence, the same sable German shepherd she'd seen the first day she'd ever set foot on the Playground site. Girlie had wanted to step toward the dog that first day, but hadn't. Now the dog was trotting to her, and the dog was Mona.

"Hi, mama," she said when Mona approached. She looked younger, which, of course, she was; her face darker, the gray hairs having not yet made their appearance, eyes still sharp, ears still pricked high.

This Mona didn't approach to sniff her hands for chicken residue, or settle at her feet to put her large butt on her shoe. This Mona was a stranger; kept slightly apart; wasn't familiar with her; had been programmed thus. Her mouth was open, panting, and then she let out one high-pitched bark; a bark of play or alert, Girlie didn't know.

Then Mona turned around, starting to walk away. She got about ten feet before she turned around again, expectantly, waiting for Girlie to follow her. Girlie obeyed.

They weaved through the fair, past the corn-eaters and the butter-gawkers and the little imagined boats full of little imagined souls; the Colonnade of States, and a race of female giants, made of what looked like stone, but up close, looked more like papier-mâché, hemp, and plaster. Their arms were outstretched, carrying torches. Every ten to twenty feet, Mona looked back, ears erect, to make sure Girlie was following, sometimes slowing down so Girlie could catch up.

"Good girl," Girlie said to her. Mona huffed, perhaps programmed to react favorably to user attention, and kept going.

One of the fairgoers she noticed for the first time as they hurried through the world was an older Asian man, dressed anachronistically in modern clothing, which was why he caught Girlie's eye. A khaki zip-up jacket, plaid collar. He turned a little at her gaze, and she stopped in her tracks. For a nanosecond, seeing the gold-rimmed glasses the man wore, Girlie thought it was her own father. Then she saw the man's specific, wide, aged face: the gray in his thick black hair; his warm, toothy, too-quick, too-bright smile, two dimples on either side. She and Mona passed the man. He continued smiling at nothing at all, benevolently and impersonally. The man was on the lookout for somebody else, somebody who wasn't there, wasn't coming.

Finally they reached their destination: the Ferris wheel. All the passenger cars had already been filled, Girlie saw, and they were approaching as the last car was loading, just at the tail end of the queue. Mona escorted her to the back of the line, waiting next to her like a sentinel, heeling loosely at her side as the line of people slowly filed into the car, with Girlie the final passenger.

When she reached the doors of the passenger car, she saw, at the back of the car, behind a crush of people, next to a window, looking straight at her, waiting: William.

She stared at him for a long moment, then felt a nudge at the back of her thigh. Mona was urging her into the passenger car, which was still moving. She took a step onto the car, felt it accept her weight.

She looked down at Mona, waiting outside. "Thank you," she called.

Mona watched the car move smoothly along, and when the doors closed and it finally began to lift, slowly, into the sky, she wandered away, disappearing into the crowd.

Girlie and William looked at each other across the crowd of excited passengers, here and there peering out of the window, pointing out this site and that. He walked toward her, not looking all that out of place amidst the other suited men of the period. His tie was on, here.

"Hi—"

William held up a hand. "Before you go on, Ms. Delmundo, I'm obligated to tell you that you're not speaking directly to William Cheung. I'm a programmed NPC, timed to trigger upon you activating your headset this morning. I can respond semiorganically within certain limits, having been populated with prerecorded dialogue, but you are not currently having a live conversation with another user in the field."

"What the fuck," Girlie breathed.

The program, the automaton that wasn't William, made no change in his expression. He lifted the hand he was already holding up, higher. "You may leave at any time, of course, but I do hope you'll stay until the end of this program." Then he made a show of looking out the window, slightly jostling a woman in a white dress, who politely moved out of the way so he could peer outside. The choreography of it all was making Girlie start to hyperventilate.

"Ah. Extraordinary view. To your left, you'll see the Missouri Corn Palace. It's a sixty-five-foot-tall structure made out of corn, designed to celebrate the Midwest. Another nearby attraction is a block of cheese, weighing almost five thousand pounds, to celebrate the dairy industry of America. If you want to see a three-thousand-pound statue of a maid milking a cow—both made entirely out of butter, that tour can be made available to you at a later time."

"Main menu," Girlie barked.

The program looked at her, amused. "That's not quite how this works," he said.

"What the hell is going on?"

"I did tell you Edison was obsessed with the St. Louis Fair," the program said. "It was our first finished creation together, but it was his dream, really; I was just along for the ride."

He smiled; she only saw it because she saw his reflection in the glass move. "You'll have discerned by now that I'm not a great—dreamer. I'm the kind of person who likes to make other people's dreams come true. A provider and facilitator. A moderator. Much like you."

Girlie approached him at the window. She didn't know how to interrupt this monologue. "That's not—I don't think that's true at all," she said finally. "What about—petting the tiger. Space tethers—"

The program's back remained turned to her; she couldn't see William's expression, whether what she'd said had registered at all.

They'd reached the top of the wheel's rotation. "Ah. Here we are. This is about how high my friend was when he fell off his balcony, after Reeden and L'Olifant took over his company, stripped it for parts, took its IP to use for purposes entirely contrary to his vision, then pushed him out of it," the program said, his voice placid as the artificial lake they were looking down upon.

William turned back at her, smiling the angel of history smile she knew very well by now; could conjure it out of thin air, with her eyes closed, on a bus, in her bed, in a million different worlds.

"It's just a standard vengeance tale, I'm afraid," he apologized.

She thought of Vuthy saying, *Check the news.* "What—what's—"

"I've sent off nearly fifteen years' worth of documentation, emails to internal memos, from Maurice de Coligny, containing, among other things, Islamophobic language, threats of violence against immigrants in France and Spain, racist language about his partners in China, and perhaps most importantly, descriptions of his desire to use the biometric data gleaned from Playground's users to create a more effective narrative delivery system for the, quote, nation-rebuilding purpose of his theme parks—"

"Oh, if highly lucrative historical whitewashing is illegal all of a sudden," Girlie sneered, "I have some cases to try."

"You're correct, of course, that the court of public opinion can be obliging, when it comes to charming demagogues, however culturally nocive," William said. "Wire fraud, however, is very much illegal. As is embezzlement, securities fraud, and campaign finance fraud: as in, for example, transferring over a hundred million dollars of company funds toward political campaign contributions and lobbyists, most notably targeting the regulatory agencies reviewing whether or not to classify Playground as a Class II medical device, thus limiting its commercial opportunities. Not to mention the tens of millions of euros earmarked for a certain far-right party in France, ahead of their most recent presidential elections."

He smiled. "Corporate espionage is also very much illegal. I should know, considering de Coligny first approached me for just that purpose, when Edison was still alive."

Girlie blinked at him. "What?"

"It wasn't because I was special," William continued, unfazed; it was the program talking. She was just on its route. "I wasn't the only point person on a VR team they were interested in turning. He just thought, because I had been close to Edison, and because I had expressed some—discomfort, with how erratically Edison was behaving—that I might be incentivized into giving up some trade secrets. Perhaps, they thought, if they could turn me, they wouldn't have to go through with the palaver of a buyout. Poach me, build their own.

"I refused. Tried to tell Edison. He didn't know if he could trust me; he thought I might be lying, to derail the deal; he knew I wasn't in great support of being acquired in the first place. Even though, obviously, without the acquisition, we were dead in the water. He knew that. He thought I wanted that. For him. Maybe I did, in a way.

"In the end, he chose them. Or: chose the money. Went through with the purchase. He wanted to believe. Then, presumably to cover up their tracks, they implied to Edison that I had not been entirely loyal, might have even been willing to give up trade secrets in exchange for derailing the deal. Was perhaps even a mole, for other VR teams.

"Edison—didn't believe them, exactly," William continued. "But he didn't believe me, either. He knew I wasn't a true disciple of his vision. It was always him I followed, not the grand idea. But at that point, he thought we could all be moles. Perera too. L'Olifant and de Coligny fed that paranoia. He died—angry at us." He turned away.

"The only reason I'm still here is because his will stipulated that I remain at Playground for a minimum period of ten years after the purchase, *to be the steady hand steering Playground toward its future*," he quoted, no light in his eyes.

Girlie thought: So then he did leave a note.

"You think someone does that because they're angry?"

"He gave me a ten-year sentence," William said. "Under a company I loathe. Which killed him."

"He gave you ten years of protection," Girlie shot back. "At a place he built. With you."

Then, quiet: "I saw his dad. Down there."

William looked back at her, face still expressionless, but his throat bobbed.

"France is very sophisticated in corporate espionage, you know," he explained, moving right along. "Maurice's father was, at some point during his tenure in Chirac's presidency, tied up in some scandal about Air France hiring French intelligence officers as crew members to steal corporate secrets from American executives."

William made a sound that in another person might have passed for a chuckle.

"You could also say I'm just another Englishman, at war with France."

"So you're—what—a whistleblower?"

"Oh, no," he said modestly. "No, no. I'm your run-of-the-mill arsonist. I'd very much like to see their entire company burnt to the ground."

He lifted a shoulder. "That won't happen, of course. They'll bat away these torches and pitchforks with their bottomless pockets and we'll be nothing, like the many nothings that have come before us.

But Playground obviously won't be a viable VR product for Reeden to move forward with, not with the scandals and lawsuits attached to it now. Poisoned chalice. I became, eventually, the mole Maurice de Coligny wanted me to be."

William's eyes were hard, flinty. "He didn't think we were anything at all. Edison. Perera, me. Just—resources."

Then he lowered his gaze. "L'Olifant won't fall. I don't expect that. They'll just go back to their theme parks, strengthen their local fortresses, perhaps even find some other VR company to expand with. But their strongholds will stay small, for just a while longer. And I'll take my friend's legacy with me. That's good enough."

Girlie's mouth was open; she couldn't close it. She shook her head.

"Why didn't you—why didn't you just tell me this before? Why—why all this—" She gestured around them, at the Ferris wheel.

"It is hardly unfeasible to imagine that I was not, as yet, sure you could be trusted," William said—it was his pheasants-shooting voice. She recoiled at the sound of it; at being just another American he had to mask for.

Then he lay his gaze on her, heavy.

"'Not all of us can run away to a country with universal health care,'" he quoted.

Girlie let out a wounded laugh. "So—what—me being realistic about capitalism—that makes me some type of corporate stooge, like I would've gone to *The Wall Street Journal* and fucked you over?"

"How could I know," William asked, almost calm.

"You know exactly how," Girlie snarled back; all in, cards on the table.

"When people who are not accustomed to wealth are paid a large amount of money to do easier and comparatively less exploitative work than their previous source of employment, I've found that incentivizes people to think kindly of the company that bestows upon them the privilege. When drowning people come across a lifeboat, they don't tend to spit at whoever's rowing."

Now the program that looked like William smiled, anguished. "I ought to know."

She smiled back warmly, patient and polite, so he would know she was furious. "You're insulting me."

"I had to be realistic."

"I would never have sold you out," Girlie gritted out.

The program flickered again, processing. It seemed to have no readily available answer, its algorithm not having calculated the possibility of that sentence, so it resumed its previously scheduled narrative.

"Well, Ms. Delmundo, as we're almost at the end of our nine-minute journey, I should inform you now that as of yesterday evening, your position has regretfully been impacted by ongoing layoffs at Reeden, as they reevaluate their future with Playground in light of these troubling revelations. It's with our utmost gratitude that we must now ask you to leave the premises. You will be compensated according to your contract, with one year of continued pay and benefits, starting today."

The program straightened its posture, still smiling. "It's been an honor, Ms. Delmundo."

Girlie wanted to tear her hair out. "You're a fucking coward—"

"I could have just let the light turn red when you tried to get in this morning," William exploded at last, roaring, "I could have just sent you the form email, *because of budget restructuring your position has been impacted, please know this decision bears no reflection on your performance at the company.* But I couldn't do that, could I?" He turned away, laughing thickly, bitter with it.

"If you think I'm just going to leave you here—"

"I'm not even here," William said, looking out the window, but closing his eyes.

"I don't believe you," Girlie said—and then, knowing it was true, repeated it. "I don't believe you."

"Ms. Delmundo—"

"You're in here. You're in here, somewhere. You're a fucking—"

She started laughing again, insanely. That was ableist language. Her face was wet; her nose was running; she couldn't tell whether that was under the mask, or not.

"You're here," she said fiercely, knowing it; knowing it just because. Girlie took a step forward. "Where are you?"

William had the audacity to look nervous. "Your ride is coming to its end. If you haven't yet paid the fifty cents to the operator, please know we also accept tips."

"Oh, *shut up*," Girlie growled. "Where are you?"

Harrowed, William looked at her. The shoulders of his skin slumped, like the strings had been cut.

"A place you've never even heard of," he murmured hollowly. "I'm on a sofa in—Crystal fucking Palace."

"I've heard of it," she said—angry at that too. At the idea that he thought she would have forgotten; not paid attention. "Ground-floor garden flat," she threw back at him. His eyes were glassy, pained.

"What's going to happen to you?"

"Resigned. Awaiting lawsuits. Potential immunity if I testify against de Coligny, which I will, obviously. Would have been outright deported, if I hadn't—look. Let's just say the Department of Homeland Security doesn't look kindly upon H-1B visa holders trying to take down the thirteenth most valuable company on the Fortune 500."

"You're—" Girlie's throat was closed, she was choking on her words, the reality of it, the blue-link Wikipedia-entry gravity of it. There it was: the succinct poetry of class difference. The bigness of his life, long before she'd shown up; the smallness of her ability to change it. And, deeper, there it was too: the fact that she'd made a big, stone-faced bluff about who she was, what was important to her, what she was capable of—and had been fully believed by all; by him; most of all, by herself. "Why—why would you do this?"

William shook his head. She saw then what she had always seen in him, what she had always recognized, because it was hers too; saw that he was angry, with an old, old, anger, an ancient battered secondhand thing he'd been carrying around for a long time, heavy as a wave, leveling. And there at the fleshly living core of the anger, there written on its mortal animal face, sunken deep in the still-living eyes: grief. Just a person's grief. As fathomless and everyday as a black hole; nothing to lose, nowhere to go.

"He was my friend," he said.

The doors were opening behind her, and the crowd was rushing out, pushing her backward, backward, so she had to move along with them, out of the car, leaving him standing there.

"William—"

"This ride took exactly nine minutes. Mona's escort took one minute. You now have ten minutes to depart the premises before the doors to the building lock permanently, with you inside or not. If the former, an on-call security guard will be summoned to escort you from the premises," William recited. "Once you leave, your fob will no longer function. Please leave it at the concierge desk."

She reached for the edge of one door to anchor herself, but there were too many people, she couldn't grasp it. "*William*—"

William's face twisted. "Just—take your parachute and go."

All in. "I like you. A lot," Girlie confessed at long, long last; suc-corless. She tried to shrug. "There was never a good time to say."

William was staring at her, wide-eyed, shell-shocked; then, abruptly, furious. He surged forward in the wave of that fury, and she did too, body moving before her mind, and they were kissing, in this world, all of them, and the haptics—she didn't have time to think about the hap-tics, they were kissing, kissing, his hands on either side of her head, clutching at the hair at the nape of her neck, deep, wild, unchecked, starving kisses, the first kisses in over thirty years she hadn't wanted to safe word out of, William making dark little dying groans she could hear against the mask, somewhere on a sofa on the other side of the world as night fell on him, the bright morning sun on his skin here, tongue sweeping her bottom lip, teeth pulling gently at the fat flesh there, groaning again when she flicked her tongue against his, *oh*, and shoved her hands into the back of his shirt through the neck so her fingers nearly clawed against the skin of his upper back, hold-ing him tight, pulling him down to her, closer, her neck strained from craning up for him, their bodies cramped up against the open door of the carriage, his fingers pressing down on her scalp, thumbs behind her ears, then one thumb smearing mindlessly along her cheek, catching the corner of her mouth, groaning again when she darted her tongue out to lick the pad of it, then starting to pant with a keening need so sharp and serrated it sounded like he'd been gut-shot, as he moved his thumb across her lower lip and she sucked it in against the open flat of her tongue, mouth wet and lavish, eyes on his blown pupils, his whole body pressed against hers, hips rocking up, fuck—he was hard, moving easily into the space she made by parting her legs, fitting there, then dipping his head down to lick circles at her pulse, she was right, she'd known it, it was going to be good, it—it was already good, dragging his mouth along her jaw, giving her quick desperate abortive kisses, sipping at her mouth, her neck, the base of her throat, back to her mouth like he couldn't bear to be apart from it, she hooked a leg around his, whining, she was wet, she was done for, she going to come from just a kiss, in a fake world, from a bag of pixels; from a person, a man, the rest of her life. "William—"

He jerked away, his forehead clashing onto hers, breathing out harsh gasps, shivering, his hands clutching and unclutching on her shoulders. She felt his hot breath, gusting across her face. Until finally, hearing the beeping of the overhead sensor, he wrenched himself away, pushing her out of the carriage, reeling himself back into it. The doors closed on him.

In shock, she could only stare at him through the window—at his heaving chest, his raw red mouth, his wet eyes, staring back, as he panted wildly. Her mouth felt hot, bruised, starting to rash. In the carriage he looked small, and lonely, and knowable. The screen dimmed, then went black.

· ·

Girlie tore the mask and gloves off, ripped herself out of the bodysuit, threw it on the ground, apologized to the cleaners; these ones would all be traceable, she couldn't keep them; didn't even bother to stay in her office long enough to empty it—instead, got herself dressed, remembering her bag but forgetting her jacket, followed the compulsion that told her to run to the elevator, to push the button for Perera's floor, her foot tapping against the floor, her knees jostling, breath short, "Come on, come on—"

In the mirrored elevator walls, she looked at her mouth. Not even swollen, not a rash to be noted. But her tongue felt burning, bitten, eroticized. She wanted to open her mouth and give it air, let it loll, taste the air, get some relief.

When the doors opened, she ran out, each step taxing her body—fucking cardio allergy—ran straight to Perera's office, expecting it to be locked, but knowing, somehow, that it wouldn't be. It wasn't.

Just as she thought, the mask, gloves, and bodysuit she'd used during their sessions, and which he'd once offered to her, were still on his desk, in their box, unguarded.

It was a strange sort of feeling: not to expect the worst of someone. A strange, world-dissolving sort of feeling, near to a miracle: to expect good of someone, and—. Get it.

There were several other sets there too; one labeled for Vuthy, another for Robin, other names she didn't recognize. She picked those two up too. Something raw in her chest started kicking.

Then she opened the envelope addressed to her false name. It said only, in Perera's nigh-illegible doctor's chickenscratch: *I never submitted any of your biometric data to Reeden or Playground. All clinical files herein. Godspeed, TP.*

• •

Girlie did something her generation, on the whole, avoided, and she was no exception: she made calls.

She called her bank. She called a number at Vanguard she'd only ever dialed a couple times. She called Tesla. She called Rhea, to ask for Vuthy's and Robin's contact information, so she could mail them the headsets, insured. Then she called Maribel, and asked if she wanted to go to Sephora.

"Ooh, ooh, ooh," Maribel said as they entered the air-conditioned store, gleeful, picking up two black baskets, handing one to Girlie. "I haven't been in so long! I don't know where to start. I need a new highlighter. Hold on. What's this?" She appeared drawn, magnetically, to a Pat McGrath counter display featuring an array of limited edition duochrome eyeshadows. "Ooh. Pretty," she said, touching one compact, where a rose had been carved into iridescent powder, each petal shifting pink-gold in the light.

Girlie followed her, then touched the compact next to the one Maribel was touching, a peachy-coral shade. She followed Maribel's lead, and swatched it on the inside of her wrist, cutting the vivid color straight across the radial artery.

"That is pretty," Girlie said quietly.

Maribel looked at Girlie's wrist, then up at Girlie.

"That's a good color on you," she said, very seriously. "You should get it." Instead of waiting for an answer, she took one of the compacts from behind the display, then put it in her own basket. "Highlighter! Highlighter highlighter highlighter."

Girlie followed Maribel from counter to counter, comparing the pros and cons of liquid versus cream versus powder highlighter, for Maribel's specific needs, which were not all that specific, and seemed mostly related to whichever product she found most delicious in that moment, the judder of bliss called up by one product, only surpassed by the next. "The packaging is so cute though," Maribel said, more than once, about something she didn't even like. For once, Girlie let Maribel pay, which had Maribel floating out of the store on a palpable cloud of pride.

When they were back in the car, each with a black-and-white Sephora bag nestled on her lap, they indulged the secondary pleasure of reevaluating their treasures. Girlie opened the blush Maribel had bought for her and inhaled, sharp, at the look of it, the soft shimmering dust seeming to float up, minutely, from it. "It's *so* pretty," Maribel said again. She was already spreading a drop of newly purchased highlighter onto the back of her own hand, taking care not to get any on her watch, which she'd been wearing every single day since receiving it. The entire surface of Maribel's hand glowed, like a geode from the deepest earth. Girlie took a deep breath.

"Okay," she said, and handed over the check, face down, sliding it across the dashboard like someone had done for her, a lifetime ago.

Maribel picked up the check, looked at it. Her face went white.

"I'm leaving Vegas," Girlie said, trying to remember what she'd practiced, faltering in the face of Maribel's shock, the baby-cousin look of her making Girlie's chest sore. "I'm leaving Vegas, and—I've paid off my mom's car, and covered the next six months of my share of the mortgage. This is just for you. For you, and Avery, and—your life together."

Girlie swallowed. "She's a good person. She—I mean, she's a dickhead. But she'll take care of you. She loves you. You're good for each other."

Maribel's tears were already dripping onto the check, her nose red, snot coming out of her mouth, shaking her head.

"Do you really think you have to pay me off—like I wouldn't support you without this—"

"I know I don't have to pay you off."

"This *is* a pay-off, ate—"

"The payoff is for me," Girlie said. "Not you."

She squeezed Maribel's hand. "Ading. Take the money. Build a life with her." Then her throat caught.

Girlie reached up to smooth down Maribel's hair. "You were right," she said gently, with a love so total she thought she might be cored out from it. "It's not on us to fix all of it."

Maribel was still rubbing at her face, trying to control her hiccups. Blindly she felt for Girlie's hand, clutching it back. Then she caught sight of the check and started sobbing again. This was going to take awhile. "What are you going to do?" Maribel wept.

Girlie smiled hopelessly. "Something pretty irresponsible."

"Are you going far?"

"Pretty far."

Maribel looked down at her lap, nodding. Then, she turned to Girlie and swept her up in a sudden hug, reaching across the divider, her arms wrapped around Girlie's shoulders, squeezing her so tight Girlie could barely breathe. Girlie could feel her small, beloved head, nodding fiercely into Girlie's shoulder, again and again.

"Yeah. Go," she said harshly, more harshly than Girlie had thought Maribel capable of. "Go. Get out of here."

Maribel started hiccupping again. "You should have left awhile ago. Thanks for—staying so long."

Finally, Girlie let her eyes shut. She brought her arms up to complete the hug, cradling Maribel in her arms. Feeling herself, cradled too. Maribel shuddered into her shoulder, the check damp and glowing, with a thumbprint of shimmer, crumpled on her lap.

8

An Escapement, or Deadwood Habitats

he weather was shit, and the journey took forever. There were three trains to take from Terminal 4: first the Piccadilly line, destination Cockfosters, which she wasn't going to dignify with a reaction, like every other tourist; then she got on the District line at South Kensington the wrong way, ended up going all the way to Barons Court before she realized she was turned around; too distracted by the names, the places she remembered hearing about, the surreality of it, that she was there, that those places were real, that the names existed, and people lived in them. And her, among them. Luckily she'd only brought carry-on luggage—she'd had precious little to bring, she'd realized very early on.

She got back onto the right train, kept an eye out for Victoria, where she was supposed to change. The people seemed absolutely indecipherable to her; some clearly middle-class and bored and sort of suspicious of everybody, others haggard and in their own heads, everyone also kind of—generally hot, well dressed, conscious of themselves. The men in particular were pretty good-looking. Maybe she wasn't even bisexual after all, she thought to herself with the deranged clarity of someone who hadn't been able to sleep a wink on an eleven-hour flight. Maybe she just didn't like American men in cargo shorts.

At Victoria Station, it all went downhill; she was supposed to take something called Southern Rail to Gipsy Hill—starting off with a racial slur, that was a nice touch—but the train was delayed, because they couldn't find a driver, or so she tried to understand via the fairly dispassionate announcements over the intercom system. "For *fuck's* sake," a white man in a navy peacoat hissed, and she almost smiled at him; his accent sounded a little familiar. When her train finally arrived, an hour and a half after it should have, the passengers who'd missed all the previous trains packed it up like sardines, so she sat on her suitcase by the doors, hugging to her chest the Telfar bag she'd bought years ago in an episode of consumerist solidarity and left collecting dust in her closet because it was too big to carry around as a daily work bag. Large Eggplant.

The Airbnb was a one-bedroom flat in what frankly looked like a fucking insane fairy-tale mansion but was actually, her Airbnb host had explained, in a prolix and self-important automated email, a former Georgian house now subdivided into individual apartments. The house was a Grade II listed property in a conservation area, the Airbnb notes continued, with a brittle tone of overbearing care that made her sense a fellow Virgo afoot. On the façade, smog stained and chipping, a man's gentle, forgiving face, covered in leaves, was carved above the bay window that looked into what was going to be, she realized when her key turned, her place.

The apartment—flat—was on the ground floor, around five hundred square feet, with a poky little galley kitchen, electric hot plate, and a washing machine under the sink. There was an enormous sky-blue bedroom you had to pass through to get to the subway-tiled bathroom—terrible floor plan—with a clawfoot tub that had seen better days. In the living room—the front room, the Airbnb notes had called it—the huge bay windows were covered with thick red Ikea curtains, and the blue-velvet sofa propped up against one wall gave the whole thing a corny sort of boudoir feel. There were stained-glass sections at the tops of the bay windows, over a hundred years old, little amber flowers and green leaves. The ceilings were so high she could feel all her thoughts, leaving her head, floating away from her.

She put her suitcase down, took out some of her clothes, put them in the built-in closet by the giant bed. She put the Sherlock Holmes volumes on the nightstand; she was almost finished with *The Sign of Four.*

Next to it she put down the suit, mask, and gloves; she'd brought them all, but hadn't used them since leaving Playground. She occasionally caught wind of things happening in the news around the lawsuit—**WHISTLEBLOWER GAINS IMMUNITY, DISGRACED CEO RETURNS TO FRANCE, HINTS AT POLITICAL AMBITIONS, TECH DREAMS IMPLODED, WHAT'S NEXT FOR SILICON VALLEY.** She only ever saw the headlines; she never read the articles.

It was already evening. She was, she realized a little sheepishly, somewhat too tired, and maybe too intimidated, to go search for food right away. She finished the Pret sandwich she'd bought at Victoria Station during the train delay, sitting in the new huge unknown bed, dazed with her own accomplishment.

She didn't have any plans for her days. She walked up to the Triangle, the sort of downtown—High Street—area local to the neighborhood, climbing up the surprisingly steep hill; Gipsy *Hill*, after all, she reasoned. She had to look up why it was called that; it wasn't all that complicated. "This afternoon my wife, and Mercer, and Deb, went with Pelling to see the gypsies at Lambeth, and have their fortunes told," someone named Samuel Pepys wrote, according to Google. "But what they did, I did not inquire."

There were restaurants—pubs, she corrected—she was too shy to go into alone, filled with people laughing, smoking outside, spilling beer onto the ground. She drew some looks; mostly just curious, though someone did yell out "ni hao ma" to her in front of a mini grocery store, so that was pretty regular. She spent one whole morning just strolling around the enormous park, which looked like something out of a movie, like *L'Année Dernière à Marienbad* or something; a pair of Sphinxes along a massive stone staircase; what looked like a huge cell-phone tower. She read on some placard that they'd hosted the original World's Fair, right here, where the original Crystal Palace had stood, housing the first Great Exhibition; she frowned a little, looking at the grand glass transept, which looked familiar; thought of Edison, and—. She kept moving.

She remembered the redwoods, in Perera's session. The question he'd asked her, early on; her old valentine. The long dirt path, under the canopy of trees. It started to rain, but she had an umbrella.

Another day, she found a maze of green hedges, full of screaming kids and tired parents and teenagers looking for a spot to make out; she found the large sculptures of the dinosaurs, or the almost-dinosaurs, which apparently predated Darwin, which meant someone had just imagined them, not knowing that they'd been real; all now extinct, and inaccurate, and full of strange feeling in the eyes.

She surprised herself by taking pictures. She sent some of them back to Maribel, who replied as soon as it was morning in Vegas. **Omg!!!! So cute!!**

She got her provisions at the Sainsbury's, tried to stock up on normal staples, pasta, garlic, onions, fish, you probably couldn't go wrong, but she didn't recognize a lot of the fish being sold—what was river cobbler—and some of the nicer-looking jam had little BY APPOINTMENT TO HIS MAJESTY THE KING labels on them, which felt forbidding. With a stern-faced determination produced by her American compulsion to find the number one draft pick, she bought Hobnobs, Jaffa Cakes, Jammie Dodgers, Ginger Nuts, Choco Leibniz, malted milk, chocolate bourbons, chocolate fingers, custard creams, something threateningly called a Digestive. She gave up on something called Victoria sponge, and never touched again the water colorant they were calling tea; bought a French press and a grinder, even some expensive matcha that looked like gray ash when she opened it, had been dead for ages, tasted like dirt. She had yet to find the Asian grocery stores. That was on the list. Brixton Market, Earl's Court, someplace called Tooting Broadway. At some point she'd get over the names.

One night, coming home from the Sainsbury's, ready to make her trek downhill back to the flat, she passed one of the pubs, called the Sparrowhawk; it looked warm, lit softly, teeming with alien life. Everyone was doing some sort of joint quiz, and someone was shouting, *Christina Aguilera, Dirrty!*

She caught the eye of the bartender, wiping an empty glass with a clean white cloth. He gave her a flirty little wave, beckoned her in. She smiled back. Let herself savor the eros of it, the hot living spark of it. Shook her head. Went home.

She learned which actual restaurants were good; a little Venezuelan spot with great arepas and coffee, run by a husband-and-wife team who gave her free tostones the second time she came. There was a Napoli-style pizza place run by stick-and-poke-tattooed young people in chore jackets, which claimed to be one of the "Top 5 Pizzerias" but didn't say top five of what, top five of where; it didn't rank in any of her top fives, but maybe she just didn't like her pizza floppy as a used napkin. A couple of truly terrible Japanese and Mexican places: the sushi made with long grain rice, barely any vinegar, and the less said about the textureless repudiations to flavor they were calling tacos the better, with everything on the menu spelled phonetically because presumably the word "Oaxacan" was too confrontational to the English eye.

She was starting to figure out what places to avoid, the tenor of local palate the restaurants were catering to, how to adjust for Bay Area tastebuds; that if online reviews said a dish was extremely spicy, it would be a mild to medium at best; that if a restaurant was rated five stars on Yelp by locals, she needed to knock off two stars, right off the bat. She had her first English breakfast plate at a café run by a charity that catered to domestic abuse survivors, run by an ex-Rastafarian woman with a shaved head who wasn't all that friendly to her at first, then warmed up the next time she came and ordered oxtail, and was downright chatty by the time she ordered curry goat, "You all right, darlin'?" There was one pretty-good Vietnamese place, run by an old guy and his daughter, both of whom seemed extremely fascinated by her, like they didn't get that many Southeast Asian girls round those parts; they didn't believe her when she said she was Filipino. "You don't look Filipino," the old guy insisted, like she might have been misinformed. They had meant it as a compliment, the way most assholes who said that kind of thing did, so that was also pretty regular.

Some days she stopped in the big warehouses selling antiques, peering at the furniture, the veiny marble-topped consoles, the paintings of horses in repose or greyhounds on the chase, rooms full of midcentury coffee tables, or surfaces covered in brass doorknockers, here a lion, there a wolf. She had her eye on a little entryway table, cheap, topped with marble-like Formica, maybe from the '70s, but in good shape, and charming, with a sort of glow to it; a soul, if she was going to be maudlin, which was an emotional register she was trying out of late. Instead she bought a large sturdy glass for iced coffee or matcha (could take the California girl out of; but not California out of; et cetera) that looked like it was maybe supposed to be a beer mug, had a faded illustration of a woman on it, labeled in peeling paint PEARLY QUEEN.

Other days she went into the little local bookstore, snorting a little bit at a section labeled LOCAL INTEREST AND CRYSTAL PALACE AUTHORS; snorting because underneath it, the ghost of the words BLACK AND MINORITY ETHNIC FICTION had been poorly erased.

She bought a little picture book about the Crystal Palace dinosaurs. The clerk looked startled at her accent; maybe they didn't get that many tourists. "American?" asked the clerk warily, like it was a test. "That's right," she said, raising her chin. "Thought so," the clerk said, triumphant. Now it was her turn to startle; the test hadn't been for her.

It was like this, slow and unhurried, that she passed her days; eating her fill, looking her fill, letting herself be foreign, and alone, and without context. It was like this that she came out of Sainsbury's one morning, carrying her reusable tote of rice, pasta, oat milk, salmon, eggs, courgettes, aubergines, romaine hearts, mayonnaise, vinegar, hefting the tote over her shoulder to make her way on what had become her regular walk home, when she turned her head, looked across the street, and saw William and Mona seated together outside a café: Mona, on the ground, panting; William, frozen in place, holding a coffee cup, staring at her.

"Hi," she said, when she'd crossed Westow Street, rearranging the tote on her shoulder.

On the table, there was a half-eaten pain au chocolat on a plate in front of him, an as-yet-uneaten burnt custard tart next to it, and a plate with what looked like a once-tried croque monsieur next to that, greasy fork and knife balanced on the plate edge. William clattered the coffee cup back onto its little plate. Latte art in the foam, gently disturbed; a fern.

Mona perked up at the sight of her, got herself up with not a small amount of effort, sniffing at her hand.

"Hi again, mama," she said to Mona, kneeling, not reaching out. Mona's paws were damp and muddy, stained here and there with green. There was a crumb of cheese on her muzzle. Mona sniffed her, investigative, then gave her one delicate little lick on the chin, the first kiss; then the side of her cheek, the easy second. She let her hand drift up to scratch gently at Mona's chest, up into the thicker scruff at the side of her neck. Then Mona returned to her position, turning around twice, before settling back down on the concrete.

"—. Hi. Hello," William said.

A faint shadow had grown over his jaw, above his lip; he was wearing a navy Patagonia fleece with dog hair on it and army-green nylon Adidas tracksuit bottoms, the same sneakers he'd worn to Maribel's party, now also stained with green and mud. The eyebags were still there, deeper than ever, so too the fat pockets under his bottom lashes. He was wearing what looked like one of those neo-vintage Seamaster 300s—she tried to clock this without being smug about being right, another register she was trying out of late—brown leather, warm gold on black ceramic. There was the same silicone water bowl next to Mona, calcium streaks on the bottom of it. The water was very hard here.

William, for his part, was fixated on the bag over her arm, which was bright yellow and had an orange elephant with huge eyes on one side of it. On it were the words: I'M A RELIABAG. YOU CAN RELY ON ME TO CARRY HEAVY LOADS WITH EASE. DON'T FORGET ME!

"You're. Here," he said dumbly, eyes darting all over her body, blinking several times in succession. He wasn't letting his gaze rest on her face yet.

"Well, I was fired from my old job and given a year's salary in severance, so I had quite a lot of time and money," she said, shifting from one foot to the other.

"Your position was impacted," William corrected, sounding faint. Then he blinked. "Please, sit," he said, pointing to the empty chair next to Mona.

She sat down, awkwardly putting the heavy tote on her knees, so it wouldn't block the sidewalk; Mona was blocking enough of the sidewalk as it was. "I—tried to call you," he said, faltering.

"I bet you say that to all the girls," she recited, playing the role.

He didn't laugh to make it easier for her. "No." He frowned. "The number had been—"

"The number Reeden had on file was never my real number," she said. She smiled wryly. "Aditya used to text moderators after hours."

"Ah. I thought you—well."

"Mm," she said. She was taking her time.

"Perera's here too," he said suddenly, like he couldn't keep himself from filling the silence. "Not—in Crystal Palace. But in London. On sabbatical."

"He mentioned."

"Oh," William said, wrongfooted. "Did he?"

"He shares things about himself with other people."

"He shares hundreds of thousands of pounds' worth of technology that does not belong to him, with other people," William said dryly, a flicker of the William she'd known in Vegas coming to the surface. "Allegedly."

He gazed into the distance, then scrubbed a hand over his face.

"He's very into gardening at the moment. He keeps talking about—rewilding Finsbury Park, or something, I can't make sense of it. Have you heard of deadwood habitats?" He looked down. "Says he's burnt out. But I think he'll go back to the NHS."

"Rhea's still moderating. She's trying to get the floor to unionize. I've donated to the cause," she said solemnly. Then smiled. "She said Vuthy and Aditya left. Moved to Austin."

"Oh, yes," William said. His eyes were twinkling now. "They've got a Labradoodle puppy now. Very active on Instagram."

"God."

"Awful," William agreed.

Then he cleared his throat. "So. You're—here," he said, carefully. "On holiday?"

Her hands tightened around the base of the bag. She saw that he still couldn't stop looking at it; like it was the sight of her carrying a worn-in reusable Sainsbury's bag that was the most unhinged part of this moment. Looking, too, at the soft black hair on her bare forearms: no bodysuit, no watch that morning, she was shopping around for one—the scene here was a racket, fifteen thousand pounds for a Patek Ellipse she didn't even think was nice. Jacket sleeves pushed up to the elbow. It was almost summer; not that anyone had told England. Her old tattoos were visible. It occurred to her, then, that this was probably the first time he was seeing them.

"Not sure," she said.

"How long are you here for?"

She shrugged. "Americans can stay up to three months on just the passport," she said. "Or so I've read."

"Could always find a British citizen for the fiancée visa," William joked, then turned bright red.

She held his gaze. Didn't laugh to make it easier for him.

"If only there were some unemployed pauper, willing to wed me for my incredibly stable newfound fortune," she murmured. "What bliss and succor I could provide."

She looked down at Mona, who had adjusted herself so the tip of her snout was on her feet, leaving wet marks on her shoe.

When she looked back up at William, he was staring at her; tense, frozen. She looked away, licked her lips unconsciously, sensed him track the movement.

She felt, had felt since laying eyes on the two of them, a deep, stilling calm coming over her, the pulse of it slow and even; her heart rate, her cognitive load. It was the deep end, but she was floating across it. She had the feeling of being in multiple time zones at once: there, in the not-so-bygone past; there, in the not-so-faraway future. And here: here, in the present. Here, in this one vast life of hers. She hadn't thought those things before. That life could be vast; that it could be hers.

He swallowed. "You—. Right. What—what have you—"

"Paid off some family debt, paid off my mom's car. Gave some money to Maribel. Made a withdrawal from my Roth. Haven't had to touch the 401(k) yet. There's not much in it yet anyway, no point getting the tax hit. That kinda thing," she said, trying for casual.

She shrugged, looking away into the street, the cars driving by, the people with their own reusable shopping bags and dogs big and little, whose gaze passed over them, indifferent, thought nothing of what was happening here, at this table, in front of a place called Costa Coffee. Inside her own body she began to feel, not heavy, but immeasurably, boundlessly weighted—tethered, divinely, to the earth. Everything was hardware. Someone had told her that, once. "I'm, you know," she said softly. "Trying to change my life."

William's own breath was coming sharp, fast, his chest heaving under the fleece. Mona sat herself up, shoving her head into his lap, peering at him in concern. Blindly, he reached out to scratch under her chin. She immediately put aside her concern to lick pastry crumbs off his fingers. He stared down at her as she did, like he wanted to know if Mona was seeing this too; if she could even believe it.

He looked back up, swallowed. His eyes were rimmed in red; the tip of his nose.

"You need—. You'll have to apply for a National Insurance number."

"Mm-hmm," she said, not breaking eye contact.

He stared back, then stared upward.

"You—you won't qualify for a state pension for at least ten years," he fought to say, at last. "I'll—I can tell you about cash ISAs."

Now she grinned at him; couldn't help it. "Stop, I'm gonna come," she said.

His face broke then, looking so shocked-open and happy his skin couldn't contain him, like he was going to tear right out of himself; like he'd made a frugal wish at the Fontana di Trevi, a long, long time ago, and some sympathetic minor god had heard him—given him everything he'd asked for, and threw some things in for free, just for being a first-time customer. The expression on his face: she'd seen it once before. It hadn't been for her that time; but she might have been wrong about that too.

"You're coming home with me, then," he said, brisk and formal, holding it together. "If you'll have me," she replied. He nodded, too fast, frantic; it was already falling apart. "Yes. I will." His gaze was swallowing her up; he made the world bigger. "I can confidently say there is nothing I want more."

"I've never even told you my name," she reminded him, as if she didn't know that he'd known it from the beginning.

He was shaking his head, choking out a laugh in utter disbelief, like all of this was—was—, and he was going to wake up at any moment, and there wouldn't be an American woman carrying an overflowing Sainsbury's bag sitting in front of him, offering up her entire life to him on a platter. He inhaled through his nose noisily, wiped at it with one hand. The other was rubbing at the top of his thigh, like he was cold all of a sudden, like her mouth was too far, like the reusable bag as big as Christendom was in the way, like they were going to have to make a stop at the fucking chemist's and buy condoms at Sefgrove where the family had known him for decades, like they were still in public at a bloody Costa—like they needed to leave, as soon as possible. Leave; and go home. "All right. Let's have it, then. For HMRC."

She told him. He nodded again. "Nice to meet you," he said, eyes still roving, greedy, over her face; she could see he didn't want to miss anything, was making himself remember—but was also desperate to skip ahead, get there faster; wanted to be early for the future that had never once been promised, not even imagined. "Pleasure's mine," she agreed, reaching for him, meeting him there.

Acknowledgments

As always, original debts are to my parents: my mother, through whose unshakeable faith all things are possible; and my father, through whose enduring memory all things are bearable. Eternal thanks to my extraordinary agent and cherished friend, Emma Paterson, who makes the world turn, and to my U.S. editor Laura Tisdel and my UK editor James Roxburgh, for their wisdom, clarity, and care as I worked my way through multiple worlds, trying to write this one. Thank you to Monica MacSwan, Carlos Zayas-Pons, Claire Vaccaro, Lynn Buckley, Kirsty Doole, Felice McKeown, Julia Rickard, Raven Ross, Ryan Boyle, the audiobook producers, and everyone on the extended Penguin Random House and Atlantic teams who helped bring this book into the world. Thank you to Leslie Shipman and Katie McDonaugh of The Shipman Agency for their support and compassion, especially over the last couple of years. Thank you to Chris Lupo, for his championing and vision. Thank you to Harry Cepka for nearly fifteen years of friendship, laughter, and growth. Several books and articles were of great aid in the world-building of this book, especially around virtual reality therapy, content moderation, and the St. Louis Fair, most significantly: Brennan Spiegel's *VRx: How Virtual Therapeutics Will Revolutionize Medicine*, Helen Ouyang's *New York Times* article "Can Virtual Help Ease Chronic Pain?," Adrian

ACKNOWLEDGMENTS

Chen's *Wired* article "The Laborers Who Keep Dick Pics and Behead-
ings Out of Your Facebook Feed," Eric Breitbart's *A World on Display:
Photographs from the St. Louis World's Fair, 1904*, and Robert Jackson's
Meet Me in St. Louis: A Trip to the 1904 World's Fair.

To Xena Castillo, upon whose inimitable example Mona is lightly
based, and for whom I would give up every book in the world just
to have back for an hour. To Vincent Castillo, who lights up all my
days, and taught me how to write a novel while also playing tug
with a stuffed toy. To Fabien, who makes this life worth living, and
who is always asking for a love story. And to all of the human and
animal and otherworldly companions, here and gone, who shep-
herded me through the writing of this book and the living of this
life: thank you.

100 YEARS of PUBLISHING

———◇———

Harold K. Guinzburg and George S. Oppenheimer founded Viking in 1925 with the intention of publishing books "with some claim to permanent importance rather than ephemeral popular interest." After merging with B. W. Huebsch, a small publisher with a distinguished catalog, Viking enjoyed almost fifty years of literary and commercial success before merging with Penguin Books in 1975.

Now an imprint of Penguin Random House, Viking specializes in bringing extraordinary works of fiction and nonfiction to a vast readership. In 2025, we celebrate one hundred years of excellence in publishing. Our centennial colophon features the original logo for Viking, created by the renowned American illustrator Rockwell Kent: a Viking ship that evokes enterprise, adventure, and exploration, ideas that inspired the imprint's name at its founding and continue to inspire us.

———◇———

For more information on Viking's history, authors, and books, please visit penguin.com/viking.